"Brimming with crackling tension and immersive prose, *The Ripple Effect* swept me away. The fake engagement, burly cinnamon-roll hero, and forced proximity had me turning pages late into the night. Passionate and playful, this story is a testament to loving the softer sides of ourselves." —Alexandra Kiley, author of *Kilt Trip*

"A masterpiece as fierce and stunning as the landscape in which it's set, *The Ripple Effect* hits all my must-haves—a brilliant woman trying to hold herself together, a strong man moving gently through the world, friendships and relationships in transition, and breathtaking natural beauty. Readers will fall into this book the way Stellar and McHuge fall in love—with arms and hearts wide open."

—Sarah T. Dubb, author of *Birding with Benefits*

The Ripple Effect

A NOVEL

MAGGIE NORTH

ST. MARTIN'S
GRIFFIN
NEW YORK

First published in the United States by St. Martin's Griffin, an imprint of St. Martin's Publishing Group

THE RIPPLE EFFECT. Copyright © 2025 by Maggie North. All rights reserved. Printed in the United States of America. For information, address St. Martin's Publishing Group, 120 Broadway, New York, NY 10271.

All emojis designed by OpenMoji—the open-source emoji and icon project. License: CC BY-SA 4.0

www.stmartins.com

Designed by Omar Chapa

The Library of Congress Cataloging-in-Publication Data is available upon request.

ISBN 978-1-250-91013-4 (trade paperback)
ISBN 978-1-250-28964-3 (ebook)

Our books may be purchased in bulk for promotional, educational, or business use. Please contact your local bookseller or the Macmillan Corporate and Premium Sales Department at 1-800-221-7945, extension 5442, or by email at MacmillanSpecialMarkets@macmillan.com.

First Edition: 2025

10 9 8 7 6 5 4 3 2 1

To all the women who wanted to feel the full bittersweet spectrum of human emotion—from joy to grief
to fury—and didn't think that should disqualify them
from being loved, and respected, and listened to.

And to all the readers, Bookstagrammers, booksellers,
and librarians who championed my first book. What an
amazing corner of the world you've made. I'm proud to
be invited in.

For a full list of content considerations, visit
www.maggienorth.com.

Prologue

Objectively speaking, this concert is a disaster. Which makes it exactly what I need tonight.

Earlier, when the surprise May cold snap came down in a blast of arctic air, the lead singer of the opening act kicked off their performance by drunkenly slurring, "We *hate* playing Canada." Two hours after they wrapped up their sullen set, the crowd's still shivering, waiting for the headliners to take the stage.

But I love a good disaster. My specialty is "working the problem," a skill I perfected as an emergency physician: list all possible solutions, rank them from most to least useful, and try them all exactly once. Don't freeze if one or two or six solutions don't work; getting stuck can literally mean life or death.

Crises are when you discover who *you* are—when you get to choose who you want to be.

And tonight, I need to be who I used to be. I need to get back in balance.

Because I don't feel so steady these days.

Sometimes, I'm mostly myself: little, but fierce. Still pissed off at the state of the world, if a bit tired of throwing myself into finding solutions.

Other times I feel like even the tiniest pebble tossed into my inner waters would make a ripple big enough to take me under.

So here I am, back in *my* town for a weekend, looking to soak up some chaos and energy to tide me over for a while. Everything I love is here—grumpy mountains, turbulent rivers, and Liz, the best friend who's more of a sister to me than anyone I'd match to with a cheek swab.

I wish she'd come to this festival with me. Then I'd have someone to hug for warmth—someone to hug, period—and she wouldn't be staying home to do yet more unpaid work for her douchecanoe boss. The only familiar face I've spotted in this farmer's field is an acquaintance at best, a friend of Liz's husband who goes by the frankly unbelievable name of McHuge.

He's big, sure. But I've seen bigger. Like that time an NFL defensive back gave the keynote speech at the Pacific Northwest Trauma Society conference. Or in Jason Momoa movies. Probably.

All evening, I've watched guys slap him on the back before asking if he could spare a twenty. Long-legged women wearing flower crowns leap into his arms, then walk away five minutes later with his food and tea. They all promise to pay him back; he brushes them off with hippie platitudes about energy and karma.

Everywhere I look, McHuge's head and shoulders rise above the crowd, dark-ginger curls and pale skin popping against the blue-green mountains bracketing the Pendleton Valley. We're not hanging out together, but when aggressively intoxicated people lurch in my direction, he materializes to gently redirect them before nodding and stepping a respectful distance away.

He's not my type. Obviously. I'm only watching him because I can't figure him out.

Besides his size, there's nothing physically remarkable about him. He's got longish hair and a big beard—not an uncommon look in Pendleton and Grey Tusk, the famous ski resort half an hour south of here. Prominent nose balanced by full lips. Generous auburn brows over eyes of dark mossy green flecked with gold. No visible tattoos or piercings.

He's not what I'd call pretty. Rather, he's attractive in a rough way; clean but not quite tame. There's something about the way he crosses his bulging arms and vibes to the music that makes me picture him in one of those medieval woodsman hats, playing levelheaded Little John, solving everyone's problems by giving them his stuff.

My mom was like that: generous to a fault, unable to hold on to anything if she thought someone wanted or needed it. Then along came my dad, convinced he deserved everything for nothing. A perfect match, as long as you weren't their kid.

That history is why I turned McHuge down half an hour ago when he offered me a flannel shirt big enough to fall past my knees. That, and I'm sensitive about my height. If I look too cute at a concert, people pick me up and surf me across the crowd, and some asshole always takes one of my shoes.

I took care assembling tonight's anti-cute outfit: red lips, platinum pompadour, fresh undercut. A black tank top emphasizes my newly completed left sleeve—a cyborg fantasy in shadowy gray with the Rebel Alliance symbol on the back of my wrist and Luke Skywalker's prosthetic circuits over the tender skin immediately opposite.

I look pleasingly scary, but I'm fucking freezing.

The second I glance at McHuge, toasty in his long-sleeved, high-necked fleece, he appears at my side like he can hear my brain waves. "You're shivering. How 'bout you borrow my jacket for ten minutes, and give it back once you get warm?"

Not even this miserable cold can unclench the hesitation that fists in my stomach. I don't take spontaneous favors from people I don't know. That's how my dad would reel in a mark, with favors they didn't ask for but felt obliged to repay.

"N-no, thanks," I say, teeth chattering.

A spiky-haired figure takes the stage. The crowd wakes like a beast, miserable moans giving way to a roar of excitement. Relief floods me, feeling almost warm. I'll duck up to the front—one of the rare times being tiny comes in handy—tuck myself into the crush, and get my core temperature up.

"Sorry, everyone. The Bare-knuckle Fighters have some cold-related equipment problems we haven't been able to fix. We wish we could play for you, but we have to cancel."

Disappointed wails transform to an angry mutter, then a collective scream of rage.

Bodies surge around me, knocking me face-first into Mc-Huge's chest, because of course he's right here, where I'd swear he wasn't a second ago. *Maybe he* is *that big*, I think, as my cheek mashes against his pec.

Somebody grabs my shoulder while clawing their way to the howling mayhem in front of the stage. McHuge's chest tilts hard. Shit, I'm falling, my head accelerating toward a seething forest of legs.

Before I can get my arms over my face, I'm up again, two big hands hoisting me to my feet. No, farther; he's somehow gotten an arm under my ass and I'm cradled in the crook of his elbow like a new puppy. His arm is . . . I think "thick" is the word I want? Thick and oaken, dusted with springy ginger-blond hair that teases the back of my thighs.

"Are you all right? Take any hits?"

I scan my body for pain points. "I'm good. Damn, that was close. Thanks for the lift." Up here, I see things I missed before. His beard is trimmed around those full lips with surgical precision. The harsh artificial lighting gives everyone here a zombie complexion, but when I look at his face, my imagination superimposes a fringe of pale-ginger lashes, hair a couple of coppery shades darker, beard two tones deeper still, face and arms covered with a dense lacework of golden freckles.

Someone jostles him. For a second, I'm afraid we'll both fall.

The smallest cloud crosses his placid expression as he sets his feet wide. The next person who bumps him bounces off, landing on their ass. His lips twitch microscopically.

He liked doing that.

Now *that's* interesting. Underneath the Friendly Giant personality he wears in public, there's something steelier. Something that doesn't give.

Maybe he's a *little* bit my type.

The crowd pushes toward the exits, rushing to get away from the trouble seekers up front with their chaos dreams of smashing guitars and starring in blurry social media videos.

"You have unusual eyes," he says, like he's too tall to have seen them before this moment. "Pale blue. Like whitewater."

Compliments aren't my thing. "You can put me down now."

He looks at me for a beat. Two. Three. Then sets me down carefully, one armed.

Okay, that was hot.

"How are you getting home?" he asks.

"The buses."

"Those buses?" He jerks his chin at the public transit parking lot, where there are enough buses to handle a slow trickle of people, not a full-on stampede. They're all jammed with bodies. The drivers honk ineffectively at the swirling, pushing crowds, unable to leave so more buses can pull in.

He watches my face fall. "I'm heading south," he says. "I can drop you off anywhere from here to Grey Tusk Village."

I hesitate, doing mental math. What would I owe him? "I'm in Pendleton. I can give you gas money."

"It won't cost me anything to take you."

"And it wouldn't cost you anything to leave me here, either. Take the money, McHuge."

Am I imagining the way his lips curve ever so slightly upward again?

I feel a rush of lightness, a tug in my skin that makes me want to see whether he has room inside his oversize fleece for one more person.

And I remember something else I used to do that made me feel steady—that is, before I turned thirty and decided I'd better try to have a grown-up relationship. When I wanted companionship but didn't want to roll the dice on love, I'd find someone like me who was looking for a night of warmhearted fun and nothing more.

Hookup math was simple: give as good as you get; leave someone at least as happy as you found them. I got good at avoiding people who were only in it for themselves and even better at gently turning away those whose eyes said they wanted my tomorrows.

It wasn't as good as partnered sex, but there was an equilibrium to it. I gave some, they gave some, repeat. I'd try this, they'd redirect me to that, the pleasure dulled a little by the effort of making sure everyone got their fair share. Nothing I loved was lost when it ended, because it was *supposed* to end.

I need something to bring me back to myself. After being an ER doc during the pandemic, then getting run out of the hospital by my so-called work family, I can't weather any more loss.

And I'd very much like to forget that this afternoon, going through boxes of my stuff my ex-girlfriend left at Liz's house, I pulled out an unfamiliar pair of bikini underwear with SWEET AND SOUR written across the ass.

Not my size. Not hers, either.

I realize I've been staring at McHuge's fleece too long when he strips it off and drapes it over my shoulders. It feels so good against my bare arms. This guy runs so hot, his jacket is warm on the *outside*, for fuck's sake. It smells like a mountain rescue: honeyed tea and laundry warm from the dryer. The burst of comfort triggers a wrenching shiver.

"Ready to go?" He raises his eyebrows. One of them is crooked, a white line running through the ginger, the two halves meeting slightly off-kilter. Oh, I like his face—the straight nose that says he's never been in a fight, the eyebrow that says he has. I think he's not who he pretends to be.

What I *should* do is go back to my too-expensive vacation rental, stand in the shower until I feel 50 percent sure I won't die of cold, then sleep until it's time to head to the airport for my flight back to Brittle Rock, the far north mining town where I'm the locum doctor.

What I'm *going* to do is see whether I'd like to hook up with a guy named McHuge.

Step one: I ask him to give me something. Not a fleece, no matter how amazing it is. He's given his clothes to a lot of people today, so a fleece isn't special. I need something specific. Something *I* choose.

I catch up to him to walk alongside. "What's your name, McHuge?"

"You just said it."

"Not your professional wrestling name. Your real name."

"I could argue professional wrestling names turn into real names, given enough time."

"You're funny." I keep my tone light. I asked, he refused, done. I'll give him directions to the rental place.

He looks down at me, brows drawn together. Again, I have the disconcerting feeling he senses what I'm thinking. This might be why people are afraid of gingers, and their forest eyes, and their miles of muscles that would go on and on underneath your fingers.

"It's Lyle. Lyle McHugh."

Huh. Didn't see that coming. "What's your middle name, Lyle?"

"Planning to steal my identity?" He cocks that crooked brow.

"Yes. It's because we look so much alike."

"In that case, it's Quillen."

My middle name has made me lightning fast at calculating the humiliating permutations of names and initials. "Your parents named you Lyle Q. McHugh? Were they reading too much Dr. Seuss?"

"I think by the time they got to the fifth kid, they were too tired to think it through." He doesn't look embarrassed. I don't think anything unnerves Lyle Q. McHugh.

"Meh, I've heard worse."

"Oh yeah? What's yours?"

There it is: step two in my hookup test, the reciprocal ask I'm hoping for. I usually say my middle name is Wilhelmina or Brunhilde. Any unusual name is close enough, in spirit. But for some reason, I give Lyle the truth.

"It's J. Like the letter *J*, full stop. Explaining it at the DMV is a nightmare."

"Stellar J. Like the bird." Unlike me, he doesn't make a joke about what kind of parents would name their kid Stellar J Byrd.

We reach the parking lot, weaving through rows of cars until he points his key fob at a small SUV. Inside, it's worn but clean. On the underside of the flipped-down sun visor is a photo of Lyle in the center of six Chewbacca-sized gingers—siblings, maybe. It looks like it was taken as everyone lost patience and started tormenting each other. Elbows are being thrown. Ponytails fly. Lyle alone stands still, hands folded, body blocking the brawl.

Nothing about this guy is what I expect.

I'm not in a place where I can let myself like him. But I can sleep with him, if he's willing.

"Where are you heading?" he asks, once we've joined the slow crawl of cars out of the lot.

"How about your place?"

Breath comes out of him in a catch, then a rush. He turns my way, darkness falling in his eyes of midnight moss.

"You don't owe me anything, Stellar J. I'd never . . . I'd never offer you a ride because I wanted to ask for that. I don't want that energy between us."

"That's not the energy I'm bringing, Lyle. But if the answer's no, let me out at the corner of Junction and Currie, and we'll never mention this again."

He makes a rumbling sound that shakes me all the way down and all the way back up again, like a natural disaster. I can't look at his hands on the steering wheel, big and rough like a pair of grizzly paws. I'd like to see those hands—

"Hey, you want some music?" I say it to interrupt myself, more than anything. "What do you like?"

He touches a button on the stereo. A folk-rock station mercifully takes the edge off the silence.

When we get to Pendleton, he doesn't take the turnoff, and I don't mention the fact that he missed it. We keep driving south, toward the lights of Grey Tusk.

Chapter One

I can't believe I ever subscribed to the idea that a disaster meant I could choose who I wanted to be.

My life has been a disaster for a year, and the last person I'd choose to be is the one chugging north on the Oceans to Peaks Highway, one eye on the gas gauge, one hand on the dashboard to encourage my ancient Honda.

"Honey. We're getting killed out here. I think those cyclists are going to pass us." Honey's almost as old as I am—thirty-three—and very close to exceeding my repair skills, unless I take up welding in my nonexistent spare time. She needs an emotional support person on the hills. Unfortunately, she got me, and the only emotion I have anymore is anger.

Burnout, my therapist called it, before I ran out of money and stopped seeing her. If that's what we're calling simultaneously losing your profession, your reputation, and your ability to make a living in one of Canada's most expensive places, then sure.

Half an hour from Grey Tusk, the luxe mountain playground beloved by the world's wealthiest people, the Pendleton Valley

unrolls like green shag carpet, the fertile farmland hemmed in
by mountains in every direction. A few minutes north of Pendleton, I spot the landmarks Liz gave me: two big gray rocks
on the left, then a tree that looks like a moose on the right. I
slow down—not by much; poor Honey—and turn onto a dirt
track nearly grown over with rainforest understory: maiden-
hair ferns, skunk cabbage, moss in every shade from emerald
to deep gold.

These abandoned logging roads crisscross the foothills
everywhere, mostly maintained by locals who use them for hiking, hunting, and access to the Pendle River system. This one's
old; cedar and birch trees have grown into a dense canopy that
nearly closes out the sky. Leafy arms reach into the one-lane
track to squeak across Honey's panels. Behind me, a plume of
pale dust swirls, a reminder that everything in this valley comes
from the river: the fine, silty soil, the rich agricultural land, the
abundance of life blossoming in our little microclimate.

We've got the mountain animals Canada's famous for, like
grizzlies, cougars, and wolverines—the forty-pound weasel
type, not the Hugh Jackman type, but they sound impressive.
Tourists like the big, flashy fauna, but when I used to spend time
in the wilderness, I preferred the small things. You can find a
dozen rare types of salamander and even a tiny species of boa
constrictor, if you don't think size means everything.

After ten minutes of bumping over rocks and edging past
sawn-up windfall trees, I reach a tidy clearing marked with logs
to indicate the parking spaces. I pat the dash. "Screw the hat-
ers, Honey. We made it in one pi—Ahhh!"

I stomp the brakes reflexively, and Honey's wheels skid a
little on the loose gravel.

McHuge. Or at least McHuge in vehicular form.

I mean, I knew he'd be here. I'm interviewing for a job

with him. It's just unsettling to be confronted with a van that couldn't possibly belong to anyone else, unless the Scooby-Doo gang works here.

Okay, it's not an *exact* replica of the Mystery Machine. But what else can you call a multipassenger van painted the glossy summer cream of vanilla soft serve, accented with a vintage surf-style red-orange-yellow stripe? There's a stylized sunset on the rear doors, captioned with loopy brown script: KEEP ON KEEPIN' ON. It looks like it was designed by a gray-ponytailed boomer who had one too many light beers while marinating in a Beach Boys megamix.

A round logo in the aggressively plain style you'd see at crunchy, expensive natural food stores decorates the rear sliding door.

THE LOVE BOAT.

This is what my life has come to.

But I still have two things in this world I love: my friend Liz and this beautiful, wild part of Canada. After losing everything else I used to care about, I'd do anything to keep them.

Even this.

I wait for the road dust to settle, then roll down my window, open the door using the still-functional outside handle, and step into the parking lot. I'm heading to work after this and I need to stay clean—Grey Tusk tourists don't tip when your clothes aren't spotless. I've tried a lot of different outfits in a year of working gig jobs, and this one sends me home with the most cash in hand: a fitted short-sleeved black button-down, slim black pants cut an inch above my ankle bone, and vegan leather oxfords in black and white. Black suspenders make a nice triangular gap between my waist and my padded bra. My undercut is freshly touched up with my secondhand trimmers, my hair sprayed into a pouf that filters any smile into a wicked smirk.

I look like the last person who should be working at a whitewater-canoeing-slash-relationship-therapy start-up. Then again, McHuge doesn't check a lot of boxes on the "stereotypical doctor of psychology" list, with his braided beard and California yoga teacher vocabulary.

No one's here to greet me except an enormous king shepherd dog who pops her head out of the van's open sliding door. She's big enough to bite me in half, and I respect that. God knows I'd like to bite a few people from time to time.

The dog looks me up and down, decides I'm not worth the effort, and curls back up on a towel spread across one of the vinyl bench seats.

It's fine. Animals don't like Katniss Everdeen, either.

I head along a path toward the river, stopping when I reach a clearing with a panoramic view of what Liz's husband, Tobin—also McHuge's business partner—called "base camp." It used to be part of a rustic family compound, but fewer people care to go without electricity and running water on their vacation these days, so Tobin and McHuge were able to secure prime waterfront for their don't-get-divorced summer camp.

I shouldn't make fun of it, I suppose. Last year McHuge published a self-help book that allegedly saved Liz and Tobin's marriage and made a few bestseller lists. Mostly the Canadian ones, but it's not nothing. Liz has been on me to read it, but I'm not interested in learning to get along with the people who've disappointed me.

To my left, there's an old cabin, planks silvered by age and rain, with a staircase of bright new cedar and a sign reading COOKHOUSE: STAFF ONLY. Not far away, on the edge of a wide sandy path leading to the river, is a smaller shed, its barn-style doors thrown open to reveal a pair of weathered sawhorses and a shelf crowded with marine maintenance products. A modest lawn surrounds a screened-in pavilion labeled DINING HALL / STUDIO; up the hillside is an open-air wash station next to a broad-planked outdoor shower stall. Beside that is a low, square wooden building with a bright aluminum chimney. A sauna, unless I miss my guess.

The far end of the clearing obviously used to be a volleyball or badminton area, with those two tall poles that beg for a net. The nearer end features a river-stone firepit surrounded by a dozen thick, round log stools.

If there are sing-alongs, I'm calling in sick.

Fronting the calm expanse of the river, five white canvas castles, practically big tops, rise on airy platforms of the same red cedar as the cookhouse stairs. Smart: clients want the river view, but not the groundwater seeping through the floor.

And there, at the river's edge, a tall, broad figure looks out over the water toward the tree-lined mountains and decommissioned railway tracks on the opposite shore. On closer inspection, he's standing in the river, quick-dry cargo pants rolled up to midshin.

It's either a stirring portrait of Man in Nature or a dude who's two horns and a helmet short of a viral Viking video series.

Or it's my prospective boss and the man I've been dodging ever since the best, worst hookup of our times. The memory brings a sick flush to my cheeks. We were so goddamn good together, and so catastrophically bad. I've spoken to him twice since then—once at an improv show, once serving on a volunteer search crew. Both times, I vowed not to come near him ever again. A *year* later the first sip of morning tea still tastes like him.

I want to turn around, put Honey's pedal to the floor, and run back to the delivery job that pays almost enough to keep me in ramen noodles and out of student loan bankruptcy. Keep my head in the sand till the car I can't afford to replace breaks down for the last time. Then I'll finally have no viable job prospects in Grey Tusk's bizarre economy, where the middle class is officially missing.

I'll have to leave Grey Tusk and Liz. Lose the only two things I've managed to hold on to during the total implosion of my life.

I'm angry even thinking about it, but better fuming than frightened. When I worked in the emergency department of Grey Tusk General Hospital, getting mad made me smarter and stronger. There's nothing like a burst of furious last-ditch CPR interspersed with yelling to revive a stubbornly arrested heart, or a heartfelt curse to finally pop an IV into an elusive vein. Anger makes you want to throw things, and problems need you to throw things at them, so they pair well.

But there are no solutions to throw at my finances, except one. It means a whole summer next to McHuge, who I usually try not to come within talking distance of. Ten weeks of being a camp doctor, which puts a stethoscope-shaped rock in my stomach.

I assess the soft deep sand leading to the shore, then pull off one oxford at a time and balance them on a log with my socks tucked inside. McHuge is already a piece of grit in my metaphorical shoe, rubbing me wrong with every step. No need to add real sand to the equation, too.

He turns around before he could possibly have heard my foot-steps over the rush of water.

Still using his psychic powers for evil, I see.

I stagger awkwardly across thirty feet of loose sand while the two of us don't speak to each other, as usual.

An olive-green T-shirt with a gooftastic cartoon of a bear

portaging a canoe—carrying the boat over his head, in canoe-speak—stretches across his generous pecs, barely hugging the little bit of softness at his stomach.

"Stellar."

"McHuge."

This is our first conversation in a year, so obviously I war-gamed it on the drive here. I plan to give back exactly what he gives me. One-name greeting? Check.

"Thanks for coming out. Kind of an unconventional spot for a job interview, but I like it." He scrunches his bare toes into the riverbed. "Join me?"

Argh. He walked into the water; now I have to, too. He defeated my give-what-I-get strategy on his *second move.* Forget canoes; McHuge should take up chess.

"Love to." I roll up my pants as far as I can. Creases are better than splashes or mud.

The water's ankle deep, pale aqua, and freezing. In the tender late-afternoon light, his eyes are the color of a sunbeam hitting the waters of the North Pacific, every hue of green touched with drops of gold identical to the freckles dusted over his cheeks, arms, and knees, perfectly clear until suddenly a trick of the light hides what's underneath. His ginger hair flames extravagantly next to the darker shade of his beard.

I don't like his face. I especially resent the one deep auburn lock that's escaped the elastic to curl across his temple, ugh. And I hate how my body softens when I step closer, as if he's not the most dangerous mistake I could make. Or *re*make, technically.

Busy disliking everything about him, I forget to watch my step. My left heel hits a flat, slippery rock and shoots out in front of me. I pitch sideways toward McHuge and a million gallons of pure, clean, icy meltwater.

I'm closing my eyes against the cold that's about to shock my face when my suspenders tighten against my chest. Gravity ceases to exist.

After a careful breath, I open one eye. McHuge does indeed have the back straps of my suspenders and a generous handful of my shirt gripped in one gigantic fist, like I'm a toddler intent on running into the street.

"You good?" he asks evenly, setting me on my feet.

"I'm fine." I consider throwing myself into the river. "Thanks for the lift. You may want to move that rock at some point." I turn away to tug my shirt into place, closing the string of gaps that popped into existence between the buttons. I'm starting to think this was a bad idea.

"You sure? Your aura is very dark right now." He bobbles his head side to side. "Darker than usual, anyway."

"I look good in black," I say flatly, turning to face the opposite bank. We can talk without staring into each other's eyes.

He nods. "Did Liz explain what we're looking for, or do you want me to go over it?"

"She showed me the article." It was a long-form think piece in *Beeswax*, a major online magazine, arguing the dangers of the "pop psychology gold rush"—the scramble to stake out a niche in the rapidly growing self-help industry, consumer safety be damned. "The Love Boat," the article claimed, "is one such example."

Lyle McHugh developed a legitimate piece of psychology scholarship—which was published as last year's trendiest do-it-yourself marriage counseling manual, *The Second Chances Handbook*, under the guidance of Dr. Alan Fisher, his PhD supervisor and coauthor.

Now McHugh, a never-married proponent of "free

love," hopes to capitalize on his success by launching an unproven relationship therapy program based in a remote wilderness camp without access to medical care for miles around. It's based on tandem whitewater canoeing—a sport so difficult it's unofficially known as "divorce boat."

Dr. Fisher chose his words carefully when approached for comment. "I do wish Mr. McHugh had persisted with his PhD studies for an extra year or two, instead of leaving against my recommendations. His radical ideas need tempering and underpinning with rigorous methodology, for safety reasons. Of course, I wish him every success."

"What did you think?" McHuge shifts his feet; a school of tiny brown fish dart into deeper water. I wouldn't be surprised if he was talking to them before I got here.

I purse my lips. "It's a hit piece. The never-married thing is a total straw man. And out here, a doctor can't do much more than someone with industrial first aid training. You're not that far from the urgent care clinic in Pendleton, or even Grey Tusk General." I swallow the taste of my former workplace out of my mouth, then add, "Plus, your prof called you 'Mister,' like you didn't finish your PhD. And the writer didn't correct him."

The arcane traditions of medicine used to be one of my favorite things. I loved it when my doctor friends called me "Doctor" to convey anything from "I'm happy to see you" to "you just said something astonishingly smart." I flinched at panel discussions when one speaker unleashed an icy "I disagree, *Doctor*," before publicly scoring devastating points on the archrival seated next to them.

But if another doctor calls you "Mister," it means they want you *dead*. I caught a stinging "good luck in your future endeav-ors, *Ms*. Byrd," as I was escorted out of Grey Tusk General, and I knew my department chief wanted me to understand he'd scooped out the best part of me.

"The writer was misinformed," McHuge says mildly. "Brent and I connected. We cleared up a few misconceptions."

"Brent's article made one of your employees quit a week before launch. You don't have to be friends with everyone, Lyle."

At the sound of his given name, our heads do a move that feels choreographed, like a pop and lock—turning to face each other, holding for a tense moment, then turning away. I know how he likes being called by that name, which is why I had planned never to use it. But it flew out of my mouth like it was waiting for him.

He clears his throat. "I generally find it's better to be kind than right."

Touché. He was the kind one after I sneaked out of his bed in the middle of the night. He sent me exactly three texts: I didn't hear you go! Everything all good? progressing to Stellar J ♥ I would be very open to seeing where this goes if that's the vibe you're feeling, and ending with I think you want me to back off, and I'm doing it with peace in my heart. Take care.

He was kind. But I was right. And the two of us couldn't be more wrong for each other.

"The problem is," McHuge goes on, "Renee Garner is con-sidering a partnership with us, and she feels we need to ad-dress the criticisms wherever possible. She's at a vulnerable moment, reputation-wise."

Everybody's heard of Renee Garner. Even me, who swore off wellness culture after realizing "resilience" is code for how toxic a workplace can get before employers have to deal with it.

Renee's research on bad bosses led her to the speaking circuit, then to a media career with an Oprahesque stable of bright young collaborators. She must still be stinging over having to fire an addiction specialist whose degree came from the University of Photoshop.

"Which is where I come in," I say.

"Which is where you come in. We need a medical professional with whitewater experience."

"I haven't guided whitewater since medical school." It was good money, but the culture could be shitty and sexist at times. Tour operators prefer younger guides, who are less likely to have unhealthy adrenaline-rush habits or chronic injuries. Fun people, who can make the tourists laugh.

"I'd do the instruction. As long as your whitewater rescue certification is still good and you're strong enough to do a solo rescue, that's all we need."

"Oh, I'm strong enough," I snap back. I run. I lift. Granted, it's with a set of flaking free weights I scrounged from the free bin at the Pendleton triathlon club's annual gear swap, but my arm definition doesn't lie.

"I don't doubt it," he says evenly. "You'd be doing site prep from now until next Monday's launch. The sessions are ten days on, four days off, with an extra week between the first and second sessions to make changes if Renee asks for them. Payday every Friday." He names a weekly salary triple what I pull down as a delivery driver.

"That's . . . competitive," I choke out. Jesus. With summer earnings like that, I could take time off in the fall, figure out what to do with my life. Take a course in real estate or something else I could tolerate but never love. "What about the medical thing? The, um, clinic?"

A clinic. *Calm, I am calm, I am*—fuck, I'm flashing back.

It was a few months after I got *Ms. Byrd*-ed at Grey Tusk
General, not long after the doomed hookup with McHuge. I was
alone in my tiny office in Brittle Rock, seeing a fit-in first thing
in the morning. There was the patient, tall and burly, his florid
face turning purple from yelling, like my dad's had the night he
told my mom to get in the car, then reamed me out on the side-
walk for being a selfish little shit who only thought of myself.
And me, writing prescription after prescription to de-escalate
the situation, praying for the clinic nurse to arrive early and
help me, heart galloping so fast I couldn't breathe.

When it was over, I knew I couldn't give any more if this
was what I got in return. A year later I'm still so angry I can't
catch my breath, tucking my fingers into my armpits to hide
their trembling.

"You'd cover emergencies only," McHuge says. "Maybe treat
minor cuts and scrapes. If that works for you?" He strokes one
hand over his beard, scanning my posture like he can read
every tightened angle.

"Sounds doable." I unclench my teeth, not wanting my secrets to be legible. My dentist will be pleased.

"And there's one more thing." His tone pulls from its usual
slack Owen Wilson drawl into something with a firm pencil
point. "Distraction can be dangerous out here. To keep my focus on the clients, I need strong, low-maintenance relationships
with my employees. It goes without saying that nothing beyond
a collegial friendship could happen between us."

I slap a hand over my mouth. "Jesus, McHuge."

His hands splay open in a *welp* gesture. "I can't make a hiring decision without talking about our history, Stellar. It's one
thing for you to make sure I'm on the other side of the room
before you walk under the mistletoe at Liz and Tobin's holiday
party. It's something else entirely to expect the clients to not

pick up on the two of us avoiding each other when we're together twenty-four seven for ten days."

Excuse me. The *two* of us avoiding *each other*?

My cheeks burn hot. Sure, I sometimes look at his texts
when I feel lonely. Maybe I wanted to believe I had to stay away
for his sake, not just mine. But I guess I've been making an
ass of myself at every barbecue since last summer, keeping a
backyard's worth of people between us like he was a deadly
allergen.

The vast wilderness feels too small now that I'm standing
in it with this version of McHuge—the one who actually isn't
friends with everyone, because he clearly doesn't want to be
friends with me.

It's for the best, but I'm furious with myself for not being
smarter. If I weren't wearing my good clothes, I'd run this feeling away: crank up the pace until my brain went silent and there
was nothing but the sawing of breath in and out of my chest.

His fingers twitch. If he's considering reaching out to me,
he thinks better of it. "If you can move past that, I don't need
to look for another candidate. You're bright, you work hard,
and you're one of the most loyal people I've ever met, if your
friendship with Liz is anything to go by. You're the right person
for the job."

I can hear him holding back the words "on paper." I'm not
the person I was when I pushed his front door shut and tugged
on his belt loop that fateful night, thinking I could handle myself. And I'm not the person he thinks I am now. He's still wrong
for me, and I'm wrong for everybody. And we both know it.

"When do you need to know by?"

"As soon as possible. Extra hands would be great to have
this week, before launch. And Tobin wants to start his paternity
leave at least a week before Liz's due date."

So, two weeks. He has time to find somebody else.

"I'll think about it," I say, pivoting toward shore.

"Do that," he says, but he can read my thoughts, and he knows I turned him down.

I intend not to look back, but the deep, effortful sound he makes pulls my head around in time to see him pry the slippery rock from under the water and shot-put it a ridiculous distance into the river. It's sizable, maybe twenty pounds, and it doesn't take long before the waves from its impact are tugging the sand from beneath my feet, unbalancing me like the aftershocks from the night of the festival.

I practically run out of the water, clean clothes be damned. The closer the two of us are, the stronger this ripple effect gets, undermining us both. The only solution is to stay far, far away, where the waves he makes can't reach me.

Halfway down the dirt road, my phone dings with missed notifications. I pull over by a fallen tree to catch up. It's Liz.

> Are you at the Love Boat?

> Contractions 6 minutes apart. 37 weeks isn't premature right? Googling

> We're going in! Baby tonight (I hope)

Shit. I'm half an hour away and Liz needs me. I push my speed as high as Honey's chassis can take on this rocky road and hope I haven't missed the biggest moment of her life.

Chapter Two

The next morning is one of those crystalline mountain days, the self-indulgent early-summer beauty capped by an unlimited supply of blue that glows with a layered indigo brilliance you'll never see in the shallow watercolor coastal skies. The fresh, damp wind feels good on my skin as I run down Liz's street, slowing to a walk for the last block.

Pendleton is an Austrian postcard of a town. Fields swirl with tender green shoots that tremble and flip in the breeze, showing their pale-green underskirts. Perched above the river, farmhouses flaunt red shutters with heart-shaped cutouts and massive window boxes spilling bright blooms, their natural-stained wood balconies popping against whitewashed walls.

I like Pendleton. It's cute and quirky and quiet, and too far from the hospital for me to run into my old colleagues.

I take the steps of Liz's gabled cottage two at a time, punch the doorbell, and let myself in. "Helloooo! Everybody still pregnant?"

I was almost to Grey Tusk last night when Liz texted again:

False alarm. They shamed us and sent us home. But everything feels so REAL all of a sudden. Baby's room not ready at all 🫣

Liz appears in the kitchen doorway sporting heather-gray maternity leggings, fuzzy slippers over her swollen feet, and a french-blue top that sets off the cinnamon tones in her brown hair. "Too soon," she says flatly, frowning at my running clothes. "Honey wouldn't start again? I could have picked you up."

"Meh, I needed to put in some distance."

She meets my gaze for a moment—an extra-long moment for Liz. She's not the biggest fan of eye contact, but she does it for special people. "Yes, and I still could have driven you. As long as the kid's not actively crowning, I'll always come get you, Stellar."

She would, too. Liz and I have been best friends since I was a first-year med student and she was a freshman. I'd applied early to dodge extra years of tuition, so I was only two years older. She was standing in a corner of a New Year's keg party, her expression cool, giving off an untouchable vibe with her shirt buttoned up to her chin. Of course I hit on her; I loved a challenge in those days, and she was a pretty puzzle box for me to solve.

The next morning I was warming up my friendly goodbye speech when she looked at me with big brown bunny eyes and I realized I'd misjudged her completely. She wasn't untouchable, she was *shy*, and likely way less experienced than I'd thought. I couldn't drop this girl. I'd messed up the balance between us, and I'd have to fix it.

I invited her out for coffee. She was as careful a conversation partner as she was a lover, almost seeming to count the words I spoke so she could answer with the exact same number. In retrospect, her autism should've been diagnosed a lot sooner.

Obviously, we were perfect for each other. As friends, of course. A dozen years later, she's as ride or die for me as I am for her. The way she refused to take shit at her former job gave me a big chunk of the courage I needed to quit my own.

But our relationship has been getting more and more uneven since I crashed at her place for a month after fleeing Brittle Rock, right when she'd gotten back with her husband after a dicey separation. I owe her big time, but she seems to need me less and less. She made half a dozen new friends when I was away. She does improv comedy—gross—with them on nights when I'm grinding at my minimum-wage jobs. She won't take any baby gifts that cost money. We always joked about me delivering her baby, but three weeks ago she told me she and Tobin decided to have just each other in the birthing room.

I know she doesn't keep track of our friendship balance sheet like I do. She'd tell me everything's fine, and she'd believe it. But there's a distant early-warning bell ringing in my heart. Jen—the ex I was sure I was going to marry—found ways to not need me less than a month after I left for Brittle Rock.

So here I am, ready to build a crib. I'd assemble twenty cribs for my honorary nibling if that's what Liz needed.

"You're still calling it 'the kid'? Babe," I say, gently chiding. "What if yesterday had been the real thing and you had no name and no crib?" I head upstairs, Liz following more slowly with the weebly, rolling gait of late pregnancy.

"Well, it wasn't. And a crib isn't strictly necessary. Newborns sleep in boxes in Denmark. Or is it Finland? Somewhere progressive where people are happy because their marriage didn't have to withstand an IKEA build."

In the nursery I tear open the flat-packed box and sift through cardboard flotsam for the instructions. The first page shows a pictogram of a human holding a broken piece of wood, making a sad face. Should be fun.

No, it *will* be fun. Liz still needs me for this.

"You should charge me your hourly," she says. "You're over here when you could be working."

"No way. I still owe you for last year's extended stay."

Her face darkens. "You don't have to pay me back for that forever. You could take my help. If you need money—A loan, okay?" she says when I stiffen. "Or a gift. Ow. I need to sit down for a second." She arches her back as she settles onto the glider in front of the window.

"Your husband's trying to start a business; I'm not taking your cash. I'll figure something out." I toss the Allen key, catching it with a flourish and a smirk to detract from the bags under my eyes. Last night I took a deep dive into the parts of my finances I usually try not to look at. I've dipped into my line of credit for twenty bucks here, fifty bucks there, hoping it wouldn't matter. But actually, the laws of math are still in effect and that shit adds up.

Unless I stumble across an unmarked duffel bag of cash, my next rent check is going to bounce. A loan from Liz could get me by for now, but then what? I'd be one spiral farther from the drain, but still getting flushed.

Anyway, I'm here for her, not me. "Where's Tobin?"

She tries to balance a smile on top of a worried expression. "He's at base camp with McHuge. You know, trying to finish as much as he can before I pop. He says thanks, by the way. I've been so superstitious about putting the nursery together or packing my hospital bag or doing any of the things you're supposed to do. Yesterday it felt like I'd be pregnant forever and never see my cankles again. Now the baby could come any second and *nothing's* ready."

The skin under Liz's eyes reddens with the threat of tears. The unspoken question of yesterday's interview buzzes along the silent channels of communication we've forged through years of friendship. Maybe I can avoid answering until the build's at least partway done.

"That's why you texted me about the crib," I say in my most soothing voice. "And I'm here. The room will be ready by lunchtime. Besides, first babies are notorious for coming late. You probably have more time than you think."

She shifts uncomfortably in the chair and pushes a fist into the place where her pelvis meets her spine. "I guess the interview didn't go well if you're not bringing it up."

So much for avoidance. "It went fine," I lie, running one hand through the back of my undercut while sorting through pieces of white painted wood. "Tobin and McHuge can do better than someone who's been out of the doctor game for a year. They should look around a bit. Consider their options."

Her mouth crumples—alarming, considering how restrained her usual range of facial expressions is.

"I mean, I'll definitely do it if they can't find anyone else," I rush to add.

"It's not that. It's my stupid back. The websites that say pregnancy is miraculous and glowy are all *lying*." She shifts in the chair, wincing. "I'd never push you into taking the job, Stellar. I was hoping you'd *want* to."

Maybe I should've told Liz I slept with McHuge, because now feels like the wrong time to confess why I don't want the job. I pick up a bag with a dozen different types of fasteners. How a person is supposed to build this with pregnancy brain is beyond me.

"They'll find someone," I say, making my voice bright and chipper. "The Love Boat should advertise on medical Facebook groups. I'm sure there are tons of doctors who'd fly in for a working vacation."

"I wanted this for *you*," she snaps, voice tight. "Not for me or Tobin or McHuge. I'm worried about *you*. It's like you're disappearing. You won't let yourself have anything nice. You could get a better job, you know. One with decent hours and a livable wage. It doesn't have to be the Love Boat."

I put down the wood I'm unsuccessfully trying to match to the diagram. "You may be overestimating the job market, babe. My MD is worthless in the real world."

I can't count how many Grey Tusk employers have said I'm either underqualified or overqualified for their openings. One guy had the balls to tell me I was both. The crushing drudgery of the gig economy never feels more endless than when I get turned down for decent jobs.

I have no money and no prospects. And I'm so afraid I'm about to have no friend, although she's much more than my friend.

"No," Liz says, that sharpness still in her voice. "You could do a lot of things, but for some reason, you're pretending you can't. You like to think you're a machine"—she gestures at a series of gears inked down my forearm—"but how long can you keep this up? Financially? Emotionally?"

My stomach clenches hard. I was keeping up fine until a couple of months ago. Or maybe not fine, but the drain on my bank accounts was slow and easy to ignore. But I may be in dire straits soon, especially if Honey needs a new starter motor.

Mom pops into my head the way she does when I feel trouble's breath on my neck. Some old ghost of a program grinds to life on my mental hard drive, making me wish she'd come back for me. When I first moved here, she and Dad weren't living too far away. I knew Dad wouldn't want her to reach out, but it's a small town. Every time I went to the grocery store, I'd watch for her face, sure I'd see her sooner or later. But I never did.

Eventually, I understood that Liz was the only family I had here. The only family I had, period.

"I think . . ." Liz looks out the window, answering the things I've left unsaid. "I think our friendship may be the only thing you truly care about. And that's not good for you."

Ah. I see. I roll from my butt to my knees, full of the ignominy of having leaned on her too hard. She's got a husband, a baby on the way, a job she loves, and a hobby I don't share. I only have her. It's wildly uneven, and I'm embarrassed I didn't see it until now.

"Sorry, babe. I'm putting too much pressure on you."

"Don't do that. I didn't say it wasn't good for me. I said it wasn't good for *you*. You need something, Stellar. You have so much love and drive and *heart*, and nowhere to put them. I don't want to say gig work is killing you, because you'll argue medical definitions and I'll lose." She rolls her eyes. "But it's bad for you, what you're doing. It's like you don't feel anything anymore."

Liz is the best person I know. She's unflinchingly honest and—she'd hate that I think this—fantastic at spreadsheets. I thought she understood I can't give myself to another job the way I gave myself to medicine and then lose another part of me when it all ends.

If I burn through another job, it needs to be one I don't love.

"I don't mind gig work. I give it time, it gives me money, fair tra—"

"Aaaahhhhh," she yells, in the rudest, most unhinged interruption I've ever seen her make by a factor of a thousand. "This argument is not about late-stage capitalism! It's about you! I fucking know you, Stellar. Can you *listen* for one damn—Oh. Oh!"

She stands up, eyes wide, touching the back of her gray leggings. "My water—"

"—broke," I finish. "You nerd. Have you been having contractions this whole time?"

"I thought they were Braxton-Hicks. I didn't want to over-call it again." Her eyes fly wide. "Tobin! He's at—"

"I'll call him."

"There's no cell signal in camp," she wails. "All they have is a two-way radio in the van."

"Liz. I've got this. Go get changed; I'll find Tobin. I'll drive up there myself if I have to. We have time, I promise."

She has a couple of hours, I'm pretty sure. The person who's out of time is me. The Love Boat needs a replacement for her husband starting right now, and I promised my friend I'd do it if they couldn't find anyone else. My ride-or-die friend, who I'd do anything for.

Even this.

"DIZ!" The front door slams open much sooner than it would have if Tobin had respected the speed limit.

"We're upstairs! Baby still inside! Nobody panic," I shout back, popping the last screw cover into place and sliding the crib against the buttery-yellow wall. Perfect. Maybe in the fall, I can moonlight as a furniture assembler while I do a hospitality management certificate.

Tobin skids through the nursery door, sweat glistening at his hairline. "Is it time to go? I think it's time. Stellar, it's time, right? Did we pack a bag? Oh my god, the bag!"

Liz levers herself painfully out of the chair and falls into Tobin's arms like he's the only person who can comfort her, even though I've been coaching her through contractions for twenty-five minutes. It's fine. Nobody was under the illusion a baby wouldn't change our friendship. I'm here to make sure we weather the transition.

"Do you need to lie down? Walk around? Backrub?" Tobin unthinkingly slides a hand under the back of Liz's shirt. Although I've seen her fully naked and then some, I spin away at the raw intimacy of it.

I'll put together the bedding and get out of here.

Someone lifts the mattress as I reach for it. Someone whose thick, callused knuckles lead to a broad, weathered palm and on to bluntly powerful forearms dusted with freckles.

McHuge's startled eyes find mine. Pop; lock. An unguarded look crosses his face, like a summer cloudburst: there, then gone. I pull back, barely managing to avoid touching his hand with mine. There's a little stutter in his arm movements, like he'd rather avoid me, too.

My fingers curl with the urge to smooth his crooked left brow, to go back in time and do a better job with finer sutures. I have good hands: small, nimble fingers, a nice touch with the freezing.

Or at least I used to.

I loved medicine for the same reason I loved whitewater: not necessarily being strong in my body, although I was, but being smart and strategic. Knowing how to read a situation, knowing I could trust my judgment. I learned to time the sedation so I could get a dislocated shoulder back in the joint right as the muscles relaxed. I felt the moment when the sutures pulled just tight enough.

I look away first. Medicine and Lyle are both problems I don't know how to solve, but my brain won't stop turning them over and over, no matter how I will it to stop.

"What are you doing here, McHuge?" That was a bit abrupt; I make a *whoops, sorry* face at him. I can't use that tone at work, not if he and I are going to be professional and cordial or whatever words he used to mean *get over yourself.*

He nods at Tobin. "My buddy lost his cool. Safer for me to drive." He grabs the fitted sheet and expertly snaps it around the tiny mattress before slotting it into the crib. I object to how sexy it is that he's hardly paying attention while he does it. Giving men extra credit for doing basic chores is so tired.

Mattress done, McHuge looks around, avoiding my eyes the way I should be avoiding his. "Is there a changing table?"

"Basement," Tobin replies. "Under a few other boxes. Thanks, man." Their brotherly camaraderie squeezes my heart to the point of pain, like a boob squished cruelly by a mammogram machine. Those two seem to be weathering the baby thing just fine.

McHuge's voice drifts back as he heads downstairs. "Babe. Kitchen." On the stairs, dog claws click reluctantly away.

I steel myself and turn to Tobin. "Liz's hospital bag is packed and at your bedroom door. I'll talk to McHuge about the job."

"Oh, no. Stellar, no." Liz surfaces from deep inside her husband's embrace. "You don't have to do that for me. Not necessary."

Tobin meets my eyes over his pregnant wife's head. *Please*, he mouths, when she's not looking. He's not the type to ask for favors, but he's pretty convincing when he does.

"No, you were right. I thought about it while you were counting to ten over and over. It'll be good. I'm excited." My fist pump could be more convincing, but like Scully and Mulder, apparently Liz and Tobin want to believe.

Liz lets go of her husband and holds out her arms to me. "Thank you thank you thank you. I'm so happy for you. And it means everything that Tobin's business is in good hands." I have to lean way over her belly to hug her. She's soft with pregnancy, warm like a sister in my arms.

"Take my truck for the summer. You'll need it for hauling

the boat trailer. We have the baby seat in the Prius, anyway."
Tobin smiles beatifically, visions of safely secured infants
dancing in his head as he shoulders the bag stuffed with Liz's
e-reader and a couple of sets of pajamas I chose for their stain-
hiding dark colors.

"McHuge and I will sort everything out. You two focus on
having a baby."

"You're the best." Liz blows a kiss over her shoulder as Tobin escorts her to the door.

"Try to remember that feeling when you're naming my new
nibling." I wrinkle my nose. "On second thought, forget it. Give
the kid a decent name."

It's quiet once they're gone. I arrange an unbearably soft
sleep sack across the mattress, waiting for McHuge to come
back.

This job doesn't have to be the place I put my heart, no
matter what Liz says. I could live at base camp, eat there, sublet
my place, and save my entire salary. I'll stay professional with
McHuge and stay away from being a doctor in anything but
name. The part of my life I lived in the outdoors—lost when I
couldn't afford the gear, the driving, the time off work—I can
take back. At the end of the summer, I'll have a financial cushion big enough to protect the things I love.

And maybe I can bargain with Lyle for something more permanent.

McHuge eases through the nursery door with a changing
table under one arm and the topper under the other, like it's
nothing. Even beyond his sheer size, he fills a room. Not by
being loud or seeking attention; he has *presence*. He had it on-
stage at Liz's improv showcase last summer. I was shitty to him,
actually, almost heckling him. Fully on my "I must save us from
ourselves" bullshit.

We have a lot of problems to get past, but me being unwilling to apologize for my mistakes isn't one of them. Besides, it's not like I have to work hard to stay away from him anymore. He can do his half of that job.

"I'm sorry I ghosted you, Ly—McHuge. You were nothing but respectful, like you said. It was me, not you."

Sure, I failed at long-term relationships and then he ruined hookups for me, and was I irrationally, unfairly mad about that? Yeah. Yeah, I was, but that wasn't his fault.

"I had some stuff going on, but that's an explanation, not an excuse. I can be professional if we're going to work together."

I hope like hell that's the truth, because the one time I was alone in a room with him, I forgot myself completely. I let things get unbalanced. I didn't keep myself safe. And when I realized what I'd done, I freaked out so hard I haven't slept with anybody since.

Why couldn't I have stuck with my usual type—weedy, unimposing nerds wearing androgynous glasses and not dancing to the songs everybody else liked? Why, after so many friendly, forgettable hookups, is he the one who refuses to be ignored? Usually I keep a vague memory—an impression of facial bones, a movement of hair. Sometimes a first name. Rarely a last. But him? I remember it all, and I'm fully aware of how dangerous that makes him.

When I can be trusted to make good choices, I can allow myself to get back out there. If I deny myself nice things, like Liz said, I have my reasons.

McHuge puts the table down at my blunt declaration, his crooked eyebrow rising. "So . . . you're taking the job?"

"Hear me out first." I take a bracing breath. "I will do everything in my power to make your company succeed. I can work hard. Like every-hour-of-the-day hard. But I'm not giving or *nice* the way you are. And you should know I left Grey Tusk General under less-than-ideal circumstances."

He sobers up at this. "Were you fired?"

"No."

"Were you right?"

"Yes." I notice he doesn't ask if I was kind.

"Well then." He shrugs as if he can make the whole mess go away just like that.

"You shouldn't hand over your trust so easily, McHuge. There are good reasons you should look for someone else."

"But I want you," he says simply, and my heart lurches hard enough that I have to look down. His voice is a slow eddy, calm and welcoming; I only imagined it held a rush of current.

"You need someone with an MD and whitewater experience in time for next week's launch. I need stability. At the end of the summer, I want a chance to become an owner. Stock options for five percent of the Love Boat."

"Ten percent," he counters, without a second's hesitation.

"Ten?!" His unexpected generosity makes me faintly nauseous. "Don't you have to consult with lawyers? Or Tobin?"

"He's on paternity leave. I have his proxy vote. You know he'd give you anything you asked for."

"I asked for five."

"I'd have given you fifteen."

"You're terrible at business," I mutter. "No more freebies after I come on board."

"Okay then. Welcome aboard, Stellar J." He extends his hand, then seems to realize what he called me. A subtle flush backlights his cheeks beneath the freckles.

I take it as a good sign for our future working relationship that we shake firmly and let the moment pass.

Chapter Three

Nothing bends time like hard physical work.

It feels like way longer than four days ago that I packed everything I'd need for camp, took my valuables over to Liz's, and gave my neighbor the keys to pass on to my subletter, an Australian mountain biker and TikTok star named Br!an.

My connection to the apartment felt so breakable despite my efforts to make it sturdy. My art and furniture was scavenged from Buy Nothing groups on Facebook—nothing I would've chosen for the way it made me feel; nothing I saw and loved and had to have. I hate that I could leave it behind and not feel sad.

The thing about having a con artist for a parent is that every con comes to an end. If it succeeds, you take the money and run. If it fails, you move on, hoping to find easier marks and evade consequences. Whether we were broke or flush with dirty cash that didn't last, Mom and Dad and I moved constantly.

I saw medicine as a way to stop packing my bags with an hour's notice. It was the opposite of everything I knew: honorable money in a steady supply and a profession whose first commandment was *not* to hurt other people. If I didn't feel called to it the way my classmates with comfortable childhoods did, I could live with that. Wanting money is only embarrassing to people who already have enough.

The calling came little by little, sneaking up on me until one day I realized that every time I told a patient I would take good care of them, I was doing it because I wanted to. Because I meant it. Medicine tethered me to something deep and steady and good in a way I've never felt before or since.

I didn't want to come back to this unanchored life, closing the door to an apartment that could belong to anyone, living in a tent I borrowed from Liz, whose orbit drifts further from mine every day. But it found me anyway, like a shadow at my feet, impossible to outrun.

At least the work keeps me busy. A morning of manual labor at camp is the equivalent of a day at any other job. Afternoons scouting nearby rapids with McHuge feel like another whole day, me in a generic solo canoe and McHuge paddling his custom boat with Babe the dog chilling in the front seat. Eating dinner and staring exhausted into the campfire is at least a half day. We're still behind schedule because Tobin can't be here, but sometimes I have hope we'll be ready for launch on Monday.

The best thing about this job is that today is Friday—payday. Some employers play games, withholding the first check if you haven't worked a full pay period. McHuge paid me last night, early, for Tuesday through Thursday plus a small but meaningful signing bonus. He made a choking sound—*hrgack!*—when I buried my face in the check to inhale the scent of solvency.

I didn't care if he saw me being weird. I told him not to make me manage his airway, then took a solo paddle out to the middle of the river, one of two places to find a cell signal here, to electronically deposit the money.

For the first time in months, the volume on my financial crisis lowered from a full-on air raid siren to a manageable background hum of debt. I made my student loan payment *in advance*. I set up automatic rent checks to my landlord. I did budget math and didn't have to go for a run afterward.

Emotion-wise, I haven't needed to run at all since I got to base camp. It's been too long since I came out to the wilderness. Too many years of putting my head down and pulling the plow of my life back and forth, back and forth over the same ground. I let myself forget what it's like to have a sense of flow, like the river. That, and the daily level of physical exertion is enough to tamp my feelings down to a barely glowing ember.

I'm out for a morning run anyway, because the second place to get cell service is a fallen tree a couple of kilometers closer to the highway. It comes in handy when I want to send my daily batch of texts to Liz without asking McHuge to help me unrack a boat. Or worse, interrupting his "me time": morning plunges in the river I highly, highly suspect are done in the nude, based on the way we both screamed when I accidentally spied either an extremely formfitting white bathing suit or McHuge's pale butt cheeks flashing above the water on Wednesday morning.

It's a very good ass. Unfortunately. High, round, with the sun sort of sparkling off rivulets of water. Which makes it all the more important for me to be far, far away.

At the fallen tree, I pull out my phone, freshly charged with the solar battery. The weak signal eats a lot of juice.

5:41

> Good morning my loves! Three days old today! Sending you good vibes from beautiful Love Boat HQ, wish you were here

5:41

> I hope you're sleeping instead of replying to texts

5:42

> You never have to answer, btw! I'll text every day and you can reply when you have a minute and an extra hand. So I guess I'll hear from you when Jess is hitting puberty 😆

I met baby Jess on Tuesday. McHuge had to pick me up from the apartment because Tobin's truck was still at camp. We made a detour to Grey Tusk General—an hour and a half we couldn't really afford, given how much work there is—to visit the new family.

McHuge handed Tobin some healthy prepared meals and nonlatex balloons, then gave me side-eye when I slipped Liz a six-pack of tiny bottles of champagne. I stand by my choice. I took care of countless new parents at the hospital, plus I've delivered a lot of takeout to people with bad hair wearing bathrobes covered in spit-up. They're relieved to get the meals, but it's the booze that makes tears of gratitude well up in their purple-shadowed eyes.

Holding my best friend's baby with her new smell and her squeaky little cry was the closest I've come to crying myself in I don't know how long. Despite how exhausted they looked, Liz and Tobin seemed somehow forged into a single Borg consciousness by this experience. Watching them together reinforced the rightness of what I'm doing.

If I'm not the person Liz needs, then I'll give her the person who is.

It's what a sister would do. I think. As we were leaving, Liz's actual sister, Amber, arrived with an arsenal of snap containers filled with precut fruit and vegetables and a liter of chocolate milk nestled in a bucket of ice. "Trust me," Amber said. "It's what you need, even if you don't know it yet."

Since I've known Liz, she's never been as close to Amber as we've been to each other. But now Amber and Liz are both parents, members of a club I can't see myself joining. I'm not jealous, exactly. I'm just aware we're entering a period of friendship adjustment, and I'm determined to adjust.

I've done it before, following Liz to Grey Tusk after a couple of years of long distance, when I was training in Vancouver and she was here. She's worth the effort. She *gets* me. I may have a hot temper and keep slightly obsessive track of who owes what to whom, but she loves me anyway because I'm her best, most loyal advocate, and she's mine. I've always treasured her the way she is; she doesn't push me to change.

Except she did, that day with the crib. *You need something.*

My brain turns her words over as I shuffle in place, light brown silt collecting on my damp calves.

5:46

> Okay, better get going. The artisanal knots for the hand-lettered trail markers aren't going to tie themselves, lol. Ttyl

I know Liz would text me back if she could. I've worked in labor and delivery; I've seen how destroyed first-time parents are in the first few days.

I'd feel better if I heard from her, though. If, after my three texts, there were three replies. I get nervous without hard evidence that people care as much as I do. That's not just a me thing, either; the internet is rife with memes of cats spooking themselves over nothing and destroying entire rooms, captioned "when my friend leaves me on read."

But last year I left town for barely twelve weeks, and when I came back Liz had made all new friends. When I move back to Pendleton three months from now, will she be going for chai lattes with all the yoga moms? Will there be room for me at that table?

I don't know. All I can do is run to the tree every day and hope she texts me back sometime. Until then, I have work to do.

Technically, I'm not avoiding McHuge by doing my postrun stretch in the parking lot. I can hear him chopping the wood our chef, Jasvinder, requested for his pizza oven. *When the axe is swinging, it's safer to stay clear*, I tell myself.

I'm working on my hamstrings when a black Escalade rolls up behind the Mystery Machine. A fiftysomething woman with silver-blond hair slides out of the driver's seat and hooks her oversize sunglasses on the neckline of her athleisure top.

Sharon Keller-Yakub is the CEO-in-waiting of Keller Outdoor Epiphanies, an adventure tourism conglomerate in Grey Tusk. She's also my ex's aunt. It figures I'd run into her when my hair is sweaty and my face matches the bright raspberry shade of her yoga pants. McHuge told me Sharon was bankrolling the Love Boat, but I thought she was a silent partner, as opposed to one who turned up unexpectedly at 6:23 A.M.

"Hi, Sharon. You're up with the sun."

"I keep telling you, Stellar, it's *Aunt* Sharon. Is McHuge around?" She offers me a drink tray with three tall go-cups. "Coffee?"

Sharon's a generally awesome person, but something in the set of her shoulders is making me nervous. And she's here so damn *early*. There are a million half-done projects around camp she can't help but see.

"No, thanks. Love it, but haven't been able to drink it since I burned a hole in my stomach lining in residency. That's nice of you, though."

"Well, shit," she says, frowning. "Tea, then? I got English breakfast for McHuge. I'm sure he'd share."

"Don't tell him," I say quickly, envisioning McHuge trying to give me the whole thing, me politely refusing, and the tea going cold in the Canadian standoff. "I don't want to steal his drink. And should we still do the aunt thing, considering?" I say to distract her.

She waves an imperious hand. "Being your aunt is a state of mind, not a legal definition. Jen getting married doesn't change anything between you and me."

"Oh," I manage. I've gotten over Jen the person, but Jen-the-breakup-that-happened-at-the-lowest-point-of-my-life-after-she-swore-she-was-cool-with-long-distance still stings. I guess she's marrying the woman she left me for—a soft, pretty mom of two young kids. I've run more than a few angry miles thinking about her finding someone who didn't audit household chores and insist Jen actually complete her half.

McHuge pauses as Sharon and I approach and pushes his safety glasses to the top of his head. Though Sharon's in the lead, his gaze flicks to me first. Our eyes meet for a long indecipherable moment before he glances down to the knot I made in my peach-colored shirt, which exposes a strip of abs above my high-legged black running shorts. He's flushed from wood-cutting, so I could be imagining the deepening pink of his ears as he looks away.

I don't care what he sees. If he thinks my outfit isn't professional, he can wear a bathing suit. Or put a shirt on under those work overalls.

No one wants to see the light sheen of exertion on his bare chest or the way the cool morning light fills the hollows and negative spaces of his body with slate-blue shadows that shift as he catches his breath. And I'm definitely not curious about the woven hemp cord around his neck—usually concealed beneath one of his silly, soft T-shirts—threaded through a bleached bone pendant. McHuge shows everything, but that pendant, he keeps hidden.

"Share-bear! River goddess!" McHuge folds Sharon into an enthusiastic hug, holding his dirty hands away from her pristine white vest. "To what do we owe the pleasure?"

She sighs. "Is there breakfast?"

His crooked brow angles in a worried direction. "Jasvinder should be here in a few with sustenance." Good move from McHuge. Whatever criticism we're about to get, our camp chef's devastatingly delicious breakfast—plentiful fried protein, crispy carbs, and an obsession-worthy secret Earl Grey blend far better than a chain store tea bag—will soften the delivery.

"What's on your mind?" McHuge brushes sawdust off one of the log stools and motions for her to sit. Babe trots over from the beach, belly and muzzle wet from her morning of standing in the shallows, trying to bite the fish. I've never seen her catch one, but it's funny when she barks indignantly at them for refusing to play. She leans against McHuge and refuses to look my way.

On Wednesday night, after two full days of Babe's attitude, I asked him how to get the dog to come to me. He said, "The way to coax someone closer is to make them *want* to come."

I felt judged, but I'd also just asked him why he named his dog after a generic term of address, and possibly scoffed a little when he said she was a rescue and he didn't change her name because she had a lot on her mind. Whether or not he meant to judge me, I deserved it.

The dog and I have ignored each other ever since.

Sharon extracts a stray chunk of bark from underneath her butt and settles in. "Excuse us, Stellar. This meeting is owners only. But if you ever called me, we could hang." She can pull off slang decently well for her age.

"Stellar should stay," McHuge says, before I can make an excuse about needing to shower anyway. "She'll be an owner soon. And I value her opinion."

That's news to me, after we had words about my *opinions* yesterday. I questioned how on-brand it was for a relationship camp to have twin beds in the client tents.

"Easier to push two beds together than pull one bed apart," he replied. "People need different things at different times in their relationships."

"It's your company," I said, shrugging. "I'm not attached to any of my opinions about it."

"Hmmm," he replied, like he could hear how I'd rather not love my job.

Unnerved by his emotional X-ray vision, I went back to spreading mulch along endless paths and stringing two-person hammocks between every decent-sized pair of trees. For the rest of the day, we only talked about what work needed to be done and what new hazards we spied in the water.

Sharon looks from me to McHuge and back again, then cocks her head like, *what could it hurt.* "I'm afraid it's not good news."

My shoulders hunch involuntarily as I sit. That's the phrase my med school professors taught us to use for the worst revelations. Cancer. An aneurysm. A patient who couldn't hold on long enough for their family to get to the bedside, no matter how we worked the problem.

"Yesterday afternoon, there was an anonymous online leak about Renee Garner's possible partnership with the Love Boat. Renee responded by categorically denying she's considering us. She replied to our . . . let's say our statements of concern," Sharon says, with brutal diplomacy, "very late last night. She's pulling her people."

For a second, the sinking twist in my stomach almost freezes me. This is *bad*. Renee wasn't coming on the course herself—she's ridiculously busy, and besides, we're not big enough to handle her security detail. But six of her people, including a senior producer, were going to be here next week. Six empty spots in a ten-person camp.

McHuge doesn't say anything. He doesn't even move, with the exception of the sap-stained, callused fingers twitching in his lap. Why doesn't he react? Why isn't he fucking furious?

"But . . . but *why?*" I push myself off my stool, ignoring the scrape of rough wood on my bare thighs. I can't get stuck in this fear. My diagnostic brain needs information; my body needs to *move*.

"She's concerned we haven't addressed the criticisms in the *Beeswax* piece," Sharon says darkly.

"But we *did!*" I gesture at myself. "We hired me, we sent McHuge's PhD paperwork, we forwarded all those scientific studies."

"Apparently McHuge's singlehood reads as a 'barrier to trust' in their focus groups."

"Come *on*. That's unhinged."

Sharon shakes her head. "Let it go, Stellar. She's out, regardless of whether her excuse is true."

McHuge finally speaks. "What about the podcast?"

In exchange for six comped spots, Renee agreed to feature us on her video podcast, even if she didn't bring McHuge into her psychology cool kids' club. It isn't the big prize, but it's in Spotify's top fifty podcasts. It would have helped. A lot.

Sharon's tight jaw is answer enough. "Gone. The leak forced her hand. If she could have quietly sent her team, we'd have had a chance. But she can't publicly tie herself to a questionable venture."

McHuge looks up from his study of the firepit. "What does she want us to change? Anything she needs, we'll give it to her." Babe pushes her nose into his hand. He buries his fingers in her fur and absently tugs her ruff.

It's been three hundred–plus days since someone tugged my hair, and the last person to do it is sitting across from me, his cheeks still pink, his eyes shadowed like a reflecting pool deep in the forest of a fantasy novel. At a moment like this, I didn't expect the complicated shiver that works its way from the crown of my head to the base of my spine.

I'm envious of a *dog*, for god's sake. I pull the knot out of my shirt and tug it down over my stomach, suddenly caring what he sees.

Sharon shakes her head. "Our focus now is making sure the accusations from the hit piece don't stick. Everything we can do to make the Love Boat look professional, aboveboard, windproof, waterproof—you name it, we make it happen. But . . ."

Sharon's the type to plow ahead, not pause. Her hesitation fills me with dread, which unlocks the floodgates of fury.

"Rip off the Band-Aid," I snap.

"Easy there, killer." She gives me a quelling look. "*But*, we designed the camp around Renee. She wanted visual appeal and creature comforts, stuff that would look great and make good copy in her magazine. So we got a designer, splashed out on luxe tents, real beds, high-end meals from a trained chef. Our price point isn't the accessible one we originally wanted, but we were willing to compromise in exchange for the reach we'd get with Renee. Not many people are willing to pay that price tag on a new venture without a celebrity endorsement, though. And a pulled endorsement is even worse. We've already had two canceled bookings from the second session and four from the third. Unless we can stem the tide, we're looking at a midsummer shutdown. Maybe sooner."

A hard, deep ache flares to life behind my breastbone. There must be a way through this problem.

"You can't find any more funding for the first summer? I mean, don't most new businesses run in the red for a while?" I'm uncomfortably close to pleading.

Sharon gives me a look so compassionate I tense, preparing to dodge a hug. "I love the Love Boat, too, but this is business. If the company isn't viable, propping it up only delays the inevitable."

Sharon's wrong about me loving this project. I'm only upset because sympathy makes me feel horrible. I never come closer to crying than when someone's being nice to me.

Crying never solved anything. And I have to solve this problem, or I lose everything.

Sharon rises from her log. "Why don't we take the day. Let it simmer, reconvene on an as-needed basis. We still have a launch to prepare for," she says, looking askance at McHuge's messy pile of wood. "We're not beaten yet, kids."

For the rest of the morning, everyone acts like we're beaten.

Jasvinder tucks his long, dark-brown hair into a tight knot and furiously rechops the wood even smaller, his tall, wiry climber's frame tight with disappointment. He was hoping to parlay his work here into a foothold in the insanely competitive Grey Tusk market; no doubt he's wishing he backed a different horse.

McHuge hardly smiles when the raven he's been taming comes to eat his apple core at lunch. Babe sticks close by, leaning into his leg at every opportunity.

Those two may not be able to see a difference in me, since my emotional baseline is smoldering rage, but I'm not fine, either.

If the Love Boat folds, I have nowhere to go. Literally. At this very moment, Br!an is probably lying on my couch, feet propped on the signed sublease agreement. I refuse to turn up on Liz's doorstep—*again*—when she has a new frickin' *baby*. Any place I could rent on short notice would be insanely expensive, which is why Br!an was so eager to lock down my place.

This is the end of the road. It's this job or moving someplace affordable and far away.

Liz and I would promise to keep in touch. She'd text me as much as she could, which might not be very much, if the past few days are any indication. We'd video chat weekly at first, then less often as time went on. She'd call other people to babysit or watch a rom-com or pick her up when she forgets to charge her car battery. She'll pin someone else with that direct gaze and make a joke so dry it takes them a full five seconds to laugh.

It's those little things that cement relationships together like a thousand tiny drops of glue. Without them, the bond can't last.

By unspoken agreement, McHuge and I don't go canoeing in the afternoon. I'm guessing he feels what I feel, that the way the camp looks suddenly matters more than ever.

At four o'clock, I finish sanding the log chairs and take a break to retrieve the afternoon snack Jasvinder left after he re-chopped his kindling, unloaded his supplies, and headed back to town.

On my way to find McHuge, I take in the pale-gray after-noon sky screened with green boughs that whisper in the river breeze. The forest is alive with birdsong, still damp from last night's rain.

It felt like I was catching my breath here. I was sleeping well for once after working my ass off all day, drifting off to the sound of McHuge turning pages in the tent next to mine. Sometimes he'd murmur through the nylon walls to Babe, who prefers curling up in a sheltered spot underneath McHuge's rain fly to sleeping in the tent. The first night, I asked whether he was worried about bears, but he laughed and said both the bears and the dog were too smart to tangle with each other. I have to admit Babe is nothing if not sensible, which makes her dislike of me into a pretty stinging indictment of my character.

It actually seemed possible McHuge and I would get past the awkward, polite stage and maybe have a decent working relationship. I didn't realize how much I missed talking to some-one at work, beyond the brief, goal-oriented interactions with customers or food workers.

I like this job, surprisingly enough. And I love Liz. I love Pendleton. What would I do to protect the only things I let my-self love?

Anything. I'd do anything.

The hit piece could still do damage. We need a celebrity endorsement and a way to neutralize the last criticism in the article.

And I know how to do it.

I find McHuge stretched sideways across one of the

hammocks, feet dangling off the side, Babe curled against him. He looks up but doesn't say hello.

I hand him the snap container of food, not greeting him either. "I might have someone who can endorse us. She's not a psychologist. And she's not as famous as Renee." Hardly famous at all since she left *Cow Pie High*, the teen show she starred in until well into her twenties, but that will almost certainly change soon. "But she's better than nothing."

McHuge sits up fast, setting the hammock swinging. "Really?" His voice is half agony, half hope. Fair enough—I deliberately gave him every impression I was here to work hard, get paid, and leave the business of caring to him. I'd be surprised at me, too.

"No promises, but I can make a call. We're not going down without a fight."

And the other thing. I have to make myself say the other thing. He won't like it; god knows I'm not thrilled, either. It violates everything I promised myself about keeping my distance from him and everything I promised him about being professional and avoiding entanglement. Every hard thing about this job will instantly ratchet up in difficulty.

But Sharon said we have to be windproof and waterproof. There's one more hole we have to sew shut for that to happen.

"And the article criticized you for being single. We'll neutralize that by getting you a partner."

He deflates somewhat. "Launch is in three days. I can't just go to the outdoor store and pick out a partner, Stellar."

"There's no time for shopping, McHuge. So *I'm* going to be your fiancée."

Chapter Four

It's a whole year since Jen broke up with me instead of proposing, and my stomach still doesn't like the word "fiancée." I press a hand to my belly, soothing the place where the memories of her letting me go pinch the hardest.

"Fiancée?" McHuge's voice swoops high, then stalls. "Like, me and *you*?"

"Yup." I hold up my fingers to tick off reasons why. "A girlfriend isn't good enough. They can still say you've never been married. A wife is a no-go; the timeline's short even for Vegas. You can't invent an imaginary partner, because that journalist guy, Brent, will go looking for confirmation." Naturally, McHuge invited the journalist who did the hit piece to join the inaugural session of the Love Boat. At no charge.

I spread my hands, shrugging. "That leaves me, your real live fiancée."

He looks at me like I've lost my mind, his sleepy chill completely destroyed. "Okay. Apart from the fact that faking an engagement is ludicrous, it's . . . I mean, you and me, pretending we're in *love*? We'd have to sleep in the same tent. We'd have to . . . touch, in front of people. I mean . . ." He rolls his shoulders down and back, shivering like I personally have walked over his grave.

Annoyed by his repulsion, I snap, "I'm an amazing tentmate. I keep my gear tidy, and I don't snore. You're not the only one who'd rather not get engaged. But we have to do it, McHuge. You know we do."

He stares into the distance for so long I think he might be dissociating. Finally, he says, "I don't like lying."

"Fisher lied. The article lied," I point out brusquely. "We're not obligated to play by the rules when everyone else is cheating. Besides, it wouldn't have to be a lie. You ask me to marry you, I say yes. Boom, engaged."

"I can't ask you to marry me," he says, a cornered, desperate note in his voice.

I throw up my hands. "Fine! I'll do it. Lyle Q. McHugh, will you marry me?"

His head turns sharply, his eyes dark and wary. I never intend to use his real name, but it's like I'm possessed. Every time it flies out of my mouth, I feel one step closer to summoning the specter of our hookup.

If I'm honest, that ghost haunts me all the time. After McHuge, the idea of going back to the one-night stands that sustained me before Jen seemed stupid. The thing that spooked me about him was the sense that even the tiniest of his caresses weren't part of a deal where each person got an equal share. They felt like he wanted to give these touches to me, and only me, unconditionally. All those bodies of all those people giving no more than what was fair—it stopped feeling safe and familiar and started feeling sad and unfinished.

And I couldn't afford to be sad, so the only solution to that problem was to swear off sex entirely.

Snack forgotten, McHuge shifts forward in the hammock, eyes fixed on the spot where his feet now touch the ground. "Are you any good at acting? Can you make people believe?"

I look at him sideways. "Acting runs in my family."

He strokes his beard, giving a brief, rumbling exhale, then levers himself up and heads for the parking lot.

"Where are you going? We still have tons of work to do."

"I need to think." He pats the pocket where he keeps his wallet. His keys live under the sun visor of the Mystery Machine. Any passing teenager could boost the van for a midnight joyride, which McHuge naturally insists would never happen.

He pauses midstep. "Oh, and Stellar?"

"Uh-huh?"

"*Yes.*"

He doesn't even look at me when he says it, just whistles for the dog and walks on, arms tensed like he wants to heave this fucked-up situation into the deepest part of the river. A minute later, the Mystery Machine rumbles down the road toward Pendleton.

It's hardly the engagement I used to imagine. I mean, I certainly wasn't envisioning anyone going down on one knee on the Kiss Cam at a hockey game.

I did think the moment might be sweet, though. Maybe some kind words or a nice gesture. And McHuge probably didn't picture someone glaring at him and barking, "We have to do it."

I look around. One hundred crappy chores need my urgent attention, but they can wait.

I'm going into town, too.

It's a relief when the Mystery Machine pulls back into the parking lot a little after 7 P.M. I've been back for over an hour,

even though I went to Costco on a Friday afternoon, which is a
live-action preview of the breakdown of Western civilization. If
you cut the line in there, someone will cut *you*, and they already
have a three-pack of J.A. Henckels knives in their cart to get the
deed done.

I was starting to think McHuge might not come back at all
and conducting arguments with myself over what he meant by
that *yes*.

Not that I was upset to watch him walk away—no more
than anyone else would be to see the calmest person they know
storm off in a self-imposed time-out. I was unsettled, though.
Even when he's gone, he's here, like one of the negative spaces
on his body I can't stop looking at.

McHuge doesn't come find me, so I don't seek him out, either. I already wolfed down my share of the grilled Halloumi
and vegetable skewers Jasvinder left for us in the cookhouse,
so we won't be eating together.

We can't avoid each other forever, though. I already tried
that, in case he doesn't remember, and this is how it ended up.

When I come back from the wash station after brushing my
teeth, there's an orange sack on the ground between his tent
and mine. An unexpected surge of relief crashes over me. It
looks like he hasn't changed his mind about the engagement. I
check the tag: he dropped eight hundred bucks on a six-person
tent, so while we'll go broke very slightly faster, we'll have some
breathing room.

He also bought two camp cots. Our place will be a low-
budget version of the client tents, which I like. We can push
the beds apart and tell the guests we won't judge them if they
don't judge us.

I'm snug in my own tent, wearing my sleep shorts and my

worn WOMEN BELONG IN THE RESISTANCE T-shirt with the silhouette of Princess Leia, when the front flap of McHuge's tent zips open, then shut. I think of the drawstring bag tucked into my backpack and mentally push that task to tomorrow. I don't know how to give it to him, and besides, I won't be able to sleep for hours afterward if I do it now. In the morning, when he's rested and has had a chance to reboot his internal Zen—that's the right moment.

"Stellar."

His voice comes through my tent walls, startling me out of my exhausted half sleep. I pray the rustling of my sleeping bag covered my embarrassing squeak of surprise.

Jesus Christ, McHuge, is the right response to getting abruptly reawakened by the person who's been giving me a taste of my own avoidance medicine for half the day. But he'd prefer kindness, so I suppress all responses that start with profanity.

"Yes, McHuge?" I reply through the nylon barrier.

"Did you make the call?"

"Yes." I have a phone number that should work, but it's fifteen years old. If all else fails, I can reach out through her talent agency, like I did when I was seventeen and clueless.

That was two days after I refused to drop my entire life for the "fresh start" Dad promised after finishing his five-year sentence for wire fraud. I'd worked hard to show Mom we were fine without him—pulling straight As, working a retail job for extra cash and discounted clothes, keeping the house clean and getting meals on the table when Mom had her sad spells.

But instead of realizing we didn't need him, Mom kissed *me* goodbye, told me I didn't need her the way Dad did, and left me to dodge Child Protection Services until I got to university in the fall.

I should've known. Before he went away, he'd been teaching me how to tell when the con got too big or the mark got wise. When I got wise to him, there was nothing he could do but run.

Alone and more than a little panicky, I left a message for the half sister whose TV show Dad made me watch, though I'd never met her. I wasn't sure she knew I existed, but thirty minutes later my phone rang, and someone said, "Hold for Ms. Summers."

Then the voice of Deanna, the tall, pratfall-prone 4-H enthusiast from *Cow Pie High*, said, "Hi, it's Sloane Summers. Is this Stellar Byrd?"

When I got over my stunned silence, I didn't ask for help right away. I wanted to prove I could be useful and trustworthy before telling her how bad things were. It went well, I thought. I texted her a selfie of me in a hoodie from the university I'd be attending in the fall. She laughed at my Canadian accent. I promised to email her my contact information but decided to wait a day so I didn't look desperate.

The next morning, I woke up to a curt email from her agency. Ms. Summers thanks you for taking her call. Regrettably, she has nothing to offer you, financially or otherwise.

My chest felt crumpled, like trash. Sloane had a fierce mom, a career she was hoping to move to the big screen, and a deep desire to avoid any connection with her bio-dad. I, on the other hand, had a sketchy past, an uncertain future, and a wardrobe from the supersale rack at the Gap. Of course she knew I needed her to give me things, and I had nothing to give in return.

A couple of months later, Sloane sent a message to my university email address. There'd been a mix-up; could I give her my new number to call? When I sent a brief reply—thanks, but no thanks—she was confused, then upset. She left me an emergency contact number to use "if ever you need anything, Stellar."

She'd been right the first time, though. We had nothing to offer each other.

With my mom, I hadn't needed enough; with Sloane, I'd needed too much. I learned two good lessons that summer.

"And?" The painful hope in McHuge's voice brings me back to the present.

This is what loving a job does to you: it hurts you. It's fine for me to like being here, like the work, even get along with McHuge, but I need to not get emotionally enmeshed.

"It was late Friday afternoon in New York. I'm hoping to hear back tomorrow."

He heaves a slow sigh. It's very que será, será. "Okay. Thank you."

"Just looking out for my job."

The sound of the river fills the silence. Babe grumbles softly from where she's settled between our tents, snapping the air like she's chasing a pesky insect.

"Is that all, McHuge?"

"We can leave the rest until morning, if you're tired."

"Tired" is not the word. Even if I hadn't shoveled, raked, and hauled since sunup, today's emotional roller coaster would have worn me out. But.

"I don't like leaving work undone. Let's do it now."

He makes a soft, pleased rumble, like he was hoping I'd say that. "Okay. Good. I was thinking we should agree on what's going to happen between us. And what's not."

"Draw all the lines you want." And I'll draw my own in return.

"I don't want to pretend when we're not in public. Anything we do, we do for the guests."

"Fine with me," I say.

"Good."

His obvious relief offends me. I'm not a difficult person. I only argue over things that matter.

"I'll tell Sharon about the engagement," he offers when I don't speak.

"I don't think we should tell anyone."

A note of anxiety colors his voice. "Do you think she'd tell us not to?"

"No. She's pretty pragmatic, and she did tell us to do literally anything. But she might want plausible deniability if this goes wrong. Tobin, too."

It feels serious now that we're discussing potential downsides—like keeping secrets from Tobin. And Liz. I don't always tell her what's going on with me if the time isn't right, but I've never withheld something that could affect her family finances before.

"So only you and I will know it's fake," he says.

"It's not *fake*. People are allowed to get married for reasons that aren't love. Companionship, finances, tradition, kids. Businesses. Any reason they want, except maybe immigration. If the couple says it's real, it's real."

"Valid," McHuge says, somewhat reluctantly. "But it does need to look like we at least *want* to get married. If we bump into each other in front of the guests, we can't sprint in opposite directions."

"That was *one* time." I was working down by the shore and didn't realize he'd joined me. His footsteps are light and sneaky for a man of his size.

"You ran into the river to get away from me, Stellar."

"I was startled!"

He sighs. "You wouldn't have been so startled if your body recognized mine."

I plaster both hands to my forehead and keep my mouth shut. I can think of at least five ways to respond to that statement, all of them far too revealing. "Fine. We can do chores together over the weekend. I'm sure the startle reflex will settle down after we throw some accidental elbows while raking. What else?"

"We should talk about . . . touching." I feel the solar storm of his blush from here.

"Easy. We won't be doing that." I know the engagement was my idea, but I draw the line at making out. That's basic preventative medicine.

"I think we have to. We supposedly had a whirlwind romance. People will expect an occasional peck on the lips, minimum."

"A *peck*? No one says *peck*, McHuge. Were you born a hundred years ago?" Although if he *were* an immortal time traveler, his Summer of Love vocabulary would make perfect sense.

His sigh sounds like he's let his head fall back in aggravation. I really do bring out the best in him. "*I* say peck. And we should peck, or people will get suspicious."

I think of his lips, soft against mine. His eyes at close range, like a pair of chemical weapons. "No, thank you. You can . . . you can put your arm around me and leave it there. That's a love thing."

"I put my arm around a lot of people."

"And *leave it there*," I say crossly. "I've seen you put your arm around Tobin for five seconds. Liz, maybe a little longer. Leaving it there for like a minute? That's a love thing."

Silence falls, and I realize I just told McHuge I've watched how long he puts his arm around people.

He clears his throat. "Last thing. We need a relationship story. People will be curious about our history."

I'd rather not talk about my history. People claim they won't judge you by your past, but if that were true, they'd look at your actions and keep their questions to themselves. My past is a knife, the kind of thing you don't hand to just anybody—as I learned the day I left Grey Tusk General, when my department chief said he guessed my apple didn't fall far from my dad's tree.

"You're an improv comedy teacher. You can improvise," I point out, very reasonably, in my opinion.

"Yes, and you and I could end up telling two different stories."

"Couples tell separate versions of the same story all the time. That's why they come to relationship camp."

"Brand-new couples are not *supposed* to need relationship camp. We're supposed to be—"

All over each other, my imagination supplies when he breaks off.

"So we tell them the truth. Or a version of it. You and I had a thing last year, but the timing wasn't right. We ran into each other through mutual friends, one thing led to another, yada yada, I asked you to marry me."

I'm worried about the drawstring bag. It could easily fall to the bottom of my backpack. I'm not 100 percent certain where it is, now that I think of it. I should make sure it's not lost. It was only sixty dollars, but I'm not made of money.

I unzip my sleeping bag, flick on the solar lamp, and rummage in my pack. My hand finds the stiff, cheap felt bag exactly where I left it. I open it and shake my gift into my palm.

"Everything good?"

"You're worried about believability, and I have something for that. I'm coming over. You decent?"

"What?!" Hurried rustling comes from his tent.

"You'd better not tell me you sleep in the nude, McHuge." Although he didn't wear anything when he was with me last year.

Get your mind out of the gutter, Byrd.

"I'm putting on a shirt, give me a minute."

"No need to get specific." I unzip my door and shove my feet halfway into my boots. Babe lifts her head as I cross the ground between my tent and his. It's late, but I don't need a flashlight; the sun never fully sets at this time of year this far north.

By the time I'm at his door, he's got it unzipped. Behind him, the solar lantern illuminates details I've been careful not to notice before tonight: dark-green sleeping bag, extra long; vintage trekking backpack covered in pockets, most of them open; a shadowy pile of books in one corner.

"Are you coming in?"

"No," I say. "We're too tired for a slumber party. Give me your left hand."

He holds it out, palm up. I put my hand in his and turn it over, taking the "will you marry me" handhold I was taught to use to look for veins. I've held thousands of hands this way. When I'm starting an IV, I always know what to say: *Nice and still now. Relax the hand. Little poke—one, two, three, ouch! All done.*

Tonight I have no idea what words to use. Even if I were good at easy intimacy, I'd still be shocked by the first touch of his broad palm against my own hand. Even if I weren't avoiding his eyes, I'd still be preoccupied with the calluses below his fingers and the tiny, almost imperceptibly raised scars that tell the story of a life lived outdoors. His skin is as warm as I remember from that night at the festival. He smells clean, like tea and toothpaste.

I touch the ring to his left fourth finger. He startles a little at the kiss of cool steel.

"What—"

"Don't freak out. It's from Costco." *Damn it.* "I mean, I know our conversation this afternoon was weird. We kind of argued. A little. No one wants their engagement to be like that, no matter why you're doing it. So I thought we could . . . try again?" I don't slide the ring on. I'm not sure what I'm waiting for, but I'll know it when I see it.

"You got me a ring?" He looks at the black steel band, then up at me. His face is a collection of inscrutable lines in the twilight, everything straight where it's usually curved, still where it's usually mobile.

"Yeah. I picked a rounded profile, so it wouldn't catch on things. Smooth, like a river stone. It reminded me of you, I guess." I shrug. "You want a relationship story, so . . . this could be ours."

"This could be ours," he repeats.

"Yeah. I asked you to marry me, you lost your cool—"

"Stellar."

"You did, though," I argue. "You know I'm right. You went off and thought about it for a while, you came back, I gave you this ring. And when I did, you knew we could pull it off. Because we *can* pull this off, Lyle." And if we do, I get to keep everything I've been afraid to lose. No hard choices, no slow friendship fades.

He uncurls his fingers. I only have to wiggle the ring over his knuckle a little bit, then it slides home, clasping him like it's made-to-measure.

I didn't expect this moment to have such weight. I didn't expect our eyes to pop and lock, and lock, and lock.

It's too much. "Screw that sales guy who didn't think I could eyeball the size," I announce, sweeping the mood away like it's good weather and I'm La Niña. "That ring is perfect."

"Yeah," McHuge agrees, his face carefully blank. He tugs his hand out of mine, and the moment ends.

I was right about one more thing: I lie awake for hours afterward, replaying his hand sliding away from me.

Chapter Five

Morning on the Pendle River is so beautiful I can almost forget my launch day nerves.

A gold rush of sun sparkles off the water where the barest morning breeze strokes it to life. A stone's throw from shore, a pair of loons dive for fish, their sleek bodies curling under the surface, then popping up in unpredictable places a minute later.

The air is hypersaturated with scents and sounds, so full it can hardly hold them all: cedar, damp earth, liquid birdsong. Every winged dinosaur in the valley is staking out a musical claim to a mate and a nest, the trees full of flashing wings in black and brown and white, green and violet and red.

I'm no expert, but I can identify chickadee calls and the gurgle of baby crows hidden high in a cedar treetop. And Steller's jays of course—everyone points those out when you're named Stellar J Byrd. Bold and pretty with their stiff black crest and lightning-blue plumage, they're smart enough to steal a chunk of your sandwich if you're not careful.

Unless you're McHuge, in which case you would give the birds your lunch and go without.

As if to prove my point, McHuge leans to his right, reaching out one long arm with a handful of apple slices. He spends some time arranging them on the stool two seats away from where he's sitting. When he's satisfied, he turns back to his breakfast bites—hammy, eggy, creamy little mouthfuls wrapped in golden pastry that I can't get enough of. It's been a while since I've had an obsession with a new food—the kind where every time I taste it, it's just as good as the first crispy, buttery, shockingly satisfying bite. I've got a huge crush on these things.

I've long since polished off mine, but McHuge still has two left. I'd steal them if Jasvinder didn't make McHuge's with mushrooms.

"Did you make a *happy face* with your—"

He only has to look my way, grinning, and I fall silent. He doesn't smile much, I realize with a burst of surprise. Or maybe he doesn't smile *this* way. Like he's truly happy, instead of trying to give you something. The microcurl at one corner of his lips holds a hint of mischief and excitement that's almost boyish, despite the fact that he's six feet one million with a beard straight out of *Game of Thrones*.

Sure enough, thirty seconds later, the raven he's been befriending drops down at the edge of the clearing, tilting its head before cockily hopping closer. The dog raises one eyebrow, then the other, but her chin stays on the ground.

McHuge sits still, body loose, stealing sideways glances from under his lashes. He could physically take anything from anyone in this clearing, but what he wants is to style fruit into an emoji this bird can't even read.

I check my own posture: hunched, my arms wrapped protectively around the plate balanced on my knees. The sheer volume of physical work at camp has me painfully ravenous.

I'm desperate to take another bite, jam in as much as my mouth can hold, guard it from any creature who would steal from me.

But I have to stay still while the bird hops sideways with its shiny black eye pointed at us, its neck dipping toward the freshly sliced honeycrisps. McHuge *tames* things like the fox teaches the boy to tame things in *The Little Prince*, which I sneaked a look at yesterday when McHuge left it open in the pavilion. He sits a little closer every day, coaxing, making everyone *want* to come to him.

Except me, with my thorns.

The raven's wings beat an abrupt staccato. It alights on the stool, drops a shred of red fabric from its beak, then snatches as many apple slices as it can hold and takes off.

"Did you see that? It's trading for the food." McHuge grins down at his meal with open-faced delight. A smile like that is wasted on a three-sectioned tin camping plate, but I guess he'd rather put it there than give it to the person who takes cheap shots at his food art instead of being curious about what he's doing.

It's sad, actually. Not pathetic or uncool or any other meaning of the word. Just plain sad—a slow rain that doesn't come with any anger to keep me dry and hot.

The great thing about having been so damn broke for the last twelve months was that I didn't have space to think about what I wanted beyond a bank balance without a minus sign in front of it. I didn't have to worry about what kind of person I was becoming, or who I might like to be for the rest of my life.

It was a relief, after losing the career I'd grown to love, not to have to look for the next thing.

Not to have to search for myself.

But the past week of working here, and especially the last two days of staying near enough to McHuge to cram for our en-

gagement exam, might be bringing feeling back into my soul. It's
no rosy burst of undiluted joy, either. I feel like a cramped, frozen
limb, with the deadened sensation giving way to pinpricks that
promise a world of pain before I'll be able to bear any weight.

This is *my* company now, my new chance. Do I *want* anything beyond money and security and guarding what's mine?
And if I do, will the same hurts happen to me all over again?

I blink when a breakfast bite lands on my plate.

"Hey," I blurt, dismayed at how my mouth waters. "This is
yours. Besides, I don't like mushrooms."

"I asked Jasvinder to make them all without mushrooms."

"Why?!" The breakfast bites are good, but they don't war-
rant the cry in my voice.

"Because fungi aren't your jam," he says slowly, like it's obvious. "Eat it. I had plenty."

I hold out my plate. "Take it back."

"No. It's for you."

"I don't want it."

"Yes, you do. I saw you looking at it. If you're not hungry,
just compost it."

I can't compost perfectly good food—not after the way I
grew up. I can't leave it here for animals to find. And he won't
take it back.

I stare at the breakfast bite, flooded with agony where
there used to be numbness. He's kind and I'm not. He gave me
the thing I wanted most, and I have nothing to give back. No
scrap of red fabric, not even a slice of apple. I would never have
thought to give him something just to be nice.

I feel terrible. Everything around camp suddenly looks like
it could be better. Especially me.

"I'm going to finish redoing the ropes." I talked him into
letting me do fancy, aspirational knotwork around camp, but it

isn't as easy as it looks, and I've been struggling to get it done. In the face of his generosity, the least I can do is get working.

I stuff the breakfast bite in my mouth and stand up fast, as McHuge does the same. Next thing I know, my feet are tangled with his and my plate is on the ground. He pins me to his chest with a palm between my shoulder blades, one hand still gripping his own plate.

My first thought is *At least I didn't jump back this time.*

My second is that it's not *how* he smells—like canoe repair compound, Earl Grey, and mountain wind—that's so intoxicating. It's the emotion it pulls from my soul, this strange, unidentifiable longing I used to feel on the first day of school. It's a sense of things coming together for a brief moment in time, planets swinging close in their orbits, tides flooding high and receding low.

I step away carefully; McHuge steps back, too. Sadness, again.

"Thanks for the catch," I say. His look of surprise gives me a burst of painful sparks. I should thank him a few times this morning. Get him acclimated to hearing nice things from me before the guests arrive, so he doesn't do the facial equivalent of jumping away from me.

I scoop up my plate, stash it in the cookhouse, and head toward the sleeping area. On the way, I run a few mnemonics about McHuge, like the one I made for the birth order of his six giant ginger siblings. Bruce, Morag, Brigid, Angus, Lyle, Tavish, Elspeth: Bring More Bread And Let Toast Explode. It's not my best work, but I didn't have time for anything else.

McHuge ambles up to the green sign I'm readjusting, which is mounted to the tree with rope, because McHuge would never poke a hole in a friend. GROOVER THIS WAY! it says, groover being the inexplicable whitewater word for outhouse. Also scattered around camp are a selection of McHuge's favorite inspirational quotes. From here, I can see CHALLENGE YOUR REALITY and HAVE THE COURAGE TO BE BAD.

Ha. It takes way more courage to be good than bad, to show your soft belly instead of your steely spine. Although by that metric, McHuge is the brave one around here.

"Looks nice." His voice is a natural disaster. It raises the hairs on my arms, gives me the sensation of gathering electricity in the air.

"Could be better," I say, undoing a lumpy knot and trying again. "I want to send the right message."

"What message is that?" He makes an amused huff, tracing a freckled finger along the rope. I thought his hands were blunt and pawlike, but I was wrong. Their roughness doesn't erase their elegance and deliberation.

I look back at the rope. "These knots say, *Your eyeballs matter to us. What you put in them should be beautiful and luxurious. We know you have a choice of outrageously expensive experimental relationship therapy, and we thank you for choosing the Love Boat.* Ha!" I exclaim, when the knot settles into the right lines. Thirteen more to go.

"I'd rather go for more heart and soul, less eyeball and wallet."

I stare at him, amazed. "You have *no* idea about people, do you?"

"I have a PhD in psychology, Stellar." Is there a trace of annoyance in his voice? A barely noticeable rise in his shoulders? They're good shoulders—built by a generous hand, muscle on muscle topped with pale, freckled skin like the glaze on a cinnamon roll. I'm learning to diagnose their hidden messages: the easy, satisfied roll of a steering stroke in the canoe; the loose happiness when he plays chase with Babe; the square strength of a hug with Sharon.

I shouldn't care that I'm the one who tightens his posture instead of loosening it. I should care that whatever I can discern from his movements, he can probably discern twice as much from mine. When you're with people day after day, they see things. Weaknesses. Soft spots I'd rather not reveal, because those are easier to defend when nobody knows where they are.

It's fine if we're colleagues, but I need to not forget how he got under my defenses last time. That can't happen again.

"Maybe we've met different people, because the ones I know want *everything*. If they think they're owed something they don't get, that's when trouble happens."

"You think a lot about give and take." He doesn't say it judgmentally, but maybe I'd rather he did. I'd like to find his boundaries, but he's a cloud, leaving me swiping at nebulous arms of mist.

"Everyone cares about that. I've never gone to a restaurant where someone said, 'I had the pasta but got charged for the wagyu filet, seems fair.'"

"I'm sure the guests wouldn't give you a hard time about knots." He puts a shoulder against the tree, leaning into my field of view so I can't avoid his gentle concern. "It's okay to let it go, if you want to."

Ugh, sympathy. I want it; no, get it away from me. I'd die of relief if he hugged me; I'd kill him if he made me cry with his stupid *caring*.

"I'll be fine. It's the service industry. It's not that different from delivering pizza."

"The river is not pizza, Stellar. It will give you more than you ever expected, but you have to be open to receiving and giving back."

It's the first Zen-like thing he's said in days. When did he drop his groovy persona around me? "I'm sure the river and I will get along, in that case."

He breathes out like he was hoping for something and didn't get it. "Okay. Show me how you tie those knots."

I make a shooing gesture. "I can handle it, McHuge. There must be other last-minute things you want to do."

"Nothing more important than this," he says, undoing the lowest one himself. "The knots matter to you, so that's what we'll do." He's a lefty, so the black steel ring winks in and out of view as he follows my directions: twist, loop, around, and through.

When he pulls the rope into a tight, flat, flawless double infinity shape, something inside me loosens. I don't know why it's better when he gets it right than when I do, but it is.

"It's perfect. I . . . you didn't have to do this."

"I know."

I haven't yet learned to diagnose whatever's in his eyes when they lock with mine. Suddenly I wonder what I would do with his body, if I had the right. What he'd do with mine. I can't quite breathe, imagining the touch of his stomach against my own, the spring of his hair in my fist, the whisper of his fingers underneath my shirt like a prayer.

An old-fashioned alarm clock sounds from the sleeping quarters. My eyes wander to the neon-orange tent now visible through the trees—tall where McHuge's and my solo tents were small, wider than our two spaces put together, bright and dangerous as a red sky in the morning.

"Time for me to pick up the guests," he says, stepping back. "We're ready, Stellar. I promise you can take a break. Chill in a hammock. Go for one last solo paddle."

"No, thanks. I have work to do."

He sighs. "Yeah, I figured. See you in ninety minutes."

With each guest that steps out of the Mystery Machine, McHuge shines brighter. By the sixth and last, it's like looking at the sun.

I position myself at his left side, feeling the pressure of living up to his rainbow-tinted McHugemanship. He *likes* people; I only *used* to like people. I'm a grumpy former ER doc, not a soothing psychologist who's also a seasoned tour operator. During the years I looked at rashes and performed CPR and delivered pizza, McHuge ran every river around here hundreds of times while writing a semi-best-selling book.

The greatest thing about finishing my residency was sloughing off the me who was vulnerable because I didn't know what I was doing. Becoming a staff physician meant I had the armor of knowledge and position to protect me. I'd paid my dues, and I could reap the rewards.

But here I am, already indignant at these people for making me taste the old fear again. It's sharp and sour the second time, long past its sell-by date. But this is customer service, so I swallow instead of spitting.

McHuge claps his hands to get everyone's attention, which has the secondary effect of making the couples look for each other before the briefing begins. He's jammed a straw cowboy hat over his loose curls, the chin strap dangling to midchest. In the afternoon sun, his moss-green hoodie makes his hair seem to almost glow by contrast.

I become aware that I'm staring at him the way all the other couples are staring at each other, which is technically the right thing to do, but also feels embarrassing and weird. I transfer my attention to the guests instead, for safety.

There's a pair of older women looking formidable in multi-pocketed vests and weathered boots—they must be our last-minute additions Lori and Laurie Mitchell, although Laurie specified that she prefers "Mitch." Lori's tall and slim with fine, chin-length blond hair, her fair skin weathered by sun and smiling. Mitch is shorter and blockier, with barely creased brown skin, her tight gray curls cropped close in a no-nonsense style that suits her wary expression.

The pair in their twenties, Petra and Trevor, lean into each other awkwardly. On their intake form, they said they're best friends who always wondered if they'd make a good couple. For the sake of our reviews, I hope they do, although they don't seem to fit together particularly naturally. Tall and tanned with curly brown hair, Trevor tries to smile while he fishes for a strand of Petra's straight dark hair that's wafted into his mouth. Petra steps on his foot when she tries to help him, her olive skin flushing. They glance around the circle like they want to check out how other humans do intimacy.

The fortysomething white woman who's struggling to close the Mystery Machine's sliding door must be Willow. The man who exited ahead of her would be her husband, Brent, the journalist who wrote the hit piece. I would have argued against comping their trip, but it happened before I came on board. At least he won't have an excuse to get McHuge's qualifications wrong this time.

Unlike the other clients, Brent hasn't looked to see where his spouse is. She tries the door one last time, then gives up without asking him for help.

"Welcome to the inaugural session of the Love Boat!" McHuge has a deep, steady hum to him, like an engine that's warmed up and ready to run. He's wearing the perfect Cape

Canaveral expression: looking joyful and optimistic the way people were in the 1960s when a TV camera as big as a lunar module was trained on their faces.

I'm not great at smiling on command, but I clasp my hands and try my best. I wish I were wearing a mask, so I could do whatever I wanted with the lower half of my face.

Maybe I do miss *one* thing about being a doctor.

"I'm Lyle McHugh—"

"McHuuuuge!" Brent interrupts in a hooting bellow, like he thought of it himself.

"People also call me McHuge, which is fine." No one else seems to catch the microscopically pained note in his voice.

I narrow my eyes at Brent. He's at that high-risk age for acting out, in my experience: grappling with milestone birthdays that start with numbers higher than four, struggling to feel relevant in a world where Nirvana and Lenny Kravitz are dad music.

Guys like this were the most likely to invite me in "for a slice" when I was doing deliveries. On my last day as a working doctor, a guy like this screamed, *I pay your salary, and you'll do what I tell you.* But #NotAllMen, I guess.

"I'm stoked to introduce our talented and dedicated team here at the Love Boat. If you need anything, don't be afraid to approach any one of us. We have some awesome experts to make your stay as special as it can be."

I refocus away from Brent. I have to look the part, which is not an angry part. I can do this.

"In the kitchen and driving the van, the very talented Jasvinder Singh. You'll want to remember that name for when he opens his Michelin-starred wild cuisine restaurant."

Jasvinder inclines his head like the fussy chef he is.

"Keeping you safe on water and land, my fiancée, Dr. Stellar Byrd, MD."

His arm comes around my shoulder, like we planned. We even specified his left arm, wanting the ring to be obvious. I imagined it being sterile, clinical, and over very quickly, like a minor procedure with no sedation.

But it's been so long since anyone held me this way.

I didn't plan for the feeling of his fingers wrapping around the front of my shoulder and squeezing, crinkling my plain black T-shirt against my skin. He feels so warm against the cold illustrated metal of my tattoos. It does something to my brain that makes me lean into his side and reach up to cover his fingers with mine. Against the pressure of my shoulder, his serratus anterior muscle tenses in a startled jump.

I'd forgotten how *intimate* this is. You can kiss a stranger and you can hug a friend, but you don't stand with your arm around someone unless they're special to you. If we weren't standing in front of six strangers, I could turn my head and breathe him in—convert this deep, peaceful feeling into a spark and see what caught fire.

Pretending I have to wave at the clients, I duck away from his hold. I can't look at his face, no matter how much I want to see his reaction.

"Hi, everyone, I'm Stellar, like Stella with an *R*. Try to keep all your blood on the inside for the next ten days." It's an old joke, a favorite for patients with lacerations. My delivery is rusty, but the clients chuckle. I feel McHuge giving me a curious look: Stellar Byrd knows a *joke*?

Maybe this will be all right.

"And this is Babe," McHuge says as the dog trots up beside him, his voice reassuringly normal. "She's a serious type, but if you keep trying, she'll warm up. Take a look at the color on your luggage tags before you head to the pavilion for refreshments, so you know which tent will be your recharging station.

Orientation is at the firepit in thirty minutes. Come dressed to paddle. No whitewater, but be prepared for a current and a breeze."

McHuge and Jasvinder turn toward the pavilion. I'm the only one watching as Brent examines a tag on a stiff new backpack, then tugs Willow away from the van door.

"Let the staff deal with that. I don't want to be last in line for snacks."

"Don't you think we should let the paying customers—"

"Leave it, Willow. Just because we're not paying doesn't mean it's free."

She lets him pull her toward the path like my mom let my dad pull her into the car that day, and I have to set my feet hard to keep from getting swept into the past.

My brief burst of optimism fades like a firework, leaving the smell of cordite and rage. This will not be all right. This will be *hard*. Every second of this cruel summer will be hard, and the guest I'm dreading most hasn't even arrived.

For the millionth time, I wish I'd never offered to call anyone. I wish when I'd called that number, Sloane hadn't called me back. I wish she'd endorsed us from a safe distance, instead of insisting on attending.

My body needs something to do, right *now*. Something to defuse the time bomb ticking in my chest. I'd go for a run, but I can't sprint away from launch day unless I don't plan to come back.

I snatch a duffel bag whose tag sports a yellow square. It's maybe thirty pounds—not heavy enough. Pawing through purple triangles and red circles, I spy a second yellow-tagged bag and heft that one, too. The weight settles my spine, replacing the burn in my heart with a burn in my traps and delts. I'll carry as many bags as I can before McHuge gets to them, and I'll feel better. Calmer.

I'm about to head down to the tents when, one by one, the people on the path look toward the crunch of heavy tires overlaid by a smooth, eight-cylinder growl.

A shadow-colored Range Rover pulls up in the parking lot, its rear passenger door perfectly aligned with the short pathway to the clearing. The echo of the driver's door closing has the hushed, smug whisper of cocktail party conversation in rooms with plush Persian rugs. It's the kind of fancy whose understatement contains plenty of statement about the kind of people inside.

She's here.

Chapter Six

Before the driver can make it around the car, the rear door swings open. A pair of long, taut legs wink into existence, clad in multipocketed canvas expedition shorts that hit at the precise point on her midthigh where a pair of six-guns should be strapped. Those cream socks ruched over black leather hiking boots will stay clean for about six minutes out here. Her cropped olive-green jacket sits just off her shoulders, her body-skimming tank top teasing her Hollywood collarbones and news anchor arms. The breeze feels engineered to ruffle her thick platinum bob.

The entire camp stands riveted by the performance. Valid—Sloane *is* an actor. Or she was, and she will be again soon, if *Nighthawke*—her new movie—does well. She plays the titular character, a dystopian future James Bond type. In the trailer, she's dirty, bloody, and constantly biting some kind of ordnance.

She's far from dirty now. Sloane Summers is seven years older than me—forty, if her birth date on IMDb is correct—but my sister's skin is as smooth and glowing as the epidermis of a freshly decanted cyborg.

"Ahhhh, Lara Croft!" Lori blurts, pointing.

"Lori!" Mitch mutters, grabbing her arm.

"But . . ." Lori mimes operating a video game controller.

I can't help barking out a nervous laugh.

Sloane's dawn-sky eyes swing to me, jumping from my identical pale-blue irises to my hair, chin, clothes, shoes. For a long, silent second, her flat mouth makes me think she's going to get right back in the car and drive away.

But she tips her head back and laughs, throaty and musical, and *wow*, can she project.

Everyone laughs with her. Even me, albeit through gut-churning emotion. I knew we looked alike, but actually seeing my cheekbones on her face feels like staring at an alternate-universe version of myself.

What if *my* mom, like Sloane's, had had the good sense to leave my dad in time to keep his name off my birth certificate? What if Mom had taken me far away, and we, too, had had lawyers to keep us safe?

A stupidly handsome man, maybe thirtyish, joins Sloane. His light brown skin and wavy black hair shine with the same Hollywood glow she has, and in the most moneyed flex I've ever seen, he's holding a smartphone with no case. Dereck Burgos plays Nighthawke's doomed lover—a very James Bond touch, killing off the love interest—in the film that's supposed to launch both of them to silver-screen stardom. According to the websites I definitely do not use to stalk Sloane's career, they've been dating since filming wrapped last summer.

"Hi, everyone, sorry we're late! I'm Sloane, and this is Dereck. We're so excited to be here!"

McHuge makes his way through the swarm of curious people. Sloane's cut her hair since *Cow Pie High*, and her face has morphed from its softer, rounder teenaged shape to a sharper cheekbones-forward look, but she's recognizable enough that some of the guests are squinting, obviously trying to place her.

"Dr. McHugh! I can't believe it's you," she squeals, pulling him into a hug. That's another favor I owe her—for acting like McHuge is a celebrity in front of the other guests.

Delighted, he squeezes her in return. I see the moment Sloane stops acting and lets her back bow into the pleasure of McHuge's embrace.

I can't imagine he's gotten less good at hugging since last year. It's like he can sense some change in your vibrations when he's reached the perfect amount of pressure, holding it steady until you're high on wraparound warmth and security. Sloane laughs as she steps away, glowing. Dereck pockets his naked phone and reaches out for a quick handshake.

I dart forward. "Welcome to the Love Boat! I'm Stellar. I'll bring your bags to the Sunset Dome."

"I can carry my own—" Sloane begins, reaching for the designer-logoed weekender topmost on the stack assembled by the driver.

"I insist," I say, grabbing it.

"Of course. Thank you." Her gaze moves from my service-able French braid, across the darkening roots of my under-cut, to the stainless steel barbells in my cartilage piercings. Her eyes pause on a twining hexagonal circuit in my sleeve tattoo. I feel the differences between us settle hard on my shoulders.

"The camp is *beautiful*. I can't tell you how excited I am about your program." She's got a sanitized, placeless accent that immediately makes me hyperaware of the way I pro-nounce the letter *O*. Canadian accents are cute. I prefer not to be cute.

Dereck seems less excited to be here, tapping his phone restlessly through the pocket of his streamlined joggers. "Where can I get a signal around here?" He sounds straight out of Brooklyn or the Bronx or possibly Queens—someplace where, if you guess the wrong borough, they never speak to you again.

"We encourage clients to unplug, but if you need to call or text, we can drive you to a place where there's reception. Usually."

"What about streaming?"

"Um, that can be tricky on the cellular network up here. But we have a movie night planned, weather permitting."

"Right." He drops behind, waving his phone overhead, trying to catch stray bars.

We enter the clearing for Sunset Dome—an audacious name for a tent, but McHuge claims language inspires thought.

"I'm sorry our flight was delayed," Sloane says. "I hoped we'd have some time to hang out privately."

"It's fine," I say, not meaning for it to sound like "*fine*," but it does. "I appreciate you being here."

A faint line dares to pop up between her eyebrows. "Stellar. I don't know why it feels like we're fighting. I'm not here for that. I'm here because I promised I'd always help you, if I could. And because I'd like to get to know you."

I hoped for something from her once. Since then, I've learned you can't solve problems by trying the same thing over and over again.

I set Sloane's luggage on the raised platform, unzip the front opening of her tent, and heft the bags onto the chest of drawers to the right of the entrance. "Sloane, if you're worried I'm harboring resentment, that's really not the case. I know the value of your time, and I promise to pay you back the second

I'm able." Sloane might call this a favor, but we both know I've taken out a loan against our scrap of shared DNA.

Like mine, Sloane's features aren't exactly pretty. A hundred years ago, her high cheekbones, strong nose, wide mouth, and Dad's square jaw would've gotten her called *handsome*. An injured expression works well on her precisely because you'd expect a face like that to stay stoic.

"You don't have to pay me back for anything. You're my only—"

My finger flies to my lips: *Shhhh.*

Her voice drops to a barely audible whisper. "Sister."

The Love Boat crew all know who Sloane is, but she and I agreed not to reveal our relationship to the other guests. An endorsement will look stronger if it's not a family affair.

"I already have a sister," I say, because Liz would call me her sister too. "Like I said, this means the world to McHuge and me. We're here to provide a transformative experience and to ensure our future brand will reflect positively on yours. For now, I'd better let you change. I suggest a long-sleeved sun shirt, a hat that won't blow away, and water shoes. Don't put sunscreen above your eyebrows; it'll get in your eyes. I'll see you at the shore in five."

Sloane's chin tightens a fraction, her lips pressing together.

I know that face. I've seen it in the mirror during my residency, on days I ducked into the bathroom to stop myself from crying after particularly harsh criticism from my staff. It's not sad, though. It's a Terminator robot calculating where it can reacquire Sarah Connor.

"Sure," Sloane agrees, sounding damn disingenuous for someone with years of acting experience. "Oh, isn't it pretty in here. You did a beautiful job."

Until this moment, I thought the tents *were* beautiful. The Sunset Dome is every shade of orange, from the pale-coral gauze draped in generous swoops against the white walls to the warm ginger-brown of the rug. It's stuffed with luxe throws and fat cushions Jasvinder taught me to fluff, then chop with my hand to make soft folds. There's real furniture—a metal dresser with faux leather pulls, a pair of canvas chairs in bright tangerine.

But Sloane standing here with her sleek neutral outfit and her lips pressed together makes the Sunset Dome look lesser-than. Country. Cheap.

I can't imagine her staying at my crappy apartment. Or see myself in her Malibu guesthouse, picking out the perfect shoes for a dinner that costs more than I make in a month.

I don't want a future where I'm eager to keep in touch with her, like I was eager to be hired at Grey Tusk General—excited to join committees and take the projects no one wanted and let a million sketchy things slide in the name of paying my dues.

A year from now, I don't want to look at our texts and realize I'm initiating all the conversations.

It's better if we understand exactly what we have to offer each other and for how long. It can be like a one-night stand: she wants forgiveness or whatever; I need a celebrity jump start for the Love Boat. We can part ways once our conditions are satisfied.

"Who's in the tent next door?" Dereck asks, ducking through the flap.

"In the Sky Dome? Our guests had a last-minute scheduling conflict and won't be here." Goodbye to Renee's team, hello to my new secret bedroom. Chores mean McHuge and I get up

first and go to bed last. No one will know if I bunk in there for
a night or six.

"Would you mind if I use it? Sloane and I prefer to stretch
out."

My fantasy of curling up safely alone wafts away, replaced
with a sleeping bag barely an arm's reach from McHuge.

"It's fine if that's not possible," Sloane says, her eyes flicking
to Dereck. He flashes a frighteningly white smile but doesn't
quite meet her gaze.

"We want you to be comfortable. I'll bring your bags to Sky
Dome right away."

Outside, I turn back. Sloane looks at me as if I might've
changed my mind about sisterhood. Not likely.

"Don't forget to keep the door closed. You'll spend hours
chasing mosquitoes if you don't."

The silver zipper neatly seals the barrier between us.

Next session, we need to shorten the time between arrival and
orientation. Thirty minutes turns out to be long enough for
nearly half of our clientele to pull me aside.

Mitch says Lori can be forgetful—do we have spare sunglasses and water bottles, in case her wife's go missing? Meanwhile, Mitch's diabetes has caused nerve damage in her feet,
says Lori; I need to watch her when we're portaging.

Lori strikes me as someone who's never been embarrassed about bodies—hers, or anyone else's. I get the strong
impression that before this trip is over, she'll have sponta-
neously shown me her entire butt for some quasi-medical
reason.

I don't laugh when Brent jokes that doctors are bad for his
blood pressure.

When everyone's seated at the firepit, the Love Boat's

multifunctional hub for socializing, briefings, and group therapy, McHuge claps his hands.

"Now that we're all here, quick reminder of the nondisclosure agreement covering course materials and privacy. Without safety, no one will be comfortable sharing during the debrief. Likewise, we ask that no one takes photographs during paddling. We don't want the focus to shift from how you feel in the moment to how you'll look in an image that lasts forever."

Brent obtrusively nudges Willow, who looks sadly at the waterproof camera bag at her feet. She brightens when McHuge says photos are fine in camp as long as the subjects consent.

"Let's introduce ourselves. We'll have lots of time to grow into besties, so keep it to name and hometown." McHuge gestures to Willow on his left.

She's got a sweet smile to go with her wavy brown hair and soft face. "I'm Willow. Brent and I live in a suburb of Chicago, but I was born in Stockholm."

Before the murmur of interest has died down, Brent fluffs the thinning top of his salt-and-pepper hair and launches his own intro. "Brent Torquay, senior writer for *Beeswax* magazine. I've been stationed in New York, Tokyo, and London, among other places."

Silence follows Brent's recitation of his résumé, but he's set the tone.

Mitch coolly discloses that she's the vice president of internal communications at Vancouver International Bank; Lori grins and says she's retired. Petra and Trevor are both grad students in Boston. Sloane says she's in the "entertainment industry" in LA, prompting another round of stares and whispers. Dereck proclaims he's an actor, then looks disappointed when no one asks any follow-up questions.

McHuge pulls a stack of shiny cards from his pocket and

hands them to Dereck. "We'll go over the curriculum, but here's a quick-reference for day-to-day. Take one and pass them on."

The cards are basic black print on white stock, the design spare and fancy like a spa menu. I scan the first side.

DAILY SCHEDULE

7:30:	Hot water delivery to tents
8:00:	Breakfast (Pavilion)
9:00:	Morning yoga/meditation (Pavilion)
10:15:	Bell rings—meet at the clearing dressed to paddle
12:30:	Lunch on the go
3:00:	Return to camp, afternoon snack
3:30:	Debriefing Circle
4:30:	Sauna (optional), personal time, journaling
6:00:	Dinner (Pavilion)
7:00:	Campfire

I flip over the card.

CURRICULUM

Days 1–2: Get It Together

Days 3–4: Get Out of Here

Days 5–6: I Get You

Days 7–8: We've Got This

Days 9–10: Capstone river-running trip

Most of the guests tuck their cards into a pocket. Brent photographs it front and back, then stuffs both card and phone into a waterproof pouch with a shoelace-thin lanyard that will be killing his neck by Wednesday. Trevor and Petra huddle shoulder to shoulder, reading intently. They look fresh and eager. Younger than twenty-nine.

Or maybe it's that I feel older than thirty-three. I once read a study showing that doctors' DNA ages six years during their first year of training—too much stress, too little sleep—and that was *before* the pandemic. Maybe I'm grumpy because my brittle geriatric DNA wants everyone to get off my lawn.

Trevor's hand shoots up. "Will there be additional printed material? Something more detailed, like your book?"

"Amazing question, Trevor. I don't want people to be distracted by the future instead of staying in the present, so I'll explain quickly now, then more as we go. I recommend you try to build an *emotional* foundation versus an intellectual one. The Love Boat is about exploring how you *feel*. You feel me?" McHuge glances around, nodding wisely.

McHuge the public speaker is a tightrope walker: mystical, but not so far out that people feel uncomfortable; unique but recognizable; intelligent yet approachable. He's managing to give every vibe anyone could possibly want while making the balancing act look easy. I think I'm the only one who wonders what would happen if he fell.

"What I love about the Love Boat is that we're all seeking a higher plane of connection. As such, it's important to anticipate highs and lows as we learn. A very typical pattern would be to start strong, feel great, love everyone, and bask in some beginner's luck. That would be the 'Get It Together' phase." He taps his card.

"After that first win, we might struggle as we take on bigger challenges. We're still learning, but it can feel like we're stuck or even losing ground. It's very emotional. You might be tempted to blame your partner."

"'Get Outta Here,'" Lori supplies cheerily. "Mitch and I felt that way the entire first year of our son's life. Luckily, we were too tired to research divorce lawyers." Mitch reaches for Lori's hand and squeezes, her brown cheeks flushing deep pink.

I'm calculating the over-under on when exactly I will be seeing Lori's butt when I happen to glance over at Sloane. She's sitting stiffly, a cardboard smile in place of her previous high-wattage grin. I was wrong about the universal intimacy of the arm around the shoulder thing, because Dereck's arm hangs from her body like the physical embodiment of a recurring argument.

"Exactly, my friend," McHuge says, giving Lori an apprecia-tive nod. "That's when journaling can be most transformative, so I may assign a reflection or two.

"The good news is there's nowhere to go but up. At the I Get You level, you and your partner engage in deep relation-ship exploration. This stage is my favorite. Very, very spiritual and satisfying. And last, you'll use that deep understanding to perform together: We've Got This.

"The highlight of the course is our overnight trip with loaded canoes. I don't know about you, but I'm pretty excited to camp out. Any questions?"

Brent raises his hand. He has a way of leading with his chest that reminds me of my neighbor's rooster in Pendleton, strutting around the yard, crowing at all hours. "Would you credit the Love Boat's curriculum for your quick engagement? Congratulations, by the way."

McHuge looks at me, eyes wide. He wanted us to sit on op-posite sides of the circle so the clients wouldn't be up against a wall of instructors. Now we're too far apart to coordinate a response.

"No," I blurt, just as McHuge starts to say "Yes," then panics and changes it to "Um."

Brent frowns like he's unearthed an interesting puzzle piece. "Yum . . . ?"

"Inside joke. Off the record," I say, fully talking out of my ass. I have no idea about journalism. "Let's save the personal

questions for later. Right now, does anyone have concerns related to the curriculum?"

No hands go up. As everyone stands to head down to the
beach, McHuge and I exchange a glance. That was close, but I
think we weathered our first test as a "couple."

"Yum," Lori whispers, nudging me as she walks past. "You
two are such cute little lovebirds."

I can't blush like McHuge, so I try for a knowing smirk. It
seems to work; Lori winks and moves on.

Only nine and a half more days to go.

Chapter Seven

Down by the shore, there's plenty of oohing and ahhing over the big sky and the bald eagle riding the thermals overhead. The wind carries the tang of evergreens; if I take a mouthful of the water, I'll discover the same sharp, wintry taste on my tongue.

We're at the north end of the Pendleton valley, where the golden-green floodplain dissolves into white-tipped crags skirted in birch and cedar. Wide-open valley views narrow into near focus: you can only see *this* hillside, *these* trees, a single set of rapids before the river disappears around a bend.

I like the mountains for that. They don't let you have all of themselves for free.

At our beach, the river is flat and wide, still a touch muddy from spring floods but clearing into its signature pale, chalky blue. The top half of a cedar trails in the water nearby, its trunk twisted and split by a winter storm, spiraling strands of bark and wood still connected to the stump. It's broken yet whole, a tree yet not a tree. *Greenstick fracture*, I think, my doctor brain flaring to life like a computer virus.

McHuge and I are treating this outing like low-stakes skill building, but today will define the rest of the session. We're about to discover the difference between the experience levels people reported on their intake forms and the levels they actually have, which is always an issue on adventure tours. We want everyone to come off the water feeling good, which will be hard to pull off if we have struggling newbies next to bored experts.

I badly want everything to go right. No cracks, no flaws, nothing to criticize or exploit. No accidental swimming. One hundred percent satisfaction.

Lori and Mitch stand slightly away from the main group, scanning the setup and chatting quietly. I get the feeling Mitch prefers to hang back in a group until she knows who the assholes are. Her eyes linger on Brent.

You and me both, Mitch.

Willow's eyes pop as McHuge effortlessly pulls a tandem canoe from the rack at the shore, then plucks a paddle and a life jacket from the supply shed. Brent notices and frowns.

Meanwhile, McHuge is playing himself to perfection. "All right, my river otters. First and most important lesson: You will never step in the same river twice. A river is time, and you can't go back in time. It's forward—or nowhere." He likes to keep up the hippie-dippie Child of the Universe persona in public, unlike when we're alone.

A sudden memory ripples through me: the two of us, alone. McHuge stretched out on his giant bed, hands reaching for the rustic, branch-like slats of his headboard. Eyes dark, voice darker: *Call me Lyle.*

It's the worst thing to think about while watching sunny McHuge standing next to Sloane, whose first name was literally Sunshine—my dad's only legacy—before she changed it, presumably replacing Dombrowski, her mom's last name, with Summers as a nod to her past self.

I'm a pale copy of her in every way. Smaller, less shiny, nowhere near as warm. Even my name was chosen to contrast with hers: sunshine and stars, day and night.

I have no right, no *reason* to be jealous that in under thirty minutes she's managed to establish the easy, friendly vibe with him that I couldn't figure out in an entire year.

Sloane catches my eye and manages to nod without a flicker of a muscle: yes, she is carrying on saving my livelihood, my home, and everything I love.

I don't need to feel so guilty. I didn't promise her anything. But she *is* doing me a solid. If she's not going to get the sisterly love she came for, I could spare some genuine gratitude, at least. I could try not to be angry with her for the childhood she didn't choose any more than I chose mine.

I take a deep breath, conjuring a dim, gray memory of the Stellar who felt compassion for imperfect people, including herself.

"Gather 'round the tandem," McHuge continues. "That's the two-person canoe. This course is about relationships first, canoeing second, but we need fundamentals in place for both.

"A whitewater canoe is *different* from regular canoes, like a committed partner relationship is different from friendships or familial bonds. The steering is trickier and the stakes are higher. If your partner performs well, you look good. If you tip the boat and go for a swim, you take them with you."

He looks around the circle for effect. "*And* it can be the deepest, most connected relationship of your life. You, your partner, the boat—you become one entity. Solo whitewater paddling is a compromise between power and steering, but with two people you can have both—*if* you can move in tandem. Today's lesson is about Getting It Together: learning what you're starting with and imagining where you can go from there."

The clients push closer as McHuge demonstrates the thigh straps that hold paddlers in a half-seated, half-kneeling position, his big gestures bringing his body to life. His straw hat dangles down his back, the chin strap stretched across the base of his throat with enough pressure to lightly dimple his skin. My fingers twitch with the urge to smear extra sunscreen across his cheeks so I can stop watching for new freckles to appear.

When the demo moves to the canoe's flotation system, Brent turns to the helmet locker and starts browsing. McHuge must see what's going on, but he's not intervening. And now Dereck, who wasn't looking keen to get on the water in the first place, is glancing that way too.

I work my way unobtrusively around the circle to put an end to the distraction. I wish we'd made Brent pay for the course. The Love Boat needs money, for one thing. And in my experience, people can't tell the difference between something they got for free and something that has no value.

At the hospital, I did tons of work for free, thinking it was earning me something. Respect, gratitude, collegiality, whatever. But actually, I was convincing everyone I had no idea of the value of my time, so they shouldn't value it either.

Brent taps a helmet against Willow's arm until she accepts it, then disappears back into the wide locker.

"We won't need helmets until tomorrow. Brent, how about you rack those back up." McHuge says it kindly, but a miserable flush climbs Willow's cheeks. Brent rejoins the circle, hands empty, and nudges her toward the locker.

I sidle up to Willow, smiling through my fury. "I'll take it," I whisper. "Don't miss the demo." Looking relieved, she hands it over. I silently will her to join the circle between Lori and Mitch, but she slips in beside Brent, putting her hand into the crook of his elbow.

I think the demonstration she needs is how to leave her awful husband, who's sandbagged her twice and we're not even on the water yet. Brent strikes me as no different from a lot of men who like to treat women like we don't need autonomy or respect. No different from my father, who thought my mom should give him everything, including the decision to abandon her daughter. His daughter.

But it's not helpful to wish Willow would tell Brent where he can shove that helmet. *It's better to be kind than right,* my inner McHuge advises, impatience coming through in his imaginary tone. That, and it's better for the guests to feel smart, give us five stars on Tripadvisor, and refer their friends. That's what'll keep the Love Boat alive.

"Time to get zipped and clipped! Any time we're in the red zone—meaning whitewater and areas where it's possible to slip, trip, or drift into whitewater—we keep our helmets buckled and life jackets secured. As I said, no helmets today, so my . . ." McHuge coughs to cover his hesitation. "My lovely fiancée will put you together with a life jacket and paddle. Choose who's sitting in the bow, or the front, and who's in the stern. The stern paddler has more power to steer. The bow paddler's momentum makes the steering strokes effective, and they watch for obstacles ahead. Suit up, friends."

Tomorrow, McHuge and I will be in separate boats, but today we're demonstrating the tandem positions. After taking care of the guests, he hefts a tandem into the water and holds the stern so I can get into the bow. Babe gallops past, leaping into the bow with a shower of water and mud and wet dog smell.

"Out, Babe," McHuge says, pointing at the shore. "Next time, buddy."

Babe gives me a sour look. She squints at the shallow water, then jumps out and slopes off toward camp, ears down, belly dripping. McHuge launches us, then jumps in the stern like a bobsledder. I have to kneel in the puddle Babe left behind.

"Which side do you want?" I dip my paddle right and left.

"I'm easy."

"Stern picks," I say, still irritable about Brent.

"You can choose."

This feels like a test where every response teaches him something about me. Maybe I *want* the camaraderie Sloane had with him, but that's not an instinct I can trust. He and I are nothing alike. At best, we're opposite sides of the same coin, looking away from each other for a damn good reason.

"I'd rather you chose, McHuge."

I feel his silent sigh. "Left, then."

He takes a stroke, the boat leaping with a surge that tugs in my belly. He's good at following my lead, synchronizing his rhythm to mine so closely the splashes blend into a single heartbeat.

I wish I could watch him paddle and feel it at the same time. When we scouted the local rapids, his body was one with his boat and the water in an almost mythical way. He's a fish— still until the moment he flicks his tail and disappears, mercury scales swirling into silver water.

"Circle up, everyone!" McHuge has to shout to reach Mitch and Lori, who are goofing around halfway to the middle of the channel. At this volume his voice has the commanding reverb of a Harley, and feels just as fascinating and dangerous.

Wait, *fascinating*? I put some snap into my softening spine.

Knock that shit off, Byrd, I tell myself. We'll teach steering strokes for an hour, play in a baby current upstream, then drift back to camp. I'm not going to accidentally fall in love with him in one afternoon. Or ever.

It takes some time to circle everyone up, given that we have to go get Brent and Willow, who are spinning hopelessly. Trevor and Petra are concentrating so hard they don't even look up when I call their names. In close quarters, the guests bump into each other with every wave, looking like rainbow molecules in canoes that match their tent colors.

"We're going to do a little warm-up," McHuge announces. "Everyone has to sing *all* the words and do *all* the actions, or I lose my place in the song and start again. You put your paddle in, you take your paddle out . . ."

He leads them through a canoeing version of the hokey pokey involving a lot of silly facial expressions and splashing. Sloane and Dereck nail all the moves like good little triple threats; Lori sings with maximum gusto despite not remembering any words. Everyone else looks like they want to die.

"There," McHuge says. "Now you don't have to worry about looking stupid, because we've already looked sillier than you ever will when you're paddling."

I dip my paddle in the water, hoping that's true.

I'm the last one to take my seat for the debrief, my hair still sending cold drops down the back of my spare fleece. McHuge must've changed in the breezeway—the covered clotheslines where we hang wet gear at night so it'll be slightly less wet by morning—because he's mostly dry, too.

He wasn't happy when we pulled up on the beach, bedraggled and defeated, although I'm not sure how I know that. His displeasure is a ghost, there in my peripheral vision, gone when I look directly at it.

Jasvinder comes around with steaming tin mugs of tea. Their waft of bergamot and honey reminds me of McHuge's clothes, which were already in the tent when I moved my gear in this morning. I curl my hands gratefully around a mug, soaking up the warmth.

McHuge rubs his hands together and glances around. He doesn't have to be loud to make everyone look his way, it turns out.

"Welcome to Circle, everyone. We're here to share with each other, learn from each other, and support each other. I'm a positive psychologist, which means I'm interested in the study of happiness and mental health. So let's start by talking about what went well today."

Mitch raises her hand. "It was great to be back on the water together." Understatement of the century. Lori and Mitch are light-years ahead of the others. The invisible strings that connect their movements speak to the depth and breadth of their life together. It's going to be tricky to keep them challenged while the newbies build skills.

"It was great to be on the water for the first time." Trevor shares a look with Petra like they have a secret clasped between their palms. They weren't naturals, but they stuck it out like it was their job, never getting snappish.

"Me and Sloane made a good team," Dereck chimes in brightly, which surprises me. He seemed miserable all afternoon, constantly cold even after McHuge loaned him his wind shell. "I love working with her. I'd like to do it a lot more."

They beam at each other and we all suffer cardiac arrest. Dereck has underwear-model smolder and eyelashes thicker than some people's hair. Sloane has a Matt Damon quality of being very interesting to look at until she smiles, at which point everyone plucks their heart directly out of their chest and hands it over. If their movie has anything like this kind of chemistry, their careers are going to go stratospheric.

Sloane's "secret" came out this afternoon, when Lori cocked her head at Sloane's windblown Deanna-like hair and shouted "*Cow Pie* Deanna!"

This led to fifteen minutes of excited clamor in the middle of practicing draw and pry strokes and an argument between Brent and Willow. She said he used to love that show; he insisted he'd been in college when it aired and would never have watched it. *Cow Pie High* was never as big as *Degrassi*, but everyone except Brent has been finding reasons to stand next to Sloane, hang their gear beside hers, and generally fangirl all over. There was an intense game of silent musical chairs before Circle, everyone lingering to see where she'd sit, then scrambling for nearby logs when she made a move.

"Good insight, everyone," McHuge says, nodding. "Learning a new skill can be frustrating. It's important to maintain focus on enjoying the activity and each other. Brent, Willow, what went well for you?"

"*We* didn't tip," Brent says, right to the still-dripping McHuge.

It takes a great deal of effort—and the knowledge that McHuge is already mad at me—to keep quiet. How Brent gets any scoops when he walks around pissing off every single source like this, I'll never know.

"Moving on," McHuge says. Am I the only one who felt the micro-bite in his voice? Looking around at the guests' rapt faces, I think so. "What felt difficult or challenging to you personally? No fair critiquing your partner."

An uncomfortable silence grips the circle. Everyone made

mistakes, but Brent and Willow blew right through Get It Together and landed firmly in Get Out of Here.

We'd all wished we couldn't hear his voice cracking across the water. "Left, Willow, paddle left! Dammit, right, right, *right!*" They were the only couple who got worse as the afternoon went on—bad enough that McHuge and I paddled over to sort them out after a pair of bird-watchers turned their binoculars our way.

The closer we got, the more dysfunctional they became. Willow stabbed her paddle into the water with panicky inefficiency; Brent yelled about the boat's defective steering. As we came alongside, Brent switched his paddle to Willow's side, leaned out, and dug hard. The overloaded right side lurched downward like Brent had pressed an eject button.

I didn't even think, just grabbed for their left gunwale and shoved it down as hard as I could, desperate to put the bottom of their canoe back in the water and save them from a first-day swim.

"Stellar! What the—" McHuge yelped as our boat, bound by the laws of physics, bucked us out in the opposite direction.

McHuge and I surfaced at opposite ends of our canoe, shocked into breathlessness by the freezing river. Willow looked like she wanted to cry. Brent shrugged. "I told her to paddle on the left, but . . ."

He hadn't even used Willow's name while he threw her under the bus. The injustice burned worse than the water in my nose. Breathless with cold, I gasped, "*Wife*. That's your wife. You're talking about. My guy."

Goodbye, five stars.

McHuge papered over my mistake by demonstrating two types of water rescue, but I could feel everyone's pity and blame.

In the here and now, the quiet rolls on. Everyone's very interested in the ground.

McHuge catches my eye meaningfully in the signal we agreed he would use only in an emergency: *Help me out.* Debriefing isn't in my job description, but I'm not eye-arguing this with him on the day I sent him swimming.

"I tipped my canoe. Our canoe," I correct myself. "I don't feel great about it. It's rough to be the only one who tips when you're supposed to be the instructor."

Humility isn't my style. I had to be self-assured in department meetings at Grey Tusk General if I didn't want my points swept aside by men questioning my math or complaining that I was "emotional." Exposing myself to criticism is physically painful, but it's my fault McHuge's curls will be wet all night, so it's only fair.

"Don't be embarrassed." Lori reaches out to squeeze my arm. "Everyone tips sometimes. Well, Mitch and I don't," she says, grinning at the round of chuckles.

"Lori and I don't tip because we're past that point in our lives," Mitch says. "Our bodies aren't as forgiving as they used to be. It's why we looked for a trip where there's a doctor. But if we didn't tip back in the day, we knew we weren't pushing ourselves enough."

The dam is broken: one by one, everyone shares something they screwed up. McHuge lets the guests do most of the talking, but the few words he says somehow prompt them to make his points for him. He makes everyone feel brilliant, his green eyes twinkling gold in the dappled late-afternoon light.

By the end, I'm hypnotized into believing a tandem canoe is an exact metaphor for a relationship. Then my eyes meet his across the clearing, and I remember how we clambered into our half-swamped canoe and didn't talk the whole way back to camp.

The guests scatter after McHuge's closing meditation. The hammocks are calling, and Jasvinder has built a fire in the woodburning sauna.

"McHuge. I'm—"

"Later, Stellar. Okay? I'm not mad. I'd just rather wait until we have time. And privacy." He scoops five mugs in each hand and heads for the cookhouse.

High in my chest, I get a pulse of something both good and bad. When he says "privacy," he means the tent.

The one tent we'll be sharing for the first time tonight.

Chapter Eight

The people who will make tomorrow's bad canoeing decisions sit around the campfire, lightly stunned from exhaustion and Jasvinder's simple, unbearably delicious evening meal—fresh wild salmon with homemade dill and caper aioli; plentiful fingerling potatoes with a touch of Brazilian barbecue spice; flame-roasted asparagus glistening with butter sourced from an independent creamery north of Pendleton. Dessert was a delicate lemon tart that melted in my mouth like morning fog under fresh sunshine.

The combination of sun, exercise, and Jasvinder's hot chocolate with optional "rations" of opalescent violet-flavored liqueur is catching up to everyone. Now that McHuge has put away his harmonica and the rhyming song portion of the night is over, the guests are stifling yawns, with the exception of Trevor and Petra, who somehow found the twentysomething energy to go for a romantic evening paddle.

I probably shouldn't position myself so my peripheral vision catches the way McHuge's loose ginger curls flirt with the firelight, or the way his hoodie is giving outstanding shoulder. Or, since we're supposed to be engaged, maybe I should?

I catch him evading my gaze as he brings his mug to his lips, and I think I see . . . *something* in his expression as he turns away. A flicker like a glow of eyes shining back at your flashlight when you step out of your tent in full dark. It's gone in an instant, leaving me wondering whether it was all in my imagination.

McHuge pushes up from his stool. "Hot water at the wash stations in five minutes," he announces, heading uphill to turn on the on-demand water heaters.

Everyone gratefully levers themselves up. "Put your cushions in the overnight bin, thank you," I call, jogging after McHuge.

He and I run through the evening chore list—mostly making sure nothing gets wet, catches fire, or tempts the bugs and bears. Jasvinder's already packed up the food and dishes to take back to his commercial kitchen in Pendleton, where he does most of the prep. I scan the clearing, put away Brent's cushion—no surprise there—and douse the fire with water hauled from the river.

And then there's no reason not to go back to my tent.

Correction: *our* tent.

McHuge and I arrive at the same time, both of us stopping awkwardly ten paces apart, like this is a duel.

"You can change first," he says, indicating that he'll wait outside.

A gentle raindrop hits the bridge of my nose, then another. Not far away, a flashlight bobs along the path to the groover. We can't negotiate who gets to use the tent in front of witnesses who think we're engaged. In love. Banging each other's brains out.

I lower my voice. "It's going to pour. We should both go in, or one of us will end up steaming up the entire tent."

He blinks, crooked eyebrow reaching for the sky.

At least it's dark enough that he can't see my burning

cheeks. "Oh, for god's sake. You know I meant we're going to get wet."

I wouldn't have thought that eyebrow could go higher. It can.

"I mean *rained on*," I snap, stomping to the tent. Perching my butt inside, I pull off my boots and tuck them under the overhang before scooting my legs through the door.

The sound of McHuge zipping the flap closed feels uncomfortably final.

And then it's just the two of us, looking anywhere but at each other.

Our domed tent with its tight, angular rain fly isn't like the client tents with their miles of headroom and luxe textures. McHuge thoughtfully got a six-person size with front and rear entrances, but it still feels small with both of us in here. It would be small with just him, his stooped head threatening to bash the orange nylon ceiling every time he turns to avoid my eyes. There's barely room for our backpacks, our camp cots—no fancy bedroom furniture for us—and the microscopic twelve inches I insisted on putting between our cots after McHuge hypocritically wanted them to be closer together than the guests' beds.

McHuge drops onto his cot, facing the back entrance. "You go first. I won't look."

We should have discussed a lot more in advance. I didn't think to put a Just One Tent Protocol in place, but I feel its absence now.

"We'll take turns. You go first tonight, I'll go tomorrow." I flick on the solar-powered lamp, hang it from the loop at the tent's peak, and reach into my backpack for my e-reader.

It's a long minute and two fake page turns before he believes I mean business. I don't love that I'm making him uncomfortable, but I can't handle an entire summer of his automatic self-sacrifice.

I hear the uncertainty in his movements: a shift of weight as he makes sure I'm not looking, a rustle of ripstop nylon as he leans forward, then stands up.

It was a mistake to grab my book instead of my headphones. The night we hooked up, I left the room to take a shower and told him I hoped I'd come back to find him naked, which I did. I didn't see him getting undressed, much less hear him, so now I have no reference point for the whisper of his shirt and the snap of his pants, the chime of his ring against some metal fitting on his pack, the unmistakable sound of skin on skin as he puts on whatever he wears at night.

He makes a sound as he settles into the warmth of his sleeping bag, a low breath of comfort and pleasure. Suddenly I'm not in a brightly lit tent, politely facing away from him. I'm back in a darkened room, his face framed by my thighs, my soul pinned by that same sound, held firmly by the deep weight of it. My skin shivers in a wave from my heart to my fingertips.

"I'm good," he whispers, and I think about how many things those words can mean when two people are alone together. We're talking to walls instead of each other, the familiar antagonism not feeling half as safe as it used to.

I set down my book to grab my sleep shorts and shirt. Much more of him is covered than if he were chopping wood in his overalls or skinny-dipping in the river, so it's not wrong for me to face his side of the tent while I change.

He's on his side, his curls caught in an elastic at his nape, tense shoulders golden where they've caught the sun, then suddenly pale where they haven't.

His gear is a touch messy in a way that's untamed and endearing rather than sloppy, because he's clearly trying to get it together. He's left his backpack unzipped, his things peeking out the top: a red-and-black checked overshirt, a beaten-up pair of

Levi's, a black beanie, and a couple of those small drawstring sacks outdoor stores sell as backpack organizers. A carabiner clipped to an axe loop holds his bone necklace. The pendant is a salmon vertebra, I'd guess. A peace sign is clumsily etched inside its round, concave body, like someone used a woodburning tool.

The largest backpack pocket, also unzipped, bares the edge of a battered hardcover notebook and a pair of black-framed glasses that look adorably nerdy. I immediately want to see who he is when he's wearing these.

I turn away instead. "You want the lamp on?"

"No. I'll probably go to sleep after we talk."

He sounds tired. Lucky him. I'll probably lie awake, every nerve ending angry from whatever he's about to say. *It's not going to be like the hospital*, I tell myself. We signed the paper-work; I have the right to purchase my percentage, and no one can take that away. I'm sure of it.

But I was sure about other things, too. My clinic. My mom.

I flip the light off and climb into my sleeping bag by feel. "Let's get the fight over with, then." The client tents are a rea-sonable distance away, but we're both keeping our voices down.

In the dark, his sigh is so close. "Not everything has to be adversarial, Stellar. I'm not upset about today. Tipping is simply a sign that we need to do better."

"I know my whitewater technique is a little rusty, but—"

"It's not our technique!" He so rarely breaks through his calm persona that his passionate whisper hits like a shout. "It's that I can't read you. I can't predict what you're going to do, so I do the exact wrong thing."

His words serve me an unexpected burst of loneliness.

Liz and I could read each other when we used to do over-night trips. I loved knowing what she was thinking when she glanced at a hazard. I loved that she always knew what steering stroke I wanted her to do without me asking. I miss the deep happiness of being out here with someone who knows me.

"I'm sorry I tipped us. That was my fault, and you paid for it. I won't make a move like that again. But tomorrow we're paddling solo, anyway."

"Yes, and as much as we planned for me to do all the instruction and debriefing, I'm occasionally going to need your help. We can't discover we have major philosophical differences in the middle of running a rapid. We need to build trust *now*. I need you to open up," he says firmly. "Stop hiding behind that unbreakable shell."

"Oh, *I'm* hiding? Interesting, because which one of us does the Summer of Love act with the clients and then drops it the second we're together? Why am I the only person who gets pushback from you, McHuge? Do you even believe any of that positive affirmation, universal love, higher consciousness shtick?"

"If you're asking whether I was born this way, the answer is no," he says. His flat calm makes me regret being forceful the way a return of hostilities never could. I've poked something important to him. Maybe even something sore.

"And yes, I *choose* to do this, but that doesn't mean it's fake. Being different is a gift I give people, Stellar. I make a space for them to be as weird as they want to be in a world where it's safer to be ordinary."

An unpleasant jangle of fear vibrates down my spine. It's safer to be a lot of things. Safer to be at home working a job I don't care about instead of in this tent trying to launch something I'm afraid I could love. Do I have to offer up *everything* for this company? My history, my heart, the safety of being angry instead of the vulnerability of terror or grief?

He releases a long breath. "And I push back against you because I've seen you fight fair even when you're angry. If I offered you a silver platter with an engraved invitation to take advantage of me, you'd put something of yours on the platter and shove it back in my face. So if you want to lie there under your thundercloud—"

"I do not have a *thundercloud!*"

"—that's fine. As long as you're kind to the guests, you don't have to perform niceness to me. But you and I need a connection. Our business depends on it. Safety and lives depend on it. Give me something I can work with. Tell me about Stellar J Byrd. If possible . . ." He hesitates. "Trust me with something you regret. One true thing you and I can build on. And I'll give you the same."

There's nothing I hate more than people who give me something I didn't ask for, then turn around and claim I owe them something in return, like my dad reeling in a mark.

But McHuge isn't doing that. This is a deal, negotiated up front. We both know the terms.

I swallow hard, finding myself wanting to be honest with him the way he's honest with me—with everyone, really; I'm not special to him. He's such a good person, while there's nothing about me that's simultaneously honest and good.

I'm the kind of person you turn into when your dad's a third-rate con artist who spent most of your teen years in prison, then screwed up your life even worse when he got out. Suspicious. Guarded. Not very nice. I don't trust most people enough to be their friend, let alone their girlfriend.

Although McHuge doesn't want honest and good, does he? He wants honest and *bad*. That, I might be able to do.

"Something, Stellar," McHuge says into the lengthening silence. "*Anything.*"

"I'm thinking." It comes out testier than I mean it to. Fury is so ingrained in me, sometimes it's hard to turn it off.

"Why don't I go first then," he whispers.

My skin pulls tight under my shirt. Outside, it's still twilight, but in here the darkness is the perfect density to hold a whisper, making words last long after the sound dies.

Even with the visual impact of him covered by night, McHuge still has the power to wallop me with that gentle *why don't I go first*. With him, the most unexpected things reach inside my heart and hammer something that echoes and echoes.

"The worst thing I ever did," he says conversationally, "was fracture a kid's skull for taking something from my locker. He was hospitalized for a month. I almost went to juvie."

"Holy shit. You?! No." Shocked, I roll onto my side, facing his half of the tent. "Really?"

"Really," he says, calm like we're discussing the time he smoked a cigarette and learned his lesson like Deanna in Season 4 of *Cow Pie High*.

"What did he take?"

"A family photo. He didn't want the pic—he wanted to fight me."

"Were you the school badass?" I try and fail to imagine McHuge with an attitude. McHuge hurting someone.

"No. But when you're my size, it's kind of all people see. I was like Everest—they wanted to fight me because I was *there*. There was this kid a grade ahead of me who goaded me for months. Stepped on my feet, knocked my lunch onto the floor, dumped milk into my backpack. He was looking for the red button, and he found it. He even threw the first punch."

"*He* started it, and he was older, and *you* almost went to juvie?" I'm angry for little Lyle McHugh, who even then was big Lyle McHugh.

"He gave me three stitches in my eyebrow. I gave him major surgery and an ICU stay. And it was worse because I chased him. He was running away, and I—" He clears his throat. "It was super hard on my family. My younger brother Tavish was sick at the time. Leukemia. My mom was so pissed at me for taking her away from his chemo to go to my legal appointments. I never wanted to feel that way ever again. And mostly I haven't. I try to be the bigger person whenever I can."

He tries hard to be kind, instead of right. God, I'm an asshole.

The only thing I can think to say is, "I'm sorry that happened to you."

He takes a long breath, in for maybe fifteen seconds, out for the same length of time. "Thank you," he says simply.

And now I'm on the hook. He shared his, now I have to share mine. I want to; I'm afraid to.

"Promise you won't tell." My voice sounds small and uncertain, two things I hate being.

"Promise." He's not making fun of me even a little.

"The stupidest thing I ever did was steal a liter of milk." I wince, glad he can't see me. "No, forget it. I'll think of a better one."

"Sounds like a good story to me."

He's so convincing. After a year of trusting hardly anyone—not even myself—I'm perilously close to believing anything he says. Just the thought is dizzying and dangerous.

"It's ridiculous. It's *milk*."

"Somehow, I don't think it's about the milk."

It is and it isn't. "Five years ago, the media got a tip about Grey Tusk General. Their chief of emergency medicine hadn't hired a female doc or approved a rotation for a female resident in sixteen years."

"I remember that. It was national news."

"It was," I say, bitter regret rising in my throat. "They did good crisis PR: Fired the old chief, hired me and another new female grad named Kat, and hunkered down until the news cycle moved on. They made all the right noises about culture change, equality—all the DEI buzzwords. They told us we were lucky to be there."

I *had* felt lucky. I'd wanted to live near Liz, but with three years of residency training instead of the more desirable five, I never thought I'd get a position with the exciting scope of practice Grey Tusk had.

"It took me four years to figure out Kat and I were getting the shaft." My hands clench around my sleeping bag. "Twice as many night shifts, weekends, and holidays; all the unpaid committee work that didn't count for promotion; none of the shifts with senior residents who could lighten the workload. I spent months putting together the data, then presented my findings to the department.

"My colleagues couldn't deny my numbers. But they could, and did, vote down my motion to investigate how it happened. And refuse to make up the financial and career damage to me and Kat. *We need to put the past behind us*, they said.

"But I couldn't. I'd given everything to that place. The only thing that got me through the pandemic shit show was feeling like even if I'd lost faith in the system, I could believe in my colleagues. I trusted them when they said they were 'immunocompromised,' so would I please intubate their COVID patients. I put my life on the line for them, and in return they acted like their bad behavior wasn't a problem, but my being angry about it was."

I thought helping them meant one day they'd help me in return. I thought they *cared*.

But I was a mark.

"Then one night I went to the doctors' lounge for a snack.

In the fridge, there was milk for coffee. All the staff doctors contributed to the coffee fund. That was the rule. Forty bucks a month—not cheap. But I couldn't drink coffee. I'd been doing all the work my colleagues didn't want, and on top of that, I'd paid for their coffee with my money, my time, my body, my *soul*. And I just . . . reached for a carton of milk. Put it in my backpack, zipped it up, done.

"When I turned around, my department chief was standing in the doorway. The *way* he was smiling." I shiver, remembering. "I could've fought back when he asked me to resign, but for what? A job with people who hated me for holding them accountable? Doctors are supposed to be better than that. They're supposed to do no harm. I *loved* being a doctor, and after they took it all away . . . yeah. I was so ashamed of getting taken for a ride, I didn't even tell Liz. I left town and told my *best friend* I wanted to explore rural medicine. Pretty fucking sad."

I lie there, eyes dry and hot. McHuge doesn't rush to fill the silence. I love that about him—that he's willing to let things take as long as they take.

"They didn't steal everything," he says, after a while. "They took a lot, but you kept yourself. When you walked out the door, your talent and drive and creativity went with you. They lost a lot when they lost you."

The simplicity of it takes my breath away. I've heard "it's their loss" before—when I've gotten dumped, been passed over for an award, suffered injustices large and small.

But "their loss" isn't the same as "you kept yourself—good job you."

I swallow. "No one's ever said that to me before."

For the first time, I believe the hospital lost something when they lost me, *and they know it*. For the first time, I realize that when Liz said *you need something*, she understood I was afraid I couldn't hold on to anything—including who I was.

McHuge makes a considering sound, slow and deliberate. "Someone should have, because it's true. If you could go back, would you do it differently?"

"No." The word is out before I even know I'm going to say it. "I mean . . . mostly no. I'd leave, but I'd try to preserve my job options. Every hospital within a couple hundred kilometers of Grey Tusk knew my name after that. I was the angry woman who made damaging allegations against a department that needed to stay trouble free. I bean-counted everything and bitched to the scheduling coordinator and wanted to get as much milk as I paid for. 'Stellar Byrd, milk vigilante: do not hire.'"

To my amazement, he laughs. Until this moment, I would've sworn he laughed all the time. Now that I hear *this* laugh, I know I've never experienced the real thing before—warm and low like an outboard engine thrown into gear.

"Stellar Byrd, milk vigilante," he repeats, and I can hear his smile through the soft patter of drizzle. "Well. I'm glad I got the chance to hire you, Stellar Byrd. Going to steal any milk?"

"Are you kidding? Jas would murder me. I may not be afraid of you, but I *am* afraid of him."

I'm not sure that's exactly true, though.

After tonight, I don't know if I have it in me to be angry with McHuge anymore. His laughter shrank my fear and shame into a shape that was tiny and bittersweet and more than a little sad. That version of me I told him about—she tried so hard and cared so much. I feel her stir deep down, the Stellar who believed in things.

Even if McHuge himself doesn't scare me, the possibility that I'm about to start believing in things and putting my heart on the line again—*that* should scare me plenty.

Chapter Nine

I've never been a good sleeper, so it's a surprise when I drift from soft blackness to the sun filtering through the bright-orange walls of my tent.

Correction: *our* tent.

My eyes fly open at the sharp realization of exactly whose pencil is scratching along industriously behind my back.

Last night's confession rushes back at me, along with the world's worst vulnerability hangover. I don't know why I didn't make up some bland fake story about a dating disaster. He'd never have known, and I would have stayed safe, a dragon atop my hoard of ugly truths.

I roll over, cracking one eye.

McHuge sits on one of the camp chairs, wearing nothing but a pair of olive-green shorts, those professorial square black glasses, and a headlamp trained on a hardcover journal with FIELD NOTES embossed in gold on the cover. He doesn't sit on so much as *inhabit* the chair, relaxing bonelessly into the canvas fabric.

His shorts are *short*, or maybe it's that his legs are long, stretching out for ages. The hair dusting his thighs is gold rather than ginger, his skin a light champagne color interrupted by a density of freckles above his knees. His farmer-tanned torso gives the impression of useful power, and plenty of it; but his belly is soft, rounding a little over the waistband of his shorts.

If he were a truck, he'd be a vintage pickup, cherry red, with a bed made of wooden slats: somehow very cute with all those rounded planes, but underneath the hood he's got twelve cylinders if you should need them.

I'm seized with the desire to press my face into his stomach, to feel the comfort of him against my cheek, to hold on tight until I feel better.

"Marcus Aurelius, huh," I croak, because I absolutely cannot continue to lie here and drink him in.

He looks up, eyebrows cocked. "Good morning to you, too. And I like the classics," he says, tapping the slim volume of *Meditations* underneath his field notes. "Marcus Aurelius happens to be extremely relatable for someone who lived two millennia ago. Feeling connected to people across time makes me more empathetic toward all people, which makes me a better therapist. 'Kindness is invincible . . . what can even the most malicious person do if you keep showing kindness?'" he quotes.

Trust McHuge to be a better person before breakfast than I am at any hour. Trust him to be relentlessly analog, writing on recycled trees instead of a device.

"Taking notes?"

"Nope. Making lesson plans. Remember the Class 1 rapid with friendly eddies a kilometer or so downstream? We can split the clients into two groups and still be close enough to help each other with rescues. In the debrief, we can talk about hopping from safe haven to more dangerous waters and back to the next safe haven in your marriage, the same way you hop from eddy to eddy in whitewater."

"McHuge," I say carefully. "You're not *making this up* as we go along, are you? Is that why there's no printed curriculum?" Last time I worked as a guide, our trips were planned down to the exact weight of the food. I assumed the Love Boat didn't give out reading material for the usual McHuge reasons, like *expanding to fill the present moment*, or *paddling your own river*. But this sounds like not even *he* knows what we're doing.

He squints up at the roof of the tent, then switches off his headlamp and reaches for his pack. I refuse to feel regret when his navel disappears under a well-worn Rolling Stones T-shirt.

"I once lived with someone who shopped for food every day, instead of once a week. Arie's explanation was *How do you know on Sunday what you want to eat on Thursday?* Likewise, I don't know what our guests will need tomorrow until I see what they learn today. I also need to accommodate my coworkers, the weather, the terrain. So I shop for lessons every day."

"Arie was your girlfriend?" I have no reason to be sour about any of his partners, past or present. No standing to be jealous of a woman who picked him the freshest fish for that night's dinner.

"Boyfriend."

"Oh! I didn't know you were . . ."

"Pan," he supplies. "And poly. But I don't know if I'll look for a polycule again. You know, your identity evolves over time, and sometimes you can't predict where it's going until you get there."

"Yeah, totally." That would be the "free love" bit from Brent's article, I guess. I did not have "discuss the many facets of queerness with a guy I thought was cishet" on my bingo card for today. It's uncomfortable to discover my assumptions about him were wrong.

"I should put the hot water on." I wriggle out of my sleeping bag, trying to act nonchalant. He didn't care if I saw him in just shorts, feet bare. What do I care if he sees me in my Leia T-shirt? My boobs are small enough that a bra is optional, anyway.

"I'll give you a hand," he says, tossing the books onto his cot, then pushing himself out of the chair. He takes off his glasses and rummages around in his backpack for a good minute before coming up with the case.

"Shouldn't you put your field notes somewhere safer? Maybe type them into your phone and back them up to the cloud once in a while?"

"I'm not good at typing," he says, wiggling his thumbs. He doesn't have to say they're too big. I look away and try to breathe normally.

"Besides," he continues, "what do I need to protect them from?"

"Your tendency to misplace things. Bears. People whose names start with *B* who've already tried to invade our privacy."

He laughs. "No one wants my notes, Stellar."

I shake my head. "You should take better care of your intellectual property, and not just because it's *my* future intellectual property. You had a best-selling book last year. Your ideas are worth more than you think."

"You can't copyright an idea, only a method. And my methods are only worth anything if I sell a book proposal or Renee decides to partner with us, in which case the lawyers take care of that. Our guests are ordinary people. With the exception of Sloane and Dereck, who presumably have better things to do than sneak around."

The fact that McHuge thinks Sloane is automatically trust-worthy pokes me in a spot that I would dearly like not to be sore. Maybe that's why I snap, "And the exception of Brent, who has tons of incentive to sneak around, collecting dirt for an-other clickbait article. You've seen how he treats Willow—what makes you think he'll treat us any better?"

"I wasn't under the illusion that only unproblematic people would come on this course, Stellar. And you're right, their dy-namic is a yellow flag."

"But," I prompt, when he stops.

"*And*," he replies, giving the word a little heat, like a pitcher warming up his arm, "it's not yet a red flag. Right? There are a lot of reasons someone might not be their best self on the first day. They're feeling vulnerable. They're worried they'll be the worst paddlers. They can't see each other's faces in the canoe, so they lose that avenue of communication. They're afraid, so it comes out as safer emotions—anger or judgment. We can't know what's inside other people's marriages, Stellar. We can't know what's inside their hearts."

I don't know whether he purposely raises his crooked eye-brow, but that fractured arch, split on the day he decided to become the person he is, says *As both of us should know* better than any words.

"But what if what's inside their marriages is bad?" *What if what's inside their* hearts *is bad*, my brain howls.

We had this saying in the ER: *For you, it's a regular day, but for the patient, it's the worst day of their life.* It's supposed to help us not take bad behavior personally. Toward the end, I questioned that wisdom. What does it do to people to work in a place where the person who's allowed to be having their worst day is never you? What do you do when you're supposed to reset the bad behavior column to zero every day, but for you, everything keeps adding up?

At some point, the balance tips, and I never again want to be surprised when that moment comes.

"Then we can help them," McHuge replies. "*If* we stay curious, not judgmental. I'm curious about you, actually. I'm thinking your reaction has more to do with Stellar than it does with Brent and Willow."

"Always the psychologist, McHuge," I say, yanking open my pack and pulling out fresh day clothes. "So I'll be the ER doc: Sometimes danger signs don't mean anything. But I take them seriously anyway. Check and double-check them, get ready to react in case they *do* mean something."

"I'm allowed to play roles other than psychologist, Stellar." He steps between our beds, looking the tiniest bit pissed. "I'm allowed to be your friend. I'm allowed to be worried about you as a person. I see how hard it is on you to be this angry, never trusting anyone or anything."

I step over my cot to where he's standing in the relatively high-ceilinged center of the tent. "It's easy for you to be perfect. I'm sure *you're* never angry. But when *I'm* angry, that tells me to pay attention. It saves me. Sometimes you have to choose between being a nice person and protecting yourself." My mom was never angry—not when I got held back in second grade after changing schools too many times, not when my dad's irate marks pounded on our door in the middle of the night demanding their money back, not when we got run out of town. She never used the power of anger to protect herself. Or me.

McHuge reaches out, hesitates for a second, then cups my elbow. I don't know how to describe the sensation except to say he's *gentling* me, like I'm a skittish thoroughbred and he's the horse whisperer, coaxing me close enough to smell the goodness of him: zinc and bergamot and mountain wind.

"I'm not a perfect person. I've made mistakes. I've been taken advantage of. But I've gotten more wins than losses from believing people are essentially good."

When he lets go, I want him back.

"No one's asking you to be perfect, Stellar. I've counseled a lot of doctors in the last five years; I know how hard it's been for you since 2020. A lot of people let you down. But you can trust me. I won't ignore problems because I'm afraid of a bad review from Brent. Or from any guest, for that matter."

He's being so kind, but instead of being happy and reassured, I feel tears push to the surface. "Can we get rid of him? Send him home with an apology and a gift card? I have a bad feeling about this, McHuge." If Brent were a rapid, I'd portage around him. Too many hazards, no tongue of safe green water to get us to the outwash.

"I . . ." He exhales like the forest—trees shifting with a gust of wind, then settling again. "I don't see how we can cancel his trip. But almost everyone responds to kindness. And I promise I will manage him."

I sigh, hands on my hips, eyes on the orange floor. "He already has something bad to write about. We swam on the *first* day, McHuge. And it was my fault." Outside, steps crunch past on the path. "Argh, someone's up. We're late with morning chores."

"One bucket of water won't make or break the session. I'll get started; you get dressed." He grabs a gigantic pair of wool socks and unzips the door. Sitting with his feet outside and butt inside, strapping on his frayed, well-loved pair of river sandals, McHuge looks up. "And a swim isn't a failure. An expert can keep you from tipping, but sometimes people need to go in."

Babe trots over with a low, pleased *woof*. McHuge gives her a good-morning ear rub, then stands, ducking a little to see inside the tent. "You're still upset. With any other coworker, I'd bring it in for a hug. I don't want to presume, but . . ." He cocks his head in invitation.

He hugs everyone at the Love Boat except me. Tobin, Sharon, even fussy Jasvinder, though our chef insists on taking a few moments to prepare himself first.

Minutes after he cupped it, my elbow still glows with calm; imagine what he could do to my whole *body*. But I don't know how to get from where I am to where he is. How do I let go of anger when it's the only thing anchoring me?

We've been sharing a tent for fewer than twenty-four hours, and already I'm in danger of forgetting that his compulsion to give everything to everyone is the worst possible match for my desire—my *need*—to keep things balanced. I could never relax and feel safe around him; I'd always worry he'd find someone who needed him more.

He straightens up, his head disappearing behind the triangular lines of the rain fly. "Cool. I won't ask agai—"

My face is in his chest before he's finished talking, my neck bent to lay my forehead and nose into the negative space between his pecs, my hands flat against his stomach. His body tightens in surprise, then softens, letting me press farther in.

It's not a hug. He's outside the tent; I'm inside. I don't put my arms around him, and he doesn't put his around me. But his hand comes to the back of my head to brush through the softening length of my undercut, gentle and deliberate. It feels *stupid* good, all tingles everywhere.

He's altogether too skilled at fiancé touches—first the arm around the shoulder, now this. You can't get this kind of contact from just anyone. It's *rare*.

My brain stops boiling like a patch of dangerous current. I want to stay here and think until things make sense.

I tried trusting people at the hospital, and ended up getting gaslighted and brushed off.

But McHuge isn't brushing me off. *Yellow flag*, he said. *I will manage him*. And he does have a way of managing people. Including me. So if I'm going to start trusting things, maybe I can trust that.

"I wish we'd agreed to use nicknames for each other," he says softly, fingers riffling through my hair. "If we had, I'd say *It'll be okay, Stellar J*." The way he says my name sounds different than it does in my head. It's not sharp like a crust-stealing scavenger, but soft—a trill of birdsong.

"I already call you 'McHuge,'" I mumble into his xiphoid process—the little knob of bone that sticks down from the bottom of the sternum. It's a landmark for CPR. If you want to restart a heart, you find that bone first.

"You can call me Lyle, then."

Startled, I take my face out of his chest. That night echoes between us, from his eyes to mine and back again: *Call me Lyle.* Time circles back to that breathless moment of possibility when we knew something would happen, but it hadn't happened yet.

For a second, I don't know what's real between us.

"We would do this . . . for the guests?"

Under my hands, his body loses its softness. "Sure. For the guests." His lips press tight. "I'd better get that water going."

And then he's gone.

For the rest of the second day of camp, I think about that moment, even when I'm yelling, "Set your angle of attack, power, *power*, let the current turn you. Yes! Don't fight the river! Don't fight the river"—then watching as boat after boat wobbles, tilts, and flips its frustrated occupants. I remember it when I'm standing with my arm around my co-instructor, whose name I don't use, because I don't know what his name is anymore.

In the evening, we stay away from the tent since it's important for the guests to see us together. And every moment I'm not there, I think about the tide of his stuff creeping closer to mine, just like the tide of his presence is wearing away the shores of my self-preservation.

Chapter Ten

Situated on the highest part of the camp's grassy open area, the pavilion commands a dramatic view of the Pendle River. Sunrise drenches the far bank in buttery light; in the evenings, the sun sets over the mountains, bathing base camp in golden rays.

For morning announcements, McHuge likes us to stand on the west side of the building, framed by cedar posts and the stunning panorama. I wish we'd decided this particular routine would be more businesslike, so I don't have to spend another day thinking about the negative spaces his body leaves in mine after he presses me fake-fondly to his side.

"Day three, my brethren. The one we've been waiting for." He says this unironically, because of course he does. "I promise the Get Out of Here phase will be one of your favorites. In retrospect."

Everyone laughs nervously except Dereck, who gives a miserable shiver. He spent an average amount of time in the water yesterday, but the cold bothers him more than most. Probably because he's so ripped. He and Willow could set up a thirst trap photo shoot at a moment's notice—if she weren't more interested in artful crops of the worn-out paddles McHuge mounted on the repair shed—but Dereck's lack of body fat is a serious drawback in these waters.

"Knowing what's coming will help you navigate this phase productively. Expect to wonder whether this course is doing anything for your canoeing skills or your relationship. You might find yourselves arguing, competing for leadership, or uncovering differences of opinion. It can feel pretty heavy.

"My best advice is to not set unrealistic goals. Today is not about improvement. It's about understanding why you came here, establishing your ground rules, and figuring out how to deal with conflict. Stellar and I will be offering support on the water, but first, we'll meet back here for morning yoga and meditation thirty minutes from now."

The guests bus their dishes, then disperse to the tents; I race through morning chores and head out for an early run. I watch my step on the stony, pitted road—I can't get injured between now and September, or I won't be able to work.

At the tree, I text Liz. She's read my messages, but no replies yet.

How's it going? Are you sleeping at all?

Halfway through composing a chatty update about the Love Boat, I blink when three dots pop up. Liz is *replying*. I grip my phone like a drifting astronaut who's just reestablished contact with her ship.

No. This child hates sleep. Possible she also hates me. Unconfirmed

The only place she'll sleep is on Tobin's chest. I shouldn't complain, because at least she's sleeping instead of screaming, but I'm irrationally jealous. Why won't she sleep on *me*

> Babe! You're alive! Sometimes babies like to switch parents that way! It's hard and I know you're doing a great job

> Liz? You still there?

Sorry, everyone's a critic when you have a newborn and I started crying when you said I was doing a good job. I cry every day. Is this normal?

> You're doing an AMAZING job! The hormones can be pretty gnarly for a few weeks, but get Tobin to keep an eye on your moods in case we need to start thinking about PPD

Thank you so much 🤍 Don't know what I'd do without you! Wish you were here, but also so glad you're there, if that makes sense? Honestly don't know how to word anymore after one hour of sleep in the last 48

> I'll text you every day. You're doing so good!! Gotta run (literally)

My throat stings with gratitude as I run back toward camp. The last time I was away from her, she revamped her entire life. This time, the Love Boat will keep us connected, and I'm thankful.

The rhythm of my strides punctuates the soft morning, the *crunch crunch crunch* of gravel marking every footfall.

Running is hard, and I like it that way. My favorite part is dialing up the pace until my brain goes silent and I'm reduced to a pair of eyes that can still see beauty even though they're bolted onto a body preoccupied with pain. The fingers of wind running through the trees meet the burn of breath whistling into my lungs. Four brown songbirds swoop and loop across the road, flapping madly before tucking their wings to glide, and my desperate desire to walk eases a little.

It helps. It helps a lot. Preemptively exhausting myself is the only effective preparation for another day of soothing fragile egos, building up discouraged swimmers, and refereeing other people's emotional dynamics.

And it gives me time to think about what to call my business partner. I like to use people's preferred names, but the thought of calling him Lyle conjures a pleasure-pain so keen my breath halts in my throat. I can't fall back on "babe" because of the dog. Yesterday I tried calling him "love," which sounded fake even to me. Plus, he made that *hrgack!* sound again, so that's out.

I walk into camp, hands on hips, just as Brent walks away from yoga-slash-meditation, leaving his equipment on the pavilion floor.

I automatically look to the tall ginger figure holding a spray bottle of tea tree oil.

I'll manage him, moss-green eyes tell me. Lately I can't think of a damn thing to say when his dawn-forest gaze pop-locks with mine. The moments are getting longer, our gazes holding instead of moving on to the next thing. Heat blooms under my skin when his eyelids fall a fraction. He *looks* like a Lyle to me this morning, which seems like a bad thing.

"Good yoga?" I attempt an unobtrusive swipe of my brow and come away with a smear of road dust mixed into sweaty mud.

"Eh, it was only their second time. Some people were into it. Others are, shall we say, new to the discipline." He cracks a smile that's different from his usual unruffled serenity. This one hides a little hook, something sharp and steely. It's conspiratorial, like we're sharing a private joke, and it plucks an echoing string inside my chest that better not be my heart.

I like that smile. Yes, I do, and I should've seen it coming. Should've realized last night or this morning or half a week ago that summer would be long, and I'd need to force my brain to remember—and convince my body to forget—that I've already been down this road with him.

But none of my vital organs are cooperating. I have to clench my thighs against the memory of moments when it seemed like the real him peeked through—when wild power surged behind his kiss, dangerous and past the edge of control, making him growl and yank me close before he remembered he was supposed to be giving.

I need to firm myself up on the inside. I want a heart that won't scuff after meeting a steel-toe boot, not one soft enough to hold an impression of Lyle's fingerprint. It's nice that we can laugh about the business, but it doesn't have to mean anything deeper.

His winking smile fades into an expression of gentle invitation. "You should come salute the sun with us tomorrow. You might like it."

"No, thanks. Running filters my personality. Makes everything less scary."

"You're not scary. You're . . ."

"I'm begging you to not finish that sentence." I don't need

him to embarrass us both by fumbling for something nice to say. Besides, I like being scary. "I'm going to shower and change. Anything you want from the tent?"

We've figured out discreet ways to ask for privacy when guests may overhear us. Unfortunately, ginger skin is the least discreet organ system ever. Lyle's face may be composed, but his pinkened neck tells me he's involuntarily pictured walking in on me. And now I've accidentally imagined that scenario too. Fantastic.

"There is something, actually. If you see my field notes, can you stick them in my pack? I tidied up before campfire last night, and now I can't find them." He's diligently keeping his stuff contained, though I told him I didn't mind. His gear is like him—never quite neat, but never messy either, some perfect shade of clean yet tousled that pleases me to look at. It feels friendly, like I could let go of my rigid tidiness. Which I won't.

But I could.

"I haven't seen it, but I'll keep an eye out."

I'm about to leave when I remember the knots. How it felt to watch his fingers fly through twists and loops, how it untied my stomach to have him do something he didn't care about at all because it was important to *me*.

I pivot back around. "I could help you look."

Oddly, this doesn't feel like I'm paying him back for the knots. It's more like I *feel* his frustration and anxiety.

He shakes his head. "You don't have to."

He said those words the night of our hookup. One second I was sunk in the deepest postorgasmic bliss I'd ever experienced, muttering, "Stop. I'll fall asleep before I can do you," as he stroked my hair.

The next, he was murmuring, "So fall asleep," and that's when I lost my damn mind.

My other partners had all understood the one-night assignment: a vaguely clinical exchange of I-do-this-to-you and
you-do-that-to-me to establish that neither person was a selfish
asshole only interested in their own good time. A touch *here*, a
redirection to *there*, everyone's pleasure dulled a little by the
effort of paying attention. That's how it was the first time with
someone, which—except for my relationship with Jen—was my
only time with someone.

With Lyle, it was exactly what I didn't let myself want. He
deflected all my attempts to please him, and I shouldn't have
liked it. I should have known better than to float on the high
of his undivided attention, the languor mixed with desperate
anticipation, the freedom to be wholly in my body. I touched
him only because I wanted to, accepted the gift of not worrying
about anyone's pleasure but my own.

But when he tried to skip his turn, I popped up from his
king-size mattress like a frenzied jill-in-the-box. That was
a trap and it was absolutely fucking not happening. There
would be no outstanding balance on my account at the end
of this night.

"You don't have to," he said. In response, I practically barked
orders at him: "Reach up. Hold the headboard. Don't let go."

It was hot, until it was over and I realized I'd done the same
thing I did with Jen. Maybe Lyle was her polar opposite, but it
didn't matter—I was making a balance sheet with someone who
didn't understand give and take. Worse, his best friend was
married to mine. An eternity of uncomfortable encounters at
backyard barbecues loomed like a prison sentence.

I left him sleeping. Left his kind, confused texts on read.
Double-checked the guest list on every Evite for a whole year.
I made sure we were nowhere near each other at 11:59 on New
Year's Eve—or at any other time. I tried not to wonder if the

people who came after me had heard, *You don't have to,* and taken him up on it.

We're not going to sleep together again. But if we're going to work together for the summer, and if I'm going to own a piece of this company by fall, we can do better than giving only what we have to.

I take a step toward him. "Wouldn't it be better if we searched together?"

"Mornings are busy. I should have been tidier, anyway. Go. Shower while there's still time."

He sounds as chill as ever, but I know he likes to write in his book the same way I like to run. If I couldn't find my running shoes, I would lose my damn mind.

"I have time for this. Come on, Lyle." I extend my hand. "Five minutes, then I'll shower whether we've found it or not. You'll feel better."

I wait, knowing he'll have trouble taking instead of giving, remembering how much he liked what I gave him with my hands and mouth after he said I didn't have to.

Gingers aren't the only people who blush around here, I guess.

"Don't leave your girl hanging, bro," Dereck says glumly, heading up the path to the wash station, wearing every piece of clothing he owns plus a towel as a scarf. Poor guy.

I know Lyle only reaches for me because a guest saw us. The only time I've held his hand was when I slipped on his ring.

His palm is dry, his fingers rough from work and water. Given our size difference, it shouldn't be possible for him to put his hand in mine, but that's the feeling I get as my fingers curl around his. This time, he doesn't pull away.

This gesture is so small, and so big. I can count the hands I've held in my lifetime without running out of fingers. Even in middle school, my friends and I thought holding hands was immature. But holding Lyle's hand, I suddenly understand that when you grow up, this touch is reserved for people on the very highest tier of devotion, like your children.

Or your lover.

This barely puts Lyle and me on first base. *Barely.* So why are all the parts on second, third, and home base snapping to attention?

It's nothing. It's a favor for a coworker, a show for the clients. I'm not the one who's supposed to feel better.

But I do.

Scheduling our first road trip to bigger rapids on the first day of Get Out of Here seemed like a bad idea to me. After yesterday, every couple but Mitch and Lori is balancing on a razor's edge of annoyance, one unlucky wobble from shouting things that can't be taken back. But Lyle thinks a success today will help the guests get through this difficult phase.

The access road to the rapids is hillier than most. The Mystery Machine can't handle the towing, so I'll follow behind in Tobin's truck with the boat trailer.

Sloane's voice startles me as I'm checking the ropes securing the canoes. "Hey, McHuge. Mind if I ride with your girl?"

I stick my head out from behind the trailer in time to see the rest of the guests' shoulders collectively slump. They're getting used to being in her presence, but there's still a fair amount of fangirling. It's useful, actually—no one but Brent has asked a single question about me and Lyle when Sloane's been around.

"Lyle has activities planned. You shouldn't miss them." This morning, I glimpsed the words *Car Games: Ideas* in his round, spiky handwriting, which reminds me of apples and arrows.

I wasn't snooping; I'd found his field notebook splayed open

between my backpack and the back door of the tent like it had
flown there in a tidying frenzy. He has enough ideas, analysis,
and local whitewater wisdom in there to run Love Boat sessions
for the entire summer without repeating a single activity. When
the first AI goes rogue, takes over the world, and wants to up-
load McHuge's personality into the database, those notes will
be its source material.

"I don't mind." Sloane smiles with all twenty-eight teeth.
"We'll get in some girl time."

Dereck playfully tugs the loop on the back of Sloane's life
jacket. "I'd rather ride together, Sloanie."

"Next time. I owe you one," she tells him, with a meaningful
look. "All good, McHuge?"

"Far out," Lyle says distractedly, clipping Babe into her
doggy life jacket. She loves to ride in the bow of his boat,
mouth hanging open to taste the wind, but she's a sinker, not
a swimmer.

It sounds less than groovy to me. If Sloane and I get close,
what's the endgame? She flies me down to LA and puts me up in
her guesthouse? She takes me out to the restaurants it's safe for
a movie star to frequent, which are not going to be cheap, fun,
hole-in-the-wall places where I can pick up the check?

Even if the Love Boat can eventually offer her something
prestige-wise, I'll never be on her level money-wise. Sooner or
later, generosity goes sour when it only flows one way.

But I resolved to be nice to her. Also, Petra's watching us,
her eyes flicking back and forth between our faces. We look
much more alike now that the river's washed away Sloane's
makeup and blowout.

"Hop in," I say, opening the passenger door so I have an
excuse to turn away.

"I love your truck." Sloane runs a hand over the dash, then

doesn't seem to know what to do when it comes away filmed with road dust.

"It's not mine. But yeah, it's cool. Do you mind if I don't talk for a minute? I need to concentrate on this stretch of road." I follow McHuge out of the parking lot, taking it easy on the narrow track with the loaded trailer.

"Whatever you need. But then I get a free question. Anything I want." Sloane turns her dusty hand over, turns it back, then seems to give up, wiping it on her white shorts. The mark looks the way McHuge's handprint still feels on my palm—permanent, the kind of thing that won't wash away.

"Ask away," I say when we reach the highway, thinking she'll pick something gossipy and light. The size of Lyle's junk, maybe.

Instead, Sloane opens with, "What's your mom like?"

There are reasons I don't talk about my parents. First, one of them is a sociopath. Second, people act like I shouldn't be over it. They rush to console me, or cry and need to be comforted themselves. Or they get an awful little glow in their eyes, like they're imagining who they'll tell—in *strictest* confidence, mind you.

Sloane may be the only person who won't do any of those things. What could it hurt, to give her this one piece of myself?

"My mom was—" I stop short. She hasn't died, even if it feels that way sometimes. "I mean, I'm sure she still *is* generous to a fault. She loved feeling useful. She wanted things to be nice for us. Always a jar of wildflowers on the table, you know? She could do anything with a can of soup or a box of mac and cheese plus whatever produce was marked down."

She lost herself when my dad went to prison. I learned to trim the bad spots from half-price tomatoes and pluck the mushy tops from last week's asparagus before tossing them into the Kraft Dinner, thinking it was what she wanted.

But Mom needed someone to need her like Dad did. And by the time she got herself together, I could make my own macaroni.

Sloane stares out the windshield at the layers of color unrolling in front of us: gray asphalt, green cedars, pale pearly clouds. "Do you ever hear from him?"

No need to ask who.

"No. Dad's figured out I have nothing to offer him."

She flinches at my phrasing. "Touché, sister mine."

The silence stretches long enough that I think we may be done here, which is both a relief and, strangely, a burden.

I'm considering whether I can figure out Tobin's antique radio when Sloane abruptly says, "My mom's one rule about Gerry was that he had to make the first move. If he wanted to know his daughter, he had to do the work." She looks straight ahead, face impassive, sun-bleached blue eyes flat.

"I was eighteen when he contacted me. You're still kind of stupid at eighteen, you know? Like, I'd made myself an imaginary dad from all my friends' dads. He'd laugh as loud as Zarah's dad, he'd nap on the couch with me like Julia's. I was a romantic, and I was on a teen drama, so I was sure he'd have a sympathetic backstory.

"He asked for money so fast, Stellar. He didn't even wait for the second phone call."

A pained *oof* escapes me. I planned to wait for that second call myself. Sloane would have seen right through me. I'm glad we've entered a series of the Oceans to Peaks Highway's famous twists, and I have an excuse not to look away from the road.

"Yeah." She nods. "He disappeared when I told him my money was held in trust until my twenty-fifth birthday. I've never had my heart broken like that, before or since. It took a lot of therapy to understand how very, very lucky I'd been.

"And then, four months before my twenty-fifth birthday, you called my agency. The day we talked, he reached out, too. My mom and stepdad thought he was dangling you as bait. My manager agreed. You don't know how I regret what happened, Stellar. You were alone."

I'm as over it as I'm ever going to be, but Sloane's story gives me the numb, electric sensation of pushing on an old scar. "You were right to be cautious. I should've guessed he'd come for you."

"And I should've come for *you*." Her voice throbs with regret.

I remember myself at twenty-four, newly graduated from med school, nowhere near as smart or tough as I imagined. I was afraid my dad would come back to haunt me, and afraid he wouldn't, because then I'd never see my mom again.

That was when Dad landed in my inbox for the last time. I hear you're a doctor now. So proud to be your father, he wrote. We need to put the past behind us. Family should help each other.

For days, I deleted his email, then recovered it from the trash. Eventually I sent him a screenshot of my six-figure student loan statement and thanked him for helping with my debt. I was angry; I *wanted* to drive him away. I still cried when he didn't answer.

I imagine Sloane at age twenty-four, not so different from me.

"I was okay." I don't know why my voice wavers. I *was* okay. August rent was paid, my job would cover food, and I'd learned the utilities wouldn't get cut off after one missed bill. I contacted my university, told them my family was relocating to Australia, and arranged to move into my dorm a week early. It worked out.

Sloane shakes her head. "I know it's weird, but I had you investigated. You weren't okay. But by the time I figured it out, it was too late. You were so angry."

"You didn't owe me anything, Sloane." Nothing like what I owe her now.

"I know," she snaps. "Jesus, Stellar, is it always pay-to-play with you? I guess the only way I'm going to get anywhere is to be as blunt as you seem to enjoy being. So I'll just say it: my mom's sick."

I've seen photos of Sloane's mom on her daughter's red carpets. Sloane looks like her: tall, regal, with killer legs and a sneak-attack smile. But she also looks like our dad: cheekbones, jaw, shoulders, ankles. He's in her bones. In *our* bones.

"Shit, I'm sorry. Is it bad?" I don't know Sloane, but I know about the end of life. Empathy comes in a painful rush, another frozen limb reawakening.

"Chronic leukemia. She has a few years, give or take. But it made me think about family. You and I don't have forever to forgive each other. And sooner or later we won't have anyone who shares our fucked-up history, because I don't know about you, but it doesn't look like I'm having kids."

I slow down as McHuge switches on his turn signal ahead of another narrow, overgrown logging road. "I don't want kids either."

"No, I want them. But I'm forty, and I already tried. Two years of mechanical duty fucking with my ex, six months of IVF. One morning I went to my egg-harvesting appointment and realized our marriage wasn't worth another round of giant needles. Got home early and found him watching soccer in his underwear. He'd told me he had a casting call that couldn't be moved. He didn't even *like* soccer."

"What a *dick*," I say, before I remember I'm not that kind of friend to Sloane—not a trash-talking, ex-bashing friend. Not any kind of friend. "You probably shouldn't tell me this."

She tilts her head, hair falling across her pale electric

eyes. There's a streak of dust on her cheek from the hand she
didn't get quite clean on her shorts. "Telling you is the *point*,
Stellar. Marriages come and go. Careers don't last. Friends sell
your secrets to the tabloids. Sisters . . . I think those might be
forever."

That strikes a fucking painful chord. My failed relationship,
my failed career, and the friend I'm terrified to lose: apparently,
Sloane has all those pain points, too. *Stars: they're just like us.*

"I think you'd be a good sister," she offers, her voice shaking
as we bounce over a rocky section of road. "Loyal, judging by
how long you can successfully hold a grudge, my little star."

She earns a glare for calling me "little," but she only grins.
"Don't you want to text each other on our implanted micro-
chips in thirty years? I'll bitch about my hip pain and how the
lines around my mouth make me look like Dad. And you'll say,
'Shut *up*, I have the same lines.'" Her half-shouted "shut *up*" is
very me.

I bark out a laugh. "So what's the catch? We become friends
or . . . what?"

"No catch." She shrugs. "I'm not going to rage quit the course.
Or tell everyone you're faking your engagement."

"What?!" The truck lurches as I reflexively tap the brakes in
terror. "Why would you say that?"

"I'm an *actor*, Stellar. I know fake relationships, on-screen
and off. But I won't tell anyone. I won't even tell McHuge you
like him."

"I don't *like* him," I snap, flushing when I realize I've fallen
into her trap. "Because I *love* him." My voice goes strangled over
the word "love."

Sloane laughs. "Did you seriously think sleeping in the
same tent was enough to fool anyone? Please tell me you have
an exit strategy."

I give up trying to maintain the pretense. "What do you mean, 'exit strategy'?"

"If you're fake dating, you either have to fake break up or you get found out. Usually the latter."

Sloane's forecast puts an icicle of fear right through my heart. Lyle and I can't fake break up in the *first session*. And we absolutely cannot get found out—not with Brent in camp.

I peer through the Mystery Machine's plume of dust. We're a few minutes from the put-in spot—not much time.

"Say you couldn't fake break up. How would you work that problem?"

Sloane considers. "I'd make people think there's more to the relationship than they've seen."

"And how do you do that?"

"Easiest way? Get caught kissing."

Chapter Eleven

It's impossible to steal a private moment with Lyle during the day. Every single guest wants to eat with him and paddle next to him and ask him a million questions. Especially Brent, who made a point of casually inquiring about our engagement in every conversation.

My chance finally comes during afternoon snack. By the time we paddled back to our beach, every couple but Mitch and Lori was somewhere on the spectrum between putting on a brave face and openly speculating about pushing each other's beds out onto the highway. Now they're drowning the day's sorrows in Jasvinder's lemon-ginger scones with vegan clotted cream and cranberry-cognac jam.

I corner Lyle in the parking lot, checking over my shoulder before whispering, "I've been waiting all day to get you alone."

Lyle fumbles the canoe he's racking, dropping the deck plate on his fingers.

"Shhhhhh—" he hisses, and for a second I think I'm finally about to hear him swear.

"—oooooooot." He sticks one finger in his mouth, face creased in agony.

I throw my load of paddles into the trailer with a clatter and dart over, tugging at his elbow. "Spit that out!"

"A little dirt is good for you," he mumbles, shoulders hunched with pain. "Natural."

"You already eat enough dirt. And the human mouth is a hotbed of microbes."

He draws in a sharp breath as I take his hand and palpate the finger as gently as I can. "Sore here?" I look up at his pinched expression. Fingers hurt more than anything, except maybe the heart.

"A little." His voice is strained.

"How about here?" Eyes closed, he shakes his head. "Good. Skin's not broken. No dislocation. No displaced fracture." I flip his hand over, pleased.

When I look up, he's watching my face, an odd look in his darkened eyes. "You have good hands," he says. "Strong. They're very . . . kind."

I cringe at the bright, hot discomfort of his praise. I don't deserve to be called "kind" by Lyle McHugh.

"Good, because they're not very pretty." Prominent knuckles, short bare nails. Doctor hands.

"There's a difference between pretty and beautiful," he says softly, and I don't know why I almost feel like crying.

He runs the pad of one thumb over the purple marks dotting my nail beds. We both have them—there are a million chances a day to catch a finger between a boat and a paddle, a boat and the trailer, a boat and pretty much whatever. "These bruises never seem to hurt you."

I make a dismissive sound, not sure what else to do when he's laying whispering touches across the part of my body with

the highest concentration of nerve endings, with a few excep-
tions. Lips. Tongue. And then there's . . . I take my hands back
and shove them in my pockets, dismayed at how fast my imagination went everywhere it shouldn't have.

"They hurt. But you learn not to say *oops* or *ouch* when
something surprising happens. It freaks out the patients."

He gives me an incredulous look. "You know it's not normal
to pretend you don't feel pain."

"It is what it is. And we're getting off topic. Sloane knows,"
I say in a low voice.

"Sloane knows . . ." He glances around nervously. "She *knows*?
You told her?"

"No, I didn't *tell* her," I snap. "I don't tell anybody anything—
you know that. She guessed. And she thinks others may suspect."
They might, too. At lunchtime, Lori nudged me and suggested
Lyle's lap would be softer than the log I was sitting on, then died
laughing when I looked at his shorts, then quickly down at the
log, and said I didn't think so. "You don't *think* so, huh," she
teased, winking. "Do you *know* so?"

Ironically, I know plenty about Lyle's lap—it's his love I can't
answer questions about. I remember only too well it was me
who suggested this charade, me who talked him into it. The fake
engagement could save the business, if it holds. But it could hurt
him, too. It could hurt us both.

Also, it feels uncomfortably like a con. Isn't this what Dad
did, creating an illusion to throw over people's eyes while he
rifled through their wallets? Isn't this what the old boys' club at
the hospital did, gaslighting me to serve themselves?

This is different, I promise myself. This is a PR response to
a criticism so flimsy that I can't believe we ever had to answer
for it. We're not stealing people's life savings. We're not faking
our qualifications or tricking people into buying a defective

product. Lyle's relationship status will mean nothing once this company's found its legs.

Even if Sloane was right and no deception lasts forever, the plans for our breakup can wait. Right now, we need to plan for our romance.

"Does anyone else know?" Lyle asks, face pinched with worry.

"Well, we can't exactly take a poll. But we could do a better job selling our engagement. We could, um. Kiss."

Sloane gave me a two-minute primer in the truck: Start slow. Keep the contact light; deeper moves can look awkward. Focus on posture and facial expression instead of overselling what's happening with your mouth. Pick a time and place that suggests you *weren't* trying to get seen.

I try to remember when I've seen her kiss Dereck, and can't. But those two have nothing to prove, I guess.

Lyle frowns. "You said you didn't want to kiss."

"*You* said you didn't want to know me at all," I shoot back. "Of course I didn't want you to kiss me."

"I didn't . . ." He grips a rung of the trailer until his knuckles shine white in the green-tinted daylight under the forest canopy. When he speaks again, his voice is as soft as his fist is tight. "I didn't mean it that way. You wouldn't even stand in the same room as me, Stellar. At Liz's improv showcase, you did a heck of an impression of somebody who wanted me to go away forever. When I said the thing about us not wanting to know each other, I was saying it first. So you wouldn't have to."

Trust Lyle to try to give me everything, even a way out of a difficult conversation.

"You don't have to say uncomfortable things on my behalf. There's enough awkwardness between us that we can share the pain."

I do like his smile when it's subtle, with a slight press of his full lips, a little crinkle around the eyes, and a lift of his crooked brow that looks like a laugh instead of an exasperated question.

"So," I say, already regretting having volunteered to say uncomfortable things. "We should, um, plan to kiss a few times. In front of people. Well, not in *front* of people, but where they might see us accidentally on purpose."

He nods at a blue-and-white baseball cap on one of the logs surrounding the parking lot. "Willow will be missing her hat any minute now."

"You want to do it *now*?" I thought we would work the problem a little before plunging in. Everything feels suddenly too large: the truck, the trailer, the sway of wind-tossed branches overhead, Lyle.

Lyle.

I swear his warmth radiates across the careful twelve inches between us. Suddenly I smell not the lemons and sugar I could be eating, but the earth underneath our feet, his damp, clean hair, and what's left of his sunscreen after the water has had its way.

We stand there, the sounds of wind and river and a rise of laughter from the clearing coming and going. He looks down, and I look up, and something hovers shimmering between us. He's still got a hand wrapped around the square metal rail of the trailer. With one quick move, he could bracket me in. The idea puts a shiver between my shoulder blades.

"Do you . . ." I clear my throat. "I thought you wanted to kiss me now?"

"I'm not kissing you, Stellar," he says, voice rough. "We've done that before, and you sneaked out of my house without waking me up or leaving a note. You didn't answer any of my texts. I was worried I hurt you. Or scared you."

I let myself scoff a little. "You couldn't hurt me, Lyle. And I don't scare easily."

Am I sure, though? Didn't I imagine him giving everything away, unable to hold on to anything, not even me? When I imagined him letting me go, was I so scared I decided to let *him* go, instead?

It was nice having a safe little fantasy that he had feelings for me, and never having to find out whether he'd keep me in real life. It was nice thinking I had something, without ever having to risk anything for it.

His breath comes out in a rush. "And how was I supposed to know that? People get nervous around me; it happens. Or maybe you didn't want to tell me I wasn't gentle enough when . . ."

I want to run my thumbs over his cheeks where they're stained crimson. No—I want to fit my cheeks to his and *feel* the heat of whatever he didn't say. But unless he bends down, I can't physically do that, so I touch one hand to his chest, right where my cheek would land if I stepped forward and leaned in.

His black T-shirt is soft under my hand. It's faded at the neck and sleeves where his life jacket doesn't block the sun; there's a fingernail-sized raised circle at his neck where his peace sign must lie. Under a decal of green cedars framing a night sky, my fingertips find the good hardness of his chest, the shift of cotton against his skin, the subtle change in tension as my hand lands, and stays.

"I wasn't hurt." Not in my body, anyway. "But if you don't want to do this, we won't. We'll figure out something else."

"I didn't say I don't want to." His voice drops to a deeper hush, vibrating against my fingertips. Vocal fremitus, it's called—the vibrations you feel through someone's chest. I was taught to diagnose what's underneath: liquid, solid, air? He is in every way solid, if these vibrations mean anything. I can't imagine someone steadier than him.

My heart jumps against my ribs, a hundred beats per

minute. Maybe faster. Sloane described kissing as something choreographed and unemotional, but if it were, I wouldn't feel so scared with every second it doesn't happen. I wouldn't want him to lean into me and wrap me up until I could breathe again.

He looks at the ground, eyes obscured by ginger-gold lashes. "When someone walks away, I don't chase. It's not something *I*"—he gestures at himself like he's Frankenstein—"can do and still be the person I want to be. So even if it's not real, this needs to come from you."

"Right." I ghosted him then, so if he makes the first move now, the balance sheet will be all off. That's why he couldn't propose. That's why he can't kiss me. It makes perfect sense.

Except how am I supposed to kiss him if he doesn't help me? I can't reach his face way up there. He has the power to equalize us physically; I don't.

Restlessness rises up my chest and over my back like high water. Even though it's the end of a long, physical day, the urge to run grips me like a fist. I have to get this over with *immediately*. We'll probably be terrible together, which will be good, actually. Then we'll never have to think of kissing ever again. We can find something else to convince the clients we're in love. I don't know what, but I can work the problem.

"This way," I say, stalking toward the log where Willow's hat still sits. She's probably forgotten it's here. No one will see this ridiculous display, and that's for the best, too.

I scramble up the log's fourteen-inch girth. "Now we're equal," I say, taking him by the shoulders.

I pull him in fast and lay one on him, framing his face with my hands to hide the fact that we have no idea how to act like we're in love.

His body stiffens, arms held slightly away from his sides. His lips are closed hard, like he's dry-kissing his grandma.

This is a disaster.

I grab his elbows, bringing his hands around my back in a way I hope looks sexy. His stiff limbs poke me in all the wrong ways.

"This is like kissing a frozen steak," I mutter. "Relax your mouth, please."

"I *am* relaxed," he grits out, teeth clicking against mine. "What, am I supposed to use tongue in front of the guests?"

"It might help!"

"*Fine.*"

He goes soft, and the world tilts.

No, that's not right. It's not the world tilting, it's me, dizzy with this unexpected pleasure all light and fizzy on my lips, rising straight up to my brain. There's an art to the way he follows when I move, giving us power and momentum while I steer. His mouth is firm and sweet, his tongue like a surging forward stroke, clean and unhurried.

He knows how to move in tandem, I realize. He paddles like he's dancing with the boat, and he kisses like he's dancing with me.

The breeze shifts, and I'm caught in a riptide of the sharp scent of cedar and sun-warmed skin. I'm swamped, hit broadside by a rogue wave.

I turn my head to take more, sliding my thumbs beneath his ears and my fingers along his neck, seeking the hammer of his pulse under my palm. He's so urgently *alive* against me, his heartbeat vibrating into my mechanical ink. My stomach swoops like I'm falling, so I press my body to his steadiness and don't stop, don't stop. He's holding us up, rescuing us, our mouths fused like I wished him into existence.

It's exactly like it was a year ago in that I'm immediately starving, and nothing like it was a year ago in that nobody's

wrestling for control. He's not trying to give with no expecta-
tions, and I'm not fighting to give back what he gives me, no
more and no less.

This time, both of us know he's going to take, and I'm going
to take charge. The thought brings a tingling heat to my skin. He
makes a sound—half low hum, half sharp exhalation—at the feel
of my teeth on his lip. He's so warm under his shirt, and hot, and
hard, and soft. His arms turn from pointy Ken-doll appendages
to living muscle, hooking up my back and over my shoulders,
pulling me in and under like we've slipped below the waterline
where civilization ceases to exist.

"Oh! Oh, excuse me, I'm so sorry!"

Our eyes fly open. Willow. The hat.

My heart is booming, the big hard slams visible through my
shirt. I'm breathing fast. If I saw myself in the ER, I'd put myself
on oxygen and order a dozen tests, because I am not well.

"I forgot my—Never mind, I see it. Sorry!" Willow stammers,
snatching her hat with a swish and scampering away.

Lyle has the presence of mind to let go slowly. I forget how
Sloane said we should break apart—*something something lingering look*, maybe?

Sloane's all about how things should end. But this doesn't
feel like an ending at all. The two of us stare at each other as
our arms come back to our own bodies. It's like we broke the
seal on something, and now we have to buy it.

"Will *that* do it?" There's a waver in Lyle's voice like this
kiss nearly killed him, too. It occurs to me that he has an acting
background, if you count improv comedy. He could probably
pretend he's okay when he's not.

But me? I'm not okay at all, and I'm sure he knows it.

Chapter Twelve

Everything bothers me this morning.

For one, yesterday's kiss was a huge fail. Yes, Willow saw Lyle and me all entwined and losing our heads, but for the rest of the evening, everyone else saw us passing dipping sauces for Jasvinder's spring rolls without letting our fingers touch. I can't blame Lyle for keeping his distance. I forgot everything Sloane said and basically tried to eat his soul like a mythical night-traveling monster.

For two, it's the fourth day of the course, which is the day I always get grumpy and homesick on an expedition. I get past it in a couple of days, and by the end I never want to leave. But today, adventure is outweighed by the desire to sleep in my own bed, alone, instead of a too-small tent where Lyle's absence pushes against my edges almost as much as his presence.

Last night, he caught me reading his copy of *Meditations*. I picked it up after evening chores, mostly because it had migrated underneath my cot, but then I started hearing Marcus Aurelius's words in Lyle's voice and I didn't want to stop. When he came in I pretended I was only reading to pass the time, but I'm no good at acting and we both know it.

I lay awake for a long time, keenly aware of a particular lack of privacy I hadn't thought much about before I kissed him. I kept thinking about his lower lip, for some reason—how I'd thought it would be soft, but it had been so firm. Biting was definitely not in Sloane's Hollywood kissing manual, but the memory—my teeth, his mouth, the rush of his breath when I'd taken his lip and held it not quite tightly enough to hurt—lit my skin from the inside.

And I couldn't do a damn thing about it. Not in a rustling nylon sleeping bag an arm's length from the sounds of Lyle's 100 percent awake breathing pattern.

Morning chores couldn't help but be weird after a night like that. It's almost impossible to keep secrets in camp, which makes me worry about who else has figured out mine. Ours.

For example, Petra and Trevor go for a private paddle every night, looking giggly and excited. But when I brought hot water to the Rainforest Dome this morning, she opened the flap wide enough for me to see their beds were pushed as far apart as possible, like they're coworkers sharing a hotel room.

I found a tin mug in the jumble of shoes outside Brent and Willow's tent, the dregs of last night's bedtime drink crusted inside. I instantly imagined Brent denying the mug was his, Willow looking down miserably and saying nothing, and me having to go for a long run. Lyle would have to have another word about food attracting hungry animals.

And when I stopped outside Lori and Mitch's tent with a soft call of "Hot water," Lori burst out of the tent bare-ass naked to prove my instinct about seeing her butt was right on. I advised her to cover up to avoid mosquito bites; she giggled while making sex faces at a mortified but still-smirking Mitch. They may be the only people in camp who are getting any.

And now, a short drive later, we're at the launch point for the Rolling Stones, a rapid named for its long, straight, forceful series of standing waves, which can also be called a tongue. Never let it be said that paddlers don't enjoy a vintage concert T-shirt and a good strong dad joke.

"Circle up, my siblings," Lyle says, raising both hands above his head like he's making himself big to frighten off a bear and managing to look more like a teddy bear. "Today we are ready to challenge ourselves in body and spirit! As we discussed last night at campfire, the Stones has the gnarliest waves we've ridden so far. More hazards, too. Don't be fooled by the gentle outwash—unless you tuck into an eddy, the current will sweep you away from your friends.

"We're looking to follow the tongue—smooth green water that's usually heading where you want to go. The tongue can be mellow and gentle, but also exciting and unexpected, and even euphoric by the end."

I'm going to die. How can he *say* things like that and not remember what he did with me—what we did with each other?

"Remember, there are no gold medals for coming first! Stay with your friends. Bring it in for a group cheer!" He sticks his hand into the center of the circle.

I nudge my shoulder into the tense gap that's persisted between Brent and Willow since the tin mug talk went exactly as I predicted.

"This won't be a problem for us," Brent says, talking over my head like I'm not even there. At least he's saying something nice to his wife.

He promptly ruins it with, "*I'll* get us through."

I breathe through my nose, trying like hell to dispel the familiar, electrifying surge of anger. The fateful night I stood in front of that refrigerator, staring at the neat rows of 2 percent milk and 10 percent cream, this same injustice crackled through my heart like 200 joules of direct current, defibrillating the monster inside.

That time, it lost me my job. This time, I'd be wise to learn my lesson and shut my mouth before I alienate a man with the power to help—or hurt—the Love Boat. As Lyle would say, I'm not in a position to judge their relationship.

But I *am* in a position to judge the dynamic in their boat, and it's lopsided as hell.

Willow's shoulders roll inward, and my fists clench. Every straw is the last one with me, it seems.

"And, um, we forgot to tell you!" I blurt. "Today everyone's switching positions! Bow paddler goes to the stern, and vice versa. Everyone gets to do the other person's job and, uh, take their perspective."

All eyes turn to me. No one says a word. Lyle's uneven eyebrow is way, way up. I'm surprised, too: I said I didn't care about the instructional side of things, and guess what, it looks like I do. I really, really want this to work.

"It's gonna be, um, so fun!"

Unlike when Lyle says something is fun, no one looks like they believe me. Even when people don't agree with his definition of "fun," they believe he's genuinely into whatever it is.

There's a lot of groundwork to Lyle's persona, I realize. Underneath the relentless chill, the old-school catchwords, and the vaguely spiritual pronouncements, there's a willingness to give and give again. People feel safe with him.

I haven't laid that groundwork, and it shows. When I run out of cheery, positive things to say, they glance over at him for confirmation: *Are we really doing this?*

Stay with me, Lyle, I plead with my eyes. I shouldn't have sprung this on him, but he won't call out a co-instructor's mistake in front of the guests. I'm the only one who can say I was wrong, and with every second that ticks by, I'm more convinced I'm right.

It's not even the halfway mark of the course, yet nobody questions which paddling position they take anymore.

Like I never questioned anything at the hospital until it was too late.

Lyle dips his chin almost imperceptibly. It may look unintentional, but he has incredible control of every part of his body. I try not to sag with relief.

"Thanks for catching that, Stellar. This is great real-life training that could come in handy on river-running trips like the capstone. It's important for *all* of us to experience our partner's role firsthand, even me. That's why Stellar will be today's lead instructor, and I'll be taking a back seat."

I blink in surprise. This must be what he means by *yes, and.* At this moment, I wish I'd paid more attention to his improv sayings. Or read his book. A kind person would have done that.

Sloane appears at my side as everyone else is heading to the water. "Do we *have* to switch? I'd rather not."

The spiky burst of irritation in my belly is sharp enough to feel like fear. My authority with this group is tenuous as hell. If Sloane and Dereck bail out, no one else will participate either. My debut as lead instructor will turn into my curtain call.

That's what happened to Kat, the other woman who got hired at Grey Tusk General. She was named chair of the equipment committee that year, and suddenly everyone discovered a brand-new willingness to go to the mat for specific brands of video laryngoscopes and disposable suture trays. The previous chair's emails had dropped straight into the void; Kat's became reply-all slugfests.

She lasted six months before the department chief removed

her, saying he needed someone who could "keep the peace." As far as my male colleagues were concerned, the precedent had been set: a woman couldn't handle a committee, like a woman couldn't carry a superhero franchise if even one of the sequels failed to break box office records.

Sloane should understand what's at stake for me, with her gritty female-led film that screams "series potential" and its risky gender flip of the promiscuous gentleman spy trope.

"Is there some reason you can't?" Oof, there's so much *history* in my voice.

"I'm more comfortable in the bow."

"The point of the exercise is to be uncomfortable."

"Please, Stellar. It wouldn't have to be a big thing."

"But it *would* be a big thing," I whisper, impatient to get going. Other guests are already launching their swapped boats.

"And what if I can't?" Her sharp tone brings my head around, but her expression stays mild and inquisitive, like she's asking me for stroke correction.

"You *can*. You're strong, you're skilled, you have great instincts. Unless there's something you're not telling me?"

Her mouth tightens. "Forget I asked." She stumbles a little on the rocks as she wheels away, leaving me unsettled.

Lyle's canoe drifts in from behind me once I get onto the water, Babe studiously looking away as usual.

"It's not too late to back down, Stellar. Save this for another day."

"Is it *that* bad of an idea? Because if it isn't, I'd really appreciate your support."

"I'll always back you up, Stellar J. If you've got an idea of what you want the clients to learn from this, in the water and out of it, then we're on."

I tip my head at Brent and Willow, still on the riverbank.

Brent makes impatient gestures, deliberately rocking the boat as he climbs into the bow, making it hard for Willow to hold the canoe steady from shore. Establishing a precedent, no doubt.

"People get used to seeing things from their own perspective. They wouldn't be half so likely to want their partner to 'Get Out of Here' if they had any idea of the work they were doing. We need some of the dynamics around here to switch up."

He nods slowly. "So, *they* need the dynamics to switch up—or *you* need that?"

"Everybody needs that." It's true, but there's a guilty little itch behind my breastbone saying I'm doing the right thing for the wrong reasons.

"Okay. I believe in you. You know what you're doing."

On the short paddle to the rapids, Lori and Mitch switch it up like pros, pulling ahead with a smoothness that makes the others hustle to prove themselves. Brent's getting a big dose of what it's like to be the bow paddler, namely that Willow can critique his every move from the stern while he can't even see her.

"I'm doing my best! I don't have eyes in the back of my head." Willow greets this protestation with the disbelieving silence it deserves, given how he's expected her to have eyes in the back of her head for the last three days.

It's delicious.

We come ashore above the rapids to scout the hazards. After we reconvene in a big friendly eddy that exits directly into whitewater, all eyes turn expectantly to me.

Lyle always says something inspiring at this point.

"Um . . . we'll go ducky style, one after the other. Leave two boat lengths between each canoe. Everybody, uh, listen to your partner and take their perspective. Have some fun, and when you get to the outwash, thank your partner for all the work you didn't even realize they were doing. Let's go!"

I meant to lead everyone down the rapids single file, but before I've even turned around, Brent barks, "We're first." He switches sides and digs in, turning his canoe toward the eddy line where calm water meets current.

"I'm not ready," Willow yelps, nailing Brent with a stream of water from the tip of her paddle as she scrambles to switch to the left.

"Brent, wait," I say, swiping for their gunwale, but they're out of reach.

"This is why I take the stern, so someone's in control," he snaps, turning to face her. The nose of their canoe swings hard to the right as Willow's steering stroke goes unmatched by Brent in the bow.

"Control *yourself*," Willow bites back.

"Watch your line, watch your line!" I yell, paddling after them.

The accelerating current whips the nose of their boat into the rough, splashy flow at the edge of the tongue. Water sluices over the sides of their canoe. The lower they ride with the additional weight, the faster their boat fills.

I put my hands out to the side to signal *stop*, but Sloane and Dereck have already followed me like the next ducklings in line.

"No! Wait. Everybody wait," I shout, but Dereck and Sloane leap forward as Brent and Willow's canoe sinks out from underneath them.

I can't hear what Dereck exclaims, but he's pointing his paddle at Willow's helmeted head bobbing toward shore. Sloane interprets this in the paddling tradition: Dereck's pointing where he wants the boat to go. She's incredibly strong, her hard dig easily overpowering Dereck's. He shrieks in dismay as they enter the tongue broadside to the waves.

"Fuck!" Sloane sounds like it physically hurts her to switch to the left. Suddenly, her big strong pull is gone, replaced by a cramped half stroke that does nothing to get them out of doom's path. They disappear over the crest of a standing wave, reappearing on top of the next one as an upside-down boat and two more bright helmets floating in the current.

Source control, I think, an emergency checklist flickering to life from behind a long-closed door in my brain. A surge of anxiety accompanies the list, like when anything about my medical career occurs to me. But I have no choice.

Get help. That comes first. Then source control to stop the hemorrhaging.

I turn to hail Lyle, but he's already signaling for the remaining clients to stay where they are. Lori and Mitch are heading back to the put-in spot, presumably to portage past the rapids on the pathway next to the river. Trevor and Petra seem distracted by something upstream. They're out of the way for now—or are they? Inexplicably, they look at each other, then start paddling. They tip almost as if they're trying to, Petra's paddle flashing as they tumble into the churning water.

Everyone's lost their minds but me, but at least Lyle's coming down to help me with the murder scene at the outwash.

Sloane shoots me a pissed-off look from beside her boat. She's functionally been my family for a little over twenty-four hours, but I can read *I told you* so on my sister's face. Dereck has managed to climb back in the boat, shivering as he bails with a plastic measuring cup tied to a rope.

Willow might be in control of her waterlogged canoe if Brent were helping her, but he's whirling around in the water shouting "My shoe! I lost my shoe," while Willow screams back, "Don't put your feet down! Float on your back!" Some distance downstream, Trevor and Petra are swimming for shore, their abandoned boat bumping gently in an eddy near the outwash.

Mitch and Lori tromp out of the foliage carrying their canoe. Lori can't see much with the hull over her head, but Mitch surveys the carnage with a dispassionate look, the canoe braced on one strong shoulder. "That went poorly."

I bristle, very much aware that I liked Mitch's blunt, critical style before she directed it at me. "Everything's okay! Stay cool while we sort ourselves out!"

Sloane glares at me, shivering. "Easy for you to say from up there," she gripes, just as Dereck accidentally nails her right in the helmet with a cupful of water. Sloane floats for a second, eyes closed, then ever so slowly reaches up and pushes her sodden bangs out of her face, coming away with a gritty handful of sand from the bottom of the canoe.

"Oh, shit. Sorry, Sloane." Dereck leans way over to see whether she's okay. The canoe ejects him, soaking Sloane again. Dereck comes up spluttering, then draws a mighty breath to scream, "*Why* is this country so fucking *freezing*?"

A *look* comes over my sister's face. I've seen that look in the trailer for *Nighthawke*. I've seen it on myself, and it's never not meant trouble.

She kicks herself onto her stomach and heads for my canoe.

Chapter Thirteen

"Don't do it, Sloane," I warn, as she closes in on my boat like Jaws. We're in a calm patch at an elbow in the river, the water deepening from the foamy pale green of the rapids to a more tranquil sea-glass shade. Tall spikes of purple loosestrife show their first few flowers near the flat brown shore, the muddy sand quickly giving way to aspen and baby cedar trees framed by distant snow-dusted peaks.

I can't make any big moves when there are this many people in the water. Also, paddling away from a swimming client seems like a bad PR move when Brent's watching.

"Sloane! Don't do it! I need to be in my boat so I can help—"

She levers herself out of the water, pressing down hard on the gunwale and sending me flying.

"Nooo—" My yell cuts off as I go under, replaced by bubbles and rushing water and the ice-pick ache of glacial runoff against my forehead. The noise of my thoughts subsides, turning dull and muted like the knock of a paddle against a canoe.

When I come up, all I can hear is my sister laughing.

"Sloane! You psychopath! What did you do that for?" I whip a curtain of water in her direction.

"You looked too dry. Also too warm. So I decided to help out my s—uh, my instructor in her moment of need." She splashes me back, then turns around and soaks Dereck, who's clinging to the side of the canoe.

"Hey!" Dereck protests. "What did I ever do to you?"

"You dumped a pound of sand down the front of my shirt." Sloane scrapes her fingers under her collar and comes away with quite a bit of evidence to support her accusation.

"I did it by accident!"

"Yes. Me too." Sloane backstrokes away, laughing. As she passes Brent, floating on his back with his toes in the air, Sloane pulls off his recovered shoe and keeps going, waving it in the air.

Within ten seconds, everyone's splashing and screaming. Even Lori yells bloodthirsty sports chants from the shore, kicking big rooster tails of water that only hit her and Mitch, and also Dereck, who's sourly paddling toward land.

Downstream, Trevor and Petra have made it to the riverbank. Their excited jumping settles into a surprised stillness, then he pulls her close, fastening his lips to hers in a back-bending, mind-melding kiss for the ages.

I look away, feeling like I've invaded their privacy. Remembering how when I kissed Lyle, the whole idea was to get someone to invade ours. I wish I could take that kiss back. It feels cheap compared to the real thing.

Lyle pulls up in his canoe. Babe leans down to give me a businesslike lick on my cheek, and I draw back, startled.

"Babe thinks that was a good exercise," Lyle says. He smiles as Sloane sneaks up behind Willow, toppling her into the water with a shriek.

I look up at him, feeling so strange. I want his praise very badly, but I may not deserve it, considering.

"Really? Was she listening when I hijacked your lesson and made everyone do something they'd never practiced before and didn't want to do?"

"No. But she can see people are turning something bad into something good. She likes a therapeutic breakthrough as much as the next dog."

I look again, but with Lyle's eyes. I've never seen Sloane laugh as hard as she's laughing now, playing keep-away with Brent's shoe. Willow's gotten her hands on a bailing bucket and is very capably defending her position halfway up a large boulder. Lori's chafing Dereck's arms in a motherly way.

"Sometimes . . . sometimes people need to go in," I say, holding on to his gunwale, stunned to hear his words coming out of my mouth. *Huh.* When I look up, Lyle's smiling, but his eyes darken like they did after we kissed, smoldering an inch away from mine.

For a second I think he's going to lean down, and I'm going to pull myself up, and we're going to make that first kiss irrelevant, right here, right now.

And that's when I spot a one-person kayak heading our way.

My asshole detector starts alarming. No one should be coming down the rapids when we're in the water. We're not blocking their line of descent, but even so, they should give us a chance to get clear, for safety.

The paddler parks their boat in an eddy, then positions a a long-lensed camera to capture action shots for a flotilla of bright-blue boats assembling above the rapids. Their optic-yellow safety gear shows beautifully against the pale foaming water, the dark-green forest, and the gray rocks. Even their paddles have blue shafts and yellow blades.

Until now, I liked how Lyle's aversion to photos made the Love Boat feel less performative than other expeditions I'd worked on. I'd seen people's faces fall when the photos weren't what they'd hoped, as if one image of themselves making an awkward move had the power to erase every moment of joy they'd had in the boat.

Up against the other group's sunny, unified colors, our rainbow fleet looks amateurish. A little like we bought the canoes secondhand and couldn't get them all the same color.

I shake the water out of my whistle and give one long blast.

The water fight dries up when people realize what's happening, and the fun evaporates completely after the first two-person kayak successfully challenges the rapids. The paddlers have the inefficient movements of beginners, but kayaks are nimbler than canoes. The Rolling Stones look a lot easier for these people than they did for us, with our switched-up boat positions, bad timing, and sketchy communication.

At the outwash, the paddlers' heads turn to our bunch, soaked and shivering, half the boats still not retrieved. Much like the unfortunate action shots I'd seen on other expeditions, their pitying frowns show us what we look like.

Sloane limply tosses Brent's shoe at him and wades toward land. Brent swipes for the shoe, misses, and has to swim after it. On the shore, Dereck strips off his sodden shirt, balls it up, and throws it to the sand like he's done with this forever. Even Lori takes an apprehensive step back, joining Mitch at the forest's edge.

When the next kayak reaches the outwash, Lyle shudders like the *Titanic* throwing its engines into reverse. "Stellar. I need you to get back in your boat and rescue the canoes. Make it look like we meant to stop here. Please. As fast as you can."

"What's wrong?" He so rarely asks for anything. To hear him sound unnerved . . . it's unnerving.

"No time. Go," he says, a desperate undercurrent in his voice.

My boat is near the sandy bank. It'll take me a couple of minutes to swim over and get back in with no help.

A third kayak arrives in the wash, bearing an instructor type and a straight-backed person who's not paddling particularly hard.

"Having some trouble, *Mr.* McHugh?" the stiff man enunciates over the rush of whitewater, pale lips pursed in satisfaction. The man's voice is pleasant, yet I've never heard so many insults packed into so few words. His diction is precise in the way of people who want you to know their vocabulary words have more syllables than yours.

It can't be. Then again, who else but Lyle's douchecanoe of a PhD advisor would call Lyle "Mister" with the same malice he flaunted in Brent's article?

I pause my life jacket–hampered front crawl to take a closer look at the one human on earth who truly, deeply hates Lyle.

He's maybe fifty-five or sixty, villainous in a picky, particular way: navy wool shirt double-buttoned at the wrist, hollowed cheeks, fresh shave. Yellow sport lenses shield his flat, dead eyes. Somehow, he gives a neon whitewater helmet the vibe of a Tilley hat with the chin strap pulled tight.

In his outsize custom canoe, Lyle is taut with stress. I'd be rigid, too, if someone had pulled "Mr. McHugh" on me for the second time.

"Professor Fisher," Lyle replies. His courtesy makes me want to swim over there and capsize the professor's boat the way Sloane tipped mine. I couldn't tip them, though. The kayak is wide and flat, with two full-grown men as ballast. I don't have the power to defend Lyle, like I didn't have the power to defend anything else I loved.

In an instant, I'm furious. Rage pours from my heart like an oil spill, contaminating everything in sticky blackness. Any spark now will send me sky high.

I bolt my mouth shut and focus on breathing through my nose.

"Well," Fisher says, glancing delightedly down his long, thin, sunburned nose. "Too bad we caught you at such a *difficult* moment. But no better time to introduce you to the River of Love, our research-expedition-slash-relationship-counseling pilot project. Over the next year, we'll publish three to five papers in major journals, then follow up with *my* second book."

All the locks holding my mouth shut fail at once. "What?! You can't publish *our* idea. That's plagiarism, you jackass."

The professor fixes his fishy eyes on me. "The idea was generated and refined in *my* lab, under *my* supervision. I have a right to use it. Perhaps more right than you do, Miss . . . ?"

I turn to Lyle, who looks stricken. "Is that true? Can he . . . can he do that?"

Before he can answer, another tandem kayak successfully challenges the Stones, the bow paddler whooping with exhilaration.

That voice. For some reason, I know it, but I can't put a face to it until she whoops again, and the rest of the group whoops back.

I picture a white woman on a stage, wireless microphone in hand, the picture cutting between her open-mouthed excitement and the studio audience's wild, screaming applause.

And there she is, drifting up to the professor, her cheeks round with a huge smile.

Renee Garner. That is Renee Garner, who screwed us by pulling her people out of our course at the last minute, apparently so she could join forces with the person whose lies made our company look bad in the first place. The other team must be able to handle her security when we couldn't—yes, there's a boat full of earpiece-wearing goons in an eddy.

It's too much. Instead of doing one of the few things Lyle's ever really needed from me, I float there, stunned. Fisher has our idea, and our location, and our fucking celebrity endorsement. I'd bet my boat he's got a generous research grant. No wonder people are backing out of the Love Boat. He's probably stealing our guests, too.

Renee turns her big smile our way. "Great day on the water! Are you all having the best time, too? Oh!" She takes a surprised breath. "Dr. McHugh. So nice to run into you."

I let out a high, disbelieving laugh just as a familiar voice says, "*Stellar?*"

My heart drops through my body like a rock. I wish I could sink to the bottom of the river with it.

"Kat," I say hoarsely to the person bobbing in a solo kayak. "It's been a while."

She looks the same as the last time I saw her at Grey Tusk General. Better, even. I'd shared my investigation with her; she'd promised to have my back in the departmental meeting. But every time I spoke up, she said nothing. Over and over, I tried to catch her eye as the painful realization bloomed like a bloodstain: she was looking away on purpose, protecting herself while I hung my ass out to the breeze.

I want to help Lyle, but Kat knows things about me that could do a lot of damage if she said them in front of Fisher. I kick away from the boats, drawing her with me.

"You're doing . . . the same thing we are?" she asks, biting her lip. "I'm the team doctor for the River of Love. Are you the doc with your crew, too?"

"Seems like it," I say grimly.

"Oh, that's good. That's great," she gushes. "I heard you were working for . . . you know what, it doesn't matter. I'm glad to see you're back in medicine."

I feel the tug of my old life like there's a suture knotted around my breastbone, and Kat has the long tail wrapped around her fist.

And the worst of it is, I want what she's got. Everything I loved and lost: belonging, fellowship, the secret language of medicine. Colleagues excited to share an impossible blood gas result or the subtlest triangular whisper on a chest X-ray, almost missed—a bad diagnosis caught in the nick of time.

"Thanks." I can't trust myself to say more.

"Do you need help?" She looks around, clearly uncertain whether she should do her job or mine.

No way am I getting in her debt, now or ever. "This is actually a planned exercise," I lie. "The whole point is not to help them. So thanks, but no thanks."

She blinks at the sawn-off barrel of my refusal, her smile faltering. Guilt nips at my conscience. What happened with the milk wasn't her fault, and of the two of us, I could argue she was smarter. She kept her head down and kept her job, while I exiled myself to Brittle Rock to finish burning out.

I want to get back to Lyle. He's probably refusing to defend himself against the professor. He needs someone angry and quick on her feet who'll say the things he can't.

"I should g—"

"You never answered my email," Kat interrupts.

"I never got an email from you." The department deactivated my work email the day I left. A few months later, I blocked the hospital domain on my personal email. My therapist said it was better for me not to see that no one had reached out to say *Hi* or *How are you* or *We miss you*, not even the nurses. Sometimes I'd get fury-inducing donation requests from the hospital's charitable foundation, or an announcement about someone's promotion that brought a toxic flood of longing and shame.

"I'll resend. Things have changed since you retired from the department," she says brightly, as if I chose to leave and they threw me a nice party. "I'm the head of human resources now. It's a whole new ER. Clean slate."

The sting of it, especially coming from Kat. She should know only *some* people get their slates wiped clean.

"Kat, I can't—I have to go."

"Check your junk folder!" she calls, paddling off after the rest of her crew.

I swim back to Lyle, who's floating on his own, Babe worriedly licking sunscreen off his cheek. "Hey. Let's regroup and reset. Take lunch, maybe."

He watches Fisher and Renee skim away, saying nothing.

On shore, Sloane's stripped down to her sports bra, wringing half a river out of her sun shirt. Brent limps dramatically out of the water, one shoe in his hand. Trevor and Petra have made it back to the group, but they're unhelpfully gesticulating to where their canoe is drifting toward a sieve—a downed tree whose branches dip dangerously into the current.

We look bad. We look weak. Like they can push us up against a locker and take our lunch money anytime they want it. Like they already *did* take our lunch money.

We are so, so fucked.

Chapter Fourteen

A fire ban came down this afternoon, so when campfire time rolls around, the guests glumly stare at Lyle's alternative: a light bulb, a battery-powered fan, and a metal ring festooned with pieces of yellow, orange, and red cellophane that together give the flickering vibes of a low-rent production of *Lord of the Flies*.

"S'mores aren't the same when you don't toast them over the embers," Brent comments idly.

Willow rises from her seat across the firepit—quite far from her husband, I note—marches over, and snatches his share of Jas's homemade bourbon-vanilla marshmallows with lightly spiced dark chili chocolate and gluten-free shortbread.

"I'll eat yours, if it's not good enough." He's so stunned, his finger and thumb stay in an empty C shape long enough for her to peel back the wrapper, take a huge bite, and pointedly lick chocolate off her upper lip.

At Circle, she eviscerated him with a devastating recital of the support she needed, and didn't get, as the stern paddler. No one came to Brent's rescue, not even Lyle. Definitely not me, especially after this afternoon's long, chatty exchange between Brent and Fisher, who know each other from the hit piece.

I ended up having to lead most of the debrief. Fair enough, since I engineered today's tragedy, but Lyle was worryingly absent from the process. He seemed absent from *himself*, unable to muster a single groovy comment.

The one thing I was right about: today was a nice segue from Get Out of Here into I Get You. Our group rallied bravely, portaging their boats to the top of the rapids and posting a mood-boosting second run, swim free. Mitch and Lori ran the rapids with Lori in the stern, and Mitch agreed to check in with Lori before making decisions for both of them. Dereck's frosty mood thawed somewhat once he got dry and warm, although he elected to walk to the fallen tree to check his messages during the first half of campfire.

Trevor and Petra couldn't praise each other enough. Their blushing glances during campfire made me wish I'd stocked the first aid kit with complimentary earplugs as well as the gross of condoms Lyle crammed between the bandages. I can't be the only one thinking about blocking out their inevitable all-night bangfest.

I make a weak excuse about a scraped canoe so I can drag Lyle down to the beach. Lori wolf-whistles as we leave the circle of artificial firelight at the same time Petra and Trevor head for the tents.

It's a nice night to discuss the demise of our hopes and dreams—clear, with delicate summer stars lining the southern horizon, a fresh breeze blowing away the mosquitoes. Far above, the cedars sigh at the river, too old to bother with our pesky, fleeting human problems. A million tiny frogs fall silent as we approach the shore, then start up one by one, too young to be cautious for long.

"Hmm," Lyle says, stroking the gash in the bottom of Trevor and Petra's purple canoe. "Not too bad. A little epoxy and it'll be good as new."

"It doesn't need fixing, Lyle." I have to chase him up the beach to the repair shed. "We need to work the Fisher problem. We'll call Sharon first. She can activate the lawyers, and they'll call—"

"The lawyers won't call anyone, Stellar." Lyle emerges from the shed with a headlamp, heavy-grit sandpaper, and an epoxy kit, the breeze toying with that one curl that wants to live free. His mouth matches the flatness of his voice.

"It's *our* idea! We have to protect it." My stomach twists, remembering how I told Kat we'd tipped our boats on purpose. Their group hauled their boats back up the rapids for a second go, too. All of them purposely tipped, frolicking in the water afterward.

They helped themselves to our lesson the way my old colleagues carved scoops out of all the things I hadn't realized I needed to guard. If we do nothing, Fisher will grind us under his shoe and walk away with our company.

Lyle lets out a long breath that sounds like the tide—cyclic and inevitable. "I don't know if we can, actually." Back at the beach, he strokes the bottom of the canoe with the sandpaper, his opposite hand gracefully splayed along the upside-down hull. "I pitched Alan—Dr. Fisher—the Love Boat as a potential PhD project."

"His name is *Alan Fisher*? Please tell me everyone called him 'Anal Fissure.' That guy deserves a pain-in-the-ass name. And so what if you pitched him the idea? He turned it down, right? So it's yours."

His laugh isn't the one I like. "It's complicated. Anything he touched when I was his student, he can claim ownership of. I can't prove he didn't give me verbal feedback on the idea in the development stage. So even if I sued . . ." He shakes his head, the slope of his shoulders slack and defeated.

"I'm so sorry, Stellar. I never would have developed this idea if I thought Dr. Fisher had any interest in it. If he even *remembered* it. I pitched him so many ideas. Developed so many proposals. All shot down. The Love Boat didn't even get past the one-page summary stage. It was 'too radical, too impractical, too expensive,'" he says, imitating Fisher with fussy, nasal, entitled perfection.

"I did that for a year and a half, then told him I had to quit my PhD if we couldn't agree on a topic. He didn't love the idea for *The Second Chances Handbook*, but I was teaching two sections of Psych 101 and contributing to four other students' research projects, so it would have been devastating for the lab if I left." He blows on the hull, sending dust flying, then squeezes some epoxy into a container and mixes it with quick, practiced strokes.

"And then . . . the pandemic." He looks at me apologetically. "I know it sucked for you, but the shortage of therapists and huge demand for relationship counseling created the perfect market for a scientifically proven do-it-yourself marriage manual.

"Everything changed. Now I was Fisher's protégé. *We* had a bright future together. After the agents and publishers came knocking, suddenly he was saying I couldn't graduate. He wanted me to stay on and develop a licensed program based on the handbook. I had to petition the chair of graduate studies to get my degree. Dr. Fisher was . . . not happy."

"The hype was about you, not him," I say, puzzle pieces falling together. "You were young, you were innovative, and, I mean . . ." I wave at him in a way that I hope conveys general attractiveness, versus me specifically being attracted. "You're the new face of science. If I were a journalist, I'd pose you in a T-shirt with your beard braided and your hair untied, like . . ." I turn my shoulders to three-quarter profile, arms crossed sternly, eyes challenging an imaginary camera.

"There were a few of those." In the deepening twilight, I can just make out the flush climbing his neck as he layers epoxy onto the hull, his big hands working fast and sure. My throat tightens. He's so tender and fastidious, like the boat is his patient.

"I bet. And Fisher would have done anything to keep *his* name on the things *you* did."

"Dr. Fisher's actions were human and understandable. I'm not angry."

I smack a hand to my forehead. "Are you shitting me right now? You should be *furious*. *I'm* furious. Anyone would be furious for you."

"I'm hardly the originator of wilderness-based therapy, Stellar. The Love Boat can patent a specific therapeutic method, but that's it." His eyes shine with regret. "All we have is you and me."

He meticulously recaps the epoxy before placing the twin tubes on the hull with a movement that smacks of finality. "I'm sorry, Stellar. This isn't what you signed up for, and I wouldn't blame you if you decided to leave the Love Boat. All I ask is that you give me time to find your replacement." He sounds tired. Defeated.

I imagined so many ways this business could fail—ways I might not give enough or be enough.

I never dreamed it would be *taken* from me. I never imagined watching Fisher paddling away beside Renee the way I watched my dad's taillights turn the corner, my mom in the seat next to him.

Everything I hoped for—the money, the security, the soul-feeding *something* Liz wanted me to look for—dangles out of reach, like that horrible fucking guy has my dreams on a string and is jerking them away every time I jump.

I press my fists to my face, knuckles mashing my eyebrows. "People like Fisher always win, *always*. I can never beat the assholes, no matter how I try."

And Lyle's not helping me fight. He's just letting everything go. Letting *me* go.

Anger floods my heart, pumping through my limbs in a muddy maroon tide. I need to move, tire it out, cool it down. And the river's right there, calm and cold. I charge in, shoes and all, so I can bounce around in the shallows shaking my arms.

"Stellar," Lyle says, wading in after me with a look of alarm in his mossy eyes, but I wave him away. I can't let him touch me. I *can't*, because I might spread this to him.

Worse, I *want* to spread this to him, because I'm right, and he's delusional. I want him to stop being goddamn *kind* and letting things go. He needs to fight for this company. I need him to hold on to *something*, for once.

I need him to hold on to me.

And I'm afraid he can't hold on to anything. He's not even angry with Fisher for convincing Renee Garner that his theft is better than Lyle's creation. We're in trouble, bad trouble, and I have to—

"I have to go for a run," I say, pulling out of his reach.

"Is that why you run?" he asks, concern etched across his forehead. "You literally run away from whatever's bothering you?"

"I run back again," I snap. "Running helps. It keeps me out of jail. It gives me the strength to control one thing in this world, even if it's only me. Even if it's only the desire to go around stealing milk. Or pushing people into the water." I imagine my hands on Fisher's kayak, strong enough to flip him and hold him upside down, so he has to abandon his boat *and* the idea he stole.

"Why would you want to push someone in the water?" He doesn't sound horrified or judgy, just curious.

I shift from foot to foot, like I'm still thinking of bolting, but also thinking of staying. "For *justice*, Lyle. To show the assholes some consequences." I kick the water, miserable. "But I can't. I'll never have that power. Not socially, not physically."

Water curls around my feet, no warmer than it has to be to keep flowing. It never yields, not one degree, and never will, not until the glaciers that feed it are gone.

I wish I were half as strong. You don't fuck with the river.

I look over my shoulder, expecting Lyle to end this conversation. He'll say something about energy or balance and head back to the campfire. But he tucks his thumbs in the pockets of his shorts and waits. The warm western sky touches him with liquid gold, underlining the shadow on his T-shirt where his bone necklace hides, lighting up his freckled collarbones, glowing from his hair.

I can't be imagining the look on his face, like he wants to chase me even when I'm furious and freaking out. As if he *likes* me when I'm angry—wants me to march out of the river, climb up on a log, and kiss him hard.

"You could push *me* in the water, if you needed to." God, the softness in his voice. Withstanding his compassion is the hardest thing I do around here.

I set my jaw, trying to set my soul along with it. "I don't want to."

"Why not?"

"You're too strong. Too big. I could work out for a million years and you'd still be twice my size. I don't want to feel stupid when I push and you don't fall down."

He wades closer, catching my hand and bringing it to his chest. I can't help spreading my fingers into the soft cotton of his T-shirt, over the skin and negative spaces I imagine underneath. He looks down at my fingers across his sternum, then back up, a strange light in his eyes. "Try it, Stellar J."

"Ugh. Fine." I sigh, making my shove sullen and half-hearted.

The whole time he's falling, I'm certain he'll take a step back, grab an overhanging branch, pull up at the last second. I believe it until a sheet of freezing water soaks me up to the nipples.

I scramble to where he bobs in the shallows. "Shit, Lyle! You didn't have to actually fall down!"

He lets me pull him to sitting. "How else would you have known how strong you are?"

I respect him, so I don't roll my eyes, but it is a very close call. "Cute, but you let me knock you over. I couldn't actually do that to someone your size."

"You could do that to *me*," he says, his eyes fixed to mine so firmly it feels permanent. "Why does power only count if you take it from someone? Why doesn't it count if someone gives it to you? Shares it with you?" He gets to his feet, rivulets sluicing off his water-darkened hair. A sharp shiver grips my spine at the way his T-shirt clings to his shoulders, his chest, the curve of his belly over—

I stop the downward slide of my gaze.

"It doesn't count because if they give it, they could take it back. They *will* take it back, if I don't bring what they want to the table."

"And what if I like what you bring to the table? What if we're stronger together?"

He's standing so close, his head tilted down, mine tilted up. I'm hot and cold, desperate to both cool off and steal his heat. I want to drag him to the tent, skip evening chores, and earn every sly comment at breakfast tomorrow—and I want to stay here and push this moment as far as it can go, until he's looked at every ugly thing about me and not turned away.

"All right. If we're stronger together, then *you* push *me* in the water. It's only fair."

He takes a half step backward, face blanching. "No, thanks."

"Why not?"

He shakes his head. "People get scared when I'm forceful. I'd rather find ways to be kind, even when others aren't."

I frown. "So when you're most generous, that's when you're most furious?"

His eyes darken. "Not always." The yogic breath again, and suddenly I see it: he's angry too. He hides it so well, I didn't see it. *Nobody* sees it. I accused him of having a fake personality, but it wasn't the weird stuff that was fake.

It was Lyle admitting to every emotion but one, afraid to be angry.

And me denying every emotion but one, angry because I'm afraid.

We need a place where we can be brave, and we need that place to be with each other.

I grab his hand and put it on my body. His thumb brushes the tender skin of my neck, fingers meeting the strap of my sports bra.

"What are you doing?" His breath turns unsteady, his eyes shadowed like the river at dusk—quiet green water not without its secrets and perils.

"Push me in. Believe I won't run when you're angry." I tug his hand over my shoulder, the heel of his palm tucking in below my deltoids. "Trust me to be as strong as you say I am."

He hesitates.

"Don't pretend you're fine, Lyle. You're furious! You deserve to say it out loud."

"I'm furious," he says softly, as if testing the feel of the words in his mouth.

"He *hated* that idea."

"He hated *all* my ideas. He ignored me until my research went viral, then tried to stop me from graduating. I want to shatter his goddamn boat with my bare hands. And maybe I . . ." He takes his hand back, looking at the broad palm, the fingers cocked with angry intention. "Maybe I could. Maybe I *would*. Maybe it'd be exactly like when I was seventeen."

"Or maybe," I say, my voice vibrating with urgency, "that was half a lifetime ago. Maybe you're older, and you can trust yourself to handle it. Trust *me* to handle it."

Our eyes meet, his face full of hope and fear, his lips pinned between his teeth.

I nod.

I'm sure he's going to push me, but his arms sweep me up instead. And then we're spinning and falling, together.

His back hits the river first. Displaced water rushes at me from all sides. I come up coughing, chest tight with cold. "What the hell? This was supposed to be only me."

"No. This was supposed to be *us*, together."

I blink gritty-feeling drops out of my eyes, the water blurring my vision. When he says *together*, it doesn't sound like this is strictly business.

It doesn't feel like it, either.

I've wanted to not want him this way. I've tried to ignore

him, dismiss him, feel anything but this yearning that won't stay down no matter how I try to defeat it.

But maybe I was wrong. Maybe we have something we can grip with both hands. Something solid, that wants to be held.

The gentle current ripples at my back, floating me into his lap. His body tenses, his eyes casting downward to my lips, droplets glistening like diamonds in the rose-gold bands of his lashes.

Nothing has to happen.

But when my vision clears and my eyes meet his, I want it to.

"You don't have to give everything to everybody all the time. You could keep something for yourself." I bring my thighs to either side of his, wrap my arms around his neck, and inhale chocolate and spice from his lips. It's another of those lingering, breathless touches I've never shared with anyone but him. I don't want them from anyone but him.

"Stellar," he says, and the thing about Lyle is that when his voice goes low, it goes all the way down to the center of the earth. It's a tectonic plate shifting, groaning under the heat and strain, forecasting the big one. More than ripples—a tsunami. For my body.

For my heart.

"I'm afraid we won't be able to hold on," I whisper, my lips so close to his, there's hardly a point in keeping them apart. "But I want us to try. If all we have is you and me, then I want us to promise we won't walk away from this. Or from each other. Anyone can get in a boat and talk about love, but they can't be the Love Boat, because they aren't us. No one can beat us as long as neither of us walks away."

"I wouldn't walk away. Not ever," he says, a little breathless.

Every movement of his chest moves mine. Every piece of our clothing is wet and clinging, needing to be stripped off.

His back burns underneath my hands; below the water, my skin sings with cold, the ache between my legs promising to wake up in a burst of sparks if he gives it some heat. I've never wanted anyone the way I want him, here, now. I want hours of his skin underneath my lips. Days of watching his mouth fall open and his eyes drift shut. Weeks of him whispering my name, and me screaming his. His body and mine, everywhere, forever.

"Let's get out of the river. Go . . . warm up." It's clear what I'm asking for.

I'm not sure why that was the wrong thing to say, but he tenses underneath me, pulling his face away with an indrawn breath.

"You're right. We should get warm." He sets me aside, then stands in a single smooth motion. I take the hand he extends downward, flying to my feet when he pulls. The loss of his touch is a wretched, bone-deep chill.

"You want the shower, or the sauna? Pick one and I'll take the other." He sloshes to shore.

I scramble after him, embarrassed and confused. "Um, I thought . . ."

His hands clench. "Yes. I know. But we've gotten cold and impulsively fallen into bed once already. We can't go through that aftermath again. Not here. The guests *have* to be our first priority."

I wipe hot shame from my face with the cold, wet collar of my shirt. "Yeah. You're right. I'm sorry, I shouldn't have . . . I shouldn't have."

"I'm not judging you for wanting what you want. And I'm not asking for forever."

We both look at his ring, then at each other, the jolt of the empty symbol passing between us.

"But I'm at a place in my life where I need sex to mean something. Something *good*. For everyone involved. Is that what you want from me?"

I used to think I didn't want meaningful sex with anyone. Then I thought I wanted it with Jen. Then I tried not to have it with Lyle. Now . . .

Now it's been fewer than two weeks since I sat in Liz's nursery, not trusting myself to make decent decisions about one-night stands, much less sex that came with a future and not just a present. It might feel like we've known each other forever, but there's plenty we don't know about each other.

I want him, but he's right. You can't apply the same fix over and over and expect a problem to solve itself. That's not how it works.

The only solution I can try is honesty. He deserves to have that from me.

"You probably guessed I've been . . . struggling. For a while. I haven't been able to think about what I want in a lot of ways. Including sexual ways. It hasn't been an issue since . . . for the last year, honestly." I watch his body shift as he does the math from the night of the concert to now: one year.

"That's fair," he says, his voice threaded with compassion. Oh, god, here comes the rejection. "I'm glad you told me. And I think it makes even more sense to stick with the boundaries until you know what you want."

Until you *know*, he said. Not *until* we *know*.

I nod, my insides jumbled up and aching. "Okay. I'm sorry that got out of hand. I'll take the shower." I shiver, but it's his body I'm imagining under the gloriously warm water, not mine.

"It wasn't just you. I was there when it got out of hand, too," he says, striding away. "I'll see you in the morning."

We'll see each other during evening chores, and at the wash station, and in the tent, but I know what he means.

A year ago we had sex and both of us woke up alone.

He'll see me in the morning because this time, we have no choice but to wake up together.

Chapter Fifteen

I wake up too warm, legs broiling, arms cool where I must've unzipped my sleeping bag in the night. Dawn is considering its options, trickling through the western wall of the tent enough to illuminate Lyle sprawled out on his stomach, limbs draped over the sides of his cot.

His body is intensely relaxed, somehow boneless in the way of small children who've passed out harder than an adult is capable of anymore. Or maybe harder than *I'm* capable of anymore, after a decade of night shifts where the best I could hope for was a few minutes to be horizontal, rest my tight, aching hips and knees, and try not to feel so old before my time.

Before last night, I'd never had to dread the uncomfortable first conversation after someone turned me down. But Lyle, being himself, made sure nobody went to bed angry. When I came into the tent, braced for awkward pleasantries, he was in bed. Eyes at half-mast, he watched as I silently zipped the front flap closed and tucked my toiletry bag away.

"Waiting up for me, Dad?" I sniped, as if I'd ever had someone do that for me.

He answered seriously. "We all need someone to watch our backs. Even someone as strong as you."

I thought about all the times he'd had my back out here. If I'd had a disagreement with a bear on the way back from the wash station, he'd have realized I was taking too long, gone out after me, and made himself the bear's problem, too.

We were just two people bears should not mess with, especially if they found us together.

Together. The idea wrenched my heart with the fierce relief of a dislocated joint sliding back into place. I climbed into my sleeping bag so I could press my hand secretly to my ribs, checking if my heartbeat felt as changed on the outside as it did on the inside.

He looks different this morning. Familiar in a way that seems . . . well, the word that comes to mind is "dear." It's sweet and old-fashioned, like I'm Anne Shirley standing at the garden gate after three books of insults and rivalry, looking up into Gilbert Blythe's face, and seeing something that was always there. There in herself, there in him, waiting to be discovered.

I let my gaze drift over his body, the hills and valleys of him softened by gray morning light. When I get to his face—his somehow very *dear* face framed by messy auburn curls that have sneaked out of his ponytail—his eyes are open.

"Oh! Sorry," I whisper, feeling a bit like a creeper. I could mistake the darkness in his eyes for desire, if I wasn't careful.

He shifts his hips a little, but doesn't roll onto his back. I know what that move means. I recognize the quiet, bitten-off sound he makes, too.

Boundaries. Whatever he's hiding, it's not for me. I have no right to his body or his soul. They're a package deal, the only thing he doesn't give away for the asking.

"What do you want to do today?" he says softly.

The dawn chorus of birdsong is loud enough to give us some cover, and we're far enough away from the other tents that he doesn't need to whisper. But he does, like he wants us to share secrets. I want to open my mouth and let him lay soft words right on my tongue, so they can strike a sweet, tingly path down to my stomach. Which is right behind the heart, anatomically speaking. Close enough to touch, which he and I have been careful to not do since we got out of the water.

"Slip & Slide," I say, naming a popular rapid about thirty-five minutes north. "We need a confidence builder after yesterday. Lower level of difficulty, same paddling configurations. Let them learn a failure isn't a permanent mark. Fun, easy play, low stakes. Show them what they've learned. I Get You."

He nods softly, not quite fully awake. "Yes. Slip & Slide," he says, a little bit of morning roughness taking his voice down to a pitch that makes my whole body hum along with it. "I'll add it to my notes. We can work the lesson into the morning meditation."

He shifts his hips again and I have to get out of here, even after lingering in the shower long enough for some self-care last night. Maybe he'd like some privacy, too. It couldn't take him long—well, that's projecting. It wouldn't take me long, in this tent that smells like him, where I can think of his darkened eyes and that catch of breath in his throat that could have been a waking-up sound and wasn't.

Damn it.

I have work to do. Things that aren't torturing myself over Lyle McHugh.

"Look away. I'm getting up." I'll leave the tent so he doesn't have to show me anything he'd rather keep safe. And if sadness squeezes my throat at the thought, I kind of deserve it.

An hour later chores are finished, Lyle's setting up for yoga, and I'm out for my run. The moment in the tent is safely banked, like money. Or maybe like fire.

I want this run to settle me down, but the farther I go, the more restless I feel. Most days I'm kicking into a higher gear by now, my stride unlocking from a tight jog to a strong, comfortable run, fully transitioned from knowing I *should* do it into *wanting* to do it.

Five more minutes, I tell myself, but already my feet are slowing, dust kicking up in front of my toes as my footfalls change from *go* to *stop*.

I stand head down, hands on hips, trying not to listen to the yearning tug between my shoulder blades. Lyle said he didn't want impulse to be what brought us together. Impulses lead to consequences, and I don't need more of those. The Love Boat needs us both to be rational and consider every move.

Lyle wants his feelings to mean something, and I don't know what this homesick longing means, or who we are to each other at this moment.

But I can feel who we might be.

The fallen tree where I can get two bars isn't far. I'll text Liz, then turn around and discover what's calling me home.

Sixteen minutes later, I'm unrolling a mat in the empty spot beside Sloane, where Dereck usually sits. I hurry into a meditation pose: back straight, eyes closed, palms open.

I've done yoga before—any class with "power" in the title, I've tried.

In those classes, the message I internalized was to *not* listen to my body. I'd drive myself through fatigue and pain. I'd plug into the atmosphere of competition: who could do the quickest, springiest asanas, who was the most flexible, even who could sweat the most and not clean it up (somehow always a man).

It felt a lot like work.

A soft footfall breaks through the soundtrack of birds and water. I crack one eye to see a gentle smile under a ginger beard as Lyle indicates a coaster-sized green card he's placed near my mat: SEEKING BALANCE, ADJUSTMENTS WELCOME.

I glance over at Sloane's mat. Her card is flipped over to the yellow side: NAMASTE, NO ADJUSTMENTS TODAY.

Giving in to my second impulse of the day, I keep my card on the green side.

"Let's move into downward dog, if that pose is available to you," Lyle says. "There's never shame in deciding your body isn't ready for this pose today, like there's no shame if today isn't your day to run a rapid. Today is the first day of I Get You, so honor the spirit of appreciation and collaboration in this stage by knowing yourself first. Be gentle with yourself first."

I push into down dog, the old competitiveness curling through me like smoke from a snuffed candle, ready to reignite if I put a match too close. I force my elbows to straighten and rotate inward, push my heels down, hips up, index fingers forward.

I cut my eyes to Sloane. She looks like she should have Hollywood-perfect strength and flexibility, but she's on her back, knees moving from side to side in a windshield-wiper motion.

Lyle interrupts the sound of agonized breathing with a low, Zen-like stream of instruction. "The perfect form is the one your body wants to take today. Not the form it took yesterday, or the one it will take tomorrow. Work with your body, not against it."

My right shoulder hurts; it always does when I make downward dog look "correct." I let my arm uncoil a little, allowing my elbow to bend slightly.

The relief is immediate.

As Lyle's footsteps traverse the room, I close my eyes and breathe. Is this how it's supposed to feel—slow and almost pleasurable, a wave cresting and receding?

Over the past year, I've felt like a buzzing, smoking machine about to start throwing parts. Maybe I could unplug for a second. Cool down enough to undertake repairs.

Unplug, ha. I'm becoming more McHuge-like all the time.

"Think about being strong and feeling easy at the same time. Bow and stern, power and steering. Partners, working together." His footsteps stop at my mat. A moment passes where I think he's checking my form, but then there's a flutter of sensation that grows firmer as his thumbs find the crest of my pelvic bone, palms settling up my waist, fingers wrapping around my hips.

He has my back. Literally, this time, but it doesn't feel different from when he threw his weight behind my canoeing idea yesterday. It doesn't feel different from when I asked for 5 percent of his company, and he gave me 10. There is no difference. It was only different in my mind.

He pushes up and toward my heels, and I'm floating. The ease of it floods me with pleasure, bone and muscle falling into place like a video of a shattering cup played in reverse. His ring presses sweetly against the crest of my hip bone, the metal warm through my shirt.

"Find a way, with yourself and with each other." The voice is McHuge, the hands are all Lyle. Warmth and power and giving with an open hand. "Water goes where it wants, does what it wants, pushes anything and everything out of its way—and carries what it needs."

He eases his hands away, the pleasure of his touch still sparking along my skin, lemon yellow, soft and zingy at the same time. He gives everyone these thoughtful gestures. Maybe we all feel like they're saying, *I care for you, body and soul.* He's one to talk about things being *meaningful*, when I never know whether the touches he gives me mean I'm special.

Afterward, people float toward the tents, sighs drifting

back from the trail. I tidy the stack of yoga blocks in the lean-to beside the pavilion, its new plywood unsoftened by weather and time.

"Brent," I hear Lyle say through the screened windows. "Hey, Brent! Don't forget your mat and props."

"Oh, yeaaah," comes Brent's voice, in full *who, me?* mode. "Can Stellar grab them?"

My teeth clench. Lyle will say it's fine. He'll "manage" Brent by tidying the props himself. He'll give yet more of himself to a man who doesn't deserve any piece of someone as good as Lyle.

But that's not what happens.

"You could ask her. But Stellar would definitely question why you didn't tidy your own space. If she knew I'd reminded you, she'd ask why you didn't apologize and take care of things right then instead of leaving your mess for someone else. And if I were you, I wouldn't know how to answer her, you know? So I recommend doing it yourself."

Slow, petulant footsteps drag back to Brent's prime spot on the river side of the pavilion. I can hardly keep from bursting out of the lean-to to watch Lyle's victory.

When I've redone Brent's deliberately sloppy mat roll—it's a start, at least—I find Lyle waiting by the pavilion entrance.

I hoped he'd still be here, yet I feel strangely bashful. "You have a lovely touch," I tell him, fingers drifting to my right hip, where I still feel his ring.

A patient once said that to me when I was a medical student inexpertly examining her lymph nodes. I immediately changed my palpation, trying to be more clinical. A *lovely touch* felt like something people would demand whether or not I wanted to give it, or—worst of all—something they'd deliberately misconstrue. Patients already took advantage of how little clout I

THE RIPPLE EFFECT   191

had, without the power "Doctor" would lend to my name. Especially the male patients, who grabbed me and made jokes about sponge baths and "accidentally" pulled their hospital gowns up so their genitals sagged out the bottom.

It seemed there was always someone who wanted to take something I hadn't offered. I probably made the only choice I had when I turned myself into someone a little too mechanical. Someone not quite human enough.

I can't change the choices I had then. But maybe I have different ones now. Maybe I can be strong and easy at the same time, like the river.

Rosy apples bloom in his cheeks. "That's a nice thing to say."

"You're a great instructor. I'm sorry I never came before—"

"Hey," he says, the side of one index finger inviting my chin to lift, until the upward angle of my face matches the downward angle of his, eyes to eyes, everything lining up. If we were two halves of a broken bone, an orthopedic surgeon would call us "anatomic"—perfectly aligned. One day, they'll have to look hard to know the bone was ever fractured.

"It's a new day, Stellar J. You don't have to apologize for anything that happened yesterday."

"You were right, though. Last night. We need to be sure, and I'm not. Not yet. But I want you to know—every time I touched you this week, I meant it. It wasn't meaningless. Not to me."

All those moments of contact I couldn't get from anyone else—it wasn't because they were ways you touch when you're in love. It was because they were ways I touched *him*.

"Hm," he responds, more a breath than a word. His eyes flick to the floor, then right back to my face, as if I'm too bright to stare at for long.

I know what I want this moment to mean. This can't be for the guests. It has to be for us.

"Your move," I say. It's his boundary; I can't be the one who pushes it.

He steps back. At first I think he's letting go, but when he perches on the windowsill, holding out a hand, I understand he's keeping the moment together. Giving me a chance to heal it.

I step between his knees, tucking them on either side of my thighs. I hover my hand in front of his chest. "Can I?"

At his nod, I trace the decal on his brown T-shirt. It's a bear's footprint, toe beans etched with the rings of an ancient tree, a seedling rising from each. It feels contained yet limitless, exactly like the sensation I have as I lean forward, not quite letting my lips touch his.

"Lyle," I whisper, watching like a doctor. Watching like a lover who knows the double flutter of his jugular, the flare of his pupils, the heat that would rise in the hollow of his palms if I wrapped my hands around his.

He leans forward the last indefinable, dizzying distance.

The way he tastes is a revelation, something inexpressibly Lyle underneath Earl Grey and honey. It feels right to go as slowly as he would go, ask as gently with my mouth as he would ask with his, let go of giving and taking so I can put everything into *feeling*. *This* feeling, like I'm coming alive, body and soul.

The heat of our first kiss meets the balance of this one: I give and am given, I take and am taken. He's huge against my body, taking up space yet making a place for me, powerful enough to give his power away.

I breathe in the tang of glacial melt that's softly touched a million roots, picking up their steady evergreen patience; there's skin and zinc and biodegradable shampoo as well. He smells like adventure and home. My body surges with ripples of sensation, every inch of skin feeding a stream that swells to a river of wanting and needing and not quite having.

He makes a sound, barely above a whisper, but I feel its vibration through my sports bra, the rumble of impatience short and sharp as he fumbles with the hem of my tank top. He's soft and rough at the same time, the smooth skin of his shoulders under my hands a tingling contrast to the callused fingers that blaze a path across my ribs, cup me over my sports bra, squeeze until I gasp into his mouth. Against my stomach, the evidence of his desire presses into me when I push closer.

Briefly, wildly, I consider whether we have enough yoga mats for me to be on the bottom without my back sporting telltale floor marks.

"Oh! Sorry, you two. It's just me. I have a semi-urgent issue to discuss when you have a minute."

The screen door slams behind Sloane before Lyle can pull his hand out from under my top, tugging the hem down as he goes. I'm not sure when my eyes closed, but they pop open inches from his laughing gaze. When I pull back, my favorite smile teases his lips.

Last time, I wanted to be discovered in the act. I should have been more careful what I wished for.

"I'll . . ." I swallow, still tingling, not ready to let the moment go. I tug my shorts away from the ache between my legs at the exact same moment he adjusts the front of his shorts to make room for what I've done to him.

"I'll speak with Sloane," I say, backing up half a step to glance at my watch. "We can still ring the bell at ten if we move."

His eyelids are heavy. He's not being very yogic about his fast, uneven breaths. The situation in his shorts is not improving, and now he's smiling like he caught me checking out said situation.

"We can ring it when we're ready. No point in rushing."

Chapter Sixteen

For once, I don't hurry along the path from the pavilion to the clearing. My head needs a minute to come down from the dopamine rush Lyle put into my blood; my heart needs to get a grip on reality.

Two fingertips trace my lower lip, where the memory of his mouth still presses against mine. The path his hand took under my shirt feels luminescent, like trails of glowing plankton on night paddles along the Pacific coast.

When I proposed the fake engagement, public displays of affection felt like far too much.

How is it possible that eight days later they don't feel like enough?

Sloane thinks the kiss was fake, obviously; her reaction was as bland as if she'd found us scrubbing the floor.

It felt real to me, though. And if Lyle's reaction was any indication, it was plenty real to him.

But it was also impulsive. We didn't plan to kiss or make sure we'd get caught; we just did it. In the moment, I felt sure; now I'm second-guessing everything.

It makes me want that exit strategy Sloane mentioned, except I don't want the roads that go to fake breakups or other disasters. I want an off-ramp from this gray area to somewhere solid. And I have no idea how to get there.

I wouldn't even know who to ask for advice.

For a second, I feel so lonely I grip my chest, pulling the skin with my fingertips to ease the ache beneath. Sometimes you need help to work the problem, but there's no one in camp I can pour my heart out to.

If Liz were here, and if she weren't wrapped up in parenthood, I might tell her. It's been a long time since I had good problems to share with her, instead of the lopsided parade of tragedy that's my half of our friendship.

But Liz doesn't know about the fake engagement. Sloane's the one who sniffed that out, and she and I haven't really talked since our conversation in the truck. I don't see a chatty, intimate relationship in the cards for us, anyway. Gossip sessions are almost impossible when we're surrounded by people twenty-four seven, and I'm working from before she gets up until after the guests go to bed.

On top of that, Sloane already has the advantage over me in the secrets department. She knows something that could bring down my business; I know a slice of her life story *People* magazine could have told me for $7.99.

She's growing on me, though. She's too perfect for me to pour out my heart to her over Lyle, but we could aim for a clean slate, like Kat talked about. I'll stop throwing out her Christmas cards unopened; this year, she'll add a handwritten line of greeting and scrawl a big letter *S* over the preprinted signature.

As I cross the clearing, Dereck exits the path leading to the tents, his Louis Vuitton weekender bags slung over his shoulders. He's dressed in dark jeans cuffed at the ankle, a soft-looking camel cardigan over a white T-shirt, chunky-soled loafers, and expensive, sinkable sunglasses.

These aren't paddling clothes.

And the low hum in my ears isn't blood rushing underneath my skin, but the engine of the same black car that delivered Dereck and Sloane four days ago.

I blink. "Where are you going?"

"LA," Dereck chirps, striding jauntily toward the parking lot. "Flight's in three and a half hours. Oh my god, thank you," he gushes, setting down a bag to accept a steaming, green-logoed go-cup from the driver. "You don't know how I've missed these." He sips it reverently, coming away with foamed milk on his sculpted upper lip.

"Is everything all right? Is it Sloane's . . ." I glance around, not sure what I should say about her mom in public.

"It's fine; nobody died. Sloane will explain," he says, one foot already in the back seat.

I hate surprise goodbyes. If someone's leaving, I like to know the details in advance: when they're going; how long they'll be gone. If someone doesn't share their itinerary, that rarely means anything good.

If Sloane's mom is fine, then she's leaving because she wants to. She's letting me go even though she *promised*.

"Where is she?" I bark.

The front flaps of the Sunset Dome are tied open in defiance of my warnings about mosquitoes. Sloane's suitcase is flung across one of the canvas chairs. The dresser drawers are all open, the contents jumbled like she's so desperate to get gone she doesn't care what gets left behind.

"Sloane. What the hell is going on?"

She picks up a pair of underwear, shakes it, then throws it onto the heap in her suitcase and reaches for another pair. "Dereck says he returned my AirPods, but I can't find them. The car's leaving in five minutes. Can you recheck the rest of the tent while I do the drawers?"

Is this how it ends between us? She casually asks me to find her missing stuff in the last seconds before she goes back where she came from, like I owe her my help but she doesn't owe me an explanation?

My vision tingles, graying at the edges. I squeeze my thigh muscles to force my blood pressure back up, a trick I learned from a surgeon who was in no mood to have another medical student faint into the sterile field. Losing a pair of guests in the middle of the course—I'm sick at the thought. This is my fault for asking her for anything when she had nothing at stake.

"Can you please stop staring and help me?" She throws another handful of lace into the suitcase. It'll never close over the mess bursting angrily out of it.

"Just go, Sloane," I say flatly. "Buy new AirPods at the airport and the Love Boat will reimburse you. Get your sh—stuff together or you'll miss your flight."

I won't ask if she's still planning on endorsing us. I won't beg her for anything ever again.

An engine revs, then tires crunch in the parking lot as it hums away.

Sloane crumples the sun shirt she's holding and throws it against the back wall of the tent with a growl. "Asshat. He took my damn AirPods."

It's never silent in camp, but this moment feels unnaturally hushed, the sound of the river receding until all that's left is Sloane's breathing, and mine.

I recover first. "What in the actual fuck happened here,

Sloane? Make it make sense that we are looking for your head-phones when your boyfriend just drove away without you."

Sloane shakes her head, mouth pinched. "He's not my boy-friend."

"You and Dereck *broke up*? Like, *this morning*?" Jesus Christ. Twenty-five percent of our participants have broken up, and half of those have left the course, and we're barely at the five-day mark? This deal is getting worse all the time.

"We didn't break up. We were never together."

I sit down heavily on the unused bed. "But . . . all the mag-azines. The paparazzi photos." I shouldn't tell her I read those articles. You don't do that unless you care about someone and can't quite crush the stubborn wish to revise history.

Sloane smiles tightly. "How do you think I knew those tricks for fake relationships?"

I stare at the sunburned tops of my knees. All I can think to say is, "Why?"

"Why what? Why did he leave? According to him, he was cold and bored and missed LA, and the small chance that I could help his career wasn't worth another week of sand in his crevices. He must've ordered the car last night. And this morning, when I was at yoga, he was packing. The little shit."

"I'm sorry he didn't like the course," I say stiffly. "And I'm sorry he broke up with you. Or didn't break up. Are you also leaving? Because you need to call another car, if yes. Lyle and I have other guests; we can't spend the day driving you to the airport."

She drops her forehead into her palm. "What day is it to-day? On the course, I mean."

"Day five. The first day of I Get You."

"Great. Thank you. And when is the day *you* get *me*, Stellar?

Can McHuge make us one of his twelve-word plans, so I know when I graduate to someone you trust for even one second?"

"Are you leaving or not?" The words come out harsh and bitter, but Sloane could do me the courtesy of fucking filling me in before hitting me with personal criticism.

She shakes her head. "Your parents really fucked you up, didn't they?"

I draw back, stung. "Half of them are your parents, too."

"I know!" Sloane whispers furiously. "I know that. It's why I'm here. I'm sorry I screwed up, okay? I'm sorry I took my last chance to get to know you instead of letting you give me the Heisman"— she hunches over an imaginary football, holding out an arm as if to push me away, like the figure on the college trophy—"forever. And I'm sorry I dragged Dereck along for the ride, but I didn't think you'd let me come by myself. He made me promise to ask for his character to come back from the dead in the next movie. If there *is* a next movie. Because . . ."

She presses her lips together, taking a shaky breath.

"My team covered it up, but I broke my pelvis this winter, glade skiing. I was filming GoPro footage for my social media, trying to build up my reputation as an action star. And now my hip might not heal enough for me to do action sequences. I can't even run very far anymore. It would be easy to recast my role. I'd be what Timothy Dalton is to James Bond. Forgotten. A blip."

She turns to the back wall of the tent, looking toward the river through the wavy vinyl window. "I know what this means for your business, so Dereck agreed to say he left for family reasons. He'll stick to the story if he doesn't want his character's body to get launched into the sun in the opening credits of the sequel."

Sloane looks over her shoulder at me, arms wrapped across

her stomach. The abdomen is the most vulnerable part of the body, with no bones to shield it. Predators instinctively go for it; vulnerable prey know to cover it up.

"If you want me to leave, I'll go. I'll still endorse the Love Boat any way you want. Send me the photos and text for my social media accounts. God, my publicist is going to be so fucking mad at me for making her reschedule all those interviews and then coming back a week early."

Sloane's retreat hangs between us, a negative space wanting to be filled. I don't have the luxury of letting her pursue me anymore; I have to ask her to stay, or ask her to go. I have a chance for pleasant Christmas cards, or I could aim for something more. A big sister. An advice giver. A relationship that means something.

Sloane walks over to the far corner of the tent and picks up the tossed shirt. Now that I'm paying attention, I notice how she balances on her right leg when she bends, keeping the left one straight. I remember her struggling to transfer her weight in the canoe, consistently stiff when she stood up, stumbling on a flat trail.

Her invulnerable life was a figment of my imagination and an illusion she worked hard to maintain. Now we both know each other's secrets.

And maybe we both need things money can't buy.

"I wish you could have told me about your hip."

She busies herself folding the shirt into thirds, then into a neat square before pushing aside the heap of underwear to lay it on the bottom of the suitcase. "Well, I couldn't. My team's trying to keep it quiet. And it's not like you tell me anything without a court order." She looks up, the sullen, stubborn line of her mouth far too familiar.

I'm not going to help fold her panties—neither of us wants that—but I grab a shirt from the rifled drawers and smooth it out on top of the dresser, trying to replicate her technique. Her face softens when I put the shirt back in the drawer instead of in the suitcase.

We fold a few more things. Eventually, she says, "My accident happened on the last run of the day. Late afternoon, almost sunset. It was a while before someone found me. I thought no one would come, and I . . ."

I've seen traumas like the one she's describing. The fracture is dangerous, but it's the cold that can kill.

"It can't be fun for you to get chilly out on the water."

"It isn't," she says, and I hear the echo: *It was a while before someone found me.*

She smooths a pair of underwear, folding and tucking the ends to make a tight little envelope.

"You'll need a partner in your canoe," I say slowly. "Which would have to be me. If you're good with that." Days on the water together. We'd talk a lot while we paddled between rapids. We'd get closer; we couldn't help it.

Sloane's hands fall still, her Marie Kondo act forgotten.

"And I'm guessing Dereck was helping you with your hip physio. Or he should have been. I can do that, so it's easier for you to sit strapped into a canoe. If you want to be here, Sloane, we'll find a way."

When she looks up, her face is wet. "It's good to have someone here I can trust. It's good to have *you*."

"Oh, shit," I say, alarmed at the answering tingle in my tear ducts. "We don't have to make it a big deal or anything."

I can see her coming, yet I'm still startled when her arms come around me. She's laughing and crying at the same time, rocking us side to side. "You're a tough one, little star. At least, you want people to think you are. It wouldn't kill you to shed a tear once in a while."

"It might," I say darkly, but I'm silently replaying my new nickname. *Little star.* Small, but fiery.

I like it.

With one fewer rescue paddlers, Lyle and I postpone the trip to Slip & Slide and spend a half day on the wide, calm water near base camp, practicing assisted rescues with the guests. If they can help each other, we can put me in Sloane's boat and feel confident safety isn't being compromised.

Simulated rescues are cold work, with everyone in and out of the water all the time. After a late lunch, we opt for dryland games to warm up and give everyone a break.

Lyle shuffles through his field notes and picks a game I'm certain he invented while high: compliment badminton. I'd like this game a lot better if I got to observe, like Lyle does.

"Sloane has great hair!" I shout, as her racket catches the soft, high shot I sent her way.

"Petra has a giant, sexy brain," Sloane purrs somewhat prematurely, making Petra miss her swing.

"Sloane! You're not supposed to give the compliment until after they hit it," Lori scolds. "That being said, feel free to hit it to me anytime." She bats her eyelashes like Betty Boop.

Petra retrieves the birdie and serves it over the net, where Willow, Trevor, Mitch, and Sloane stand on the other side. Lyle referees from a canvas chair beside center court, scratching debriefing notes in his book.

Badminton is a surprisingly fast-moving game. It doesn't take long before we run out of things to say about people's looks, style, and canoeing technique.

"No repeats," Lyle cautions from the sidelines the second time Lori says Trevor looks better with his new five-day beard. "Penalty to Stellar, Lori, Brent, and Petra."

We groan, having already racked up several penalties for sending shots out of bounds (me, three times), hitting Lyle in the forehead with the birdie (Petra), and distracting teammates with interview questions (Brent).

"Your penalty: you must sing to the other team, with complete seriousness, the first verse of 'I Want It That Way' by the Backstreet Boys. *Complete* seriousness," Lyle cautions.

Right away, Brent says, "Not familiar with it. I was more into grunge in the nineties."

"Grunge, my ass. You owned the *Millennium* album on cassette *and* CD," Willow retorts. "And remember when *Spiceworld* got stuck in your car stereo for three years and you never got sick of it?"

A flush creeps over the collar of Brent's navy-blue polo shirt. For once, he has nothing to say.

Willow relents, her face softening. "'I Want It That Way' was your go-to lullaby the year Cayden had colic. I love that song."

"I sang him 'Seven Nation Army' way more. No, I *did*," Brent insists. Does he really not understand why Willow's face cycles through fury to a worrisome blankness? I'm no expert on love, but from what I've seen, the real damage in relationships doesn't happen when people are merely angry with each other. It happens when they stop caring at all.

"Penalty first. Arguments later," Lyle says, humming a note to get us started. When we've finished humiliating ourselves, he hands the birdie to Petra. "Pro tip: Try digging deeper for compliments. Beyond what you can see on the surface, what is there to like and admire about the people around you?"

Petra lobs the birdie over the net. It's closer to Sloane, but she doesn't make a move—*how* did I not notice the way she favors that hip?—and Mitch steps into the gap to send it back with a clean snap of her wrist, sand spinning under her feet.

"Mitch takes no shit!" Petra says, then slaps a hand over her mouth, flushing.

"Excellent, Petra," Lyle calls. "Keep going!"

"Sloane looks better after losing 180 pounds of Dereck," Mitch sings.

"I want Lori to be my mom," Sloane says, and my heart squeezes for Sloane and her real mom.

It goes fine for a few turns, until Brent yodels, "Sloane may yet bring her career back from the dead!"

"*Brent!*" Willow snaps, snatching the birdie out of the air with one hand.

"What? It's impressive."

"Should I assign a penalty for delay of game?" Lyle muses, stroking his beard.

The chorus of "No!" is loud enough to echo off the mountainside.

The game restarts in a hurry, but I miss the birdie when Trevor bats it my way, because I'm still looking at Lyle. He created this opportunity for everyone to hear good things about themselves, and he looks happy with how the game is going, but I can't shake the feeling he wants to play. I don't think it's a coincidence that the man who gives far more than he gets invented a game where everyone ends up getting something good.

I pick up the bird, grab a spare racket from the bin, and walk over to Lyle. Dropping both in his lap, I say, "Your turn, McHuge."

I use the name on purpose—not to be mean, but to call attention to the persona he wears when he denies himself all the things he makes sure other people receive. All the things people need from the ones they love.

He turns the plastic feathers between his fingers, an unreadable expression on his face. "I'm not playing."

"You are now," I say. "Don't make me assign a penalty for delay of game."

Everyone needs love and praise. Everyone needs give and take. And I intend to see he gets them.

"Play, McHuge!" Lori calls. "Play! Play! Play!" she chants, until everyone joins in, cheering wildly when Lyle stands up, racket in hand.

"Lyle is kind *and* right. Most of the time," I say, as he serves to Lori. He turns to me, so startled he doesn't notice when Lori hits the birdie right back to his feet.

"When McHuge flips a canoe during a rescue, it's so hot I almost wish I was straight!" Lori yells to general laughter, not waiting for him to serve.

Lyle's cheeks blossom with telltale crimson, like a desert after rain. "Lori always speaks from the heart," he manages, hitting the birdie to the other team.

Mitch hits it back to him. "McHuge makes impossible things possible," she says, the tiniest quaver in her usually imperturbable tone.

Oh god, I think they're both going to cry. Even my throat is tightening, seeing him clear his throat several times in a row.

By the time everyone's had a turn complimenting Lyle, he's totally undone, waving his arms and shouting, "Game's over! Stop, stop. Take ten minutes for a bio break and meet at the firepit for debrief."

On her way by, Sloane whacks me lightly on the ass with her racket. "Nice," she says, sotto voce, tipping her chin at Lyle. "Very believable gambit. You learn quickly, grasshopper."

"Grasshopper?! Go f—Uh, fix yourself up, and I'll see you at the firepit." Sloane laughs like a loon, perfectly aware I almost told an alleged client to go fuck herself. It's not a phrase I've ever said in anger. I only use it with people who understand that I mean, *I trust you to give back as good as you get.*

I hang around the badminton court, waiting for a chance to talk to Lyle, but the guests surround him, pelting him with even more compliments as they meander toward the firepit.

I gather up the rackets and tuck the birdie back into the can with its eleven companions, ready for a summer's worth of fun. It was a good game. I liked watching him get praised far more than I liked any compliment people paid me—and they said some nice things. They're good people.

He looks back once, the slanting afternoon light sharpening his features into an arrangement so beautiful my chest aches. Clutching half a dozen rackets to my chest, I give him a half smile and an awkward little wave, like I'm hoping the captain of the football team will notice me in the stands.

It feels real when he smiles back, real when my belly flutters like I'm the kind of teenager I never was the first time around— hopeful. Openhanded. Kind.

Well. Damned if I'm not half in love with Lyle McHugh.

Chapter Seventeen

It's a dim morning in the forest, aspen leaves rattling and twisting in the wind. The horizon's turned a smooth, uniform battleship gray, the color of weather that's here to do damage. Every now and then, the warm breeze has a cool bite to it, a lazy little threat that says *Pay attention.*

We should have been here an hour ago.

Lyle and I unlash the boats at the put-in spot for Slip & Slide. It's a hundred-meter portage to the water's edge, down a rocky, uneven trail. I wouldn't have picked it if I'd known about Sloane's hip, but Lyle promised the guests this trip after postponing for rescue training yesterday, and we don't have a reason to back out.

Someone's already been here—a big group with a tall trailer, given the depth of the tire tracks and the freshly broken branches overhead.

Lyle slings the last canoe down to Brent and Willow. He takes a deep inhale, smelling the wind. Our eyes meet, his full lips pressed together. We both know it's going to rain hard, and soon. River conditions could change fast. We may have to get off the water early, which would suck after yesterday's limited paddling.

Meanwhile, because I'm canoeing with Sloane, Lyle will take over today's lesson. *My* lesson.

For a person who swore not to get emotionally involved with this job, I'm not very chill about someone else getting the glory for my work, even if it's my future co-owner and the world's kindest person. It smacks of the hospital, and while I hate that Grey Tusk General seems to still be happening to me, I can't make it stop.

But this isn't Lyle's fault, or Sloane's, or mine. I can roll with it in the short term.

I climb up on the trailer to secure the ropes so they don't whip around on the drive back to camp.

"Need a hand?" From the ground, Lyle casually reaches up to check a knot beside my head.

"I've got it, you show-off." I've never asked him how tall he is. When guests demand a measurement, he only says, "This tall," or sometimes, "What would a number change?" At this moment, I wonder if he's one of those shape-shifting giants of Norse legend, stretching into whatever size the situation demands.

"I like how thorough you are, Stellar. You're a good partner." I expected him to give my banter back. Rookie mistake— Lyle only gives sincerity. His serious expression fills me with a warm rush of pleasure to counteract the falling temperature.

It's a mistake to watch him tug my knots, his movements sure and strong. I'm too exposed after yesterday's kiss. Too hot with him all up in my personal space. Anyone could see me and know what I'm thinking.

Including Lyle.

"Oh. Um, thank you. You as well."

"You don't have to say it back. You can take the compliment

straight up. You deserve it," he murmurs as I secure the last rope. His breath on my ear sends a shiver tumbling from the nape of my neck to the base of my spine.

I could turn to him and watch the dappled light playing in his hair, smell the tea he sneaked into his water bottle. My arms could drape across the sweet spots between his neck and shoulders. He could lift me off the trailer and slide me down his body until my feet meet the ground, like this is one of the rom-coms Liz makes us watch when it's her turn to pick the movie.

We could do all those things, and I wouldn't know what any of it meant, like I didn't know what it meant when he hugged me at campfire last night, or whispered "Good night" from his sleeping bag without making one damn move on me.

The guests are right there. Any one of them could step around the trailer and get an eyeful of our "engagement" playing out, just like our rules specified. So who is this for?

I want what he gave me a year ago: his attention, his care, touches that felt like gifts with my name on them. I also want rules of my own that say what we do in private is for us, *and* what we do in public is for us, too. No gray area.

"I don't think we should . . ." I gesture helplessly, "*whisper* at each other. It's distracting, and we should be paying attention to the guests." I jump down without his help and rub my arms to erase the goose bumps.

His crooked brow angles down. "You good?"

"No. Yes. I don't know." I step away from him. "We'll talk later."

A wolf whistle sounds from the trailhead.

"Lori!" Mitch hisses. Babe crashes out of the underbrush, looks to see who whistled for her, and takes off again when she sees it wasn't Lyle.

Lori removes her fingers from her mouth and grins. "Oh,

come on, Mitch. The lovebirds are having their first fight. It's cute. Remember when we'd kiss and make—"

"Lori," Mitch says, more gently this time. "We're embarrassing them." Lori's hands drop to her sides, her expression turning uncertain. Mitch takes her hand and squeezes. "It's okay, love. They're shy. Not like you and me."

By now, everybody's wandered around the back of the trailer to take in my stiff spine and Lyle's worried frown. The effect is like a purifier for every couple's dynamic, bringing their essence to the surface.

Petra wraps a hand around Trevor's waist and smiles up at him. He lowers his lips to her ear, his upstanding brown curls caressing her shiny, straight dark locks.

Brent slings an arm around Willow. "You'll learn to use reason when you disagree, not emotion." Under the weight of his arm, Willow clenches her jaw, looking like she's not feeling very *reasonable*.

Sloane catches my eye, pretending to adjust her life jacket as a cover for drawing a thumb across her neck: *Cut it out. You're supposed to be in love.*

That's the problem, isn't it? I never meant to love any of this, and now I'm ride or die for both this man and his incredibly random adult summer camp.

"Sorry, everyone. We were . . . discussing the weather. Let's get onto the water before it rains. One canoe at a time down the trail, and watch your footing." I make sure Babe's not in the way, then rap twice on the van's rear doors to let Jasvinder know we're clear.

Sloane dawdles by the orange canoe, letting everyone else go ahead. I pat my hip and raise my eyebrows. She nods at my interpretive dance: she'd rather no one saw her struggle.

We take our time on the way down, stopping often to rest.

At the shore, everyone's ranged along the waterline, watching something I can't make out through the wall of shoulders. Could be some kayakers freestyling in Slip & Slide's friendly play spots, which would be fun to see. I slide through a gap between Lyle and Lori.

She snags my arm as I squeeze by, her face crinkled with regret. "I didn't mean to embarrass you. Sometimes I forget not everyone has the same sense of humor."

"It's fine, Lori. No harm done."

"Good. I'm glad. Do we know those people? Are they waiting for us?" she asks, pointing across the river.

My heart drops hard at the sight of bright-blue kayaks.

A man wearing yellow sport lenses turns his dead eyes our way, then leans back to speak to the person in the stern of his kayak.

Fisher. *Again.*

Dinner was a silent affair after a rainy day of paddling filled with waiting and a debrief in the shelter of the pavilion where everyone had to shout over the downpour. Campfire was canceled, obviously; Lyle's cellophane "fire" was no match for Mother Nature's water.

After dinner, Jasvinder volunteered to dry everyone's clothes at the twenty-four-hour Laundromat in Pendleton. People almost cried, they were so happy to be getting clothing that isn't permanently damp. Lori handed over a garbage bag of stuff while dressed only in a towel, much to Mitch's dismay. After that, there was nothing for the guests to do but climb into bed and make the most of the solar lights, which hadn't recharged well under the dark afternoon skies.

The silver lining in the crappy-ass weather: Lyle and I finished evening chores an hour early. We played Rock Paper

Scissors Lizard Spock for who had to go to the breezeway and hang up the last of our soaking clothes after chores. I won, so I'm waiting for him in the tent, wearing my driest wet T-shirt.

Fucking Anal Fisher. Liz and I have a long-standing name game with people we hate, but never have I felt the rightness of one of our revenge nicknames with this intensity. I loathe him and Renee Garner and his gang of jerks, hogging the rapids shamelessly at Slip & Slide, having the loudest possible fun. Even Renee looked uncomfortable with how long Fisher forced us to wait as they set off down the tongue one boat at a time, meandering from eddy to eddy with no regard for courtesy.

We sang songs and played bumper boats, but games get old fast when you're parked above the rapids, going nowhere. Even faster when the light, indecisive cloud cover gets its act together and starts seriously drilling down rain like it could do this all day.

Brent started commenting about how the Love Boat was supposed to be original, but Fisher's group seemed to be doing the exact same thing in the exact same place as us. I wanted to dunk him for being a jackass and dunk him again for being right. I struggled to smile through the acid in my stomach as Fisher made a mockery of our originality—the one thing Lyle and I were banking on to save this company.

When the tent flap finally unzips to reveal a dripping Lyle, our lamp is beginning to waver.

"We have a lot to talk about," I say.

In reply, he strips off his T-shirt, holds it outside, and wrings a waterfall from it before tossing it over one of the ropes under the rain fly. He steps inside, doing a hell of an impression of a Viking fresh from a character-building dip in the North Sea, frigid water dripping from his hair and beard.

I force myself not to look at the droplets sliding down his

chest, over his stomach, and under the waistband of his orange shorts. It's embarrassing being so transparently hot for him when I don't know whether he returns the feeling. When I think about it, Lyle's desire for "sex that means something" could translate to anything short of ghosting. Friends with benefits. A situationship of some stripe, where I'm heart eyed and he's just being . . . kind.

"Talk," Lyle says, uncharacteristically short, eyes raking down the portion of my tank top visible above the edge of my sleeping bag. I refuse to cross my arms over my breasts. Let him think anything three-dimensional down there is because I'm cold.

"Get out of your wet clothes first. Then we can talk about—"

"Our discussion at the put-in."

"—Fisher."

He crosses his arms. "We don't need to talk about Fisher."

"Yes we do."

"I don't *want* to talk about Fisher."

"You're soaked, Lyle. Get changed."

"I gave all my clothes to Jasvinder. This is what I've got." His eyes smolder, a spark among the green.

"Get into bed at least," I say, retreating into safe grumpiness. "If you get hypothermia, I'll have to do all the chores."

"Is *that* the only reason you care if I'm cold?" Lyle swipes a washcloth-sized travel towel across his arms and chest, his back muscles popping and flexing in synchrony.

I roll over to face the wall and definitely do not imagine what's happening behind my back. "Of course not! God, what is *wrong* with you?"

"Nothing."

"Something," I argue. "You'd think you were—Oh my god. You're angry. You're *angry*. Today sucked, and you hated it. Right?" It's inappropriate to be this excited about negative emotions, but this is Lyle. It's a banner day.

"Yes," he groans, to the sound of his shorts hitting the floor. "They were so rude. On *purpose*. I just wanted to live my life. Is Fisher going to be shitty about me leaving until the end of time? Will it ever, ever stop?"

I wait for the sound of legs sliding into his sleeping bag, then roll over. He's rubbing the space between his eyebrows with two blunt fingers. "I try so hard to believe people are good. I give them so many benefits of the doubt. But I'm running out of kindness for him, Stellar. What is he doing to me? Who am I turning into?" He breathes in for four seconds, out for eight, eyes scrunched shut.

Me. He's afraid he's turning into *me*, and I don't love how that makes me feel. If I've been angry, it's because I had a damn good reason. The times I got angry were the times I *cared*.

"It's not a moral failing to be angry, Lyle. Sometimes it's a sign that something's wrong. Like the fact that we ran into Fisher's group at the Stones on Thursday, then Slip & Slide today. I think he's trying to rip us off." Saying it gives me emotional vertigo, like my hospital-induced paranoia has finally gotten the better of me, and also like I've already waited too long to speak up. If I allowed the warning signs of trouble to slip past me again, I couldn't bear it.

Lyle rumbles in disagreement. "Those are popular places for whitewater beginners. I'm not happy with Fisher, but I'm not convinced this is more than a coincidence."

"But *something's* happening. I swear he was waiting for us at the put-in spot. What if he wants to see our original stuff and build on it for his research?"

"They could have been briefing or playing games, like us. And they went down first. They didn't see what we did," Lyle notes, letting the last of the air out of my argument.

This feeling is so familiar—the sense that something's

wrong, but it's too small to pursue. The worst thing about finding out how badly my Grey Tusk General colleagues had stuck it to me was knowing I'd ignored my internal warning bells. What was one more night shift, or one fewer weekend off, in any given month? *It all evens out over time. Stop counting, Dr. Byrd*, my colleagues said, using "Doctor" to mean *This is beneath you.*

In retrospect, I *wanted* not to know. It was easy: I considered the magnitude of everything I had, and how lucky I was to have it, and decided my worries were tiny by comparison.

But it's the small thefts that get past you, not the big ones. You can lose everything one carton of milk at a time and not notice until it's all gone.

"So what do we do if we see him again? Call Sharon, maybe?"

"I don't think Sharon could help," Lyle says, anger seeming to leave his slumping shoulders. "We just need to keep doing what we're doing. That's how we keep the Love Boat alive."

I know he's not trying to placate me. He'd never take advantage. But I can't block out the echo of *Stop counting, Dr. Byrd.*

"Come over?" he asks after a quiet minute, sidling his sleeping bag to the edge of his cot and patting the vacated space. "We don't have to do anything. But we should talk about what happened at the trailer, yeah? And I don't know about you, but my day sucked. I was looking forward to spooning this girl I know. I think we've done pretty much everything but that, come to think of it."

"All right, all right, you don't have to lay it on so thick," I say, swinging my legs to the floor so I can hop across the gap without getting out of my sleeping bag. "And we've spooned."

"Have we?"

No sooner have I perched my butt on his cot than he puts one thick forearm across my waist and flips me to the little spoon position. The press of my spine against his stomach and chest feels insanely good, like the wildest comfort fantasy I ever conjured on long nights at work, dreaming of somewhere dark and enveloping where no one could page me.

I curve into him, wanting more. "We have. You were sleeping." I was the big spoon that time. I laid my forehead against his back, closed my eyes, and concentrated on feeling every place my skin touched his, thighs to chest to fingertips, until his breathing fell into a rhythm so deep and slow and hypnotizing I knew I had to leave before I fell asleep myself.

"I wasn't," he says, lips soft against the sensitive spot below my ear. "Not at first."

I suppress the way my neck wants to arch back and open up underneath his mouth. "Lyle! Were you checking to see if I remembered?"

His cheek curves against my undercut. "Maybe."

"I remember everything about that night," I say, strangely sad. I remember his texts—three lonely shouts into the void, still unanswered. "I'm sorry I pulled you into my mess back then. Maybe I shouldn't be pulling you into my mess now."

"You don't have to be perfect to deserve love, Stellar. Theoretically," he adds, when I tense.

"Yeah, but you didn't want distractions or complications at the Love Boat, and I'm . . ." I sigh. "I'm complicated. What happened to me at the hospital . . . it's kind of still happening in my brain. It's why Fisher makes me lose my mind. It's why I like things to be balanced in relationships, so I have proof everything's fine. And now we're kissing in public and doing *this* in private," I say, wiggling my ass against him, "even though at my job interview we agreed there couldn't be anything between us. It's confusing. I'm confused."

"Do you want to stop doing this when we're alone?" He tucks his face into the crook of my neck, tightening his corded forearm across my stomach like he definitely does not want to stop.

My chest squeezes with all the things he doesn't do at this moment. He doesn't stiffen, or move away from me, or get a *tone* in his voice. He's made of spaces I want to curl into—the hollows on his body where shadows collect and the places inside him where my heart seeks shelter from the glare.

"No, I don't want to stop. But if we keep going, I need to know that when you touch me, whether it's here or in front of the guests, it's because you want to."

"I think you know I want to, Stellar." His voice is low and slow, dark with promise. "Especially if *you* want to."

My breath goes shallow in my chest. "But would that be meaningful enough for you if that was all it was? I don't want to screw things up by promising too much too soon. I'm not ready to talk about commitment or . . . words like that," I finish awkwardly. "All I can promise is my best."

I turn to my back and look up at him. He's still on his side, my head pillowed on the bulk of his biceps. I've never seen anything like Lyle McHugh on a narrow camp cot, his damp hair a banked fire, his eyes burning as he takes me in. The open sleeping bag falls away from his torso, the waistband of his gray boxers becoming visible. With the rain drumming on the fly and the light barely illuminating his features, it feels like we're alone.

Truly alone.

Not trying to be seen together, not forgetting we could be discovered.

"I'll take that deal," Lyle says finally, with a crooked smile. "I couldn't ask for better than your best, Stellar J."

I know I'm lost even before I put my hand behind his head and pull him down.

Chapter Eighteen

There are a few sensory moments in my life that stand out for the way they brought me unexpectedly to life.

When I was sixteen, there was the boy whose kiss I thought would be wet and mechanical like all the others, but by the time he pulled his puffy lips from mine, I would've said yes to anything he asked.

In my first year of university, there was the girl who looked down into the nonexistent gap between our bodies and whispered, "Can I?" and the thrill of anticipation was almost better than getting the very first orgasm I hadn't given myself.

And then there's this moment, the lamp dimming as its battery burns down and down, the white noise of fat raindrops on canvas and the steady sluice of runoff hitting damp earth. In our private universe, the slow swipe of Lyle's thumb against my upper arm is as shocking and sweet as a tongue between my legs, giving so much more than it should be able to.

The stillness between us makes the smallest movements more powerful than I ever could have dreamed. Simply imagining my hands drifting across his topography—it lights up my palms, the inside of my wrists, the creases of my elbows.

My nipples push hard against my oversize tank top; his knit boxers are putting on a three-dimensional show. Between the two of us, there isn't a single body part that couldn't be revealed in the space of one hot moment, but neither of us makes a move.

"Stellar J," he says, his hushed voice reverberating in my throat. He brushes across and down the tender inside of my arm, where summer color fades.

His chest is warm under my hands like campfire embers: easy and mellow, with dozens of glowing nooks where you could toast a marshmallow to sweet perfection. But when I serve him a "Lyle" in reply, his eyes flare to life with a thousand golden sparks, like someone stirred up the fire until our faces got as hot as mine feels now.

"This is . . ." His voice cracks. "This is what I think it is? I don't want just tonight. I don't want this if we don't . . . if we don't care for each other, Stellar."

Damp curls tumble across his cheek. I tuck them behind his ear, smiling when I discover it's slightly pointed, like he's part elf, part giant. "I promise I've got your back, Lyle. Not just for the Love Boat. Not just for tonight. For everything."

I stand up, step out of my sleeping bag, and toss it on my bed. When I turn back, he's sitting up, his bone pendant tucked into the notch above his sternum. I step wide around his thighs and settle myself onto his lap, running my hands down his neck to rest them across the poetry of his collarbones.

He makes a low sound, a catch and release of breath as if I should be more mindful of how substantial I am, how much weight my body and my actions carry, and I love it.

"Not too close. Not too fast," he says, the words tight. "I'm . . . if I'd known earlier, I would have . . . give me a minute."

I'd give a lot to see him lose control, but I back off with my hips, moving my focus to the cord around his throat. Understated, biodegradable, and on message—it's very Lyle. "Where'd you get this?"

"Tavish. My brother. He made it for me after . . ."

After his legal troubles, I'm guessing. "You've worn it for a long time."

"It's important to me." He sends a hand down to adjust himself, and I could combust with the heat of watching him— *feeling* him—touch his body that way. His breath eases a bit; mine is ruined.

I fit a fingertip to the hollowed center of his pendant, trying to stay on topic. "But does it feel good to wear?" It would feel complicated to me—an earnest gift with a fraught message. *Don't forget to be peaceful, McHuge.*

"Feeling good isn't always the point."

I thought as much. "Can I take it off?"

"It won't get in the way."

"It gets in *your* way," I say. "It feels bad, and I want this to mean something good." I find the knot at the back of his neck and lift it, questioning. Almost before he's finished nodding, I have it undone, and I'm leaning into him so I can toss it at his pack.

"Fuck, you smell amazing," he says, his nose at the corner of my jaw.

"I smell like you, after a week in your tent," I say, and bite his earlobe. He tastes like raindrops fallen from leaves: green and wet with a touch of sweet summer.

He jerks under my fingers, and there's a swell of something hard against my thigh before it falls away again, like a shadow of some rare beast turning under the water. I want to chase it, but I remember what he said about coaxing. About making things *want* to come to you, instead of forcing them.

So I let myself go soft and put my lips against the fullness of his mouth, licking into him like an invitation, letting that be all there is until we're both trembling, necks twining as we seek every last drop of each other. Every inhale is a gasp, every exhale a sigh. He's got one big hand up the front of my shirt and the other up the back, deliciously roughened fingers spread between my shoulder blades. It's like we're outside the river of time, tucked into a safe eddy while history goes on without us, and it's impossible to say which of us is more responsible for the wet spot on the front of his shorts.

He lets go of the breast he's been palming, the nipple tucked between two fingers, and I whimper, disappointed. His handprint feels cool and lonely on my skin.

"Come back."

"I will." He reaches over to the far side of his bed, coming up with a square package between his finger and thumb. His hand shakes as I reach for the condom.

"Did you get this from the first aid kit?"

"You saw those, huh?"

"I'm the camp doctor, Lyle. I went through the kit my first day here. Two dozen condoms is twenty-four more than the Red Cross recommends, by the way."

He shrugs one shoulder. "I didn't want to presume everyone was monogamous and prepared. It seemed like a good idea to have options available."

"Did it seem like a good idea to have options in *our* tent? Were you feeling pretty sure of me?"

"No." He looks down, golden eyelashes fanned against copper freckles. "But I was hoping."

Ah, the way he says *hoping*, like it hasn't been half an hour or a day and a half or two weeks. In his voice, there's a whole year. There might be forever.

My heart slams hard, once, like it skipped a beat. Skipped a year.

"I'm trying not to rush things, but this condom should go on soon. Being this close to you . . . there are probably some swimmers escaping. Or so my high school sex ed teacher always said." A smile hooks one corner of his mouth, which is pinkened from kissing me. He's so comfortable in his body, so secure in the idea that what's happening doesn't have to be perfect. I can't help but feel easy, too.

"I can put that on." Beads of moisture break out across my chest at the mental picture.

"Better not," he says, his hands urging me off his lap. "Maybe next time."

Nobody shucks their shorts with the natural ease of Lyle McHugh, I discover. He doesn't pull in his sweet stomach or flex his glorious chest or make a joke to ease the tension, just fists himself and adjusts before tearing open the package. It's like he was born to be naked, and clothes are a convention he adopts to make other people comfortable.

"Have you by any chance lived in a nudist colony?"

"I wouldn't say I *lived* there. It was more like a short-term residency."

I laugh because it's delightful, and because of course he did, and because he's rolled the condom on with two quick movements, which gives me a lingering clench between my legs. "Very nice," I say, admiring.

"If you're worried about . . ." He makes a vague gesture, having apparently hit the limit of his comfort. "I won't, uh, jackhammer or anything."

"Lyle," I say sternly. "I've seen you naked before. And do *not* make me explain the powers of the human vagina, given a considerate partner and a decent amount of foreplay. I *am* a doctor, you know."

He gives a full-throated shout of laughter with that special low tone caressing the last notes. I don't have an exhibitionist kink, but would I like everyone to hear how I made him laugh? Yes. Yes, I would.

He comes back to bed, stretches out, and pulls me on top. Heat shimmers in my blood, tingling against the cool air as I strip off my shirt. He blinks like a teenager who just undid his first bra, reaching up to palm my small breasts and smiling when I gasp.

"I'm very thankful this happened while we still have light," he murmurs, his gaze loving me up and down. His fingers stroke the barely-there curve of my waist, his thumb circling the dip of my navel as he hefts my legs across the splayed length of his own heavily muscled thighs.

In his blown pupils and half-mast eyelids, I see exactly how thankful he is. I feel it too, sinking into the safety of him, the beauty of him, the care that wraps around me, sweet and hot like spun sugar, daring me to burn my tongue. He's in no rush to move on, making sure he hits every sweet spot again and again until I'm aching for him. Everywhere he's not touching me, my skin tightens with need.

"By 'decent amount,' I didn't mean 'until I die,'" I pant, leaning down to kiss him.

"What *did* you mean, then?"

I intend to answer, but all that comes out is a sound of surprise, because he's fixed his fingers across my leg and has slid his thumb inside my underwear, his ring dark against the pale crease of my thigh. His touch makes me forget everything I know about anatomy, replacing it with the instinct to push back against the gorgeous pressure.

"What was . . . what is *that*?"

He laughs and does some kind of sliding, beckoning finger movement that jolts me like lightning. "Oh," I say, shocked, the word so nakedly hungry I'm almost embarrassed.

I roll off him and onto my side, pulling him to face me so I can take him in hand while he takes me in his. Not because I want things to be even, but because I want to hear him make that low, strangled sound and see his eyes go dark and fucked-up when I change the pressure, then change it back. He doesn't tell me I don't have to, doesn't try to stop himself from having this. The moment takes us both in a stomach-dropping sweep, like a tongue of blue-green water whose smoothness disguises its elemental power.

It's never been easy for me to get out of my head at this particular moment of sex, when it's too soon to know if a climax will happen for me. One-night stands made that easier sometimes. I knew I wouldn't have to have any uncomfortable conversations beyond *You go ahead, I'm fine.* I wouldn't worry I'd be caught and released by someone I wanted to keep. A single night could still be fun even if I didn't hit the biggest waves.

But this isn't like the sex that came with expiration dates. Before tonight, I've never been afraid of endings. If this means something, but I can't be the person he's expecting, then what?

"Hey," he whispers, pulling me back into the moment. "Where'd you go?"

The urge to say "nowhere" pushes in my throat. It would be safer than honesty. But to say "nowhere" here, now, to this man, would dishonor what's happening.

"Sometimes I don't . . . get there. I don't want you to think it's because of you."

His eyebrows draw together, one perfect, one marked. "Last time, you didn't?"

"No, no, I did." My cheeks and chest heat with the memory. The moment I thought I wouldn't, he hitched my thighs higher over his arms and gave me patience, creativity, the willingness to *try*. More than enough to make me scream for real.

"Well then," he says, with a smug smile I've never seen on his gentle face, and I can't help but laugh. "Does this feel good, what we're doing? You want to keep going, stop, try something else?" The crease between his brows is curious, not judgmental. It's shockingly hot. I lo—I really like him.

I like him so much, and I want this to be *something*. I want to hold on to this, and him, and myself, and not let the fear of losing it stop me from reaching for it anyway.

"Keep going. I could do this for a long time, even if nothing else happens for me."

"I would literally love to do this with you all fucking night, Stellar."

I can tell when someone's rushing, trying to get me off so they can tick a box. But Lyle's face, his eyes, his sounds—he really means it. The way he touches me feels like it's for both of us. Like he gets off on the drift of his hand across my belly, thrills at the way my abs jump at his touch, loves the evidence of my pleasure soaking his fingers.

This is enough. More than enough. This sparkling current I'm riding is steadier and better than a lot of orgasms I've had with people who said they loved me, and I want to feel the hell out of it for as long as I can.

I can tell by the rasp in his breathing and the glitter in his eyes that he's here with me. "You good, Stellar J?" His eyes flutter closed as I give him a double tug that makes him arch and thrust into my hand, but he has the trick of me now, and he doesn't waver.

I don't realize how far gone I am until I try to answer and what comes out is, "Don't stop. Don't stop."

"I won't. But you can't do *that*"—he gives me an eye-crossing double tap, calling back to what I gave him—"anymore. For the moment. If you want. Not to stop," he gasps, breath breaking in time with my hand. "In fact. Let go, maybe? Just for a minute." He nudges my arm.

I take my hand away, letting him touch me without touching him in return, and it feels terrifying and amazing. What if I wasn't in control? What if I really let go? I could let him steer us through this current, keep me safe, care for me. Take me over the edge and back again.

For a moment, I'm dizzy with desire and fear.

He must see something change, because he brings his face to mine. His lips trace a curve behind my ear and down to the corner of my jaw. "Hey. Stellar J. It's you and me. We have time for whatever we need. Let go. Let it go now."

Everything's surging inside me, pushing hard and high like a flood, sparkling like sun on water, and I want to believe him. I want to believe in whatever this is.

"Okay," I whisper, drawing out the word. It's not agreement so much as surrender, letting myself *have* without fretting about the cost. Letting him give.

He turns me to my back, hooking a thumb in the waistband of my boy shorts, waiting for me to raise my hips before easing them down to my thighs, my knees, my ankles, the floor.

And when I have nothing left to hide behind, he pulls me back on top. I close my eyes and forget the math, leaning forward to brace against the soft solidity of his chest, pushing until he pushes perfectly back.

"You look so good when you get what you want," he says tightly, roughly, his fingers playing me with steady rhythm. "Tell me what you need."

"Hold on," I gasp. "Hold on to me." He wraps an arm around my back, gripping between my shoulders, his fingers splayed behind my heart.

Alive. I'm alive, and I feel everything.

And I let go, let myself break, break, break across his hand, singing like ice in springtime as it comes apart.

As I come apart.

He lets it ride until I'm good and done, more than done, every last drop caught and savored.

I open my eyes. He's flushed, muscles tensed, agony written across his forehead. I've never seen anything so glorious as Lyle McHugh in the palm of my hand.

"We don't have to do—" he starts, but I'm already reaching back to take him in hand, then taking him inside myself, slow and sweet. The sound he makes—a broken half groan accompanied by a tortured stretch and turn of his pale, beautiful neck—is worth everything to me.

"I get to have this," I tell him, settling in, rocking in the gentle postorgasmic current. "I get to give you this. It's a gift to know you this way."

His fingers tremble on my back. I reach for one hand, then the other, pulling them down to my ass. I'm rewarded by another one of those sounds, more fragmented words, a rough bump upward that takes us both off the mattress. He's trying to watch, but he can't keep his eyes open; with every few thrusts he gasps, and they fall closed. He can't hide a thing, this one. Even the rosy tint of his skin tells me it won't be long.

"It's . . . was it like this . . . for you? Like *this*?" His hips shove up again, harder this time, messier and with less control, and I can't help the ragged sound I make when he finally takes what he wants.

"Yeah," I say, and I'm full to flooding with him and with a tenderness so sharp it aches. "It was good like that for me. So good, Lyle. I think it's because I—"

No—I'm not quite ready to open my hand and let that go. Not yet. "Because I care for you so much," I whisper.

The impulse to have him for myself, all of him, is unstoppable. I drape my body across his heaving chest, easing my legs to frame his thighs, moving just enough to make him shake. I know I've done the right thing when I wrap my arms around him tight and he curls around me in return, every muscle tight, burying a hoarse shout in my hair.

Afterward, I scoot down his body and rest my face on the little curve of his stomach, knees bent where my legs run out of cot, feet kicking idly. "Can I?" I ask, nuzzling into his belly.

Lyle snorts a half laugh and busies himself removing the elastic from my topknot so he can spread out my hair, stroking it with leisurely twists of his wrist.

I like it here. His legs are iron underneath my chest, but against my cheek he's soft and safe.

"What you said, about caring for me," McHuge says.

"Yes?" I realize I've tensed when he gently tugs my hair, encouraging me to relax again.

"You're supposed to say it's good with me because I have a monster in my shorts. You're supposed to tell me my tongue is magic and my fingers play you like a Stradivarius." I can't see his face from here, but there's a smile behind his lazy words.

"If there's anything big about you, it's your head right now," I scoff, more of a bite in my voice than I intended.

"Hey now," he says, tugging my earlobe with such obvious care I have to shut down the tingling behind my eyes. "I'm telling you I liked what you said. I mean, obviously I did. But if I said 'I love you, too,' what would you do?"

Run. I'd run.

"Exactly," he replies, hearing the words underneath my silence. "So I didn't say it. We have time. It can wait until it's not the worst thing you ever heard."

I press my teeth into his right lower quadrant in reply, and he laughs. I want to drink that sound down and get slowly, grandly tipsy on its sparkle, but his confident *We have time* triggers an echo in my heart: *Maybe we don't.*

The Love Boat is precarious, whether Lyle and I hold on to each other or not. Everything ends, sooner or later.

We can't waste any of the time we have.

"What if some things can't wait?" I purse my lips and direct a stream of breath due south. Under my breastbone, there's a satisfying twitch.

He comes up onto his elbows, still-damp hair in wild ginger coils, the bulk of his shoulders giving way to sharply corded stretches of arm, freckled on the outside, pale and secret on the inside. "I'm thirty-four, Stellar. Hardly eighteen anymore."

"When do you think you'll be eighteen again?"

"Hmmm, fifteen minutes?"

"What will we do until then?"

He hauls me up his body, flips us over, and slides down until *his* face is on *my* stomach. He grins up at me, a thrilling touch of wickedness glinting from his teeth. "I have a few ideas to bounce off you."

Chapter Nineteen

Morning light arrives reluctantly on the first day of We've Got This—the last phase before the capstone trip. The cloud cover is dense and low, the light drizzle nothing too unusual for a coastal rainforest. The river, on the other hand, is high and moody. Familiar surface-level sieves of rocks have turned into brand-new underwater hazards. Beneath my hiking boots, the ground squishes, the spongy forest floor saturated after yesterday's downpour.

Sloane looks stiff with the drop in barometric pressure. She, Lori, and Mitch sit together at breakfast, joking about weather-predicting joints.

Jasvinder's breakfast was the only reason anyone got out of bed. He's hooked up a waffle iron to the solar-powered battery and is doling out top-shelf morning calories: delightfully fancy yeasted Belgian waffles topped with a savory combination of shaved ham, poached eggs, and a generous ladle of silky, shiny hollandaise or a sweet-tart pairing of dark chocolate curls, whipped cream, and supremes of yuzu.

Lyle ambles to the front for morning announcements. It

feels different today when I position myself by his side, my head not quite reaching his shoulder. I'm not sure if he's consciously shifted his weight to make a space along his ribs I could tuck myself into if I dared.

I don't quite dare, but I consider it long enough that when I turn to face the room, Sloane's eyebrows arch with surprise. She and I haven't yet had a sisterly chat, given that we spent most of yesterday waiting for Fisher to get out of our way while singing "The Quartermaster's Store." My favorite verse was Sloane's *There was Brent, Brent, who we tried hard to prevent*.

Lyle clears his throat. "As expected, the river is very high today, with a big pushy current and unfamiliar hazards. Stellar and I have decided to postpone paddling until the water's friendli—"

"We can handle it," Brent interrupts. Willow pushes back her chair, grabs her plate, and heads to the fresh fruit station; he doesn't seem to notice. "We have six days of experience, and *my* guidebooks describe the rapids at all water levels."

"Guidebooks can't cover everything. Trees fall. Rocks roll downstream." Lyle speaks affably enough, but after last night I've discovered a new ability to diagnose tiny changes in his body language. His hipshot posture fractionally straightens, his shoulders pulling back and down: he's not happy.

"We'll inspect the rapids," Brent argues, frowning as Willow finishes loading her plate and walks to a different table. "I don't get the problem."

"I can see that," Lyle says, a snap in his voice like an elastic band hitting its breaking point. It's more surprising than scary, but the guests' eyes widen. Lyle flushes a deep crimson, flicking his eyes at me in the signal to jump in.

"What Lyle means is this is a *relationship* course, not a

whitewater course. Even if we could meet our safety standards on the water today, we'd get caught up in technical elements of paddling and lose the opportunity to work on our partnerships. So we're heading for dry land. Dry*ish*, anyway." Lyle's field journal has a whole section devoted to local places, events, and challenges the Love Boat can turn to when bad weather pushes us off the water.

"Pack your phones and lots of lunch. If you need to charge your devices, plug them into the solar battery now. We'll do a shorter yoga practice this morning, then meet up in the parking lot for a mystery road trip."

The clients bus their dishes and exit the pavilion more quietly than usual.

Lyle turns to me, uncertain. "Did I go too far with Brent?"

"No. You sounded a little sharp, maybe, but no one died. It's a low bar, but you cleared it," I say, deploying one of my favorite dark medical jokes.

"Be serious." He presses his lips together. "People get frightened when I'm angry. Situations can spiral fast."

"You're fine." I rub his arms briskly, but not without care. "Our problem child pushed it too far, and Dad got snippy for one second. You're human, and Brent has thick skin. Come here," I say when his mouth stays unhappy, pulling him down for a quick kiss at each corner of his lips. "It's very hot when you stand up for safety," I whisper.

His mouth turns upward where I kissed him. "You think so?"

"Oh, absolutely. The rain's stopped—I'll deal with the breakfast cleanup if you want the outdoor chores."

I'm halfway to the cookhouse with a tub of dishes when Trevor trots up, flashing a cute smile to go with his nice haircut and good skin. Of all the guests, I've gotten to know Trevor the least, and Petra is a close second. It's easy to bond with outgoing people like Lori and Mitch, and we have to keep a close eye on troublemakers like Brent whether we like them or not. But Petra and Trevor don't make friends and don't make waves. When others are chatting around the campfire, they prefer to go paddling or take an evening stroll. Maybe I should've worked harder to draw them into the group.

"Hey, Stellar. I was wondering where we're going today."

Usually Lyle gets the curriculum questions. I might've been wrong about people being scared of him when he's angry.

I try to rebalance the heavy dishes while giving Trevor my best twinkle, the one I used when I told pediatric patients I wanted to look for giraffes in their ears. "The mystery's kind of the point, Trevor."

"Valid, but it would help Petra's anxiety if she knew what to expect."

"Oh. Right." She didn't put that on her intake form, but I can roll with it. "Tell her to meet me at the van a few minutes early? I'll brief her as much as I can."

"McHuge always briefs us before *his* road trips, though. Location, level of difficulty, hazards, learning goals."

"This *is* one of McHuge's road trips." I try not to clench my teeth at the implication that an inferior road trip must be my idea. "Tell Petra to come see me. We can talk through any specific areas of anxiety."

"Sure. Thanks," Trevor says, mouth tight with dissatisfaction. He spins on his heel, leaving me with an unsettled feeling.

The parking lot for the Pendleton Farm trail system is jammed with cars and people. A rainbow-lettered banner reading NATIONAL GEOCACHING FESTIVAL drapes between two poles planted on either side of the trail map.

"Circle up, my forest friends," Lyle calls. "Today we're

challenging the beginner courses our friends at the geocaching society have opened to the public. If you've never geocached before, it's like an outdoor scavenger hunt to find hidden treasure using your phone and your observational skills. The 'treasure' can be anything from a fun object to a secret message. Tag the location and leave the treasure for the next geocachers.

"During the We've Got This stage, you can expect fun and excitement, plenty of personal development, and flexible problem-solving within your team. Today we're doing one last exercise in self-awareness and relationship awareness by geocaching with people other than our partners. In what ways do you miss your partner's input when you're with someone else? What are you doing—good and bad—that you've stopped noticing, and what are they doing that you've stopped noticing?"

We pair off the clients and reinforce the emergency instructions: if anyone gets lost, use the emergency heading—due east—to find the main road, then turn north to get back to the parking lot.

First to go are Lori and Trevor. Lori grins when McHuge says, "May the forest be with you," although Mitch looks none too thrilled to be separated from her wife. She pulled Lori aside when we assigned the partners, but whatever she was concerned about, Lori seemed to dismiss it. I wonder if keen-eyed Mitch knows something about Trevor I don't.

"It's weird to hold a phone again," Sloane says, turning hers over in her hand as she and Willow wait a few minutes before following the first group—we didn't want everyone to clump up like peewee soccer players. The two of them pause at the trailhead to talk strategy, the occasional word filtering back to us over the hum of the crowd.

Willow points at her phone, then looks up at Sloane, lips moving. "Yeah, good idea," Sloane says, nodding. Willow's eyes widen; she shakes her head like she's changed her mind. "No, it's good," Sloane says. "If it's wrong, we'll backtrack and try again." Willow looks at Sloane like she's having an epiphany that's equal parts wonderful and horrible.

"This exercise would be better with our own partners," Brent says, watching Willow walk away without looking back. He sounds uncharacteristically pensive, and even a bit worried.

Wife, his confused expression seems to say, echoing what I told him on the first day. *That's my* wife, *and she looks happy for the first time in days, and it might be because she's not with me.*

Mitch and Brent set off, Brent clearly trying to catch up to Willow, Mitch equally obviously trying to slow him down. Five minutes later, Petra and I hit the trail. Lyle will drift between groups, helping where he's needed.

The forest is mostly cool and dim, but occasional light breaks through where larger trees have fallen, opening up space for scrubby saplings to reach for the sun. Some of the trails are wide and well maintained, rocks stacked on their downhill sides to prevent erosion; others are narrow and braided with secondary tracks that show where hikers have avoided muddy ground. Some hardy passersby have repositioned fallen trees into makeshift footbridges across puddles large enough for a protected wetland designation.

A young family crosses our path, twin preschoolers running ahead, bleary-eyed parents bringing up the rear, each with an identically dressed infant in a backpack.

I stop to wait for Petra, who's examining some days-old bear scat at the side of the trail, her shiny dark braid falling over one shoulder.

Now's my chance to get to know her, maybe. "Hey, Petra." She doesn't respond—distracted, maybe, by the shouts echoing through the trees. "Petra! You okay?"

Her head comes up, a strange look on her face. Almost . . . guilty? "Oh, yes, that's me! Sorry, I zoned out for a second."

"How are you feeling? Am I walking too fast?"

"I'm good, thanks. Whatever pace you want is fine."

"Great. Let me know if you need a break."

"Will do." She sends me a sideways glance like she doesn't know what the hell I'm talking about. She didn't come for a briefing before we set out, like I offered. Did Trevor not tell her about his chat with me?

"You and I haven't had a chance to really talk. I'd love to hear how it's going with Trevor. Everyone's rooting for your friends-to-lovers story."

That gets a small secret smile out of her. "Me and Trevor are . . . good, actually." She ducks her head shyly, tucking a stray lock of dark hair under her red bucket hat. "We have some stuff to figure out, like our work situation. But it's so much more than what I expected with him. It's kind of wild, actually."

"I'm so happy for you. I hope the Love Boat's giving you what you came for."

Petra's smile flattens for a second, then curves up with determined brightness. "Yes. It is."

Aggressive huffing on the trail turns out to be Brent. He power walks up to us, looking over his shoulder. "Come on, Mitch! We can pass these guys. I want to catch Willow and Sloane."

"Would you look at that. Another rock in my shoe." Mitch makes a big deal of looking around for a log to sit on, then meticulously unlaces her hiking boot. Nothing falls out when she takes it off.

"Where are all these rocks coming from?" Brent kicks at the forest floor, which is 70 percent sticks and leaves, 20 percent moss, 10 percent fungi, and 0 percent rocks.

"I have diabetes," Mitch lectures him. "I take my feet seriously."

I cough into my sleeve to hide my smile. We leave them arguing over phantom rocks and head for the coordinates.

A few minutes later we spot Lori and Trevor standing in the middle of the trail. He points at his phone; she shakes her head. "I've done this dozens of times. I know what I'm doing," she says. "Put the map back on your phone, and I'll show you where we have to turn north. I mean west. I mean . . . you know what I mean." Her pale blond hair frizzes out of the elastic on one side, where she keeps distractedly threading her fingers through it. A handprint-shaped smear of dirt and leaves decorates the front of her shirt, like she fell and wiped off her hand there. Her socks are wet past the ankle, no doubt from misjudging one of the deeper puddles.

"You two okay?" I put a steadying hand on Lori's arm. "I have extra socks if you need some."

"It's fine," Lori says, her voice wavering. "I just don't seem to know quite where we are. His phone is never showing the map."

A touch of impatience breaks through Trevor's good humor. "But *I* know where we are. The map app uses a lot of batteries. I'd rather turn it off once in a while. Hey," he says, looking between me and Petra. "You know what we could use? A tiebreaker vote. Petra, would you feel better if you joined us?" He throws me a meaningful look.

It could be a good idea to put Petra and Trevor together, especially if she feels like she can't share her anxiety with me. I'd rather not have another disaster like the one at the Rolling Stones, before I knew about Sloane's hip.

And god knows Lyle would endorse an enthusiastic threesome.

The new group sets off together, and I turn back toward the trailhead. Maybe I can mediate the situation with Brent and Mitch, which should be going critical right about now.

On my own, the forest feels different. I place my feet carefully on the way downhill, aware of the slippery leaves and wet unstable earth.

Slick bare mud gives beneath my right boot, shooting my foot out in front of me. I catch myself before my butt hits the ground, but down on my hands and heels, I see what I wouldn't have otherwise: an arrow made of branches, pointing off the trail. Probably one of the other geocaching destinations—there are half a dozen waypoints hidden along the trail system.

Curiosity pulls me in the direction of the arrow. At a huge hollow cedar stump, another stick arrow points toward a break in the ancient wood big enough to step through.

Inside, the small dirt floor is level and swept. White letters tacked to the walls of the makeshift room read CACHE #4: WELCOME TO THE DANCE FLOOR.

Maybe it's the secret beauty of this place, or maybe it's me being neck-deep in sentimentality lately, but my chest tightens.

"Care to dance?"

I spin around to find Lyle leaning against one softened, aged edge of the doorway, arms crossed over his WEST COAST BEST COAST T-shirt. Inside the tree, the wood matches his hair—dark where it's wet, pale where the rain has missed it, like the sun-lightened golden red atop Lyle's crown.

Last night hovers between us, delicate as breath. I remember his face softly smiling above me, below me, beside me, between my legs.

The intimacy of these deeply gnarled ancient walls hits me like the ocean at the bottom of a cliff jump. We could stream something old-fashioned and sweet. Billie Holiday or Glenn

Miller. The notes would blend with the wind in the trees, and we'd listen for the beat of our hearts to drop.

"We shouldn't get distracted from the guests." We have a week between courses; we could come back here on a nice day. Maybe eat lunch in Pendleton afterward. We could lie in the tent and dream up all kinds of things to do with the next batch of clients. We could bring them here, even.

Maybe this would be our special spot.

I haven't imagined a future like this in so long. There was only a desperate self-replicating present, day after identical day of fury to cover up the fear. The future was about *things*: money, safety, power, choices.

But my future could be about people. About courage.

I could dance.

He pushes off the doorway with his shoulder and strides toward me unrushed, eyes crinkled like he's never been so happy to see anyone, even though he saw me not half an hour ago.

We've barely touched when the shrill of a safety whistle rips through our reverie.

"Ours," I breathe. "That sounds like one of ours."

His shocked, guilty gaze meets mine. "We shouldn't have both been here," he whispers, already turning to run.

We scramble back up the trail, my runner's legs putting me in the lead, my heart galloping even faster than my feet.

Kneeling in a patch of low brush to the side of the path is Lori, face streaked with tears and snot, blowing and blowing her whistle. "Mitch," she sobs between blasts, "Mitch, where are you?"

"Lori," I shout, my hands blocking my ears. Christ, that thing is loud enough to rupture both tympanic membranes. And where are Trevor and Petra?

My mind jumps straight to the worst-case scenario: two clients missing, another hurt. "Lori, stop. Stop! What happened?"

"I don't know, I don't know," she sobs. She's covered in leaves, the elbow of her shirt bloodied and torn. Her skinned knuckles leave streaks of red across her cheeks.

McHuge pulls up, too out of breath to talk, but we don't need words. Whatever I need, he'll make it happen.

"I'm going to take good care of you, Lori. Give me some deep breaths now." I take her wrist, fingers on her pulse, my heart exploding with fear. "Focus on my finger. Now follow it as it moves. Good. Tell me your full name?"

Running footsteps catch up to where Lori, Lyle, and I crouch in the damp leaf litter. "We only left her for a minute," Trevor pants. "My sunglasses fell out of my pocket. Petra figured we'd be able to backtrack faster on our own."

"Oh, *I* figured that?" Petra snaps.

"Why are you mad at *me*? You left her, too."

"Now's not the time, you two. Go find Mitch." The sounds of their argument move away, and I turn back to Lori. Her skin is warm and pink. She's awake and talking. Her heart rate is fast but steady. No signs of a bump to the head, no broken bones, and she's moving all four limbs. She knows her name and birth date, but once I wipe her face and give her a tissue to blow her nose, she starts dodging my questions.

"What's *my* name, Lori?"

She flaps the tissue at me. "Don't be silly. I know who you are."

"Humor me." If I were in the emergency room, I'd be getting an EKG, considering an MRI of her brain, testing her urine and blood. Out here, without even a stethoscope, I'm not particularly useful.

We have to call 911.

"Lori!" Mitch rounds the corner, no sign of a rock in her shoe now. Brent follows her, gawking. I tilt my head at Lyle, who immediately moves to block his view.

"Mitch!" Lori's lower lip trembles, fresh tears pooling in her usually laughing brown eyes. "I'm having a bad day. I want to go home. Can we go home?"

Mitch doesn't look surprised to find Lori confused and bleeding on a mountain trail. She falls to her knees beside her wife, taking Lori in her arms. "Yes, baby. We can go home now. Don't cry, love."

I look over at Lyle, reading the understanding in his eyes. He's an expert on the human mind; he's figured it out, too.

Everything's about to get much more complicated.

Both Lori and Mitch decline the option to call 911, so the three of us take a rideshare to the hospital for a checkup. Everyone else piles into the Mystery Machine and heads back to camp. It's barely afternoon, but all of us are done for the day.

Lori falls asleep against Mitch's shoulder, exhausted and cried out.

"I hate to say this, Mitch, but I have to talk to Lyle about today. If that had happened on the river . . ."

"I'm sorry," Mitch sighs. "Truly. We wanted to keep doing the thing we love as long as we could. I thought it might be the last time. Guess it is. Guess it *was*," she corrects herself sadly. "I wouldn't blame you for asking us to leave."

I put my hand on her arm, giving it a gentle squeeze. "We'll need to figure out whether Lori will be safe on the capstone trip. But as long as her health checks out, you're welcome at camp tonight."

"I'd like that. She would, too. You know," Mitch says softly, glancing at the driver's earbuds, "I never would have taken up canoeing if it wasn't for Lori. Maybe you've noticed there aren't a lot of Black faces in the wilderness. But if you love your wife, you grow to love the things that make her who she is. Have you ever been married, Stellar?"

"No. I almost got engaged once. Before Lyle," I amend hastily, hoping she didn't notice my slip. "But we didn't have time for each other's hobbies." I hardly had my own hobbies, those two years with Jen. My extracurricular activities were the hours upon hours of unpaid work for the department—research, teaching, administration. Medicine was the beginning and end of many of my colleagues' lives. My life, too.

"Lucky you found McHuge, then," Mitch says. "And lucky I found Lori. She's so smart, my Lori. Did you know she was a film studies professor? She could recite every line from the movies she taught. Then she'd mix up a word here and there. Neither of us thought too much of it until one morning she decided to bake bread, then forgot it in the oven and damn near burned down our house." Mitch looks at her with a tenderness that might stop my heart, it's so full of love and loss.

She heaves a long sigh. "Life is strange. I thought she'd be the one taking care of me, with my diabetes. But it's the other way around. Earning money, taking care of the house, memory keeper—it's all my job now. Lori and I have to find value in our choice to love and care for each other, to honor the love we have, and cherish the memory of the love that used to be." Mitch wipes her tears with her sleeve.

I have to press my fingers underneath my own eyes to stay dry. "You two are beautiful together, Mitch."

She shakes her head. "I'm not looking for validation. I'm

secure in my choices. What I'm saying is life isn't fair. I see you watching people. I see you counting what they give you, so you know what to give back. I'm telling you time will steal that from you the way it did for me and Lori. And I don't mean you're selfish," she says, holding up a hand, "but it's obvious how much that man wants to give you that you won't take from him because you think it's going to cost too much. And I won't even mention your . . . sister? Cousin? Whatever Sloane is that you two are keeping secret."

My breath seizes in my chest. Mitch, always watching; me, never dreaming what truths she saw. "I can explain," I croak desperately.

"You don't have to explain anything," she says bluntly, re-settling Lori against her shoulder. "You rescued my wife. Cared for her when I wasn't there. So I owe you one. And we didn't tell you about her memory, so I owe you two. Your secrets are your business, as far as I'm concerned. But if I put it together, Lori might, too. And she's never been the type who can keep a secret. So while you're discussing things with McHuge, you might think about discussing that."

"Yeah. That's fair. Thanks, Mitch." My stomach burns the way it used to when coffee was my midnight breakfast. It's not that I wish Mitch didn't know anything—I wish she knew *everything*. I wish I could tell everyone at the Love Boat what was going on and be done with the deception and the worry. I'm not built for this life. Even my dad knew I was more of a liability than an asset on a con, or he'd never have let me go.

We pull up at the wide double doors of the emergency department. I make sure Lori gets a wheelchair and gratefully retreat when Mitch says she'd prefer to manage the visit on her own.

I walk to a nearby café, spend six bucks on a large Earl Grey, and settle in to worry about how many of my mistakes are coming home to roost.

Lori's official discharge diagnosis is early dementia, temporar-ily aggravated by a change in her environment.

We designed the worst possible activity for her, as it turns out. Unfamiliar forest, strange activity, new partner. She had nothing to ground herself with.

On the rideshare back to camp, we pass the geocaching festival again. A yellow-and-teal van pulls from the parking lot onto the highway, cutting us off.

From the front passenger seat, Alan Fisher turns his head in our direction, his flat expression asserting his inviolable right to rule the road. I don't think he'd recognize me, but I pull my cap down over my face anyway.

We were *just* here. That's the third time he's been where we were on the same day.

Looks like I have another thing to discuss with Lyle tonight.

Chapter Twenty

Back at camp, there are a lot of messy feelings and not a lot of moments to brief Lyle on what Mitch knows.

Campfire turns into an emotional semi-debriefing where Lori shares her diagnosis to hugs and tears from everyone. "But you'll still be coming on the capstone trip, right?" Willow asks.

All eyes turn to Lyle and me.

"Lori and I need to discuss it first," Mitch says diplomatically. But since tomorrow's the last day before the trip, there's no time to waste.

Trevor and Petra apologize sincerely to Lori, but seem to have hit a rough patch with each other. Petra's rigid and tight-lipped, while Trevor alternates between imploring whispers of "We couldn't have known" and fresh bouts of sulking every time she refuses to accept his pleas. Sloane, who's been pale and silent since seeing Lori hurt, retreats to Sunset Dome, re-fusing my offer of company.

After campfire, Lyle takes the Mystery Machine to the fallen tree so he can charge his phone while making calls. He's gone for hours, trying to put logistical solutions in place for a potentially high-needs guest on a trip with limited access to civilization.

I can't go with him—not when a client's recently visited the ER. Alone in the tent, I write pro and con lists and disaster plans in Lyle's field journal. When he gets back, I'll tell him everything, and we'll work the problem together.

I wake at sunrise to find our beds pushed together, Lyle's arm across my waist. His field notes and pen are neatly arranged under my cot, where he must've put them when he found me passed out.

My emotions are still a tangled mess, every instinct on high alert after seeing Fisher at the geocaching festival. I slide out from under his arm to make a morning trek to the groover. On the path, I catch myself scanning for tiny microphones and sun glinting from hidden lenses, feeling only more paranoid when there's nothing.

When I get back to the tent, Lyle beckons me to the double sleeping bag he's made by zipping ours together, his half-lidded eyes dark with promise. It feels good when he makes me forget how worried I am about Lori, Brent, the Love Boat. Our secrets.

Afterward he rolls us over so I can sprawl across his chest while he idly traces the lines of my tattoo—wires leading to switches in a spidery motherboard.

"Do you miss lying on top of someone after sex because I'm too small?"

He gives a quiet half laugh, mostly breath. "It's a little weird to bring up my sexual past one minute after orgasm."

I lift my head. "Dodging the question, McHugh?"

He sends me a look. "Hardly. And no. I stopped being able

to do that when I was fifteen. It was always kind of awkward at my size."

"You lost your virginity when you were fifteen?" I kept mine until university. Sneaking around in back seats took time I didn't have in high school, with classes and work and my mom.

"No."

My head comes off his chest. "The fuck! Who was banging you at *fourteen*?! By the way, we name names in this relationship. No witness protection allowed."

He smiles at my outrage, or maybe because I used the word "relationship."

"Britt Carstairs, if you must know. We were counselors at a sleepaway camp for disadvantaged kids. The pay was terrible. I think the owners' hearts weren't in it. The next summer, they renovated the dining hall into a wedding venue." Idly, he twists my hair and gives it a tug that makes my skin burst into shivers. I rest my face in the negative space between his pecs and give in to the pleasure.

"Britt Carstairs," I prod.

"Right. Well, put a bunch of horny, curious teenagers together with limited adult supervision after lights-out, and there you have sleepaway camp. Britt was sixteen, assumed I was a couple years older, and broke up with me when she realized the age difference went the other way."

"I hate her."

Underneath me, his shoulders bump in a shrug. "People always misjudged my age. When I was a toddler, people in the grocery store would ask my mom why her six-year-old was throwing tantrums like a three-year-old. My friends' parents freaked out about normal stuff like roughhousing, even though I never hurt anyone by accident. My high school athletic director got accused of falsifying my age so many times, I quit joining sports teams. There was a lot of pressure for me to live up to my size."

I feel how much he doesn't like these memories in the muscle tension under my cheek, the intake of breath as he lifts his chin. How must it have felt for a kid to always have to be the bigger person—literally?

"You must've been so angry," I whisper into his chest, even though I mostly feel sad for the little boy he was.

"Anger doesn't get you anywhere. And being big, white, and male isn't exactly a disadvantage in this world."

"No, but . . ." I'm not sure whether I should bring up what happened when he was seventeen. To me, the important thing wasn't that he got blamed for a fight he didn't start. It was that his family didn't back him up. I'm sure they had a lot going on with his brother's illness, but his own parents should've known he was still a child no matter how much he looked like an adult.

He still needed someone to defend him. He needed to believe it wasn't okay for people to deliberately push him to the breaking point, then claim he scared them when he pushed back.

Especially because I need him to help me push back now. Something's happening in camp, I'm almost certain.

"McHuge . . ."

"Uh-oh, fun's over if it's 'McHuge,'" he says, rolling us to face each other and resettling me so my eyes are level with his. Usually I hate it when people presume to move my body around, but I know he's not doing it because my small size makes him feel big. It's just something he can do to make things easy and kind of lovely.

I wish I didn't have to ruin the feeling, but it can't wait. I pick the most urgent item first.

"On the way home from the hospital, we saw Fisher's crew leaving the geocaching festival."

"Okay."

Okay? "We've seen him three times in five days. He's following us somehow. He's trying to copy the Love Boat."

He shakes his head, his generous mouth pinched into a conflicted line. "He was at a public festival on a day when any ethical whitewater outfit would have stayed off the river. It could be a coincidence."

"No. It's a pattern."

"Are you sure?" I know he can read my tiny sliver of doubt. Face softening, he says, "I'm worried about making a fuss when we have no proof. If we end up in a public battle, I'll get painted as the big scary angry guy who's out for revenge. It's better to lie low and let this burn itself out if we don't have hard evidence he's done anything illegal."

He's talking like a lawyer. Probably quoting his own lawyer from half a lifetime ago, who undoubtedly taught him not to fight back against rumors or trolls—stay quiet, and the gossip mill will find a new target.

My heart twists hard at Lyle once again refusing to defend his boundaries with anyone but me. He gives everybody everything, but he can't—or won't—give me this. He promised he'd hold on to me, and instead, he's holding on to all the voices that ever told him he wasn't allowed to fight back.

And he's wearing his necklace again today, like it's a pair of handcuffs he puts on voluntarily.

"I don't care if it's not illegal! It's *wrong*," I cry, too loudly for the fabric-walled illusion of privacy that's all we have in this place. "The plausible deniability is part of it. I've been gaslighted like this before. So have you—*by Fisher.* This is our livelihood we're talking about. This is someone possibly spying on our *home*. If they're willing to take a risk like that, what else are they willing to do?"

I hate how paranoid I sound. How flimsy and dismissible my own words make me feel, as if my old department chief might jump out of the bushes and scold me to stop being *emotional*.

An awful sense of impending doom yawns in my chest. The first time a trauma patient told me they felt like they were going to die, I—the lowly medical student—clasped their hand and reassured them we'd take good care of them. My attending physician freaked the fuck out and repeated every test, successfully diagnosing the internal bleeding that hadn't been apparent before.

We don't ignore feelings of doom in emergency medicine. More often than not, they're right.

Lyle clasps my hand, bringing it to his lips. Those lips have kissed me everywhere, said every good thing to me, told me he cared. Told me I mean something.

But now Lyle's lips tell me, "If all Fisher's team has is our geographical locations, they have nothing that matters. They don't have my field notes. They don't have our teachings or debriefings. Our clients signed NDAs; we can sue them if they steal our confidential course information. I can't believe anyone here is a criminal. Can you?"

He hasn't learned what my dad taught me at age ten: it's only a crime if you get caught, and laws only matter if you have the power to see them enforced. If we go bankrupt, who'll pay the lawyers to sue Fisher? No one.

He's right, though. We have no evidence beyond chance meetings and bad feelings, and I don't think the Mounties believe in a sense of doom the way we do in medicine.

"I believe you, Stellar. I trust your instincts. But I can't chase after someone in anger—not ever again. And *we*," he says, landing hard on the pronoun, "can't live like this. We can't spend our lives holding our arms over the things we create, or we won't be able to build anything new. We're making more than a one-size-fits-all curriculum that we can recycle over and over. You and I are special together. We'll create something unique every time. They can't take that away."

"But what if the Love Boat dies? What if Fisher kills it?" I hate my voice for shaking.

He presses his broad, hard palm to mine, intertwining our fingers. I can feel the scars that mark his fingertips where they curl around the back of my hand. "Then you and I will be all right."

Lyle doesn't understand. He was able to get out of his PhD program and make a career. He recovered.

"What if I'm not all right?" I whisper, the words small and fearful. "I wasn't last time. And if the Love Boat dies, I can't afford to stay in Grey Tusk. I'll have to leave town. Leave Liz." *Leave you*, my heart whispers.

"I hope this place doesn't die." His voice is so kind. Gentle, like I mean something to him. "But if it does, you won't die."

"But something *does* die," I say urgently. "They kill a part of you. You're not the same after that."

I've been undead for a year. Angry and afraid and ashamed for a *year*. Unable to forgive the people who were supposed to have my back, unable to forgive myself for trusting them.

"You deserved better, Stellar. I won't minimize how shitty it was for you. But I believe all the best parts of you are still there, waiting. I see them, every day. You can put yourself back together. Surgically, if you have to."

My laugh has the short wet sound of someone who's not quite crying.

"I don't want to burn our days and nights thinking about

what they're doing. Let's make *us* the best we can be," Lyle murmurs, tempting me to soften in the face of his openhandedness. But some last fragment of wrath ignites, its fire just hot enough to help me resist. I can't go along to get along the way I did at the hospital, ignoring the signs because people I shouldn't have trusted reassured me everything was fine.

Even if this time it's Lyle telling me everything is fine.

"I want to call Sharon. I'll take the fall if my suspicions are wrong, but I want her to know what we've been seeing."

"We've covered this, Stellar. Sharon can't do anything."

"But there must be *something*. What if we went public?"

"If we go public, we expose ourselves. We're faking our engagement, for—"

"It's not fake!"

He shoots me a pained look. "So you proposed because you love me? And you're definitely planning to marry me?"

I draw back, stung. He knows it's too soon. I promised him my best; what more can I give?

"Okay then," he says, releasing my hand to rub his eyes. "At the very least, our relationship history won't stand up to serious examination. Any press coverage could also expose your reputation in the medical community, however unfair and unearned. My juvenile record, too. Plus the fact that our celebrity endorsement is coming from your sister. I'm not trying to be an asshole, Stellar, but I have some experience with crisis public relations that you might not. Once your reputation gets cemented, sometimes nothing can change it. Not even the truth."

I press my lips together on a wave of nausea. He's right again: we're vulnerable, and a lot of our weak spots are my fault. I put a foot wrong—a *toe* wrong—with the milk and lost my job. What would happen if everything Lyle listed became public knowledge?

Still. "One more thing. *One* more suspicious thing happens with Fisher, and we call Sharon, fallout or no fallout."

"Deal." Lyle eases out of our sleeping bag, leaving me shivering with the rush of cold, damp air. "I'll start the hot water. You stay here. Get an extra ten minutes of sleep," he says, tucking me in so I'm cozy and contained like a kitten curled in a hat.

He only has to press his big hands on my shoulders, my ribs, my hip bones, and I'm hypnotized into a half slumber.

We didn't get to discuss what Mitch knows about Sloane, but what could he do about that, even if he wanted to? I'll wear sunglasses and stick my hair under a hat so Sloane and I look as different as possible.

And the minute we get back from the overnight, I'll call Sharon. Once the guests are safely checked out, we'll have a week and change to deal with fucking Fisher. He won't be able to follow us on the capstone trip, anyway—not after we changed our campsite at the last minute to better accommodate Lori.

It's reasonable to wait. Lyle will hold on to what matters. We'll be all right. I say it to myself again, then again, repeating it like a mantra until it's time to get up.

Chapter Twenty-one

"Oof, I'm nervous," I breathe, watching Jasvinder wave good-bye from the Mystery Machine, a cloud of dust rising under his wheels.

Lyle surveys the unruffled water, dyed a flawless morning blue by the mountain sky; Babe gives me a skeptical doggy eyebrow raise in tandem with her master. "Nervous about what?" he asks, gesturing at the unparalleled level of perfection like he's thrown open the gates to Valhalla.

Bluebird Lake is the first in a system of wide, calm lakes linked by narrow stretches of whitewater. Navigating whitewater with loaded canoes is a whole different skill, so we've chosen friendly waters for the guests' first expedition. Today and tomorrow are for fun, consolidation of skills, and a long lovely goodbye to our first session.

We'll cover three lakes today and two tomorrow, plus a surprise detour to a gnarly stretch of whitewater where we hope to see some pros kayaking over a waterfall. Then we'll pack everyone up and shuttle them to Grey Tusk, where they'll find bigger beds and better showers, but never again the caliber of food they ate with us. Jasvinder is a genius, and if a Michelin-starred restaurant hasn't scooped him up by next summer, we'll have to double his pay.

Today I'm hoping hard that there will be a next summer. The guests are excited, loading their canoes with seaworthy barrels of food, roll-top sacks of clothing, foolproof compact tents, even fishing gear. Snatches of laughter and conversation drift back to us from the shore. There's a feeling of everything and everyone coming together.

We've reduced our planned paddling distance so we can stay in a car-accessible campsite with decent cell signal in case of emergencies. Jasvinder and a friend will shuttle the Mystery Machine and trailer to tonight's campsite, which means the van can haul some of the gear and Lyle was able to clear space for Babe in his boat. This should please the dog no end.

I'm hoping for the best, meaning three couples graduating with plans for lavish commitment/recommitment ceremonies and even more lavish online reviews. Failing that, I'd accept a trip where no one gets hurt or lost or thrown out of the tent by their pissed-off partner.

But I can't quite shake that lingering sense of doom from yesterday.

"I'm sure there's nothing to worry about," I say, hopping up and down to shake the nerves out. "But it would be good if one *particular* client had reason to write nice things about us. Not saying who."

Lyle shakes his head with a soft smile, ginger curls sneaking out from under his paddling helmet. He never looks more at home than when he's in whitewater gear, paddle cocked like an extension of his arms, flashing an adventuresome grin. It makes me seriously consider fulfilling the cringeworthy Canadian stereotype of sex in a canoe.

"Whitewater rule number one, Stellar J."

"Yes, yes. Sometimes clients need to go in."

"Exactly. We're their guides now. All we can do is show them possible paths. Where they go is up to them."

As always, he's managed to gentle my vibrating parts with words that may as well be one long stroke of his hand from my undercut to my lower back.

He heads down to the shore, cupping his hands around his mouth. "Circle up," he calls, voice communication being a luxury we'll have for most of today. "Everyone in canoes, come toward shore. Let's go over the group rules. Each paddler gets to volunteer one," Lyle says.

"Stay together!" Lori shouts, almost before he's finished speaking.

"Don't run any whitewater you don't want to," Willow says from the bow of her canoe. She wanted the stern, but a coin toss was all Brent would agree to. It would have been fine if he hadn't made such a production of winning, but he did, and now her ramrod-straight spine refuses to twist a single degree toward him. Behind her, he's angling his body this way and that, trying to see around her turned back.

So close, guy, I want to tell him. *How can you be so close and still not get it?* But he remains hung up on the persona he's been defending since the day they walked into camp. In his mind, he's the strong one, the sensible one, busy living up to his version of manhood. It's not about Willow at all—and I think she's figured out how much she doesn't like that.

"Zipped and clipped in the red zone!" Sloane shouts in the hoarse, husky voice she uses for her worst moment in the *Nighthawke* trailer. Everyone giggles, because the whole point of this trip is *not* to have any heroics.

There's an awkward pause, then Petra breaks in with a

tentative, "Have fun," which falls somewhat flat until Trevor steps to her side, puts his arm around her, and echoes, "Yeah!" She smiles up at him, and I feel one notch more optimistic.

"You've learned much, apprentices," Lyle intones, to general laughter. "Here is my final teaching. The point of this trip is to show you where you can go with your new whitewater skills and your new relationship skills. The canoe will feel different when it's got more things in it than the two of you—could be camping gear, could be jobs and money and family in there.

"How has whitewater changed you, individually and together? Talk to each other, feel the silence with each other, tell each other what you want. Point out what you see. Notice how your partner sees different things or sees the same things differently."

I have to hand it to Lyle, he's got a way of making a day of hard work feel downright spiritual.

And actually, it turns out he's right. The lake system is maybe ten kilometers from downtown Pendleton, yet it smells like we're a million miles from civilization, the summer scent of warm evergreens carrying on the breeze. The rapids are fun, with narrow, canyon-like passes that feel more dramatic than they are.

Mountains carpeted in fluffy green unroll in luxurious ripples down to velvety blue water. The guests' chatter is punctuated by laughter loud enough to warn the wildlife for miles around. We don't spot the moose or bear I know Mitch is hoping for, but we see a golden eagle dive, then pull up a millisecond before it hits the water, a wriggling silver shape in its claws.

We break for lunch near a narrow soaring waterfall. Everyone sprawls on the sun-warmed rocks except Brent. He sits on one end of a log, the rest of it conspicuously empty after Willow declined to join him.

Part of me wants to see him reap what he's sown. But sometimes it's better to be kind than right.

For Willow, I tell myself, settling into the space next to him and unwrapping my sandwich from its waxed cloth. "You know, if you want Willow to look at you, the way to do that is to put yourself in the bow."

Miserably, Brent swallows a mouthful of roast beef on sourdough. "Then she'll be looking at my back." He's a dumbass, but his sad eyes and slumped posture make him almost sympathetic. And Willow married him, so she must have seen something good in him once upon a time.

"No, guy." I'm just a guide; where he goes is up to him. "Then *you* can turn to *her*. Put your wife first for once, and see if that doesn't land you somewhere different."

He freezes halfway through another bite, comprehension dawning in his brown eyes. I pat him on the shoulder, businesslike. "I'm going to go sit with the group. Maybe you'd like to join us."

Around midafternoon, Lyle slides his canoe into position beside me and Sloane, angling his head at Willow and Brent. She's in the stern, happily steering; he's turned to face his wife with a tentative smile. "Sometimes . . ."

"Yeah, yeah. Sometimes they need to go in," I say, reaching out to snag his gunwale and bring him close enough to kiss.

"What was *that*?" Sloane says when he paddles away. She's abusing her sisterly authority to tease me about Lyle every time he paddles by, which is often. "My acting tips were good, but not *that* good."

"Quiet, oh my god! Sound carries over water. I'll tell you later," I hiss, as she laughs.

The group falls silent as we paddle past a mountainside of blackened trees, a relic of the fires from new, hotter summers.

"It's so sad," Lori murmurs. Behind her, Mitch silently wipes her eyes with the heel of her hand, but she's watching Lori, not the forest. Though we try to hold on to them, the things we love are fragile. Sometimes beauty is lost. Sometimes one tree burns and the one right next to it remains standing, and even then, you don't know which of the ones that were spared will still be standing a year from now.

Sometimes you can hold on, though. I mentally tighten my grip on every beautiful thing I've found over the last two weeks: Lyle, my sister, the Love Boat. Liz was right when she said I needed something, and now that I've found my some-things, I won't be letting them go.

By end of day, we've covered a lazy eleven kilometers. We make a quick portage, then paddle across a neighboring lake to our new campsite, where the Mystery Machine awaits.

I occasionally catch the faint hum of the highway in the distance, but apart from that, it's every bit as good as the campsite Lyle originally booked. Our rainbow of boats looks so fantastic on the sandy beach, I roll my pants up to my thighs and wade into the water to take photos for the Love Boat's website, after arranging the paddles in a pretty row against a stand of trees.

"Feeling better?" Lyle asks softly, walking out to wrap his arms around me from behind.

"Okay, fine, you were right."

He laughs and then buries his face in the crook of my neck, breathing me in. "I know." His smile tugs at the tender skin of my neck, telegraphing promises for later. I catch Lori watching from shore and brace for lovebirds-based teasing, but it doesn't come. Instead, she smiles and turns to add a few more items to the laundry line Brent put up while Willow pitched their tent.

With the shorter paddling distance, we have some time to relax before dinner. Lyle strings a hammock between two trees, perches his glasses on his nose, and settles in with his field journal to make notes. Mitch declares her intention to take a canoe out and see what's biting; Sloane decides to tag along. It's a good sign that Mitch feels comfortable leaving Lori in camp. The two of them seem relaxed and peaceful, able to enjoy the trip even through the bittersweet knowledge that they're doing something for the last time.

Sloane turns out to be excellent at fishing, much to the annoyance of Mitch, who had to teach Sloane how to bait a hook but didn't get a single bite herself. For dinner, we grill fat rainbow trout on the fire-safety-compliant portable stove.

Sloane accepts the ceremonial first serving of buttery fish paired with a big scoop of rice from the preseasoned packets we stashed in the barrels—like any proper camping food, it's fast, easy, and doesn't weigh much. She takes a bite and chews reverently, eyes closed. "This isn't better than Jasvinder's food, but somehow . . . it is?"

Wordless sounds of agreement echo around the firepit as we fork up the freshest fish we'll ever eat.

After dessert—camp coffee and squares of dark chocolate—people linger at the firepit, speculating about tomorrow's surprise expedition.

I sneak off for a quick dip in the lake. I towel off my hair while standing outside the golden circle of light from the portable lantern Lyle situated in the firepit. Babe sprawls on the sand nearby. Our problem children, Brent and Willow, sit side by side on a bleached log, his arm around her. He's listening without a single *well, actually* as she chats to Sloane, Mitch, and Lori.

Whatever kind of article he writes, I don't think it will be the one he imagined.

Trevor and Petra sit apart from the main group. Despite this morning's détente, they lean away from each other, their bodies stiff. I can't hear them, but I can see Petra talking rapidly, gesturing at the other guests, then falling silent as Trevor talks over her. She clasps his hands, making an obvious appeal; he won't meet her eyes. Finally, he stands and pulls away from her, heading toward the clearing where we've pitched the tents.

A cool finger of this morning's dread draws a line across my heart.

I drape my towel over the clothesline, then head to where Lyle's double-checking the boats, making sure they're drawn up far enough from the water.

"You busy?"

"Nope," he says easily, pulling his canoe up last. "But you're very far away. I can hardly hear you." He scoops me up in the crook of one arm and plants a quick kiss at the corner of my lips.

My hand flies to my mouth. "Did you just give me a *peck*?"

"That I did," he says with lazy satisfaction. "It's what engaged people do." He stretches his neck upward to do it again, lingering this time.

I haven't seen him from this angle since last year, at the concert. So much has changed since then, but my heart recognizes both images, layering them—one over the other—into a single picture.

Lyle.

He looks like everything: Love and sex and kindness and belonging, strength and generosity and fun. Our past, our present, and all the painful things in between that give this moment a beauty so piercing I may cry.

He's looking at me like I'm all those things, too.

I'm in love with him.

Maybe I've been in love with him since the moment he pulled me off the ground and asked if I was all right on a day when I really wasn't.

I put my arms around his neck and my lips on his and don't take them off until I'm flirting with the idea of abandoning the guests for a special tandem canoe ride.

"I'm glad we waited," I whisper. "I'm glad you waited for me."

"It was a long wait," he says back. "But worth it. For you."

I kiss him again, a true peck this time. "We shouldn't court distraction until lights-out. I came down to talk about Petra and Trevor."

"Ah, that's a shame," he says, after I've filled him in on the relationship theater. "But it doesn't have to be a failure. They still learned something about themselves. And canoeing."

I love him for being idealistic, and I'm damn glad he has me to be hardheaded. "You and I can appreciate that, but they might need some time to get there. For now, I don't want them to leave with a bad taste in their mouths."

He makes a considering sound. It's low and slow, a lot like the sound he makes when he's above me, on his elbows. I wonder how quiet we can be in the much smaller campsite we're in tonight. Or in a boat.

"They could be worried about damaging their friendship. Especially because they're colleagues. We could focus on that angle," Lyle muses. "Tomorrow, we can each debrief one of them individually. See if we can help them move forward."

"I haven't done anything like that before," I say, uncertain. "I've barely debriefed with the group."

"I have some thoughts in my field journal. You can read while I heat the evening wash water. We can work up a strategy by breakfast."

We walk past the firepit on our way to the tents. I notice Petra sitting silently at the edge of the conversation. Her hands are pinned between her thighs, her shoulders rounded and tense.

I hope Lyle has a miracle in that journal.

I'm reaching for the zipper of our tent when Petra skids up to us.

"Hey! Hey, here you are!" She's breathless, eyes wide.

My mind immediately starts cataloguing dark possibilities. "What's wrong? Is someone hurt?"

She laughs brightly. "No! Oh my god, sorry, nothing like that. We need you two for a sing-along."

I press my hand to my racing heart, relieved. "We'll be there in a minute."

"No!" Petra blurts. "I mean, can you come now? We have something planned. Um, a song. A very special song we wrote, and we need you both there."

"Is this a prank on me and Lyle?"

"Nooooo," she says, too nervous for it to be anything else. Whatever—I'm up for it. If they want to dump a barrel of lake water over our heads, I'm willing to stand there and look honored. It's got an old-fashioned summer camp flavor that will make a lot of memories for everyone.

"All right. Let's hear this song." I elbow Lyle.

"Right on. Let me grab something real quick."

"Don't go in there," Petra yelps, raising a hand in a *stop* gesture. "I mean, if you don't come right now the surprise will be ruined."

There's . . . *something* in her voice.

I look hard at Petra the way I've failed to until now. She forces a wobbly smile, while Lyle's wearing a deepening frown.

This doesn't feel like a prank anymore.

"You good, Petra?" Lyle asks slowly.

"Fine. Great. We just miss our instructors, and it's our last night."

She's talking too loudly. There's something she doesn't want us to hear. Something she wants me to agree to ignore.

For a second, I want to hold on to the illusion she's offering, the one I'm horribly sure I've been falling for all along.

I lean toward the tent, listening. There's a slow, low-pitched sound from the inside, like the rumble of a zipper someone's trying to open very, very quietly, one tooth at a time.

I reach for the zipper pull, knowing I have to be fast.

"No, wait! Stellar, don't—"

I open the front of our tent, throwing the flaps wide. Halfway out the back door, Trevor freezes, Lyle's field notes in one hand, his cell phone in the other. Trevor's texting app is open, the name "Alan Fisher" visible. He's sent a batch of photos, the top one a bright rectangle of white covered with Lyle's apple-shaped vowels and arrowing capital letters.

All I can think is *It's happening again.*

Chapter Twenty-two

For a long frozen moment we stand there, Trevor halfway out the back door of the tent, the rest of us clustered at the front. Behind me, Lyle's harsh breathing makes a jagged, uneven backbeat with Petra's frightened sobs.

I want to believe Trevor's not holding Lyle's field journal and a phone full of stolen images, but every time I look, reality stays the same.

The spell breaks, everything going from zero to free fall in the space of a skipped heartbeat. Lyle steps forward; Trevor stumbles back, tripping over the fabric threshold and landing hard on his ass. He struggles to his feet, eyes darting toward where the Mystery Machine sits waiting, keys in their well-known hiding spot under the sun visor. Nothing's a secret at this camp anymore, it seems.

"I can explain! Please let me explain," Petra cries over and over.

Lyle doesn't miss Trevor's tell. He puts his body between Trevor and the parking area with two long steps. His shoulders are tight, elbows cocked, hands open; he moves with an easy grace that reminds me of the way he paddles his canoe, except tonight his economy of motion is less beauty, more beast.

"I believe you have something of mine." Lyle's expression—calm spread over fury in a too-thin layer—might have been what his high school bully saw before he turned to run, the way Trevor's running with Lyle's journal now.

I should be angry, but I can't summon a single spark. I should at least be afraid—not of Lyle; he might've developed a bark, but he'll never bite. Regardless, the situation is escalating so fast, a tipping point can't be far off. I should be worried about that. I should be furious that Trevor and Petra—if those are their real names, considering how often Petra blanked on hers—came here to steal from us and succeeded. I should be terrified to lose the work I managed to fall in love with despite my best intentions not to.

Instead, I feel a strange relief. Everyone will finally see what I saw. It wasn't paranoia after all.

I follow Trevor's clumsy retreat and Lyle's relentless advance. I can think of exactly one way to work this problem, and if that doesn't solve things, then I don't know what to do.

"Let it go, Lyle. Don't chase him."

Trevor and Petra already got what they came for, and we can't get it back. Everything we worked on this session, everything Lyle researched and reflected on and painstakingly handwrote—it's digitalized now, soaring into the ether. Already on Fisher's phone, probably. Lyle's field notes are lost in every way that matters.

Trevor turns toward the firepit, his pace picking up. "Don't touch me, you fucking maniac," he shouts. An uneasy murmur rises as the guests come to their feet, Babe rousing herself from her adoring slump against Sloane's leg.

"Those are *my* notes." Lyle's voice is so, so quiet. It's his body that shouts—the tight, controlled cadence of his steps, the bunching readiness in his thighs, the fisted hands and clenched shoulders.

All Lyle's doing is keeping pace with Trevor's retreat. But someone who wasn't at the tent might see Lyle driving Trevor toward the lake, setting him back on his heels.

"Trevor. Put the book down and step away." I hope I sound like I'm trying to help him, not trying to defuse an unstable Lyle.

"Hey, hey." Lori steps forward. "There's no need—"

"Don't get between them, love," Mitch says, low-voiced, her hand coming to Lori's elbow.

"Stellar?" Sloane asks, layers of uncertainty coloring her tone. Babe growls, tail between her legs.

My brain chugs and clunks, unable to work the problem. My heart is iced over and useless.

Anger was my best defense. It kept me nimble, fed me ideas, pushed me to keep trying. It kept me safe in moments like this, and now I don't have it.

"Come on, Petra," Trevor says, backing toward the beach. "We have to go. We're not safe here."

Petra sobs, looking around the circle of shocked faces.

"My book first, please." The more Lyle focuses on his notebook, the more our guests drift backward, eyes huge and faces slack. His ring is a dark blur on his left hand—his dominant hand. Its metal would carve a groove in Trevor's cheek if they should meet.

"The notes are gone, Lyle. They've already sent everything to Fisher. There's nothing more we can lose. Hey," I say, snapping my fingers to get his attention. "*McHuge*. Stay with me. I need you to have my back here."

Maybe getting him in touch with his anger was a huge fucking mistake. Maybe he should have stayed kind, and I should've stayed angry. Maybe our misguided attempts to help each other led to our downfall.

"Give it to him, Trevor." Petra grabs Trevor's arm to stop him from tripping into a canoe. Behind them, the lake glimmers under a cool, pale moon.

"I didn't have time to take pics of everything. We need the book. Back off, dude," Trevor snaps, his shaky voice undermining his attempt to sound authoritative. "You can't touch me. That's assault."

"Trevor." Brent makes a pacifying gesture. "I'd give him the book. When he was seventeen, he—"

"Shut *up*, Brent," Willow says, and for once, he does.

"I just want the notes." McHuge puts out a hand, palm up, keeping it at waist level.

Trevor's entire body lurches in terror. He swings the journal wildly, clipping Lyle's face with one hard-edged corner.

Lyle jerks back, a hand coming to cover his left eye.

An emotion finally comes: terror, cold and immobilizing. My limbs stay weak and stuck, my brain blank. I need to work the problem, and I can't.

"He swung first! You saw it, you all saw it, he made the first move." Trevor takes the opportunity to scoop up all the paddles from where they're photogenically propped against the trees. He scrambles around the canoes, shoving the nearest one—Lyle's—halfway into the water, dumping all the paddles inside. "This whole place is a scam! Those two"—he waves at me and Lyle—"are no more engaged than Petra and I are."

There's a moment for a collective inhale.

Willow's voice cuts through the silence. "Stellar? Is this true?" She sounds so shocked. So disappointed.

My mouth opens, but I can't speak.

Sensing the advantage, Trevor stands up straighter. "There's more. Much more. McHuge—he stole the idea for the Love Boat. Stellar's supposed to be the camp doctor, but she hasn't practiced medicine for over a year, and her dad is a convicted felon. And we can't prove Sloane and Stellar are related—yet. But we will. I'm not the bad guy here, whatever you may think."

I almost laugh into the silence. To think I was worried about Mitch and Sloane spilling the beans, and the whole time Trevor had all of our secrets and his own to boot.

Every con comes to an end, as my dad used to say.

Lyle takes his hand away from his face. With a tentative finger, he touches his crooked eyebrow, expression darkening as he finds new blood over the old scar. He's trembling, clearly furious.

And everyone's terrified of him.

"Come *on*, Petra." Trevor's poised at the stern, ready to launch.

Petra dodges through the boats, snagging a random life jacket as she goes. She's hardly gotten both feet in the boat when Trevor pushes off, leaving us literally up the creek without a paddle.

With a high, sharp bark, Babe gallops through the shallows, desperate not to miss her ride. She jumps over Trevor to take her rightful place in the bow, her claws scratching the hell out of his legs as she wrestles past.

"Ouch, fuck!" He pushes her forward, managing to get in a couple of steering strokes to match Petra's power in the bow. They're ten feet off shore, now twenty, now forty, as far out of our reach as if they were cruising at thirty thousand feet.

"Babe!" Lyle yells, splashing into the water. At his call, the dog starts jumping from gunwale to gunwale. She howls in confusion and terror—painful, grinding wails. On shore, seven stunned people watch the disaster unfold.

Petra twists in her seat. "Trevor, the dog!"

"Too late," Trevor says, his voice carrying over the water. "We're not going back."

Lyle seems to curl in on himself for a moment, then leans back and lets out a roar so huge and fearsome I couldn't even have imagined it coming from a human, let alone from him. The pain in it hurts my ears, hurts my soul, as loud as the night my father laid a double stripe of rubber down the middle of King Street so every time I came home I'd see my mom leaving all over again.

When it stops, I've got my hands over my ears and my eyes squeezed shut.

"Stellar," my sister says, stroking my arms. "It's okay, honey. Let go now."

"Stellar." Lyle's voice is shredded. He takes a step toward me, then, seeing something in my face, he steps back. "I didn't touch him. He took my notes. He took my *dog*. I didn't touch him." He reaches out, but I need my hands on my ears. I'm numb and the dog is barking and Lori is crying and I just lost everything.

Again.

The sound he makes this time is quiet, hardly more than a croak from his ruined throat. He walks out of the water, past me, past everyone, breaking into a run when he reaches the firepit.

My trance breaks. "Stop! Lyle, *stop*! Don't you leave me—"

He's gone, vanished into the woods, branches swaying where he passed.

He left me here, on my own.

A gigantic splash pulls everyone's attention back to the water. The Petra-sized silhouette in the bow is shouting at the Trevor-shaped one in the stern. She's standing up, rocking the boat, throwing paddles into the lake in the direction of a low sleek head and two flailing paws.

Babe, who isn't wearing her life jacket.

I'm down at the shore, both hands gripping the deck plate of a canoe, hauling it into the water before I have a whisper of a plan in place. I climb in, crouching low. "Brent!" I bark. "Push me toward Babe, as hard as you can." I don't trust him, but he's the strongest person here, and I need all the muscle I can get.

Actually, I need Lyle, but I don't have him. I only have me.

"But you have no—"

"Now, guy! Do it now."

Brent scrambles to obey, counting to three before launching me out into the dark water. Aiming a rudderless watercraft at a drowning dog is not much of a plan, but I don't know what else to do.

It's a chance. It's me, working the problem.

I drag my hand in the water, trying to steer without losing too much momentum. Babe spots me, gurgle-barking in my direction. She's in full panic mode, but working hard. She didn't give up and let herself sink. I won't give up either.

"Here, girl! Babe, come!" I tap the side of the canoe the way I've seen Lyle slap his thighs when he calls her. God, she's going to make it.

I reach down as far as I can without tipping, grab Babe by her front quarters, and haul with every muscle fiber I can command. She kicks and scrabbles for purchase, and I yelp as bright stripes of pain zip down my cheek, my neck, my arm. She's all bone and muscle, way heavier than she looks. I can't get her more than halfway out of the water.

I'm too small. Not strong enough. I can't hold on.

"Stellar. I've got her."

Petra's in the water, dark hair slicked to her head, a

determined set to her mouth. She's got one hand on the gun-wale, the other shoulder under Babe's hindquarters. There's no time to decide whether I trust her—there's only time to save the dog, or not.

Together we boost Babe inelegantly into the boat.

Petra grabs a paddle drifting nearby, tosses it into the boat, then climbs in as I stabilize the canoe. Babe plasters herself to my side, coughing hoarsely.

I reach for the paddle, but Petra grabs it first. "I'll get us to shore. You rest." She nods at a long jagged gash decorating my left arm from shoulder to elbow, my humanity showing beneath my cyborg-inked surface. Ribbons of red flutter across the circuits and servos, rusting the ink of my gears.

"Oh," I say, my voice distant and echoing in my ears. I plonk my butt on the bottom of the boat and stick my head between my knees, trying to force the dizziness away. Thoughts tumble through my brain on a spin cycle: I need to dress my injury. Get the dog to a vet. Get back on my feet. Protect myself.

The bow nudges soft sand. "Her arm. Watch her arm," Petra says. Before I can quite figure out what she means, I'm lifted from the boat, my legs unfolding weakly beneath me until Lyle scoops them over one forearm. He strides up the beach with me across his chest like he's carrying me over the threshold. The tea-and-sunscreen smell of his skin makes me want to cry the way I did when I was a kid, and I'd held in a hurt all day, waiting until I got home safe to let it out.

So I let the tears come, let a broken sob make its way past the gates of my self-restraint. Lyle cradles me even more gently, like I'm fragile. I know everyone will be frightened and upset to see my pain, but I can't hold it in like a doctor would. Not anymore.

"You're back," I sniffle into Lyle's chest. As far as conversation goes, it's not my best work.

"I wasn't far. I heard you . . ." The working of his throat tugs at my cheek. He's moving fast, a little out of breath. "I heard you scream. Christ, Stellar."

"Is that what it takes to make you s-swear?" I hiccup, dazed and lightheaded. He doesn't laugh.

Brent and Willow pass us, each of them holding two corners of a beach towel with the dog slung across it. Sloane walks alongside, cooing at Babe.

"I never screamed. It must have been Petra."

"No," he says, flat and definitive. "It was you."

"I'm fine." I close my eyes again. "I'm young and healthy. No way I've lost more than 15 percent of my blood volume. I just need a minute for my intravascular volume to compensate, and then I can take over the crisis response."

"You're not taking over. You're in shock."

"Class *one* shock. Mini shock," I argue, but he's loading me into the Mystery Machine, sliding me across the nearest bench seat, then arranging my head in his lap before buckling a seat belt across my midsection. Willow drops into the driver's seat, flipping the visor down and catching the keys with a flourish. Sloane takes shotgun.

"Look in the glove compartment," Lyle tells Sloane. "Hand me the first aid kit. The instructions for the radio are on a laminated card. See if you can radio the Mounties on the way. Hospital first, then vet." He unzips the kit and pulls out disinfectant, gauze, tape.

"Vet first, then hospital," I correct him. "Drowning is more serious than bleeding." Gingerly, I palpate my arm. It's reasonably dry, as I would have said when I was in the ER—although

maybe it's time to drop the medical doublespeak and just ac-
knowledge that the bleeding has stopped. I'll live.

Willow turns onto the near-empty highway, tires humming
as we edge up to the speed limit. Sloane fiddles with the two-
way radio. Behind me, Brent tells the dog she's a good girl between Babe's occasional bouts of deep, wet coughing. Lori and
Mitch must be in the back row of seats.

I haven't been this tired since residency. It would take
hardly any energy to turn my face toward Lyle's stomach and
rest there while he strokes my hair. But there are too many
problems left to work.

I pitch my voice low enough that the others won't hear me.
"Go with Babe to the emergency vet. She needs you. Sloane can
take me to the hospital, then you can meet us there to get your
eyebrow glued. Crap, where's everyone going to stay tonight? I
didn't think of that; does anyone have a pho—"

A warm droplet splashes on my forehead.

"Your eyebrow," I say, opening my eyes. "It's still bleeding?"
When I look up, a tear falls from his jaw to my neck.

"You screamed," he says dully. "I've never even heard you
say *ouch*. Nothing hurts you, and you were in pain. You cannot
fucking imagine—" His voice tightens to a whisper, then stops.

"I'm okay, Lyle. Nobody died. It's a low bar, but—"

"I left you *alone*." His voice shakes with self-loathing.
"Everyone was so afraid of me. *You* were afraid of me. And I
had to do something to stop chasing Trevor. If I'd gone after him
in a boat . . . I could have. I wanted to."

"But you didn't."

"But I *wanted* to," he repeats fiercely. "So I just . . . ran. I took
off when the *one* thing you asked me to do was stay. If I'd only
stayed, none of this would have happened. And now you're sending me away, to the vet. You give me what I gave you. Right?"

I've never seen him miserable like this, filled with what-ifs instead of calm certainty. My heart aches for the distance between us, though his body is literally cradling mine. My throat stings like it was me, not Lyle, who screamed the scream that broke the world.

But my brain is a mess, full of chaos and fear and problems without solutions. And if I don't work those problems, I have to confront what everyone knows: Lyle and I were never engaged, not really. Even if I asked, and he said yes. And I'm no kind of doctor. And our "impartial" celebrity endorsement is coming from my sister, who's hip deep in this mess now, too, about to be publicly tied to the father she's spent years trying to evade.

And I'd have to think about how Lyle and I let each other down tonight in the worst possible ways. How maybe we're not people whose strengths complement each other's weaknesses. Maybe we're just opposites who shouldn't have let ourselves attract.

"Can we talk about this later, once we know everyone's okay?"

"Sure," he agrees, not meeting my eyes. "Tomorrow."

"I wasn't afraid of you, Lyle. I never wanted you to think I was." I reach my good arm up to his chin to dash away more drops.

"I know you weren't. Of course I know that."

I thought he'd given me everything, but I was wrong.

Tonight, for the first time, Lyle McHugh has given me a lie.

Chapter Twenty-three

It's an out-of-body experience walking back into Grey Tusk General Hospital as a patient.

Outwardly, the building is unremarkable: a one-story seventies concrete box that immediately makes your eyes want to move on. The architects didn't concern themselves with aesthetics, choosing instead to clamp the heat and ventilation pipes to the side of the emergency department like tubes and wires connected to a patient.

Inside the sliding glass doors, it's a punch of industrial light and noise. On long night shifts, the soundscape made me feel like the hospital was a huge ship traversing the ocean of night: the ever-present hum of the high-volume air exchangers, the electric whir of diagnostic machines, the palpable vibration from loaded stretchers rolling across metal connecting strips in the linoleum.

This place is eerily the same, yet different. Or maybe it's me who's changed.

Physically, I'm not injured that badly. My arm hurts like a motherfucker, and I need irrigation and stitches. But I'll heal.

Emotionally, though . . . it's not the shape I'd rather be in when I run into god knows which ex-colleague in the middle of the night. Not exactly one of the triumphant comeuppance fantasies I conjured on those midnights I lay awake, too steeped in injustice to sleep.

I held my head high on the way out of this place, fueled by the fury of being right and losing anyway. Can I do the same tonight, now that I understand how goddamn sad I was then? Not to mention how sad I am now. In all probability, I've lost my business, my secrets, my last best chance to stay near my friend.

And Lyle.

I recognize the burning feeling in my stomach when I think about him, because I used to feel it all the time when I worked here. It's the sensation of knowing something's wrong and wanting to ignore it. Wanting the fantasy so badly I'm willing to overlook what's real. For an entire year, I told myself he and I were wrong for each other. What if I was right?

At the triage desk sits a nurse I don't know. His face looks tired for someone so young, brown skin pasty under the fluorescent lights. He straps the blood pressure cuff on my uninjured arm with efficient movements, empathetic in the measured way I recognize so well. He's learned not to spend all his kindness too early in the shift.

I give him a sanitized version of what happened and don't tell him I used to work here.

He gloves up, then peels back the edge of my damp, pink-tinged dressing to check out what's underneath. "There might be a wait to see the doctor."

"I understand. Could I have some acetaminophen for the pain?"

He cocks his head at the generic drug name. "Are you a health care provider?"

I take a breath, fail to find the right words, and let it out with a defeated huff. "I don't know."

His eyes narrow. "Did you hit your head?"

"No, sorry, no head trauma. I meant that I *was* a doctor. Before. I left medicine after . . ."

"After," he says, expression softening, and I don't correct his impression that I'm referring to the pandemic. "I'm sure you're missed."

I nod, throat tight, imagining a world where this could be true.

"There you are." Sloane appears with two take-out cups from the all-night Tim Hortons in the hospital lobby. She hands me the one with a tea bag tag dangling from under its lid. "I've never seen you drink coffee, but if you want to make an exception for exceptional circumstances, I also bought something called a double double . . . ?" Sloane looks dubiously at the second cup.

"It's good. It'll make you happy," I reassure her, wishing real happiness was something that came in a cup.

She takes a sip. "Accurate."

The nurse frowns at Sloane. "Do I know you?"

With dirt smeared across one cheek, a stained shirt, and third-day hair, she looks a lot like she does in the *Nighthawke* trailer. "I'm friends with someone who used to work here. Maybe we've met?" She's a good actor; his face smooths out. "Where do we wait?"

I get a cubicle not far from the triage station. Sloane helps me up onto the crinkly plastic mattress of the stretcher, where a different nurse cuts off my shirt, then slides on a patient gown, taking care with my injured arm. Once she's gone, Sloane kicks up the footrests of the wheelchair I rode here in, collapsing it with fight-sequence efficiency.

"You're a pro with that."

She smiles grimly. "Lots of practice."

We wait in silence. It's hard to keep up light conversation in the emergency room. Even if I weren't distracted by the throbbing in my arm, my brain wants to go back and pick at everything that happened.

If I'd been warmer to Petra, things might have turned out differently. *If* I'd pushed harder to get Lyle to believe me. *If* I hadn't put off calling Sharon. *If* I'd bailed out on the Love Boat at the first sign of trouble, instead of calling Sloane and faking the engagement and walking deeper into the quicksand with every step.

If I hadn't frozen when Lyle needed just one person on his side. If he hadn't left at the moment I needed him most.

If I weren't in love with him now.

Sloane's phone chimes. "Whoa. Brent has *not* learned the art of the brief text. Hold please, reading . . . McHuge and the dog are at the vet; looks like she'll stay the night for monitoring. Lori and Mitch are safe at the hotel. Brent, Willow, and Petra are heading over to the Mountie detachment to give statements. Is there anyone else I should call?"

I check the five-dollar IKEA clock above the cubicle door: ten minutes to midnight. Tobin and Liz need their rest, but it's past time I called Sharon.

Maybe the only bright spot in this whole disaster is watching my sister get flustered at being fangirled over by Sharon's husband.

"Hi, is this Sharon Keller-Yakub? Sloane Summers, I'm a guest at the Love B—yes, you can put it on speaker. Who am

I talking to? Yes, good evening Mr. Yakub, it's nice to meet you too. I . . . um, I really can't reveal how faithful the movie is to the books, but I hope you enjoy it. I'm calling because . . . oh, aren't you sweet. I have limited power to cast extras, but I'll see what I can do if there's a sequel. Sharon, could we talk business for a minute? A few things happened tonight. To put it mildly."

There's a light knock at the door. "Hi, it's Dr. Winters."

My heart trips wildly in my chest. I don't know Evan Winters that well; he joined the department after me and promptly took a two-year leave of absence to work at the World Health Organization in Geneva. He was still away when I left. But there's no possibility he hasn't heard gossip about me.

Sloane holds the phone away from her ear, mouthing, *Should I hang up?*

I gesture around like, *Seriously? This is my wheelhouse*, and wave her out of the room. She ducks through the door, her voice fading as Evan closes it.

"I hear you found yourself on the wrong end of a dog bite, Doctor."

The hunch in my shoulders unwinds somewhat at his friendly "Doctor." I could have drawn a much shorter straw than Evan.

"Scratch, not a bite."

"Let's take a look." He makes doctor noises as he presses gloved fingers to the ragged edges of skin left by Babe's claws. "Hmm. I might want a few stitches. Hang tight, I'll get a suture tray."

He's back in under a minute with a sealed sterile tray piled with disposable supplies. He rolls an equipment stand over to the bedside and adjusts the height. It's all so familiar, yet strange.

"Freezing first, then irrigation, then closure. Sound good?

I'll do my best to get your ink to line up, but there might be some spots where it's not perfect."

I was good at suturing once. Good at setting bones and reducing dislocations. Putting things back together so you couldn't tell one side had ever been separated from the other. Putting myself back together and pretending I was fine, too.

But maybe it's time to stop hiding the evidence of my own hurts.

"I don't mind if the tats get edited. And you don't need to clear your plans with me. I'm the patient."

"You're still one of our own," he says. "Or you could be, if you wanted to. Which I guess you don't. Kat says you never replied to her emails."

You could be, if you wanted to . . . ?

"I blocked the hospital domain," I say bluntly, wanting not to reveal too much. Asking for my job back, accidentally or on purpose, ranks somewhere below "self-administer random electric shocks" on my list of priorities.

"Then this will be an exciting conversation. Hold still now."

I close my eyes, letting Evan's one-sided conversation wash over me.

"Last September, someone forwarded your dataset to the hospital CEO and the dean of the medical school. Both launched investigations. Turn your head to the right. Here comes the freezing—little poke. In December, the emergency department got sanctioned by the hospital for failing to meet our mandated gender diversity targets. We'll get sanctioned again this year; no women will even apply here since you left. It's a hard sell for genderqueer folks, too. Last little poke. You hanging in there?"

"I'm good." The rhythm of his patter reminds me of falling asleep as a child with the sounds of adult conversation and television banter filtering through my bedroom walls. I worked

at Grey Tusk General longer than I've lived at any single address in my life. The language of this place is the language of
home, in a very real way.

"The university pulled the residents back to Vancouver
pending a review of the learning environment. Without them,
our workload increased by 20 percent overnight. People started
leaving for greener pastures," he says, listing a handful of men
I used to know, pausing meaningfully when he gets to my old
department chief's name. "Throw in the postpandemic labor
shortages, and we're on the verge of closing the ER some nights
and diverting patients to Squamish."

I thought I'd feel triumphant hearing about the downfall of
the place I spent so much time hating. Vindicated, at least.

But I don't. It feels good to know I left a mark here, but
mostly, it's sad to see the damage done.

"It must be hard for the people who are left."

"Yeah. There's not enough of us to go around. Patients are
angry. I've been working my ass off since six; haven't made a
dent in the waitlist. And I probably shouldn't have told you any
of this, because Kat was asking you to come back."

My chest snags on an inhale.

Come back. I've literally dreamed of this moment, where
the people who threw me away begged me to take them back
once I didn't need them anymore. Although given tonight,
maybe I *do* need them.

In my fantasies, I didn't have to choose between telling off
my enemies and coming back in a blaze of glory. In real life, I'll
get neither of those, but there would be a job, at least, if the
Love Boat died. It doesn't make my stomach feel great, but my
student loans would like it.

Evan pauses, gloved hands poised on the sterile towels he's
draped around my arm. "I heard about what happened to you,

Stellar. Words probably feel pretty empty from where you're standing, but I'd like to think I would've backed you up if I'd been here. A lot of people in the department would be glad to see you again."

"Um," I say, unable to summon something angrier, like *they can keep dreaming*, or something smarter, like *send me an offer, and I'll consider.*

I can't process Evan's pitch right now. I need room to grieve everything I hoped for with the Love Boat, everything I *worked* for, every part of my heart I handed over and might not get back.

So I ask, "What would you do if you were me?"

"Ha. My first instinct would be to tell them to go fuck themselves, honestly. But my second instinct . . ." Evan waggles his head like *Will I, won't I.* "I'd probably be curious. Maybe I'd give them a chance to show me they'd changed."

He ties the last stitch, then cuts the suture with a flourish. "Acetaminophen and ibuprofen every six hours. I'll give you a prescription for antibiotics, but don't fill it unless you see signs of infection. Bag it when you shower. No baths or swimming until the stitches come out in ten days. No strenuous exercise for a couple of weeks." He disposes of the needles in the bio-hazardous waste bin.

No exercise. No getting wet.

I should've put it together before now.

This injury is the end of the road for me. And where will Lyle find another doctor? Even a rescue paddler will be tough to hire at this point in the summer season. This situation is getting worse all the time.

"Knock, knock," Sloane sings, peeking around the door. "Sorry, that took forever. Sharon's called an emergency meeting tomorrow at—" Sloane breaks off, seeing that Evan's still here.

"Come on in. We're just finishing up here," Evan says, stripping off his gloves. He angles his head to indicate Sloane should take the chair. "I'll come back with that prescription."

The second he leaves, Sloane's all over me. "You're too fucking pale. Did he give you enough freezing? Let me see the stitches. I know a plastic surgeon in LA who can make any scar disappear."

"Jesus, Sloane. It's fine. I'm fine. What did Sharon—"

But I don't get to hear what Sharon said, because Lyle's voice cuts through the ER soundscape.

"I know she's here. She's my fiancée. *Now* can you tell me where she is?"

Chapter Twenty-four

There are no secrets in the emergency department. If anything, the thin walls amplify sound by blocking out the visuals.

Lyle's voice is calm. He's not shouting, but neither is he quiet or deferential. He sounds like he's taking up a lot of space at the triage desk, and I can't help but feel a tiny thrill for him even as a bolt of terrified energy strikes the center of my being.

"She's my *fiancée*," Lyle insists, again. "That means her next of kin is *me*."

"He's here." I sound panicky. I want more time; I want him to burst in here and pull me into his arms.

Hearing him say *fiancée* tears my heart in two. I want it to be true so badly my throat squeezes. But it's a lie—and now everybody knows it. As much as I want to believe in *us*, it's not real.

And the moment I see him is the moment we have to stop pretending.

"Don't look so surprised. He was always going to come for you, little star."

I squeeze my eyes closed. "He left me, Sloane."

"He freaked out," Sloane says gently. "He needed to cool off. He couldn't have known what would happen."

"It doesn't *matter* what he thought would happen! I asked him for *one* thing. I asked him to not let me go, and he did. Maybe we're not right for each other. Maybe we should cut our losses and end things now."

Sloane takes a measured breath like she's fighting for patience. I open my eyes to find her massaging her temples.

"What the hell, Sloane?! Don't tell me you're on *his* side?"

She sets the jaw that's so much like Dad's. So much like mine. "I'm not on his side! Honestly, if you weren't in the hospital, I would flick you right in the forehead for being stupid and stubborn." She waggles her flicking fingers at me. "He screwed up, okay? Is that what you wanted to hear? He screwed up, and you deserve to be mad at him and have him apologize and make amends to you.

"But you know what? Fuck you for never forgiving anyone. Not even McHuge, the world's kindest human, who would die before he hurt you. And *especially* not yourself. What's going to happen when *I* screw up, huh? You gonna drop me for another fifteen years and hate yourself just as long because you trusted someone who wasn't perfect? Or are you gonna grow up and give me another chance, even though your scoreboard says you shouldn't?"

She bursts out of the chair to stalk over to the supply cupboard behind my head. "Let me ask you something, *Doctor*, since you're so smart. Why do you think everyone at the Love Boat helped you after you lied to them? Willow drove you to the hospital. Mitch and Lori booked you a hotel room in case you and McHuge didn't want to sleep in the same place tonight.

Brent took care of McHuge's dog. *Brent*. They all could have told you to go fuck yourselves, but they stuck around and gave you a second chance, and they hardly know you." Boxes of gloves and alcohol wipes tumble to the counter with Sloane's aggressive rummaging.

"W-what are you doing?" I ask, stuttering.

"Your fiancé's going to be here in a second. We're making you look good. Ha!" She brandishes a package labeled STERILE GAUZE. She tears it open, wets a corner under the tap, and dabs my face, coming away with streaks of red and brown.

"You should've used a paper towel. The sterile stuff is really expensive."

"They can bill me," she growls.

"It's Canada. They don't know how." I liberate the expensive gauze from her grip and use it to blow my nose. She laughs so loudly I end up having to laugh, too.

At the nursing station, there's an escalating chorus of, "Sir, you can't do that. Sir. Sir!"

Sloane sighs, walks to the door, and sticks her head into the hall. "She's in here, McHuge." She turns back to me, brows drawn together. "You look kind of pathetic. I may be somewhat regretting that monologue. Do you want me to stay? I could take him in a fight. Not, like, a *physical* fight, but I can inflict emotional damage."

My chest constricts with her love, her care, and the pain of all the years she and I missed out on, everything pulling into bittersweet equilibrium. If I hadn't done everything that brought me here tonight, I wouldn't be with my sister.

"I'll be okay. And Sloane?"

"Yeah?" She crosses her arms grumpily.

"You're my favorite sister."

Her stance softens. She comes back to the stretcher to drop a kiss on my forehead, her voice a touch gravelly. "I know."

One minute Lyle isn't here, the next second he's the only thing in the cubicle, breathing hard, face flushed, hair escaping from its tie. An adhesive bandage covers his injured eyebrow, his face only partially cleaned up. Everything is beautiful and terrible—loving him and wanting him and knowing I have to choose what to do, who to be.

And I don't have a clue how to do it.

"How's Babe?" I ask, groping for a place to start.

"Ate some waves, but she'll recover. How are you?"

"I just came here for the snacks, honestly. Want some tea?" I gesture to the now cold remains in my cup.

"Damn it, Stellar." He's by my side, fingers hovering over the place where the bulky white bandage contrasts starkly with my T-shirt tan. His green eyes are red rimmed and dull, shadowed from within. He swallows, not quite able to mask a low-pitched sound of dismay, and then I'm gently, inevitably gathered against his chest, cradled there like I'm fragile and so, so precious. It's everything I want. Everything he could give to me, everything I'm afraid to take from him.

I hoped I was out of tears, but I feel them squeezing hot out of the corners of my eyes, dampening whatever dorky tree shirt is smashed beneath my face. If he'd asked me if I wanted a hug, I would've made myself say no. Now that I'm in his arms, I can't bring myself to let this go.

"I should've listened to you when you were so worried about spying. *Fuck* the risk to the business," he says with his whole chest. "You shouldn't have had to keep yourself safe. I should have done that. I'll make it up to you, I promise. I'll make it even."

I hear in his voice how long this night has been, how desperately he wanted to be everywhere at once for me and Babe. I feel in the careful press of his arms how much he wants everything to be all right, and how afraid he is that none of it will be. Even his sweat smells different, the sharp tang of stress cutting through his normal body chemistry.

I could be angry. I could demand anything from him right now, and he'd give it to me. But that's not who I want to be.

My big sister was right. Fuck not forgiving him. He won't ask me for forgiveness, but I can give it to him anyway. I can give it to us both, as a gift. We don't have to keep punishing ourselves—not for what happened when we were seventeen, not for what happened tonight. We can let the people who hurt us own their part.

We can have another chance.

I lay my good hand on the back of his neck. "It's nothing a few stitches couldn't fix." Evan did good work. Underneath the bandage, his tidy sutures line up nicely along the curve of my biceps, cracked circuits welded together again. They don't look like new, but there is a beauty in something that has been broken and lovingly repaired.

"No one could have seen this coming, Lyle. Not even Fisher, that galactic fucknut. You can forgive yourself for not being perfect. Running away matters less than running back."

"How do you do that? Forgive yourself, I mean?" he asks, lowering me to the stretcher. He straightens up, eyes fixed on the floor with its cracked linoleum tiles that haven't come quite clean at the edges in a long time.

"I don't know. I have no idea how to do *any* of this." The same way I couldn't figure out how to accept his love—that awkward half hug in the tent, my god—I have no clue about the mechanics of forgiveness.

My parents never gave me the chance to forgive them. They never even *asked*. After that, I tied myself in knots to make sure I never needed to forgive anyone who mattered. Love is the only problem I never learned how to work.

"You don't know how to do any of what?" Lyle says, voice low, arms crossed. "You mean breaking up with me?" His left thumb worries at his ring, twisting the iron circle up over his first knuckle.

"No," I say, testy with fatigue and pain and uncertainty. "I don't know how to tell you I forgive you and ask you to forgive me. Do you just . . . say it? Is there some kind of preamble? Do you extract concessions, like making the other person clean the gross stuff at camp for the rest of the summer? Like, what's the procedure?"

He raises his eyes to me. "You just say it," he says, his voice soft as dawn over water.

That seems fake, but what choice do I have?

"Then I'm sorry, Lyle. I let you down tonight. I never should have suggested a fake engagement or tried to hide my connection to Sloane. My actions put the Love Boat at risk, and I regret that so much. So much, Lyle. I hope you can forgive me. I hope we can forgive each other for not being perfect, and I want there to be a next time so I can do better. If that's what you want, too."

Deep breath. That wasn't so bad. I continue, "We need to work together if we're going to try to bail out the Love Boat. And if we're going to make this relationship thing work." With my good arm, I reach across the bed's guardrail.

"Are we?" His arms don't unfold, and the first slim needle of doubt pierces my heart. I see a future where he stands there and I lie here, aching for him and unable to do a damn thing about it. Eventually, I'll invent a reason to take my arm back—an itch under my bandage, a classic—but we'll both know it's a lie.

No. Fuck that future. I'm not letting go of the one I want.

"I hope we are," I say, leaving my hand where it is, willing him to take it. "We can't be engaged anymore, though. I'm not sorry we did it," I add hurriedly. "But next time I get engaged, I don't want to do it because I have to. I want to choose it for myself. And I want you to do the same thing."

"Okay." His smile is a little sad as he takes off the ring and drops it in my palm, but it's a smile, at least.

I slip his ring over my thumb. It's warm, its matte surface somehow soft. I'd swear it's got a piece of his soul in it. *Ah, don't let me cry in front of him.*

"Well?" I ask, my heart trying to climb out of my chest. It's a good thing I'm not hooked up to a monitor right now, because my vital signs would tell him everything my words left out.

"Well, what?"

"Did it work? Are we . . . forgiving each other?"

He slides his hand over mine, covering the ring and clasping tight. "Yeah. We are. You want to come back to my place tonight?"

It's not easy, this business of forgiving people, but it feels so good I can't help laughing. "Have you gotten a decent TV since last time I was there?"

"No. Television interferes with my—"

"If you say vibes, I swear to—"

"—sleep," he finishes, giving me an amused look. He leans down, coming in slow, giving me time to say whatever I need to.

His kiss is featherlight, but with a dig to it like a big cat pushing its face into your hand, seeking comfort, pleasure, relief.

Two sharp raps sound on the cubicle door.

"Sorry for the delay. I—Oh!" Evan blinks as Lyle and I pull apart. "I brought you that prescription," he says. "And a scrub top, since we ruined your shirt. Bring it back when you decide to take us up on that job offer."

Lyle pulls back at the mention of a job, wincing when he forgets not to raise his injured eyebrow.

"I will. Evan, do you have a second to look at my . . . um, my partner's face?" Partner is an ambiguous word, but Lyle hears what I mean, because of course he does. His hand grips my shoulder, and I slide mine up to cover it, his ring loose on my thumb.

"Sure. Same dog?"

"Book to the eyebrow."

Evan glances at me like he wants to ask and also does *not* want to ask. He gloves up, gets Lyle seated on the chair, and peels back the bandage on his eyebrow.

"Hmmm, yes. Little discomfort now," he says, pressing the edges of Lyle's crooked eyebrow together. "This one's been split before. Don't tell me—hockey? I can put it together a little straighter. More cosmetic," he offers.

"No!" I blurt, before amending, "I mean, it's up to Lyle." One armed, I pull myself up to sitting so I can catch Lyle's eyes through Evan's hands. "But I liked it the way it was."

Broken. Fixed. Still good.

Chapter Twenty-five

When I open the door of Lyle's Grey Tusk condo the next morning, Sharon's standing in the doorway, arms crossed, already shaking her head. She's dressed in all black, like she's attending the Love Boat's funeral.

"You're idiots," she pronounces. "I love you both, but I am *this* close to putting clauses in your contracts about your whippersnapper mistakes."

She strides into Lyle's compact condo, which is luxurious by ski-town standards, especially for someone who lives alone. The building dates back to the development boom of the eighties, its age apparent in the diagonal terra-cotta tiles and rustic stone fireplace. The tight galley kitchen flows into a living space crammed with a gigantic overstuffed couch. A shelf of textbooks covers the wall where you'd expect a TV.

Abnormal Psychology. Forensic Interviewing Techniques. Fundamentals of Family Therapy. A framed diploma from his master of arts in counseling psychology—nothing from his PhD, though. There's a print of the family photo Lyle keeps in the Mystery Machine, as well as various shots of his formerly ginger, now increasingly snow-topped parents, Babe, and himself with his buddies from his former job as an expedition guide.

Coming back to Lyle's bed with its chunky driftwood frame felt like coming home. This bed has a sense of history and permanence that felt just right when we curled up in it a few hours ago to get what sleep we could before today's reckoning.

"I'm sorry about . . ." I was going to say "the fake engagement," but that doesn't seem like a good enough way to describe how screwed we are and how terrible I feel. "Everything," I finish sadly.

"You meant well," Sharon says, more gently. "But yes, you did fuck it up. We'll see what we can do about that." Sharon unpacks her briefcase onto the wall-mounted breakfast table, which folds away when the weather's bad enough for Lyle to do yoga indoors. The dog, freshly released from the animal hospital at a cost that made me choke, perks up her ears and trots over to lean into my leg. Ever since we picked Babe up this morning, I've been her new best friend.

"Morning, Sharon. Coffee?" Lyle asks, padding barefoot out of the bedroom, hair still a little damp from the careful washing I gave it this morning, keeping the water away from his eyebrow. Afterward, he taped a kitchen garbage bag over my arm and helped me through a one-handed shower. It's humbling to be cared for by him. I mean, he shaved my right armpit today, a service I'm pretty sure most people don't request until after they're married or own property together.

The sight of him clean and combed could stop my heart. Every curl, every freckle, every line of his body feels as intimately *known* to me as the lines of my own, yet he's a brand-new version of himself now that we're not in camp. His beard is freshly trimmed into a neat square-chinned shape; his curls spill over the collar of his checked flannel overshirt. I'm surprised every time I see his jeans, new and unstained by sap and canoe repair compound. Maybe he thought wearing his black-framed glasses would draw attention away from the two neat stitches in his eyebrow, but it's not working.

Under the neck of his plain white T-shirt, there's no familiar silhouette. The necklace must still be coiled neatly on top of his dresser, where I put it last night. Good.

He drops a kiss on my cheekbone as he passes, letting the back of his hand slide down my new shirt in a way that tells me exactly how good he thinks I look in it, and how much better he thinks I'll look out of it.

Sharon's eyes widen. "So *that's* the way it is between you two. Well, it's a blessing you're banging, at least. The fake engagement brouhaha would be much worse if you hated the sight of each other. I'll take that coffee—black."

"Sharon," I moan, hand covering my eyes.

"*Aunt* Sharon," she corrects me. "Don't argue. It's been a long day, and it's not even noon. You look good, Stellar. If you do any public appearances, wear that."

I was ready to attend the emergency meeting wearing one of Lyle's shirts as a dress, since half of yesterday's clothes are in the garbage and the rest of my things are at base camp. But a little after eight this morning, a bike courier dropped off a dress bag from Grey Tusk's most exclusive womens-wear boutique, courtesy of an after-hours call from Sloane's very convincing publicist.

Inside, I found this stretchy white sleeveless top—bandage friendly, an excellent choice—a slim cream-colored wool skirt decorated with hammered bronze studs, and coordinating knee-high canvas lace-ups that remind me of overgrown Chuck Taylors. Canadians don't wear shoes in the house, as a rule, but these are new and the thick soles make me two full inches taller, so I'm making an exception.

It's a killer outfit, more Paris than Pendleton, but I miss how I looked on the river. Out there, I had helmet hair, sticky skin from layers of sunscreen, and clothes that were never quite clean. But when I looked in the wavy mirror over the wash station sink, I felt good on the inside. When I texted Sloane to thank her and ask how much she spent, she told me I was exhausting and refused to discuss it.

"Let's get started," Sharon says. Lyle sets a steaming mug in front of her—of course he keeps coffee in the house even though he doesn't drink it. Babe pushes between our feet as we sit down, curling up under the table with a doggy *harrumph*.

"Isn't Tobin coming?" I ask.

"No," Sharon says. "He wants to see the meeting minutes, but he said he's too removed from day-to-day operations to be helpful in making decisions. Now, good news or bad news first?"

"Good news," Lyle says, right as I groan, "Bad news."

"Majority vote wins. Good news first. Despite the deception—next time run that kind of thing by me first, please—you made the right impression on your clients. *Beeswax* will run a short piece by Brent Torquay tomorrow and a long-form piece in early fall. Willow Connors Torquay offered to donate the cover photo and promote it with her hundred and fifty thousand followers, so that's a big get. Sloane will cross-promote as well."

Willow is a well-known photographer with a giant following? And meanwhile I was arranging canoe paddles for cell phone photos? I look at Lyle, who shrugs.

"Laurie Mitchell wants to feature us in Vancouver International Bank's internal newsletter, which lands in two hundred thousand employee inboxes. That won't be until next month. And." Sharon pauses for dramatic effect. "This morning the Mounties paid a call to Alan Fisher's little canoe camp and detained a grad student of his—one William Trevor Butterworth—

for questioning. My source inside the detachment says his entire camp witnessed the conversation, which included the words 'assault with a weapon.'"

"That's great," I say cautiously, wanting to savor the thought of Renee watching the fracas at Fisher's camp, but knowing Sharon has another shoe to drop. "And the bad news?"

"Yes. Well. The bad news is that good publicity doesn't necessarily translate to strong sales. As of this morning, the bookings situation is still dire. The second session is operating at breakeven. Barely. The third session . . . it'd be cheaper to refund people's deposits and cancel."

I bite my lip. "What about the other sessions? The fourth and fifth ones?"

Beside me, Lyle shifts in his chair, taking a slow, stoic breath. He sounds like he does during morning meditation when he talks about accepting what *is* instead of what you wished for.

Sharon leans forward. To this point, she's been all business, but now her eyes soften. "I'm sorry, Stellar. I meant we'd be wise to cancel *all* sessions after the second. If not that one as well. We're in an incredibly untenable position, business-wise. Corporate espionage is a very difficult charge to prosecute. Realistically, we'll have to spend a metric fuckton of money on lawyers so Fisher doesn't publish our methods, then turn around and sue us for using them. Or we'll have to close down the company."

Under the table, Lyle's left hand encloses mine, squeezing reassuringly. A pulse of sadness hits me as I feel the empty space where his ring used to be.

Of the two of us, I'm pretty sure I'm more upset about what's happening. Which is unexpected, considering this is Lyle's baby, and he has no other job prospects.

But I do. Last night, I unblocked the hospital domain on my

email, feeling guilty for even considering a job that's not the Love Boat. This morning, I received a headhunting email from Grey Tusk General—an invitation to lunch with the new chief of emergency medicine.

"One last piece of bad news—"

"*Seriously*, Sharon?" I rub my gritty, tired eyes.

"Yeah, I know, it's a parade of suck. Renee Garner's team reached out this morning. Seems she's 'rethinking' her collaboration with Fisher. She had a podcast spot earmarked for him, with the recording scheduled for two days from now. She's offered it to us. Production schedule permitting, she'd air it this week. Special episode."

A seed of hope sprouts in my chest. "This is . . . bad news? I mean, this might be our only hope to stay alive past next session. We could stick it to Fisher. Take back what he stole. Renee's offering us a chance."

Lyle shakes his head. "But look at what she's *not* offering. None of her people at our second session. No long-term collaboration. She'll be in damage control mode, trying to distance herself from Fisher and maybe from the whole idea of whitewater therapy. She could help us, and she could hurt us, too."

Sharon's mouth pulls pessimistically to one side. "Even if we turn her down, we might get caught up in her spin machine. She won't air McHuge's juvenile record unless she wants me to sue her ass down to the earth's molten core. But the fake engagement, Sloane's endorsement, Stellar's employment and family history . . . all fair game."

I blanch. My lunch date with Grey Tusk General could go away if Renee Garner hinted I'd misrepresented my medical qualifications to the Love Boat's clients. I didn't, but that wouldn't matter; a rumor would be enough to sink me. Not many patients—or hospitals—would want a doctor who spent the last year making sure the General Tso's chicken was still hot when it arrived.

Sharon sweeps her papers into a tidy pile. "Let's take the day to process. Shutting down a business is emotional. It does none of us any good to pretend it's not. What?" she says, at my flabbergasted look. "Why does everyone act so surprised when I have feelings?"

She comes in for a strong hug, careful of my arm. "The two of you can let me know what you think of the podcast invite. I'm good either way, but I'm not the person who has to go on the damn thing."

Lyle makes me lie on his couch while he puts together lunch. We haven't had time for a grocery run, and he insisted only he could find his way around the remaining nonperishables. Not true—I can do miracles with a can of chickpeas and some salad dressing, but last night's disaster and this morning's meeting have left me with a bone-deep fatigue that renders me unable to overcome the couch's gravitational pull.

I pop two Tylenol and drift a little, listening to Lyle's cooking sounds while I stroke Babe's ears. The Love Boat had excellent beds by camping standards, but they were nothing compared to this couch. It's a Lyle-sized ocean of fuzzy blankets and plush pillows that might be the gateway to an alternate spiritual plane.

Lyle appears with a tray. "Mixed-berry smoothie, cinnamon vanilla pancakes, bacon, jam, real maple syrup, and steamed broccoli," he announces proudly. He sets the tray across my lap, then settles at my feet with his plate.

"Broccoli, Chef?" I ask, twirling a floret at the end of my fork.

"You need something green. Trust me, I'm a doctor."

I smile weakly. Doctor jokes don't feel very funny after Sharon's briefing. "These are good pancakes."

"From my finest boxed mix. I got the cinnamon and vanilla trick from Jasvinder."

I put down my fork at the reference to our Love Boat family. "What are we going to do?"

He takes an unhurried sip of his smoothie. "Well. I figure as long as we can find another rescue paddler, we'll run the second session. I'll take over first aid on the water."

I suck in a hopeful breath.

"If you want to come back, we'll keep you in camp, and you can do dryland days. I'd like to pay Jasvinder for as long as we can and honor our existing food orders with local suppliers. Give everyone as much time as possible to find a new situation." His sigh hitches on the way out. "After that, we take down the tents. Sell the boats. Settle our debts."

"Oh. Right." I deflate like a sad balloon.

"I know we promised to hold on," he says, putting his plate on the coffee table, then standing up to set aside my tray. He settles himself behind me, then pulls my back against his chest. "And we did. We held on as long as we could. It's not wrong to move on when you've done everything you can."

"But aren't you sad? Aren't you *angry*? This wasn't just any job for me, Lyle. The Love Boat meant something to me. You built a special place. *We* built it together."

He gathers me close, breathing in the scent of my hair, which smells like his shampoo—a citrusy blend that would go well with Earl Grey and honey. We stay like that for a minute, then two, then three, hurting for something we both love that was the perfect thing at the perfect time, until everything came crashing down.

"You want to do the podcast," he says, finally.

"Is there a thought of mine you can't eavesdrop on?"

He nudges through my undercut with his nose. "I've tried to stop, but you think very loudly."

I sigh. "That's probably true. Yes, I want to do the podcast, but it's not about what I want." I don't own a piece of this company yet. Even if I did, Lyle's shares plus Tobin's proxy vote would still make his word law.

And he has the most at stake. I spent a little over two weeks at the Love Boat; Lyle spent *a year* getting this business off the ground. Countless hours. It's *his*, in every way that matters. If he thinks it's time to close it down, only an asshole would oppose him.

"Tell me why you want what you want, then."

I turn my face against his chest. "Your way is smarter. More strategic. Financially sound. We'd live to fight another day."

"And you want to fight today." His voice rumbles underneath my back. There's so much *care* in it. He loves me for being angry and wanting to fight.

He loves me.

"Yeah. I want to fight today. Fisher won't go away just because his crimes have been exposed. He'll come after us with every handful of mud he can sling. The podcast is the only thing that could help us tell our side of the story in time to save the Love Boat. And I'd like to think if we gave Renee a chance to do the right thing, she'd take it."

It's a very Lyle thing to say. I also happen to believe it's true.

He makes a considering sound.

"And," I say, before he can jump in, "it's the only thing *I* can do right now. I can't do chores or paddle or even ride in a canoe. I can't ask you to save the Love Boat if you'll end up doing all the work. Especially if you'd rather let it go and start over. That leaves the podcast."

He tenses underneath me. "And what if Renee comes after your reputation? What if they withdraw your job offer at Grey Tusk General?"

"Well, first off, I already *have* a job I love. I wasn't looking for another one."

His soft laugh sends breath shivering down the back of my neck.

"And second, they have a *lot* of convincing to do before I get back on board. *If* I take their offer . . ." I draw in a shaky breath. "I'd rather go back because I want to. Because they're lucky to have me, not the other way around. I want the power to choose who I work with, and I want to not choose assholes."

"You should go back if you can," he says, his voice thickening with emotion. "If they're not assholes. You said the podcast was our chance—well, this is *your* chance. Anyone can see how much you love being a doctor, Stellar."

I tighten my mouth, trapping a sound I'm afraid may be a sob if I let it go. "Yes, and medicine hurt me, too." Some of the assholes are gone, but there are still people at Grey Tusk General who saw what was happening to me, and knew it was wrong, and didn't speak up.

He tenses his arms fractionally, holding my broken pieces together. "We only hurt when we care. Avoiding it won't stop the pain or the caring. You have to confront it sooner or later."

"Later, then," I say. "I want to focus on the Love Boat now, when it needs us. I care about this, too." *I care about you*, I think, as loudly as I can.

"All right," he says. "We'll do the podcast. On one condition: I do the interview. Alone. Renee keeps your name out of it or we don't play."

"No! No way. Then you're still doing everything, and I'm doing nothing."

"We need you in the wings, Stellar. If the Love Boat goes down, at least one of us should come out of this with a job and an income. It's not possible for me, but it is for you, as long as you can keep your reputation intact.

"And . . . I owe you one. You managed a dangerous situation alone last night. You gave Petra a way to leave Trevor and help us. You saved my *dog*. It's my turn to protect you for a change. Take one for the team."

It's strange, but I flinch at the idea of scorekeeping when it's coming from him. It feels like a river flowing in the wrong direction.

"I don't like—"

"That's the deal, Stellar J. That's what I'm prepared to give. Take it or leave it."

His heart beats steadily underneath my back, his chest rising and falling. If I close my eyes, it feels almost like we're two souls in one body. Two sides of the same coin, always connected.

I don't like his argument, but that doesn't mean he's wrong. He's hearing me out and compromising even though he doesn't have to. Classic Lyle—powerful enough to give his power away.

I can do that, too. I can give Lyle what he wants. Give the Love Boat a chance without knowing whether I'll get anything back. I could care enough to love something and know I might lose it. Be brave enough to get hurt and know I'll heal. I won't be the same as I was before, and that's okay. Maybe that's good, even.

You need something, Liz told me barely three weeks ago. Or maybe it was a lifetime ago.

And I need this.

"Deal."

Chapter Twenty-six

On the morning of the podcast, Sloane and I arrive at Liz's house bearing snacks.

This morning, Lyle got up extra early, kissed my temple, and was out of the condo before I was more than half awake. If I hadn't had plans with Liz, there's a good chance I would've followed him to camp, because I'm getting very weirded out by the way he's been acting lately.

At night, when we fall into his huge, soft bed, he says he's quiet because he's tired from working all day at camp, plus he's nervous about the interview with Renee.

But I know his body. It's in the way his arms come around me a fraction slower than usual, and the way he tucks his face into the crook of my neck after sex, leaving it there for a hundred measured breaths that hitch at the top.

Liz's door swings open to reveal my friend in her favorite onesie pajamas, which look substantially different given her new postpartum boobs and a light crust of spit-up.

"Hi. You probably don't feel like hugging when I smell

like—oh, yes you do, never mind." She seems quieter than usual. Not as happy to see me.

Suddenly I wonder why she didn't ask me to come over yesterday or the day before. Was it really because she had a pediatrician appointment and family visiting? Or is this the first phase of us growing apart? My stomach cramps with renewed anxiety.

"Missed you, babe. We brought doughnuts. I hope you don't mind that Sloane came with; it's her last day in town."

Liz's eyes track over my shoulder to Sloane, who looks like the movie star she soon will be in her high-necked, sleeveless black sweater with oversize white Fair Isle patterns, flowing black pants, and black platform sandals that put her a cool foot above me in height. Her softly perfect hair and glowing skin look like she beamed up to the alien mother ship to get re-cloned.

Liz looks back at me, her chin rising fractionally. "Sloane? You two are . . . hanging out?" She knows who Sloane is; we know everything about each other. And I'm sure Tobin told her my sister was coming to camp this week. But I didn't tell her Sloane and I have grown close.

"You two would probably rather catch up without me," Sloane says diplomatically, flashing a movie-star smile. "I could use a double espresso, actually. There were those two places on Main Street—Magic Beans and Jack and the Bean Shop. Which would you recommend?"

Liz sighs, brushing at a stain on her pajamas. "You may as well stay. I've already made it awkward, and nothing cures awkward once it's loose in the world. Come in."

Sloane gives a bark of laughter; Liz closes her mouth and winces. "I'm sorry. I haven't really slept since the baby. My filter is pretty damaged, and let's be real, it wasn't that strong to begin with. I'm Liz."

"Sloane. And don't worry about it. It's wonderful to meet the person Stellar calls her sister."

Liz smiles at that, finally. God, Sloane. I love her for always being the better person, but will I ever be able to repay her at this rate?

Liz waves us into the house, laying a finger across her lips. Rainbow-hued toys lie haphazardly across her precisely placed neutral-toned furniture. On one cream-colored wall, a painting hangs crookedly above a large splatter of something that's dried to a sticky sheen. A baby swing resembling a sci-fi transporter pod sits next to the couch, right where an exhausted parent could deposit the baby while desperately trying to nap themselves.

"Where's Tobin?" I whisper.

"Emergency run to the pharmacy. We're out of . . ." She blinks tiredly. "I forget, but we don't have any."

The sound of a fussy infant echoes down the stairs. Liz wilts visibly.

Sloane perks up. "Are you letting people hold her yet?"

Liz wipes her sticky bangs from her forehead. "She refuses to be put down and I've had maximum forty-five minutes of sleep in a row for the last two weeks. I'd let Stalin hold her if he washed his hands first."

Sloane cackles in delight and swans off to the kitchen to scrub up. I install Liz on the couch under the pretext of wanting to sit down myself. It's the only useful thing I can do.

"I wish I could help." I shrug my injured arm. "You know. Change a diaper or two. Be the kind of friend you actually need right now."

"Stellar." Liz nails me with her signature direct gaze. "You have like thirty stitches. Instead of fixating on acts of service, you might consider telling your so-called best friend about the important things in your life while they're actually happening."

I think I actually stop breathing for a second. "Liz, I—"

She puts a hand up, stopping me. "I mean, remember how you didn't say a single word about how unhappy you were at work until you'd already left two different jobs? I wish I'd pushed back on that. At least then I wouldn't be saying the exact wrong thing to your sister—who you swore you'd never talk to again—when she shows up on my damn doorstep. I don't *want* you to change diapers and build baby furniture because you feel like that's the currency of our friendship. I don't want baby-furniture friends, Stellar! I want to be part of your life for *real.* Good times and bad."

My lip trembles. I thought Liz understood the way I am. The way dumping my problems on her felt like too much to ask when she had problems of her own.

"I tell you everything, Liz. Everything."

"Yeah, you do, once you fix your problems all by yourself. Once you won't have to ask me for something you feel you haven't earned. But Stellar, I want you to tell me what really happened over the last few weeks. *Today,* not six months from now."

"You already know what happened!"

"*No.* I know what happened to the business. I want to know what happened *to you.* Like how you slept with McHuge again."

"You slept with him *before?* When?" Sloane walks in, jiggling little Jess in the crook of one elbow. The baby's clean, done up in a fresh white-and-orange BB-8 onesie.

"What?!" I yelp. "I never said I slept with Lyle at all."

Liz closes her eyes. "This is horrible. I've successfully tricked someone into holding my demon child, and I want to nap so badly, but interesting grown-up things are happening for the first time in weeks. Anyway, of course you slept with him before. It took me a minute, but I figured it out. The two of you acted so weird at my improv showcase. You called him Lyle, same as you did just now. Only sex can screw things up that badly. And I want to hear about it, Stellar. I think I've earned it."

I feel the same odd, uncomfortable pang I had when Lyle said he owed me one. The way I kept relationships exactly balanced got me through some hard times, but I think what I'm feeling is pain from my life no longer fitting into such a tight shape. Always exactly even, no room for either side to move. Or grow.

Liz is right. It's up to me to make our friendship go deeper than who does what for whom.

I take a deep breath. "I had a one-night stand with Lyle last summer. And I slept with him again when we were pretending to be engaged. And . . . it may not be just sex."

Liz cracks one eyelid, her gaze sweeping my body. "Interesting. Keep talking, friend."

"And an hour from now . . ." I check the time. *Fuck.* "Less than an hour from now, he's doing Renee Garner's podcast without me. I was the one who wanted to save the Love Boat, but he put himself in the line of fire because he owed me one. But I don't want things to be like that between him and me. I don't want it to be that way between me and you, either. And I think I have to . . ."

"Go and support him," Sloane finishes, readjusting the baby in the crook of her arm. "And you better get moving. There's not much time."

"I don't want to bail on you, Liz. This is the first time we've seen each other in weeks. I don't want our friendship to change."

"Too late," Liz says, one eye on the baby, whose squeaking is morphing from cute to hangry. "Everything changes, Stellar. Your life is about to change, too. Go. I'll be here when you get back."

"And I'll text you when I get to LA," Sloane says, preempting my objections. "I'll miss you, little star. You're a grumpy beast, but you do grow on a person. Take my rental car. Just don't drive it like you drive the truck." She pantomimes hanging out the window, shaking her fist.

"Hey," I protest, but both of them are laughing like idiots. "Quit ganging up on me." *Like sisters*, I think.

"Somebody has to, otherwise you'd never listen," Liz says, scooping Jess from Sloane's reluctant arms. "*Go*, Stellar. Go and get your love."

It's been dry in the valley this past weekend, golden days with pure sun shining through air untouched by humidity. Fine, pale-brown dust swirls in my wake as I bump up the road in Sloane's rented white Mini, which is no match for either the clinging grit or the pitted, gravelly terrain.

At the corner leading into camp, maybe twenty cars are parked on the side of the road—which is more or less the middle of the road on this one-lane track. There's no way I can get by.

I park behind them and gather myself for what's to come. An icy drop of panic lands in my stomach, sending frost splashing into my chest.

Am I really about to give up control of my own narrative, at a time when I've lost the power to alchemize my terror into anger? Maybe I'm not strong enough to choose who I want to be in this situation. I froze before; it could happen again.

But I have to find Lyle before the show starts. There's no time to make a spreadsheet of pros and cons.

I step out of the car, swipe my tongue over my teeth, and pat my hair. I did a quick style in Liz's bathroom, fixing it in place with some of my friend's one million hair products. My high, puffy braid is still holding. In a way, it feels like Liz is holding me, too.

There wasn't time to go back to Lyle's condo and grab the outfit Sharon liked, but maybe she'll only listen to the audio. Besides, I like what I'm wearing: black quick-dry pants, hiking boots with chunky socks, and Lyle's ring on a chain around my neck. Sloane bemoaned my fashion choices, then rolled up the sleeves of my sky-blue shirt to better show my bandage and win the sympathy vote. "At least this matches your eyes," she said, smiling at me with her matching cyborg-pale baby blues.

I look like what I am: a canoe instructor who's also a take-no-shit emergency physician.

I've seen enough film sets in Vancouver to know what one looks like, but it's surreal to see one *here*. A diesel cube van rumbles in the parking lot, giant cables snaking from its rear doors. I step over a branching array of cords feeding cameras, laptops, lights, and a sound mixing board.

Lyle's nowhere to be seen. I've never been in this place without his huge presence filtering everything to gentle golden perfection.

A tallish, slim white guy with a clipboard and a sour smirk stands at the entrance to the clearing. An earpiece nestles against his cheek, its clear plastic cord coiling down the back of his neck.

"Name." His eyes flick across my face.

"Stellar Byrd."

He checks his clipboard. "I don't have you on my list."

"I'm looking for Lyle McHugh. Can you tell him I'm here?"

"The greenroom is off-limits," clipboard guy says, his cool tone dipping to subzero. "You'll have to wait until after the recording session."

Time to work the problem another way. "Let me make a call. I'm sure I can sort it out."

"You do that. Kaythanksbyeeeee."

I stroll casually toward the parking lot while scanning the buildings for signs of a greenroom. Bingo—the cookhouse has a new generator outside and a portable satellite clamped to the roof. It's the building I'm least familiar with, Jasvinder being an extremely territorial chef. It also has a couple of burly people with headsets loitering outside the front door.

But they don't know the Love Boat like I do.

Three minutes and a quick detour through the woods later, I'm crouching on the hillside behind the cookhouse, peering through the back window. Jasvinder's steel prep table has been pushed aside to accommodate folding chairs, equipment cases, and a mountain of bags and backpacks.

In the center of the main room, Lyle sits cross-legged and barefoot on Jasvinder's anti-fatigue mat, eyes closed. He's wearing his dark-khaki Carhartt overalls over a white T-shirt, topped by his favorite red-and-black checkered lumberjack shirt. The studio makeup hones his features to gleaming edges, his straight nose more regal than ever.

I've so rarely seen him by himself. Even that first morning at camp, down by the water, it felt like the river was his buddy. He makes friends with birds, for god's sake. Right now he looks so desperately alone I consider breaking this window and tumbling inside.

Lyle rises from his meditation, exchanging courteous smiles with a woman wearing a black multipocketed apron. She motions him to a director's chair, where she twirls a few of his more rebellious curls around her finger before laying them to the side of his face.

My legs twitch. I wish I could take off down the camp road the way I've done so many times in the last two weeks. Run and run until every breath stabs my chest and I forget what it's like to see him preparing for the most important interview of his life without me.

The stylist pulls out a powder brush and tips Lyle's chin up for a spot check. His eyes rise to the window, widening when they meet mine. The stylist turns to see what he's looking at.

I duck in a hurry, flattening my back against the side of the house. *Shit. Shit shit shit.* I don't think the stylist saw me, but I'm sure Renee Garner doesn't play around when it comes to security.

A minute later, the awning window tilts open, its jointed arms preventing it from extending fully. I look up to find a pair of pissed-off forest eyes and half a head of professionally tousled curls staring back.

"What are you doing?" Lyle hisses down at me.

"I'm here to rescue you," I whisper back wildly. "Shit," I say, as voices approach from the side of the house. "Get out of the way; I'm coming in."

"You can't come in! Someone will see you!"

"I can't stay out here, or I'll get detained." My head and shoulders slide easily through the window, but my ass catches in the narrow opening. *Fuck.* Today *would* be the day I'd misjudge an opening after a lifetime of getting tapped to squeeze into friends' ground-floor windows when they lost their keys.

"I'm stuck. You have to pull."

He tugs, managing to lever the window tighter over my butt. He has to hold it open with one hand while I grab his waist and slither in, then wrap my legs around his to keep from thumping to the floor.

"Careful of your stitches," he scolds, hoisting me up by my waist. "And keep it down. There are people in the other room." He sets my feet on the floor, gesturing at the door to what used to be the bedroom. I brush off my pants, but there's a wet green smear on my shirt that's beyond help. *Oh well.*

In my pocket, my phone chirps. Lyle flinches like I farted at a funeral.

"I'm sorry!" I whisper, setting it to Do Not Disturb. "There's never service in camp."

"Renee's team set up a hot spot," he shoots back, practically exploding from anxiety. "You need to hide."

"Where?" I gesture at the open room with no closets or cupboards. "And actually, I'm not here to hide." I puff out my chest. "I'm here to do this podcast with you."

His face closes down. "No, you're not."

I send my arms wide. "Well, I'm not letting you do it alone. These people are professional interrogators. They'll lure you into a trap and add you to their taxidermy collection. You need a co-instructor to throw a question to if you get stuck."

"No, I don't. For the last time, Stellar, get out of here. You're supposed to be saving your reputation, not ruining it." He crosses his arms over his Carhartts, all stern and forbidding.

He forgets I'm not scared of him.

"You look cute. And I'm perfectly capable of keeping myself safe. I've been doing it my whole life."

"Stellar!" He throws up his arms. "You are *terrible* at protecting yourself."

"I am *not*."

"Yes, you are! At the hospital, you could've gone to your boss privately, gotten a good deal for yourself, and let your friend suffer. Instead, you fought for transparency, no matter what it cost you.

"And at the Love Boat, instead of sucking up to an influential guest, you knocked yourself out making Brent do his share. You launched yourself into the middle of a lake with no paddle, at *night*, to rescue a dog bigger than you are!"

He plunges his hands into his hair, ruining the shining ringlets. "I mean, I love Babe! I'm glad she's okay! But you cannot pretend a person who wanted to *protect herself* would've done that. Your whole profession is about caring for people's hurts, but you've trained yourself to never let anyone see when you feel pain." His eyes skip to the long bandage on my arm, then back up, his neck flushing with regret.

Chills grip my skin. I thought I was good at keeping myself safe. After all, I've been the only one doing that job since I was twelve, with the exception of Liz.

And now, with the exception of Lyle.

He takes my face in his hand, thumb stroking my cheek, fingers cupping my square Byrd jaw with a tenderness that makes me want to cry. "You're the most selfless, fair, moral person I know. You have more integrity and fire and . . . and *fight* than most people can even dream of. And you have a chance to reclaim the career you love," he says, his voice low. "Let me take care of the Love Boat. Protect yourself, for once, and let me make up for the time I didn't protect you. I have to, Stellar. If you come on the podcast, Renee will ask about Grey Tusk General and your gig work. She'll ask how you and Sloane are connected. She'll corner both of us with the fake engagement. It'll be a goddamn disaster."

He's flushed, mouth turned down, swearing. I could do what he's asking. He'll take the heat for both of us, and I can hide in his shadow.

He'd give me everything, if I let him.

I look up into his pleading face, his green eyes tired and sad. I can't mess with his makeup, but I can grab Jasvinder's kitchen stool and step up to his level. I can smooth his curls the way I saw the stylist do it, then put my thumbs in front of his ears, stretch my fingers down his neck, and feel his pulse leap under my palm. There's a gap in his left eyebrow, and I suspect the makeup artist has trimmed there so the camera can more easily see his stitches.

I think of him that night, keeping himself away from the people he loved to keep them safe. Isolating himself while I was surrounded by love and care.

We're not so different, he and I. We're both bad at protecting ourselves. But we can try to protect each other. It's harder to be soft than strong, but for Lyle, I want to be both.

"The thing about a disaster, Lyle," I say softly, "is you get to choose who you want to be. And I don't want to be the person you owe something to. I want to be the person who takes care of you. Because I love you, Lyle. I'm in love with you."

Lyle's hoarse, joyful bark of laughter unknots my stomach. His eyes glitter like a forest at dawn, golden and green, a sheen of wetness catching the light like dewdrops gathering at the tips of leaves. "Stellar," he starts, his voice pitched way down low, like a natural disaster.

"I'm not finished," I say. "I'm coming on the damn podcast, and if Renee asks whether our engagement was fake, I'll tell her Fisher's a crack in our collective asshole." He laughs some more, and I can't get enough of the sound and feel of it. "And I'll tell her that sometimes in whitewater, people need to fall in to understand the lesson they're here to learn. I had to make a lot of mistakes before I figured out I wouldn't have asked just anyone to marry me, no matter what was at stake. I proposed to *you* because I couldn't stop thinking about you for a whole year. I asked you to marry me because you're the best, kindest, most selfless person I know. And I want to tell the world how proud I am of everything we did at the Love Boat. We helped people and fought injustice and fell in love. The program worked for us, and I was actively trying *not* to fall for you. It's *that* good."

I already have his face in my hands. It's only natural to touch my lips to his mouth so I can watch the corners turn up. "Peck," I whisper, and watch the sun come out in his smile.

"I've waited a long time to say *I love you*, Stellar. So fucking long." He drapes my arms around his neck, reaches for my thighs, and lifts me into his arms. He kisses me like he's gulping air after a long, scary swim, like he wants to breathe me in again and again. Our mouths were meant to come together this way, meant to give and take everything, always, forever.

I forget about his makeup and my stitches; there's only the two of us, bodies and souls, need and love, ripples pushing us together the way we were always meant to be.

"Ahem."

By this point, I should know we're destined never to kiss uninterrupted.

Lyle sets me back onto the stool, his hands coming to my waist. Together, we turn to face the music.

Standing in the doorway to the cookhouse's back room, a protective cape over her silk blouse, is Renee Garner.

"This must be Dr. Stellar Byrd," she says, her smile big, her Texas accent bigger. "I hope you changed your mind about coming on the podcast. I'd sure love to have you."

Lyle grips my hips convulsively, but I drop another peck on his cheek. "I'd be honored, Renee. I can't wait to tell you about Lyle and the Love Boat."

"Let's get you in makeup, then. No time to waste."

Lyle and I are bustled off to separate rooms, me to get a full face of makeup, him to fix what I messed up. In my opinion, he looked better after I kissed him—a little rumpled, a little tidy.

It's weird to touch my phone at camp, but when the stylist goes on a quest for the perfect shade of eyeliner, I pull it from my pocket and type "Lyle Q. McHugh" into the search bar of my messaging app.

His three texts pop up, marked with last year's date. I still don't like how they look. Lonely. Waiting for someone to take care of them.

But I can fix that.

You up?

Chapter Twenty-seven

WHITEWATER, WHITE LIES

By Brent Torquay (photo credit: Willow Connors Torquay)

Three months ago, Beeswax *sent me on an unusual assignment: spend ten days in the Canadian wilderness with a man whose couples therapy start-up I'd covered rather harshly for this magazine. Harshly enough, perhaps, that celebrity client and potential corporate partner Renee Garner had pulled out mere days before the company's inaugural session.*

There are times in a journalist's life when they find themselves in the right place, at the right time, searching for the wrong story. The morning my wife (Ed: well-known outdoor photographer Willow Connors Torquay) and I arrived in Pendleton, British Columbia was a brilliant early-summer day. We'd tacked some extra time onto the beginning of our trip to drive the famous Oceans to Peaks Highway and enjoy world-famous Grey Tusk Mountain. I thought I'd spend the following week on the water and come home a little stronger, a lot dirtier, and in possession of a story about the increasingly bizarre lengths to which self-help hawkers will go to walk a gold-paved path to fame.

Instead, I came away with a marriage transformed in ways I never saw coming, a flourishing group chat of fellow whitewater enthusiasts, and a brand-new respect for the people who show us life's most important lessons in some of the world's most unexpected places.

And I dove down a rabbit hole straight to the dark underbelly of academia, which takes pains to paint itself as a meritocracy but has a bad habit of eating its young even after they leave the nest.

There I found a physician and a psychologist, both of whom were driven out of institutions of higher learning that like to position themselves as above the fray, but which remain rife with the same abuses of power you'll find in all the worst workplaces.

(Note: At the time this article went to press, Dr. Alan Fisher had not responded to our requests for comment. Both New England University (NEU), where Dr. Fisher is a professor in the Department of Psychology, and Grey Tusk General Hospital declined to comment due to active misconduct investigations.)

This is a story of good people trying to make the best of bad circumstances and creating the most astonishing "vacation," if you can call it that, I've ever experienced.

Oh, and there's a good whack of skulduggery.

But I'm getting ahead of myself.

At first glance, you wouldn't think Lyle "McHuge"

McHugh and Stellar J Byrd have much in common. McHugh, one of the few men I've met who understates his height (he claims six feet four inches under duress), most often comes across as a soothing Mother Earth type who would give you the literal shirt off his back. Byrd is the yang to his yin, a sharp-eyed pragmatist whose small stature belies her big presence. Along with their ninety-five-pound rescue dog, Babe, they live in a ten-by-ten-foot orange tent at the Love Boat headquarters north of Pendleton. For now, that is: the overnight fame that followed their company's dramatic first season means they'll be spending the winter in a yet-to-be-disclosed southerly whitewater destination to continue their lessons in canoeing, life, and love on a year-round basis.

They're not the most demonstrative couple when they're working, preferring to keep the focus on their guests' love stories rather than their own. But every so often, if you're paying attention, you'll catch him lifting her onto rocks, logs, chairs, or whatever will bring her face on a level with his. Or you may notice her passing her thumb across the scar in his left eyebrow—one of those ordinary, G-rated gestures that somehow make you feel you should look away. One does wonder whether they've decided to strictly limit public displays of affection so their guests don't try to measure up to unrealistic #CoupleGoals.

Despite their humble digs, McHugh and Byrd are no ordinary entrepreneurs. For example, they're considering a quickie wedding before the winter season, provided they're able to accommodate the schedules of their nearest and dearest: Byrd's half sister, Sloane Summers (yes, that Sloane Summers); Tobin Renner-Lewis, a Love Boat cofounder; Liz Renner-Lewis, recipient of the Innovator of the Year prize from the Canadian Outdoor Adventure Society; Sharon Keller-Yakub, heir apparent of the quietly dynastic Keller family of companies; and oh yes, close personal friend Renee Garner, rumored to be in negotiations to bring McHugh into her expanding stable of telegenic pop psychology personalities.

The story starts with Dr. Byrd, who thought she knew a grifter when she saw one, considering her father did time in Canadian federal prison for wire fraud. She went to medical school and earned a double qualification in family medicine and emergency medicine, thinking she'd finally acquired enough clout to put herself out of the reach of people who'd take advantage of her. Shortly after completing her training, she joined the emergency department of Grey Tusk General Hospital as one of two female physicians hired after the department suffered national embarrassment for not having hired a female staff physician or accepted a female resident in almost two decades . . .

Meanwhile, after completing his master's degree in counseling psychology, McHugh was accepted as a doctoral candidate in the prestigious lab of Dr. Alan Fisher, who has come under significant fire since unveiling his own, suspiciously Love Boat–like research expedition just as McHugh and Byrd launched theirs. Notably, Fisher had never published any wilderness-related work or paddled whitewater beforehand, according to my research. Since June, a number of Fisher's former graduate students have alleged their work was improperly credited to him during and after their time under his supervision—a big deal in academic circles.

If the story of this canoeing trip sounds more like a true-crime documentary than an idyllic vacation, that may be why the dispute between Fisher and the Love Boat was the subject of by far the most popular episode of Season 7 of Renee Garner's podcast, Garnered Wisdom. *Then again, its popularity may be due to the #marrymeMcHuge hashtag that began trending shortly after the episode dropped, along with a meme of McHugh dropping a chaste (but somehow not chaste) peck at the corner of Byrd's mouth, saying, "I waited a year for her. I would have waited the rest of my life for her."*

And you thought Canada was boring. . . .

So did the good guys win? Yes, and no.

McHugh and Byrd's story has so far followed an all-too-familiar pattern: while underlings may fall, powerful men—especially powerful white men—often get "forgiven."

Pending his trial on charges of assault, William Trevor Butterworth is prohibited from entering Canada except for legal purposes. He has appealed his expulsion from NEU. A second, unnamed student withdrew from NEU's PhD program voluntarily.

Meanwhile, no charges have yet been laid against Fisher. Although he is under investigation by NEU, as well as several prominent scientific journals, he remains an active faculty member at the venerable university.

Notably, Fisher has signed a legal settlement attesting that he will not undertake wilderness-based research in exchange for the Love Boat owners' agreement to drop a seven-figure civil lawsuit. Fisher's whitewater therapy research project also disappeared from a list of current funding recipients on the National Science Foundation website. So far, however, just two of his hundreds of scientific papers have been retracted by the journals that published them.

And where does that leave McHuge—sorry, McHugh—and Byrd?

I caught up with them in a rare moment indoors, at his Grey Tusk condo. Pressed and clean, without zinc-covered faces or emergency knives strapped to their chests, they give off something like Clark Kent vibes while still radiating the competence and closeness they leveraged to launch their company to stardom.

Byrd gives McHugh a secret smile when I ask what her plans are between now and the winter session of the Love Boat. She's gradually reentering medicine as a family physician in a group practice (a part-time pursuit for now, but she'll reconsider her plans once Tobin Renner-Lewis returns from paternity leave) while working with McHugh to compile material for their upcoming self-help book—his second, her first.

"Writing a book is a risk," she tells me. "It's a lot of work for uncertain returns. You have to love it and be prepared to give a lot to it, whether or not it gives back in the form of money or recognition." But to Byrd, the work feels more satisfying than anything except successfully executing her favorite medical procedures, which I won't describe here.

For his part, McHugh uses his downtime to occasionally dip into the thriving online community of Love Boat graduates. Their private server is cheekily named "Divorce Boat," an insider term for tandem whitewater canoeing that pokes gentle fun at the difficulty of the sport. McHugh won't confirm whether he and Byrd are considering licensing the rights to their proprietary methodology, but rumor has it they've already turned down some offers they felt were too low.

Says McHugh, "If the universe sent licensing opportunities our way, we'd ideally use the revenue to offer special sessions at low or no cost, to make the wilderness a more equitable place. Maybe a parent and teen Love Boat is in our future. But we'll see. Above all, we want to find the right *partnership."*

But don't they want to strike while the licensing iron is hot?

Byrd shakes her head. "For now, no matter what, we have ourselves, and we have each other."

They shift slightly, then settle back into the love seat, hands clasped as if each has reached for the other and found them waiting.

Couple goals, indeed.

Acknowledgments

Before I wrote my second book, I knew it was theoretically one of the most difficult books of a writer's career, but I figured I would be the exception to the rule. Spoiler: I was not. I wouldn't have been able to write *The Ripple Effect* without the help, advice, and moisture-absorbing qualities of so many brilliant people.

Stellar's former workplace is based on a Canadian hospital that made national headlines in 2019 for not hiring a female emergency medicine doctor or teaching a female medical trainee for sixteen years. I always wondered what it was like to be one of the two women hired in the aftermath of that scandal. For McHuge's part, his experience in his PhD came from many, many anecdotes from current and former graduate students. To those who shared their stories but couldn't share their names due to the risk of retaliation, I hope this book does you proud and makes your work even a little bit easier.

I owe a lot to Claire Friedman, who is always the best agent and the best person—and I never forget how lucky I am to have both. Editor Christina Lopez has a talent for saying lovely things about the manuscript while also gently suggesting thirty thousand words of cuts, and I love her for it (and for picking up all the slack as I simultaneously went through edits and a family crisis). Thanks and love to editor Lisa Bonvissuto for loving McHuge and wanting his book.

Alexandra Kiley and Sarah Brenton were the wise, kind, and true friends I could trust with this book when it was at its most messy (and I was at my most messy, too). I see you when I read this book, and love you for helping me make it into something beautiful and necessary. Special thanks to Stephanie Archer, who called it a Michelin-starred meal and also told me it needed more butter and less mushrooms. Naina Kumar and Amanda Ciancarelli read, brainstormed, and were generally the Best People.

Undying gratitude to everyone who made *The Ripple Effect* so beautiful, including Andrew Lyons for his stunning cover art, Olga Grlic for the incredibly sexy cover design, and Omar Chapa for the interior design. I'm blessed with an incredible team at SMP, including Kejana Ayala, Alyssa Gammello, Susannah Noel, Chrisinda Lynch, Brant Janeway, Joy Gannon, and Anne Marie Tallberg. Special thanks to copyeditor Megan Zinn.

No words can express my love for the whip-smart writers who blurbed this book. Stephanie Archer, Tarah DeWitt, Sarah T. Dubb, Alexandra Kiley, Naina Kumar, Annabel Monaghan, and Alexandra Vasti, I owe you all a drink and an adventure.

For Romance Reasons, I've taken some liberties with the sport of whitewater paddling. Steffi van Wijk from Madawaska Kanu and paddling instructors Mike, Erin, and Coby cannot be held responsible for any errors I've (intentionally or otherwise) introduced.

Dr. Deanna Drahovzal, Dr. Caroline Ostiguy, Dr. Dali Fried, Dr. Caitlyn Davidson, Dr. Daniel Santa Mina, and Dr. Stephanie Buryk-Iggers generously offered their time and expertise on the topics of small-town medical practice, academic culture, and relationship counseling.

Mackenzie Thunderbolt-North wanted her name to come first, and I said yes not just because she is the Plot Whisperer, but because she is a delight. And to Jackson Thunderbolt, for all the things for all these years.

About the Author

Lindsey Gibeau

Maggie North lives in Ottawa, Canada, with the man she met in ninth grade, their kid, and a rotating cast of hypoallergenic aquarium friends. Her hobbies include long-distance open water swimming, saving the world, and being relentlessly Canadian. She enjoys being autistic a lot more since she received her diagnosis as an adult.

maggienorth.com

@maggienorthauthor

maggienorth.substack.com